Midsummer Nights

Midsummer Nights

Edited by
Jeanette Winterson

riverrun

First published in 2009 by Quercus
This paperback edition published in 2019 by

riverrun

An imprint of

Quercus Editions Ltd
Carmelite House
50 Victoria Embankment
London EC4Y 0DZ
An Hachette UK company

Design and typesetting in Odile by Lindsay Nash

Printed in Great Britain by Clays Ltd

Contents

Introduction
Jeanette Winterson

Opera has always needed a story. Some inspirations are direct
- like Britten's *Turn of the Screw*, or Wagner's *Tristan and Isolde*,
and others, like Mozart's *Marriage of Figaro*, or Verdi's *Rigoletto*,
take a story and shift it.

Why not take an opera and shift it?

All the stories in this collection have done exactly that;
found a piece of music and worked it into a new shape. It doesn't
matter whether the reader knows the source or not – the stories
are wonderful in their own right – but those who do know the
operas will get an extra twist of pleasure from peering into the
forge where they were made.

The brief to each writer was simple: choose an opera, and
from its music or its characters, its plot or its libretto, or even a
mood evoked, write a story.

Glyndebourne is one of the most innovative opera houses
in the world, and for that reason a collection of new stories to
celebrate its seventy-fifth birthday seemed like a tribute to its
remarkable past and a flare sent up towards the future.

The music began in 1934, after a rather shy John Christie

had met the rather sparkling Audrey Mildmay, an opera singer. They had fallen in love, and as Christie happened to have a stately home, he offered it as a love-gift to his wife. They would start an opera house together, get a few Members to subscribe, put on *The Marriage of Figaro*...

The thing ran on rather a small scale at first, then it was interrupted by the War, but at the end of the War, Glyndebourne decided to reopen with a new commission – the young Benjamin Britten's *Rape of Lucretia*, with Kathleen Ferrier in the title role.

Brave or what? Just when everyone longed for the familiar and the known, for straightforward entertainments and light relief, Glyndebourne backed a young man writing a new opera, and did so to reaffirm culture as necessary to a civilized life.

This was no grand gesture, no posturing – it was a simple and heartfelt belief in music and its emotional power, in art as a force for good.

Seventy-five years later, still in the Christie family, and running without public subsidy, Glyndebourne offers world-class opera every year from May until August, and continues to support new work, and to stage some of the more difficult or less easily understood operas, as well as the core rep.

I think that Glyndebourne is a place where people can find opera for the first time, and fall in love with it. I think it is a place that has kept its values. Yes, some tickets cost a fortune, but some don't, and whether you dine in style or eat sardine sandwiches on the lawn, the music is what matters.

That opera is a necessary synthesis of words and music makes it so potent. The stories in this collection have the music in them. The rhythm, breath, movement of language, like music, creates emotional situations not dependent on meaning. The meaning is there, but the working of the language itself, separate from its message, allows the brain to make connections that bypass sense. This makes for an experience where there is the satisfaction of meaning but also something deeper, stranger. This deeper stranger place is an antidote to so much of life that is lived on the surface alone. When we read, when we listen to music, when we immerse ourselves in the flow of an opera, we go underneath the surface of life. Like going underwater the noise stops, and we concentrate differently.

These stories are quite different from each other, and absorbing in unexpected ways. What they share is the music, and what I hope they will prompt is a curiosity about music, in particular, opera, among readers who might think that opera is not for them. Story lovers who are also opera lovers will delight in the inventions, and be moved, I hope, by the richness of these collisions between words and music.

In the end it is all about feeling. I think we spend quite a lot of time trying to control our feelings, only to find ourselves hopelessly overwhelmed when we least expect, or least want it to happen.

For me, opera is a place where all the emotions can be fully felt yet safely contained. Certainly this has therapeutic value, but art is not therapy – at least not principally so: it is a profound engagement with life itself, in all its messiness, its glory, its fear, its possibility, its longing, its love.

And these stories here, funny, sad, wise, true, reflective, speculative, ardent, each with its own tempo and written in its own key, are ways to think, and ways to feel.

And there's Posy in the middle, drawing us in, reminding us that we are part of the picture, as well as part of the song.

First Lady of Song
Jackie Kay

My father wasn't thinking of me when he kept me alive for years. I was my father's experiment. At the end of this long life, when my skin is starting to show its age, finally, and my hair has the shy beginnings of grey, I need to speak. I've got out of the way of talking. It's so much easier to sing, *Da dee dee dee di deeeee*. Talking, I always trip myself up, make some nasty mistake. It's had the effect of people thinking of me as crazy, *doo- lah- li- lal*. I've learnt to talk lightly about things, just skimming the surface, in case I found myself in trouble. It is difficult to know where to begin – *doh ray me fah so lah ti doh* – for me there was no real beginning. I knew nothing of what was happening to me. One day, I was my old self, those years ago, carefree, spontaneous, and loving; another day, those qualities had gone. When I was first drugged, I fell into a coma, apparently. I was in that coma for a week; my father told me when I came round. He seemed delighted about my coma, he smiled, patted my head, and said, 'I think it's worked; it's a miracle.' I fled. I left my father, my mother, my sisters and brothers. I never looked back, and he never found me. Back in those early days,

I had a different name. My name was Elina Makropulos. I've had many husbands, countless children, grandchildren, great-grandchildren. Some of my children are a blur, but the pianos are vivid - the babies and the uprights, the ebony and ivory, the little Joes.

I remember time through music – what I was singing when. How I loved those Moravian folk songs, how I lost myself in those twelve-bar blues, how I felt understood by those soaring arias, how beautiful ballads kept me company, how scatting made me feel high. For years I've been singing my head off, singing my head off for years. When I sang Elina's head off, Eugenia came. When I sang Eugenia's head off Ekateriana came. When I sang Ekateriana's arias, Elisabeth came. After Elisabeth I was Ella. My favourite period was my Ella period. Every song I sang had my own private meanings: 'I didn't mean a word I said', 'Into each life some rain must fall', 'Until the real thing comes along', and even 'Paper Moon'. I'd lived so long, nothing was real. Ella seemed to be cool about that. *Bebop, doowop! Eeeeee deee dee dee dee de ooooooooooh dahdadadada bepop doowop brump bum bump.*

Now, I'm Emilia Marty. I'm in the middle of being Emilia Marty. I've returned to being a classical singer, my first love. My voice is deeper now. I've sung about every type of love through all the years. Back in those early years when I was Elina Makropoulos, my skin was pale, perhaps a little translucent. As the years went on, I got darker and darker. Now, my skin is dark black. Emilia Marty has dark black skin. I'm rather in awe of it. It is not transparent, it is not translucent, but it is shimmering. I wear a great dark skin now, like a dark lake, like a lake at night with a full moon in the sky. Way back in the days when my father first drugged me, I remember seeing the last moon I ever saw as Elina Makropoulos; the last moon before I fell into a coma. It was a new baby moon, rocking in its little hammock, soft-skinned, fresh. Or it was the paw of a baby polar bear, clawing at the sky. Or it was a silver fish leaping through the voyage of the deep, dark sea-sky. That's the only other thing that's accompanied me on my long journey, the moon. The moon has never been boring! I wrote a song for it back in my Ella days: *Blue Moon, I saw you standing alone.*

I've been lonely with my lies for years. I told none of my many children the truth about their mother. I didn't want them to carry the burden. I wanted them to think that they had an ordinary mother who looked good for her years, who was pretty healthy perhaps. Every time, I ran into an old friend or acquaintance who said, 'It's remarkable, you haven't changed a bit,' I smiled grimly and knew that they were telling the absolute truth. None of them knew that it was the truth, or how uncanny their little clichés were for me. 'You don't look a day older than the last time I saw you', 'Your skin hasn't got a single line', 'You're incredibly youthful-looking'. All were sickening sentences for me. The only change for me was my skin gradually darkening, yet nobody noticed this. Nobody lived long enough!

I'd sing my children lullabies, and chortle to myself when I got to *Your daddy's rich and your ma is good-looking* knowing full well that daddy would die first and so would baby, and that the person who should really want to cry was me – *Hush Hush, little baby.* When nobody knows who you truly are, what's the point in living? We're not alive to be alone on the planet. We're alive to share, to eat together and love together and laugh together and cry together. If you can never love because you will always lose, what reason is there to live? I have lost husbands, daughters, and sons. When my father used me as his experiment I don't imagine he ever thought properly about the life of grief he was consigning me to, the grief, handed down the long line of years, a soft grey bundle of it. After a while, I stopped loving anyone so that I wouldn't be hurt by their death. If you are certainly going to outlive all your family and your friends, who keeps you company? Only the songs knew me – only the songs – the daylight and the dark, the night and the day. Some songs lasted longer than sons. Some ballads outlived my daughters. Some lieder survived my lovers. Some folk songs lived longer than my folks, *Fahlahdiddleday*. Perhaps he might have thought of it as a gift. There is no way for me to go back and unpick the years to find out what my father hoped for me. The truth is more uncomfortable, I think. He didn't consider me in the equation. I was his experiment. He didn't know if it would work or not. Even now, all this time away, I can't stop myself from wondering about this. I cannot fathom my father.

I have not loved for so many years, I can't really be sure of the sensation of it, how it feels, if it is good or if it is frightening. If it is deep, how deep it goes, to which parts of the body and the mind? I have no real idea. My biggest achievement was getting rid of it altogether! What a relief! I remember that. The sensation of it! The day that I discovered I could no longer love. It was like a lovely breeze on a hot day. It billowed and felt really quite fine. I remember when, some time ago, I stood, a young woman at the grave of my old son, and not a tear came. I said to myself, 'He was tone-deaf that one, he could never sing,' and laughed later that night, drinking a big goblet of wine. Years later, I remember being at the funeral of my old daughter, a vicious tongue she had, that one, I said to myself and threw the rose in. *So, Goodbye dear.* I tried to remember if I had ever taken pleasure in any of her childhood, in reading her a book, or holding her small hand, or buying her a wooden doll. And though I had done those things, I think, I could not remember getting any pleasure. I could not remember getting anything at all.

People would say that I was the world's greatest singer, back when I was Ella, I had a vocal range spanning three octaves and a pure tone, my dear. They said on the one hand I seemed to feel and know everything and on the other, I had never grown up. (True, true!) I could sing the greatest love songs and yet appear as if nothing touched me, as if I'd never had sex. Nobody but myself knew the irony in the way I sang Gershwin's *The way you wear your hat, the way you sip your tea, the memory of all that, no, no, they can't take that away from me.* I sang it defiantly, despite the fact that they were taking it away from me all the time, and one husband's hat frankly had blended into another's and I barely noticed the way they sipped their tea, let alone remembered it. When I sang Cole Porter's *I've got you under my skin*, myself, to Elina, Eugenia, Ekateriana, Elisabeth, I was trying to keep myself together.

I had sex over and over again. Sometimes I'd get lost in it; sometimes it was the only thing that could go right through me, where I could banish the lonely feeling and abandon myself to somebody else, the soft skin of an earlobe, anybody's earlobe, the smell of morning breath, the hair on a chest. For a moment, any little intimacy would make me feel I was standing on a smallholding, and not out in the vast, yellow, empty plains, the wind roaring on my face, singing my plainsong. I barely remember some of my men; the love songs lasted way longer than the lovers. Some were large and some were small, but all seemed to be fertile, alas. And when child came out after child, between my legs and over the centuries, I would gaze down in a sort of trance, a huge boredom coming over me already, before the new baby even suckled on my breast. Another baby! So what! Another baby to feed and teach to read and count and watch die. I lost my children to typhus, whooping cough, scarlet fever, tuberculosis, cholera, smallpox, influenza. Many of my children died before they were ten or fifteen. I remember a couple of hundred years ago looking wistfully at my daughter Emily, and wishing on the bone of the hard white moon that I could catch her whooping cough and die, die, die. It was never for me, death, never going to be handed out to me on a lovely silver platter, not the gurgle or the snap or the thud or the whack or the slide of it, death. No. I was consigned to listening to the peal of church bells barely change over the stretch of years.

When I came to be Ella, I was so much more independent. Those were plucky, scatting days. Even the moon bopped in the sky. I was on the road forty out of forty-five weeks. I'd come a long way. I'd gone from working with dodgy numbers runners to being the first African-American to perform at the Mocambo! Life takes odd turns. In my case, *lives* take odd turns. There I was finally as integrated as Elvis, singing songs by Jewish lyricists to white America, having folk like Marilyn Monroe fight in my corner. Every time I sang *Every time I say goodbye* I felt it more than people knew. I was saying goodbye all my life. I was saying goodbye to my other selves, Elina, Eugenia, Ekateriana, Elisabeth, Ella. My own names were a kind of litany. Only the songs knew my secrets, only the music was complex enough to contain me. When I was Elisabeth, I was known for how I sang Strauss' *Four Last Songs*. One time, late in my Elisabeth day, I was performing at the Albert Hall, singing Straussy for the umpteenth time and I got to the last stanza. I felt like him; I welcomed death. I sang with true feeling – *O vast tranquil peace, so deep at sunset, how weary we are of wandering, is this perhaps death?* One of the reviewers said I'd grown into the songs over the years. Well, yes.

There's been so much to grow into over the years. I'm like an old person the way I pick out memories and cluck over them. Well, they say the old repeat themselves and the young have nothing to say. The boredom is mutual! I've got an old woman's head in a young woman's body. *Thank you for the memories!* I remember: my excitement when I first got to fly on an aeroplane, getting adjusted to the phone and its ring, having penicillin suddenly for my children, my first X-ray, how my hair felt the first time it was blow-dried, how exciting the indoor bath with running water, how bamboozling the supermarket was at first. There was nobody around who'd lived as long as me, nobody to say, I liked it before we had supermarkets, I liked it before zoos arrived, before we had aeroplanes, before the hole in the ozone, I liked living before all those things. I didn't like the poverty, the sickness, but there is still something to be said for a good cobbler, an honest loaf of bread, a cobbled street, bare oak beams, revolution. Even the words for everything have kept changing over the centuries. I've had to keep up with the Vocab. *Jeepers Creepers*. I've had to keep changing my talk. I've lived long enough to see *bourgeois* go out and *bespoke* come in.

I took a boat trip down the Vltava river in Prague, many moons ago. The food in Prague – how I loved breast of duck with saffron apples, how I loved my mother's flaky apple strudel. I remember the first time I ate a sandwich in England and even when the word sandwich came in. My favourite pie ever was way back in the nineteenth century. They don't make them like that these days! It was filled with chicken, partridge and duck and had a layer of green pistachios in the middle. I don't remember who

I was then, but I remember that pie! I remember when tea and coffee and sugar started being so popular. I remember my first drink of aerated water, ginger ale. I used to have a lovely silver spirit kettle. I remember the excitement of my first flask, how I took it on a lavish picnic. All musicians love a picnic, always have. There's always been music and wine, concerts and hot puddings, strawberries, champagne. Food and Claret and Ale all seemed to taste better a while back. As I've gone through times, I've noticed so much getting watered down. Not just taste, but ideas. Oh for the fervour and passion of Marx now. Oh for the precociousness of Pascal. Oh the originality of Picasso.

My body never changed shape or height, give or take an inch or so. It was my colour that changed, and with my colour my voice. My voice is deeper now; if it was a colour it would be maroon. I've returned to singing the spirituals that I sang back in the days when I was another self. *Swing low sweet chariot, coming forth to carry me home, swing low sweet chariot, coming forth to carry me home. There is a balm in Gilead to make the wounded whole. There is a balm in Gilead to heal the sin-sick soul.* My voice is deeper than I could have ever believed when I was a soprano. I go low, *Go down Moses,* till my voice is at the bottom of the river bed, with the river reeds and marshes.

I look at myself in the mirror. My skin is still young-looking, and a dark blue-black colour. I look about thirty when I'm really three hundred years old. I've looked about thirty all these years. These days, it's easier for me to make up my face, to add a little lipstick, a little blusher, and mascara for my already very long eyelashes. My eyelashes have grown over the centuries and are now a lavish length. People comment on them. 'I've never seen such long eyelashes,' they'll say and I roll my eyes. I've been here a long time. There is nothing new under the sun that anyone can say. I've lost the ability to be surprised – which is worse I've discovered than losing the ability to surprise. Nothing about myself interests me. I've lost all vanity, so compliments are dreary. I've lost my passion for ideas, so conversations trap and unnerve me. I've lost my love of listening to the way that people talk, because I've found, over the years, people say more or less the same thing, and expect me to be riveted – the price of food, the price of fuel, the children, the schooling, the illness, the betrayal, the blow, the shock. Specific times and events jump out at me – I remember when the abolition of the triangular slave trade was announced; when women first got the vote; when Kennedy was assassinated, when segregation and Jim Crow laws started to change. Actually, I really thought something might change properly in the Nineteen Sixties. That was the last time I felt optimistic. I've lived through so much hurt, so many wars, so much hunger, so much unkindness and cruelty. At last, it seemed to me a decade that people cared, and the talk was interesting and I buzzed and sang and actually made some friends. And the friends I made seemed to care about me, and we all had pretty good sex with each other, sometimes three or four of us at the same time. It was liberating until it became narrow and selfish, and petty jealousies and concern about money started creeping in, and all those lovely Sixties flower folk seemed to wake up and say, I want I want I want. And off they went, the marchers, protesters, petitioners, to see acupuncturists, therapists, homeopaths. So I crept off, changing my name again and my skin darkened. I bumped into one of my old friends twenty or so years later – I lose all track of time – and she had a bungalow, three kids, a garage, a drinks cabinet, a mortgage, a pension, a car and a broken heart. Her husband had gone running off with someone half her age. She looked at me wistfully and said, 'Oh but Emmy you haven't aged at all. It's quite incredible. You look exactly the same as the day I last saw you.' She stared at me, and looked worried. She was the first person that ever really knew in her bones that something was not right with me.

She invited me round to her house a few weeks later. What have you been doing, Emmy, did you get married, have children? she said. I laughed, and told her the truth. I thought what have I got to lose? I've been alive for three hundred years, I said, and she exploded laughing. 'Emmy,' she snorted, 'you always were so droll!' 'Children?' I laughed, 'I've had children, many, many children, and outlived the lot of them. Husbands? I've had husbands over the centuries, and buried them all.' The tears were pouring down my innocent friend's face by now. 'What have I been doing?' I asked her back rhetorically. 'I've seen kings and queens come and go. I've seen governments rise and fall. I used to have sympathy for the Whigs. I've lived in Czechoslovakia, America, England.' My friend's eyes glazed over. Suddenly, I wasn't funny, I was boring. She yawned. 'You're tired?' I asked, gathering speed. 'I'm exhausted. Imagine how tired you would be if you were three hundred years old.' 'Would you like a big gin?' she asked eagerly, desperate to change the subject. 'Yes,' I said. 'Why the hell not after all the things I've seen? What about you?' I asked her. The rest of the evening was spent on the husband, the betrayal, the younger woman that did not have a brain in her head, was skinny, was his secretary, how she'd not suspected a thing until..., how, how, how. I felt myself droop into my gin. I squeezed her hand and noticed that she'd got drunk incredibly quickly. (That was something that didn't happen to me, incidentally. I'd learnt to watch the goblets over the years, to hold my drink.) She leaned towards me half-sozzled, her eyes a little vacant, a little dear departed, and she kissed me, or rather her lips slid across my mouth like a small child sliding down a shoot. I kissed her back and fondled a little at her breasts and then I left, opening and closing the door of the quietly disturbed bungalow.

With such a long life as mine, it's impossible to capture it. And maybe it is of no consequence. I don't know what I've learned that is all that different from anybody here for a shorter time. I think because I've never had to get on a bus with a walking stick, never had to think about stairs, never had to buy hair dye, worry about brittle bones, never had false teeth, never drawn a pension, never been in an old people's home, never had dementia, angina, because I've never had wrinkles, bald patches, plastic hips or knees, that I have been deprived! I've never had that tender frailty I've seen in the old, that sudden lost old-girl, old-boy vulnerability, that anxiety the old have about travelling anywhere different, packing and unpacking cases. I've pooh-poohed all of that for centuries, jumping on and off boats, trains, planes. I suddenly wanted it. I wanted to become old. I wanted to know what it was like to have death ahead of you finally, that I could let go, that my hair would go grey and curly. I longed for the simple business of getting old, giving myself a break, not singing for the world anymore, not up on the big stages, staying in the big hotels, singing my heartless heart out.

Enough is enough is enough! I went back to Prague. I hadn't been there for years and could barely credit the change in my old town. Part of it had changed into Clubland! I traipsed round the old part of the city looking for the lawyer's office, through the *Staromestke namesti*, the old town Square where I stood remembering my girlhood when the astronomical clock struck twelve and one hand rang a bell and a second overturned an hourglass. I'd forgotten the clock! How had I forgotten the astronomical clock? I wandered through the Square in a daze, remembering how my father had told me about the twenty-seven people who were executed there. I walked on and on, through Wenceslas Square, until finally I found it! The lawyer's office hadn't changed names. They hadn't moved buildings! I climbed the stairs with trepidation. I had no idea how long I was being consigned to live. In the office was a woman by the name of Kristina Kolenaty. She hunted for the precious document which hid the Makropulos secret. I paid her a handsome number of Euros and fled down the steps, down the street, back through the old Square, down the achingly familiar street of alchemists, and back to my hotel. The original document told me the details of the potion my father had given me, that would ensure I lived for ever, and the details of how to reverse it. I didn't want to live for ever. I never did want to live for ever. It's a ghastly traumatic experience! There's no one to share your memories with except history books, and they get so much of it wrong. (Unbelievable, how much they distort and omit!) When I got the potion, I didn't even hesitate. I mixed the spoonfuls of X and X and Y and ZH together in the exact proportions and I threw it down my neck and I swallowed. I gulped emphatically, making a sound with it, a kind of animal sound. *Non, je ne regrette rien* I sang at the top of my voice. Then I lay down on the hotel room bed, waiting for something to happen to me, listening out for it, as if I was listening for the sound of slippers walking along the corridor. I felt a little uncertain, a little fright-ened. Nothing happened. Nothing happened for ages. I returned to my house in London and waited. I stopped singing publicly. I had no desire to be famous anymore, no desire to sing to anybody but myself in the bath. I had plenty of money. Money didn't engage or interest me at all. I gave as much as I could away.

I was beginning to wonder if the potion had worked when my first little sign of ageing came through, fresh as a snowdrop. A little grey hair. How lovely! A few weeks later another, and another. Bliss! I stared in the mirror to look at my dark face and watch the odd line arrive unannounced here and then there. Hello, little wrinkle I said gently. Well hello dolly! A while after that I got my first fuming red-hot flush. It wasn't so great, but I couldn't complain! I'm looking forward to getting past the flushes and into proper old age. I'm very much looking forward to it, creaking bones, memory lapses. What a lovely word – dotage! What jolly delightful words: old age.

Years passed in the proper way – quickly. Summer became winter became spring. Shocking, the speed of it all! A few weeks ago, I was in the queue for the first day at the Proms. I got chatting to a lovely woman with a very beautiful face. She had curly hair. Dark winged eyebrows. I could see her hair was dyed. I liked that. She had a few, maybe one or two, kind wrinkles around her eyes. She was large-ish, like me, a big bosom and belly. We talked about music we loved. Her eyes were shining. She had something about her that was quite, quite special. We'd been talking for ages before we found out each other's names. Irene, she said. Emilia, I said. I thought so, she said. I thought it was you. I was trying to work out her age; for the first time in my long life, I found myself interested in someone's age. 'What age are you if you don't mind me asking?' I asked her. 'Fifty-seven,' she said. 'Me too,' I said. I'd guessed I must be roughly that by now. We stood together promming it. She'd brought along some champagne and some very delicious sandwiches. I felt comfortable in my skin. We stood listening, rapt and happy like two women that had known each other all of her life, if not all of mine! When the Prom finished, I could sense her sadness. 'Would you like to go out some time to a concert together or for a meal?' I asked her and her smile lit up her face, the river, the night sky. I could feel something quite extraordinary happening to me. I could feel myself soften and give in. My heart, something was happening to my heart that hadn't happened for years. I could hear it thrumming and strumming and chiming. I could feel my body trembling, vibrato style. I looked at her eyes, deep into her eyes, and I felt euphoric. It was a wonder. That night I found myself singing *Good night Irene, Good night Irene, I'll see you in my dreams,* before climbing into my double bed on my own. I slept, dreaming her. 'You are quite wonderful,' I told her on our sixth date. 'Oh,' she said, smiling, shy, 'you are not so bad yourself.'

Last night, I went to bed humming an old song I hadn't sung for years. It was like I'd written that verse waiting for her to come along, and then my own song suddenly made sense. I opened the curtains before I climbed into bed. A big wise moon glowed in the sky, the same moon that had been there since time. The moon appeared to me like a listening eye. I sang to it before I climbed into bed. I sang to the moon and I sang to Irene. For the first time in my long life, I really wanted to live. *You knew just what I was there for. You heard me saying a prayer for/ Somebody I really could care for.*

Fidelio and Bess
Ali Smith

A young woman is ironing in a kitchen in a prison. But she's not a prisoner, no. Her father's the chief gaoler; she just lives here. A young man comes into the kitchen and tells her he's decided that he and she are going to marry. I've chosen you, he says. She is desultory with him. She suggests to the audience that he's a bit of a fool. Then she sings a song to herself. It's Fidelio I've chosen, it's Fidelio I'm in love with, she sings. It's Fidelio who's in love with me. It's Fidelio I want to wake up next to every morning.

Her father comes home. Then, a moment later, so does Fidelio himself, who looks suspiciously like a girl dressed as a boy, and who happens to be wreathed in chains. Not that Fidelio's a prisoner, no. Apparently the chains have been being repaired by a blacksmith (whom we never see), and Fidelio, the girl's father's assistant, has brought the mended chains back to the gaol.

But it seems that Fidelio isn't much interested in marrying the boss' daughter. Fidelio, instead, is unnaturally keen to meet a mysterious prisoner who's being kept in the deepest, darkest underground cell in the prison. This particular prisoner has been down there for two years and is receiving almost no food or water any more. This is on the prison governor's orders; the prison governor wants him starved to death. He's clearly a man who's done great wrong, Fidelio says, fishing for information – or made great enemies, which is pretty much the same thing, the gaoler says, leaning magnanimously back in his kitchen chair. Money, he says. It's the answer to everything. The girl looks at Fidelio. Don't let him see that dying prisoner, the girl says. He couldn't stand it, he's just a boy, he's such a gentle boy. Don't subject him to such a cruel sight. On the contrary, Fidelio says. Let me see him. I'm brave enough and I'm strong enough.

But then the prison governor announces to the gaoler, in private, that he has just decided to have this prisoner killed. I'm not murdering him, the gaoler says when the governor tells him to. Okay, I'll do it myself, the prison governor says. I'll take pleasure in it. And I'll give you a bag of gold if you go and dig a grave for him in the old well down there in his cell.

It's agreed. In the next act, the gaoler will take the boy Fidelio down to the deep dungeon and they'll dig the grave for the man who, we've begun to gather, is Fidelio's imprisoned husband. Meanwhile, as the first act draws to a close, Fidelio has somehow managed to get all the other prisoners in the place released out of the dark of their cells into the weak spring sun in the prison yard for a little while.

They stagger out into the light. They stand about, ragged, dazed, heartbreakingly hopeful. They're like a false resurrection. They look up at the sunlight. Summer time, they sing, and the living is easy. Fish are jumping and the cotton is high.

Then they all look at each other in amazement.

Fidelio looks bewildered.

The gaoler shakes his head.

The conductor's baton droops.

The orchestra in the pit stops playing. Instruments pause in mid-air.

The girl who was doing the ironing at the beginning is singing too. She's really good. She shrugs at her father as if she can't help it, can't do anything about it. Your daddy's rich, she sings, and your mamma's good-looking.

Then a man arrives in a cart pulled by a goat. He stops the cart in the middle of the stage. Everybody crowds round him. He's black. He's the only black person on the stage. He looks very poor and at the same time very impressive. When the song finishes he gets out of the cart. He walks across the stage. He's got a limp. It's quite a bad limp. He tells them all that he's looking for Bess. Where is she? He's heard she's here. He's not going to stop looking for her until he finds her. He glances at the gaoler; he regards Fidelio gravely for a moment. He nods to the girl. He approaches a group of prisoners. Is this New York? he says. Is she here?

Yeah, but, you say. Come on. I mean.

But what? I say.

You can't, you say.

Can't what? I say.

Culture's fixed, you say. That's why it's culture. That's how it gets to be art. That's how it works. That's why it works. You can't just change it. You can't just alter it when you want or because you want. You can't just revise things for your own pleasure or whatever.

Actually I can do anything I like, I say.

Yeah, but you can't revise Fidelio, you say. No one can.

Fidelio's all about revision, I say. Beethoven revised Fidelio several times. Three different versions. Four different overtures.

You know what I mean. No one can just, as it were, interject Porgy into Fidelio, you say.

Oh, as it were, I say.

You don't say anything. You stare straight out, ahead, through the windscreen.

Okay. I know what you mean, I say.

You start humming faintly, under your own breath.

But I don't think interject is quite the right word to use there, I say.

I say this because I know there's nothing that annoys you more than thinking you've used a word wrongly. You snort down your nose.

Yes it is, you say.

I don't think it's quite the right usage, I say.

It is, you say. Anyway, I didn't say interject. I said inject.

I lean forward and switch the radio on. I keep pressing the channel button until I hear something I recognize.

It's fine for you to do that, you say, but if you're going to, can you at least, before we get out of the car, return it to the channel to which it was originally tuned?

I settle on some channel or other, I've no idea what.

Which channel was it on? you say.

Radio 4, I say.

Are you sure? you say.

Or 3, I say.

Which? you say.

I don't know, I say.

You sigh.

Gilbert O'Sullivan is singing the song about the people who are hurrying to the registry office to get married. Very shortly now there's going to be an answer from you. And one from me. I sing along. You sigh out loud again. The sigh lifts the hair of your fringe slightly from your forehead.

You're so pretty when you sigh like that.

When we arrive at the carpark you reach over to my side of the radio and keep the little button pressed in until the radio hits the voices of a comedy programme where celebrities have one minute exactly to talk about a subject, with no repetitions. If they repeat themselves, they're penalized. An audience is killing itself laughing.

When you're sure it's Radio 4, you switch the radio off.

We are doomed as a couple. We are as categorically doomed as when Clara in Porgy and Bess says: Jake, you ain't plannin' to take de Sea Gull to de Blackfish Banks, is you? It's time for de September storms. No, the Sea Gull, a fictional boat, moored safe and ruined both at once in its own eternal bay, is less doomed than we are. We're as doomed as the Cutty Sark itself, tall, elegant, real, mundanely gathering the London sky round its masts and making it wondrous, extraordinary, for the people coming up out of the underground train station in the evening, the ship-of-history gracious against the sky for all the people who see it and all the people who don't even notice it any more because they're so used to seeing it, and just two months to go before there'll be nothing left of it but a burnt-out hull, a scoop of scorched plankwork.

We are doomed on land and doomed on sea, you and me; as doomed holding on to each other's arms on the underground as we are arguing about culture in your partner's car; as doomed in a bar sitting across from each other or side by side at the cinema or the opera or the theatre; as doomed as we are when we're pressed into each other in the various beds in the various near-identical rooms we go to, to have the sex that your partner doesn't know about us having. Of all the dooms I ever thought I might come to I never reckoned on middle-classness. You and me, holding hands below the seats at Fidelio, an opera you've already seen, already taken your partner to; and it all started so anarchically, so happily, all heady public kissing in King's Cross station. Mir ist so wunderbar. That's me in the £120-a-night bed, and you through in the bathroom, thoroughly cleaning your teeth.

I read in the sleeve notes for the version of Fidelio I have on CD that at an early point in the opera, when all four people, the girl, the thwarted young man, the woman dressed as a boy and the gaoler, are singing about happiness and everybody is misunderstanding everybody else and believing a different version of things to be true, this is where 'backstairs chat turns into the music of the angels'. How wonderful it is to me. Something's got my heart in its grip. He loves me, it's clear. I'm going to be happy. Except, wunderbar here doesn't mean the usual simple wonderful. It means full of wonder, strange. How strange it is to me. I wish I could remember her name, the ironing girl who loves Fidelio, the light-comedy act-opener, the girl for whom there's no real end to it, the girl who has to accept – with nothing more than an alas, which pretty soon modulates into the same song everyone else is singing – what happens when the boy Fidelio is suddenly revealed as the wife Leonore, and everybody stands round her in awe at her wifely faithfulness, her profound self-sacrifice. O namenlose.

Which is worse to her, the ironing girl? That Fidelio is really Leonore, a woman, not the boy she thought he was? Or that her beloved Fidelio is someone else's wife, after all, and so, in this opera about the sacredness of married love, will never, ever be hers?

Oh my Leonore, Florestan, the husband, the freed prisoner, says to Fidelio after she's unearthed him, after she's flung herself between him and certain death, between him and the drawn blade of the prison governor. Point of catharsis. Point of truth. After she does this, everything in the whole world changes for the better.

Oh my Leonore, what have you done for me?

Nothing, nothing, my Florestan, she answers.

Lucky for her she had a gun on her, that's what I say, otherwise they'd both be dead.

Oh, I got plenty o' nuttin. And nuttin's plenty fo' me.

It's famously unresolved, you know, I say. Even though its ending seems so celebratory, so C-major, so huge and comforting and sure, there's still a sense, at the back of it all, that lots of things haven't been resolved. Look at the ironing girl, for instance. She's not resolved, is she? Beethoven called it his 'child of sorrow'. He never wrote another opera after it.

Half a year ago you'd never heard of Fidelio, you say.

Klemperer conducted it at two really extraordinarily different times in history, I tell you.

I am flicking through the little book that comes with the version of Fidelio you'd just given me. The new CD is one of my Christmas presents. Christmas is in ten days' time. We have just opened our Christmas presents, in a bedroom in a Novotel. I bought you a really nice French-looking jumper, with buttons at one side of the neck. I know that you'll probably drop it in a litter bin on your way home.

Imagine, I say. Imagine conducting it in 1915 in the middle of the First World War. Then imagine the strangeness of conducting it in the Nineteen Sixties, when every single scene must have reminded people of the different thing it meant, for a German conductor, the story of all the people starved and tyranted, buried alive, for being themselves, for saying the truth, for standing up to the status quo.

Tyranted's not a word, you say in my ear.

You say it lovingly. You are holding me in your arms. We are both naked. You are warm behind me. You make my back feel blessed, the way you are holding me. I can feel the curve of your breasts at each of my shoulder blades.

Imagine all the things that Florestan must have meant, then, I say, to those people, in that audience in 1915, then 1961.

It's an opera, you say. It's nothing to do with history.

Yes, but it is, I say. It's post-Napoleonic. That's obvious. Imagine what it meant to its audience in 1814. Imagine watching the same moment in this opera at different times in history. Take the moment when Fidelio asks whether she can give the prisoner a piece of old bread. It's the question of whether one starving man can have a piece of mercy. All the millions of war dead are in it there, crowding behind that one man. And the buried, unearthed truth. And the new day dawning, and all the old ghosts coming out of the ground.

Uh huh, you say.

What if Fidelio had been written by Mozart? I say.

It wasn't, you say.

The knockabout there'd have been with Fidelio in her boy's clothes, I say. The swagger Mozart would have given Rocco. The good joke the girl who's ironing at the start would have become, and the boy too, who thinks he can just marry her because he's made up his mind he wants to.

You yawn.

Though there's something really interesting in the way Beethoven doesn't force those characters to be funny, I say. The ironing girl, what's her name? There's something humane, in the way they're not just, you know, played for laughs.

You kiss the back of my neck. You use your teeth on my shoulder. It's allowed, you biting me. I quite like to be gently bitten. I'm not allowed to bite you, though, in case it marks you.

I still have no idea whether you like being gently bitten or not.

Not long after we'd met, when I said I'd never heard much, didn't know much about Beethoven, you played me some on your iPod. When I said I thought it sounded like Jane Austen crossed with Daniel Libeskind, you looked bemused, like I was a clever child. When I said that what I meant was that it was like different kinds of architecture, as if a classically eighteenth-century room had suddenly morphed into a postmodern annexe, you shook your head and kissed me to make me stop talking. I closed my eyes into the kiss. I love your kiss. Everything's sorted, and obvious, and understood, and civilized, your kiss says. It's a shut-eye lie, I know it is, because the music I didn't know before I knew you makes me open my eyes in a place of no sentimentality, where light itself is a kind of shadow, where everything is fragment-slanted. A couple of months later, when I said I thought you could hear the whole of history in it, all history's grandnesses and sadnesses, you'd looked a bit annoyed. You'd taken the iPod off my knee and disconnected its headphones from their socket. When I'd removed the dead headphones from my ears you'd rolled them up carefully and tucked them into the special little carrying-case you keep them in. You'd said you were getting a migraine. Impatience had crossed your face so firmly that I had known, in that instant, that now we were actually a kind of married, and that our marriedness was probably making your real relationship more palatable.

Sometimes a marriage needs three hearts beating as one.

I've met your partner. She's nice. I can tell she's quite a nice person. She knows who I am but she doesn't know who I am. Her clothes smell overwhelmingly of the same washing powder as yours.

Ten days before Christmas, smelling of sex in a rented bed, with half an hour to go before you have to get the half past ten train home, I hold the new Fidelio in my hands. I think of the ironing girl, holding up the useless power of her own huge love to Fidelio in the first act like a chunk of dead stone she thinks is full of magic. I think of Fidelio herself, insufferably right-eous. I think about how she makes her first entrance laden with chains that aren't actually binding her to anything.

I open the plastic box and I take out one of the shiny discs. I hold it up in front of us and we look at our reflection, our two heads together, in the spectrum-split plastic of the first half of the opera.

So is marriage a matter of chains? I say.

Eh? you say.

Or a matter of the kind of faithfulness that brings dead things back to life? I say.

I have absolutely no idea what you're talking about, you say.

I lean my head back on your collarbone and turn it so that

my mouth touches the top of your arm. I feel with my teeth the front of your shoulder.

Don't bite me, you say.

Marzelline. That's her name.

Gershwin wrote six prayers to be sung simultaneously, for the storm scene in Porgy and Bess. As an opera, Porgy and Bess did comparatively badly at the box office. So did the early versions of Fidelio; it wasn't till 1814 that audiences were ready to acclaim it. At the end of one, all the prisoners are free and all the self-delusion about love is irrelevant. At the end of the other, there's nothing to do but go off round the world, on one good leg and one ruined leg, in search of the lost beloved. I guess you got me fo' keeps, Porgy, Bess says, before she's gone, gone, gone, gone, gone, gone, gone.

Will I dress as a boy and stand outside your house, all its windows lit for your Christmas party, its music filtering out into the dark? Will I stand in the dark and take a pick or a spade to the hard surface of the turf of your midwinter back lawn? Will I dig till I'm covered in dust and earth, till I uncover the whole truth, the house of dust under the ground? Will I shake the soil off the long iron chain fixed to the slab of rock deep in the earth beneath the pretty lavenders, the annuals and perennials of your suburban garden?

It is Saturday night. It is summertime on a quiet hot street in a port town. A man plays a sleepy lament on a piano. Some men play dice. A woman married to a fisherman is rocking a baby to sleep. Her husband takes the baby out of her arms and sings it his own version of a lullaby. A woman is a sometime thing, he sings. The baby cries. Everybody laughs.

Porgy arrives home. He's a cripple; he rides in a cart pulled by a goat. He goes to join in the dice game. A man arrives with a woman in tow; the man is Crown and the woman is Bess. His job is the unloading and loading of cargo from ships. Her job is to be his, and to keep herself happy on happy dust, drugs. These dice, Porgy says shaking them, are my morning and my evening stars. An' just you watch 'em rise and shine for this poor beggar.

But Crown is high on drink and dust. When he loses at dice he starts a fight. He kills someone with a cotton hook. Get out of here, Bess tells him, the police will be here any minute. At the mention of the police, everybody on the street disappears except the dead man, the dead man's mourning wife, and Bess, who finds all the doors of all the houses shut against her.

Then, unexpectedly, one door opens. It's the door of Porgy, the cripple. She's about to go in, but at the last moment she doesn't. She turns and looks at the side of the stage instead. Everything on stage stops, holds its breath.

The orchestra stops.

A white girl has entered from the wings. She is standing, lost-looking, over by the edge of the set.

Bess stares at her. Porgy, still at his door, stares at her.

Serena, the dead man's wife, stares at her. The dead man, Robbins, opens his eyes and puts his head up and stares at her.

The doors of the other houses on the set open; the windows open. All the other residents of Catfish Row look out. They come out of the houses. They're sweating, from the heat under the stage-lights, under the hot summer night. They stand at a distance, their sweat glistening, their eyes on the white girl with the iron in her hand.

The girl starts to sing.

A brother has come to seek her brothers, she sings. To help

them if she can with all her heart.

Everybody on stage looks to Porgy, the cripple. He looks to Bess, who shrugs, then nods.

Porgy nods too. He opens his door wider.

Freedom
Sebastian Barry

'John started to write his memoirs about 1936 but didn't
have the patience to complete them...'

- Lily McCormack, wife of John

It has been an extraordinary few days, God knows.

Just a few mornings ago, although it seems much longer, we
headed out from the little capital town called Butte into the
very lands of the Blackfoot. We were travelling for three days
then.

Butte is famously full of Irish, working on the mines, and I
was happy to be among them, but equally happy to get away.

We moved through a land that is so empty and full in the
same instance, you are also emptied of language. You become
silent. There is certainly nothing like it in Ireland. Maybe if you
waved a magic wand, in the best summer ever experienced, in
parts of Mayo, and were able to swell that landscape, you might
have something like it. But it is country that looks to me as
if it doesn't really need humans. It is large everywhere, pale
sometimes in the sunlight, with marks of fierce colour, and the
water is that deep and plunging sort that would sooner kill than
delight you. Everything is just murderously there. Everything

seems as if it is on death row, the grasses, the rocks, the snakes, the light.

At one time, my friend told me, it was only landscape and Indians there, for hundreds of years, maybe thousands. It is easy enough to imagine.

My friend wore so-called European clothes, but he is a true son of that place, his face an extraordinary dark colour, like the surface of one of those excellent pieces of hand-me-down furniture that Lily so covets. He gave his name as Mitch, a name maybe like the clothes, given to me instead of a more complicated Indian name.

But isn't John McCormack just the same thing, an Englished version of an Irish name that would have bamboozled anyone not familiar with our dark and intricate tongue? He called me John just as easy as I called him Mitch.

His English was really good, that is, his American, and I have rarely met a man so openly friendly. He shook my hand when he came to the big dusty hotel, took it in his in the lobby in front of some very disapproving bellboys, and shook it heartily, and I shook his. And then the bellboys laughed, to see the 'famous man' shake the 'poor Injun's' hand. I suppose it will be written up in the *Butte Herald* in the morning, to go with some fanciful drawing. I am sure they will work me into something of a leprechaun, and I will have a shillelagh under my arm, and Mitch will have acquired a tomahawk and a bow and arrow. They're not going to let us away with what we are, an Irishman in a black suit that's most unsuitable for this climate, and a Blackfoot man also in the wrong clothes maybe, but definitely at home, especially every yard we go from the town.

Mitch told me his people were called Siksiksa in their own language. I told him we were called Eireneach. With that established, we both felt more comfortable. He told me in 1880 or thereabouts there was a great starvation, when the last buffalo was killed, and I was able to match him with our famine of the 1840s. Then we were as good as brothers.

When we reached the area of the reservation, a certain bleakness set into things. Every scrap of wood in fences and houses looked indeed individually starved. The sun has sucked everything out of it. We must have been high above sea level because it began to be very cold, which surprised me, though Buffalo, when we went up to see the falls on the American side, was entirely frozen over still, like a dazed picture of water, not water itself. Lily standing there like Andersen's snow queen...

Mitch got the driver to take down my trunk and fetched out my big coat, with the velvet collar. He thought that was mighty fine, as coats went, and when it was on me, he stroked the lapel, like he might the neck of a horse. I was delighted for some reason I could not quite identify. It reminded me of my father at home in Athlone stroking my head as a boy. Some such. A simple, human gesture. I wondered could I ever work it into a performance, but could think of no scene in an opera that would accommodate such a simplicity.

If it was a long way to the reservation, it had been a long long way from Buffalo to Butte, and every day of it I began to miss my darling Lily more and more. Tremendously. She is my ease and my whiskey. Love is not just a fiction of romantic operas. I am well used to this task of missing her, but wish with all my heart we were still a touring couple, and that every thing I do of this nature did not involve being separated.

But then this is a thing out of the ordinary. I performed in *Natoma*, an Indian opera about the Blackfoot, so the Blackfoot wished to honour me. They wished to induct me into their tribe. And because I was deeply moved by their thought, I was willing to suffer exile from Lily, leaving her in Buffalo, which might be regarded as the last fringe of polite society. But who really makes these decisions? Vanity, homesickness, all those gods that bedevil us.

But we follow our noses. The best of life is instinct. I think of Blackfoot and Irishman in the same breath, imagining we have similar histories, involving of course the expansions of the whiteman. But is the Irishman not a whiteman? I suppose not, in some people's eyes. I remember reading in Carlyle, whom otherwise I admire greatly, that 'if the Irishman can not be improved a little, perhaps he ought to be exterminated'. This was maybe a mid-century jest. That 'a little' is very wonderful in its way, a Carlyle-ism to beat the band. Dickens, his friend, though well disposed to the poor in general, could have surprisingly caustic things to say about the Irish also. It must have been an after-dinner fashion – a temptation. The mysterious island next door. At least he said that the Eskimo, who he thought had probably eaten Franklin and his men at the pole, was 'worse than an Irishman'. I suppose that's pretty bad.

Montana is so far north it's nearly Canada, like so much of America up here is always referred to as 'nearly Canada', and always in the same doubtful tone. Canada begins on the frostline, I suppose that's the problem. The winters up here are said to be truly terrible. It's bad enough in May if you ask me.

'Your spit'll freeze 'fore it hits the snow,' Mitch said, or words to that effect. He's hard to translate. Maybe he has the same trouble with my Athlone accent, Butte or no Butte. I mean it being full of Irish accents.

He told me that no one sings in the winter out in the open,

because your mouth will fill instantly with frost if you open it. He may have been joking with me, like a Kerryman will tease the ignorant stranger. Or maybe not.

He tried to explain to me something about women being allowed to sing at festivities. That in other tribes this was not allowed, considered bad luck, but in his crowd the women were the singers, though they had to affect a man's way of singing. I was very careful not to laugh. I told him about singers in Ireland that were shy or fearful, who went behind the door to sing. I said behind-the-door singers were often the best ones. Well, Mitch didn't hold back, he laughed and laughed at that. So then we were both laughing together.

And singing is a fearful business right enough.

I thought of some of the terrible notices for *Natoma*, some attacking the libretto viciously, others praising Victor's songs, and the Indian music he had tried to incorporate, but then falling to saying that a little of the Indian thing went a long way, and that alas there had been more than a little.

Victor Herbert is a very nice Dublin man and he didn't deserve the drubbing. It killed the opera stone-dead. I will never forget the opening night, fabulous sets, the Met teeming, people fighting for tickets – interesting opera, fabulous singing from Mary and not too shoddy I thought from myself, even if the part was hopeless, in all truth. Everything fabulous, except the damn notices.

I don't think Victor will ever try his hand at another opera. Especially not an Indian one. Perhaps one with an Irish theme? Closer to home? But maybe *Natoma* was close to home. I think so.

To me there was some of the loveliest music in it I have read in a modern work. Though sadly not in my role. And Mary was lovely. I was enthralled by her. I would come off the stage at the try-out in Philadelphia, stunned by the experience, sweating like a bull (but do bulls sweat? I have never thought to find out). I would fall into bed with Lily, sure, despite my misgivings, that we would be hailed in New York, showered with the praises of the great cognoscenti. My misgivings melting before the mystery and power of Mary Garden. So it goes. The great delusions of our work. Yes, they couldn't see us off quick enough. Victor was even criticized for the subtitle, 'an American opera'. 'If the Irish cannot be improved a little...' The critics may have been reading their Carlyle.

But the Blackfeet didn't care about all that. We had mounted an opera about one of their own, and like people from a losing county at an inter-county hurling match in Ireland, they were ready to carry us shoulder-high, win or lose. It was delicious.

Not that they did anything so indecorous as to hoist us on their shoulders. A little delegation came in, composed of seven of their most important men (and perhaps one or two were women, acting like men?), in full regalia, and sat in one of the boxes. It was a stunt by the management, but the Indians didn't know or care about that. Indeed at the end of the performance, greeted by that miserable silence in the house, and then a half-hearted clapping much worse than the silence – precluding all possibility that the audience had been so swept away by emotion and delight, that they had been stunned for a few moments, and would shortly erupt into wild cheering and applause – the chiefs stood up as one. Mere dribbles of clapping rose from the stalls below, perhaps mostly out of relief at being released from the torments we had unwittingly subjected them to. But the Blackfoot chiefs stood nobly, and banged their hands together like the first people ever to applaud in the history of the world, and surely we felt their appreciation, even if it was all more than slightly ludicrous.

Afterwards they trooped back with the ashen-faced manager, and came into my dressing room, and asked me if I would come up as far as Montana in the late spring, as they would like to induct me into their tribe, as an honorary member. I was so moved I said yes. Lily was so moved by me saying yes, that later, in the glorious apartment enthusiastically given us by the Met, and now not so enthusiastically (the manager came and asked if we wouldn't prefer to be in a nice cosy hotel after all!), she was so 'moved' she nearly boxed my ears for me. But the next day at breakfast she sighed and gave way graciously to her daft husband.

Why was I so moved? It was something to do with the situation. The horrible and catastrophic failure of the opera, and then their noble behaviour. You have to work just as hard to achieve a failure as a success. Sometimes the gods will simply fly away. One moment they are by your side, the next, they hasten to the other side of the world, to La Scala maybe, to my dear Caruso possibly. But it's all the same expenditure of care and sweat, of love for the music, for the singing when it comes freely at last, the notes melting one into the other, something so intensely human it is touching on the divine. Ah, but, who knows the why and what of all this? Nobody knows. Until the poor manager opens the *New York Times*. Then he knows. His stomach knows first, then his heart, then his wretched head. Then everyone knows.

Then last night, or was it the night before (now I am on my way back to Lily in Buffalo, and I am confused by these Yankee distances), there was a beautiful little ceremony. Their chief, Running Rabbit, descendant of the famous (so they told me)

Aatsista-Mahkan – who I at first thought might be a Macken or McCann, having been given an Irish name, why not, until a girl kindly wrote down the name for me – their chief began with an oration that would have graced an Oxford graduation. He spoke in his own language, Algonquian, every bit as stately as Latin, or Gaelic for that matter. They all gathered round me for a photograph, taken by an itinerant photographer who happened to be there that day, or who had been called from far away for this very purpose. The chief held a pipe just at my left hand, for the minutes it took for the exposure. He seemed perfectly content to do so, perfectly conversant with the ways of the camera. We looked at the camera indeed like a group of fond relations, trying to stare our way into the future, as may be.

Then there was singing, indeed from a woman, in a low register, and with manly gestures, which went on for about twenty minutes. It kept itself to just the few notes, rather Chinese I thought, very throaty, and barely modulated. The effect was all in the tone, the repetition, the trancelike purpose. I thought of what Gerald Cambrensis had written about Irish music in the twelfth century, that it was incomprehensible to outsiders, but in truth of enormous complexity, and really very wonderful when the taste was acquired, and a proper knowledge of it.

I stood there, feeling suddenly in my great coat as large and black as a buffalo. I was being fired on by the song, it was slaying me, wonderfully. The last buffalo, returned to life, perplexed as ever. Suddenly Lily came rushing into my thoughts, the utter wonder of her, and my father and mother, growing old in Athlone, and my life of singing, of audiences, of strange abundance. The enormous ineluctable simplicity of the song was rending me. I was being honoured far beyond my worth. I forbid myself to have an 'opinion' of that music. All of history was in it, 'American' history, the history of the whiteman in America, of the Redman, of the Irishman that is no colour at all that any artist could name. I had a sudden and vividly clear sense of the struggle of mankind, the immense not-knowing, the immense effort put into marshalling adjectives, these good, but these bad, this sort of person good, but this sort of person bad, 'The only good Indian is a dead Indian,' General Sheridan said, and bless me, he was from Cavan, this colour, that colour, this century, that century, this sort of death, that sort of death, this life, that life, this singing, that singing, this opera, that opera.

To Die For
Kate Atkinson

'Opera does not threaten us. Fiction does.'

Frederick R. Karl,

A Reader's Guide to the Development of
the English Novel in the 18th Century

There was this old English actress called Phoebe Something-Or-Other. Hart-Williams? Hill-West? Skylar never could remember (not that she tried very hard). Phoebe Something-Or-Other was huge, like a big old toad and, on set, in between takes, she sat in a corner and did some kind of sewing. ('Cross-stitch. You should try it, sweetie.') It didn't matter who you were, star of the movie or a faceless runner, you were 'sweetie' to her. It got on Skylar's nerves. It was so *British*. She was tired of everything British, especially the weather.

They were in the make-up trailer, five in the morning in the middle of nowhere. (Kent? Somethingshire?) Wherever it was, it was green and dripping with water. Every day on location they had to stop for rain, most days they never even got started. They were shooting an outdoor scene where Skylar had to ride a horse down a hill towards a big old house. She had to cry as she rode. Then she had to jump off the horse and run towards Phoebe (who was playing her grandmother), standing on the steps of the house. They weren't allowed inside the house. Skylar would have liked to have seen inside the house.

Skylar's tears should be, according to the director, 'a mixture of joy and relief, tinged with sadness and regret for what might have been'. All that and on a horse! What did he think she was? ('An actress, sweetie?')

The script called for the horse to gallop but they'd compromised on a kind of trot because horses made Skylar want to pee her pants. They were so damn big! Skylar was barely five foot two and way under a hundred pounds. Of course, she looked *gigantic* on screen but Mom had been helping Skylar keep the pounds off ever since she won the Augusta Sweet Pea Pageant when she was knee-high to a gnat's heel.

They refused to dope the horse so she had to fill herself with Xanax and be hitched up by the horse wrangler and the chief stunt guy. Over and over, because of the rain, because of the petrified expression on Skylar's face.

Plus, she had to do the whole thing side-saddle in a dress the size of a Big Top. It was a costume drama, an eighteenth-century thing, about thwarted passion, from some novel that had won a prize. *The Girl Who Went Astray* – which was a real dumb title in Skylar's opinion. The crew called it *The Girl With Big Tits*. Some people had no manners. They *were* big it was true, they'd been paid for with the money from a Dr Pepper ad she did when she was sixteen. She was twenty-two now. She hoped that if she ever got to be as old as Phoebe someone would shoot her.

In the movie Skylar was playing a hooker who was really an heiress but she didn't know it (until the happy, happy end) because she'd been swapped at birth after her mother died, leaving only a locket behind to identify her by. (Eventually, by

Phoebe, her grandmother, etcetera). Harry, Skylar's agent, said she should do the movie so she could 'capitalize' on her accent seeing as it had taken her 'so damn long to get it right'. That was on account of her being English in her last movie as well. ('All Hollywood A-Listers do English,' her agent said. 'It's the only way you'll ever get an Oscar.') She'd played a spy in the Second World War. All very tragic, etcetera. They had shot the whole thing in Hungary. *In a Time of Madness*, it was called. (It was!) She was killed by a firing-squad at the end. They did twenty-two takes of that. By the end, the look of suffering on her face was *real*.

They were holding the premiere tonight in Leicester Square. It was the last thing Skylar felt like doing but everyone said it was going to be a big movie (not like this one, for sure).

'Selling yourself to the press goes with the territory, sweetie,' Phoebe said. As if Skylar, of all people, didn't know that!

Skylar knew exactly where Phoebe Something-Or-Other could stick her sewing. And the sun definitely didn't shine there!

Phoebe was eating a bacon roll. 'Mm. On-set catering,' she said. 'The best thing about this job.' Yeugh. Skylar tried not to inhale the scent of dead, fried pig, instead she took two Ritalin, to keep the weight down and perk her up (what more could you ask for in a pill?). Peering in the mirror Phoebe said, 'Gawd love us—' (or something like that). 'What an old crone I am.'

'You have a *wonderful* face!' Skylar's make-up girl gushed at Phoebe. 'So much character.' 'Character' meant old. Skylar didn't want to have any character.

Everyone (except Skylar) loved Phoebe. They called her a 'national treasure', like she was part of the Crown Jewels. (Skylar had been to the Tower of London, a special out-of-hours visit that someone arranged for her. It was cool.) Whenever anyone needed an English queen in a movie they wheeled in Phoebe. ('Oh, God, yes, sweetie, I've done them all, Elizabeth, Victoria, Mary Q of S, Anne Boleyn – when I was younger, of course.') The way she behaved you would think she *was* royalty.

'Soothes the nerves,' Phoebe said, waving her bit of sewing in Skylar's face. It was a cushion cover with a big pink rose on it. It was almost finished and if you stared at it long enough you felt you were being sucked *inside* the rose. 'You have trouble with your nerves, don't you, sweetie?' Phoebe persisted. The way she said it was real, real catty in Skylar's opinion. 'Well, nervous *exhaustion*,' Skylar said. 'That was what I was hospitalized with.' (It had been all over the papers, no point in denying it.) 'Nervous exhaustion is different from nerves,' Skylar pointed out. Of course, everyone knew that 'nervous exhaustion' meant you were wiped out on drugs or booze or sex (or in Skylar's case all three). She bounced right back though. Two weeks in a clinic in Arizona and she was good to go. Again.

'You know what they say about all publicity being good publicity, Skylar?' her manager, Marty said. 'Well, it's not necessarily true. You don't want a reputation with the studio. Look what happened to Lindsay. Cut down on the partying.' But, darn it, she was young! All she wanted was some fun, what was wrong with that? There were no parties out in the God-forsaken countryside. Her stunt double (yes, she had a stunt double and no, the stunt double couldn't do the horse galloping thing because the director was a realism Nazi) and her accent coach (who was on set *all the time*, it was like being back at school) wanted to take her to the local pub last night but she took a couple of Ambien instead and talked to her Mom on the phone until she fell asleep.

The hotel where she was staying didn't even have twenty-four-hour room service. It didn't actually have *room* service but Skylar's people had a word with someone and now they brought up bad coffee and limp salads to her room. Her personal trainer said she couldn't have coffee but Skylar didn't really care. Her personal trainer who, by the way, was down here in Something-shire for no reason because there *wasn't time* for Skylar to work out. No time for Skylar to do anything. So the personal trainer was doing nothing on Skylar's dollar. Like a lot of people.

'Nervous *exhaustion*. Of course, sweetie,' Phoebe said. 'I stand corrected. Silly old me. I could get you a pattern? Some wool?'

'Gee-whiz, that would be swell, Phoebe.' Skylar would rather stick pins in her eyes. She had no intention of cross-stitching big pink flowers onto cushion covers. The very idea made her mad. Or 'cross', as they said here. Ha, ha. Skylar preferred to go to her trailer between takes, kick everyone out, pop a couple of Vicodin and watch DVDs of *Days of Our Lives* that Mom recorded for her. Skylar had been in it for a year when she was thirteen, playing a kid who was a runaway. That was after years of modelling. 'The Crisco Kid' her mother called her but actually she'd lost out on that one to a Scarlett Johansson type. Or maybe it *was* Scarlett Johansson. For someone with so little past there seemed to be an awful lot of it that Skylar couldn't remember. *Days of Our Lives* got them out of the trailer park for good and Mom out of the Piggly Wiggly and now Mom was a realtor and wore red lipstick to work every day and had a real nice house in Orange County, all thanks to Skylar. 'Don't mention the trailer park in interviews, Skylar,' Marty said. But why not? It was the American dream to escape the trailer park and Skylar was the all-American girl.

She yawned and her make-up girl had to stop applying her lipstick. Skylar was so tired. She was making movies back to back because she was real hot at the moment. 'Everyone wants you,' Marty said. Yeah, sure, everyone who made money out of her. In the mirror she could see her English assistant (Christie? Kirsty?) smiling encouragingly at her. She was holding the biggest umbrella Skylar had ever seen.

'Ready, Miss Schiller?'

Skylar sighed and hitched up her breasts. 'Yeah. As I'll ever be.'

They didn't wrap until five. Skylar had to get a car back to the Covent Garden Hotel, have her hair and make-up done, choose from the dresses her stylist had been given and be in Leicester Square by eight o'clock. She had another PA waiting for her at the hotel, but he was her friend as well – Marshall. He'd been a kid actor too and a Mousketeer in the Time of Britney. Now he just got paid to hang out with Skylar to stop her dying of boredom and when her stylist wasn't around he was pretty good at picking out clothes. Plus, of course he was a walking drugstore, although most of what Skylar needed was on prescription. She had a great physician back home in LA. He was called Dr Morris and he really *listened* to Skylar and gave her all kinds of stuff that helped take the edge off and even out the day.

In the end they'd ditched the horse and Skylar just ran down the hill (pretty difficult in that dress), which everyone said looked better after all. Everyone except the director, but what did he know? He was, as they said here, a wanker. A real jerk-off. His last movie went straight to DVD and Skylar wouldn't be surprised if this one did too. 'The studio needs a tax write-off,' Marshall said, 'and honey, I think you're it.' ('Don't listen to that little fag,' Marty said. 'He pours evil like poison in your ear.' Marty could talk pretty fancy when he wanted to.) 'Remember Kirsten Dunst in *Marie Antoinette*?' Marshall said. ''Nuff said, honey.'

Her assistant held the umbrella over her while she walked from her trailer to the car. Skylar had asked for some kind of screen so no one could see her on this little journey but it never happened. So maybe she wasn't A-List enough. Someone was going to have to have a word with someone.

'Have a nice time, Miss Schiller,' her assistant said as Skylar got into the car.

'Yeah, thanks, Kirsty.'

'It's Karen, Miss Schiller. But it doesn't matter, you can call me whatever you want.' (Jeez, imagine being that desperate.) Skylar decided she'd give her something real nice when they finished shooting. She had a Birkin bag someone had given her that was worth a fortune. Skylar already had two.

'Skylar! Skylar! This way, Skylar! Skylar, Skylar, over here! Skylar, look at me, darlin'!'

You got used to it. It went with the territory, as Phoebe would have said. Her co-star (gay, married, bozo) walked down the red carpet with his hand in the small of her back. She was supposed to do the walk on her own. Harry and Marty would be furious.

She was wearing a cute Stella McCartney dress and a pair of peep-toe Louboutins that were a half-size too big. She'd had two Oxycontin and a half a bottle of champagne before leaving the hotel and was feeling pleasantly floaty. She slept through most of the movie, despite Marty pinching her on one side and Harry on the other, and before she knew it they were back in the

Dorchester for the premiere party. Marshall was there, thank the Lord, and gave her some Exefor to keep her going.

Marty and Harry were pretty happy and everyone kept saying how great she was in the movie. Of course, they always said that. She flirted a little with a lot of guys and then this one guy came up and said, 'Do I know you?' He was real, *real* English. When Skylar was a kid Mom had taken on three jobs so she could afford a voice coach to 'get the Georgia out of' Skylar and they'd done a lot of that 'rain on the Spanish plain' stuff. Skylar had thought it would come in handy for *In a Time of Madness* but the voice coach on *that* movie (another friend of Hitler's) said, 'Forget everything anyone has ever taught you, Miss Schiller.' As if.

The real, real English guy was still standing there like a dork, creasing his brow like a bad actor and saying, 'I'm sure I've seen you somewhere before,' so Skylar said, 'I'm Skylar Schiller—' all polite because that's how Mom raised her, but really, how could he not know who she was when for the last two hours he'd been looking at her face blown up a zillion times? (Although, of course, she'd been dressed down as a spy, which, according to the movie was not a glamorous occupation. No siree.)

He was ordinary-looking but there was something about him that was familiar. Skylar was pretty sure she hadn't slept with him.

He laughed and said, 'No, no, *no*, just joking, of *course* I know who you are – *God* – I'd have to have been living at the North *Pole* for the last two years if I didn't know who you were. I'm a *huge* fan, I was really concerned when you were taken into hospital, are you all better now? Is it Schiller like the poet?'

All this without taking a breath! A lot of people in England asked about Schiller the poet (and, no, Skylar wasn't related to him), no one in the States ever mentioned him. And then he was off again, '*Alle Menschen werden Bruder* and all that,' he said. He flushed as pink as a shrimp when Skylar smiled at him and said, 'Yeah. That too.' They were right, the English really did speak a different language.

She was looking around the room for Marshall to come and rescue her when who should pop up out of nowhere but Phoebe Something-Or-Other. She was dressed as if she'd been involved in a terrible accident in a fabric mill, bits of chiffon trailing everywhere. She smiled at Skylar, showing horrible yellow teeth – didn't they have orthodontists in this country? – and said, 'Have you been introduced properly to his Royal Highness?'

Well, you could have knocked Skylar down with a feather.

'I was a good friend of his grandmother,' Phoebe said before scooting off again, hanging on to her glass of gin as if she was on a Ouija board.

'So...' Skylar said. Was she supposed to curtsy? She gave a tiny little bob, just in case. 'So, Prince...' Which one was he? The one who was going to be king one day or the other one? She was suddenly aware of the big wad of gum in her mouth. It didn't seem appropriate when you were talking (possibly) to the future king of England.

'Prince Alfred, but please call me Alfie.'

'So, Prince Alfie...I didn't know they let you go to movies and that kind of stuff.' Oh real lame, Skylar, real lame.

'Oh, we get let out occasionally,' he laughed. 'And it's just Alfie.'

'OK, just Alfie.'

'I'm a huge fan, did I say that?'

'Yeah.' He looked a whole lot cuter now that he was royal.

'Skylar. Like skylark,' he said.

'But without the K,' Skylar pointed out.

'I thought you were a blonde,' he said, waving vaguely in the direction of her hair.

'I'm not really anything,' Skylar said. 'I'm whatever they want me to be.'

'Mm. Me too,' he said. 'Shall we get out of here? Go to a club or something?'

'People will talk,' Skylar said, suddenly, unaccountably nervous.

'People *are* talking,' he said.

'I have to be home by midnight, or I turn into a pumpkin,' Skylar said. She wanted him to think she was funny. Or interesting. Or something.

'Actually, I think it's the carriage that turns into a pumpkin,' he said. 'We've got one like that.'

On the Pont-Neuf, two gendarmes roller-bladed past them. They made it look chic. Only the French could do that, Campbell thought. She needed hot tea. She felt nauseous with tiredness and jet-lag. Or maybe she was coming down with something. Think how many germs you shared on a transatlantic flight. Millions probably. 'I need tea,' she said to Joel.

'Sure,' he said.

'Can we look for a café?'

Joel sighed. Campbell knew he was contemplating the unwelcome idea of negotiating food and drink with a Parisian. When they were here last time, five years ago on honeymoon, everyone had seemed charming and friendly, now the same people (more or less) were surly and uncommunicative. Between them she and Joel had pretty good French – when he was a child Joel lived in Switzerland because his father was something big in international banking and Campbell had majored in European languages at Brown before she fast-tracked law – but when they started speaking to anyone in French they cut them off impatiently as soon as they heard the American in their voices. The irony was that then *they* started talking to them in their appalling English! Twenty-four hours and the French were already 'they' and 'them' – the enemy.

'At least they don't smoke in cafés anymore,' Campbell said encouragingly.

It wasn't until they'd walked almost all the way back to their hotel near the Madeleine that they found somewhere both of them were prepared to compromise on. The window was full of exquisite cakes that were like works of art, that *were* works of art. They ignited a kind of mad desire in Campbell, made her feel so greedy that she wanted to eat every cake in the window.

'This one then?' she said, feigning indifference.

'Sure,' Joel said, not feigning indifference. He didn't have a sweet tooth.

He'd been in a bad mood ever since they landed on French soil. Their luggage had gone missing at Charles de Gaulle and it had made him endlessly fretful. But it turned up this morning at the hotel and when they opened their suitcases their neat, pressed clothes (unredeemably American) were all present and correct so he really didn't have to keep going on about it. All the time looking for something to complain about. She supposed he had been argumentative for weeks, but here, removed from his everyday New York context, his petulance seemed to pervade everything.

They'd spent their honeymoon in a quaint little hotel in the

Marais but it was fully booked this week and they had ended up in a middle-of-the-range place that seemed characterless in comparison. Breakfast this morning had been a rather spare buffet – little pats of foil-wrapped butter still hard from the freezer, greasy pastries and a bowl of fruit salad that surely hadn't been made fresh that morning. Only the coffee had passed muster, although Joel had to ask twice for a refill from the crabby woman in charge. In their hotel in the Marais they had taken breakfast in a little open-air courtyard at the back of the hotel, the walls of which were covered in vines. But that had been June and this was inhospitable November and the breakfast room was in a dimly lit old *cave* beneath the building. Their fellow guests, a German family and a group of Japanese businessmen, seemed dispirited and subdued, as if they too had realized they should never have come here.

The morning sky was opaque, the colour of Tupperware. It threatened rain all the time as they walked to Les Invalides. ('Let's not revisit anything,' Campbell had said, leafing through their *Eyewitness Guide to Paris* on the plane. 'We should go to places we didn't do last time.')

'Maybe there was a good reason for not coming here before,' Joel said as they wandered listlessly round an exhibit in Les Invalides about Paris during the Second World War. 'I mean it's pretty depressing.'

'Well, war is depressing,' Campbell said. Last time they had taken a *bateau-mouche* along the Seine and they had held hands in the sunshine and Campbell had rested her head on Joel's shoulder and felt she'd arrived at the place she was supposed to be.

*

Campbell spent so long contemplating Napoleon's weird, enormous tomb – strange to think what a small man was inside it – that when she looked around she could find no sign of Joel. They never stuck together in galleries and museums but nor did they stray too far from each other. Campbell used to think there was an invisible cord that bound them, one to another. Not this time apparently. Half an hour later and she still hadn't come across him. She went outside and hung around for a while, looking out for his familiar figure. She had left her cell in the hotel safe so she had no way of contacting him, she hadn't thought she would need to.

Then the clouds finally broke so she headed for a café. It was crowded and steamy but she managed to find a table and ordered a coffee and something big and gooey that just about put her into a diabetic coma. Back home in Manhattan she would have been eating grilled chicken or fish, a salad on the side. Here it didn't matter. Nothing mattered. Her mind felt cool and uncluttered without Joel. There were empty places inside her that he usually filled. Or perhaps there was just less of her without him. That was not necessarily a bad thing.

Five years since they were married, a big ceremony in the Hamptons, on the lawn of a house owned by friends of Joel's parents. Juliet roses, a quartet playing Mozart, dress by Vera Wang. The whole shebang. If that Campbell could have seen herself five years into the future she would have expected a child by now, a dog at least. A house with a yard. Just went to show.

She ordered another cup of coffee. Campbell never simply sat, never wasted time. There was always something to occupy her, papers or files, or if not work then a dinner party to go to, or to cook for, a movie to see, a show. Talking, reading, writing, thinking, always talking. Even when they made love she and Joel talked to each other. Maybe they'd talked too much, maybe that was why they had run out of words.

People came and went. Food was eaten, checks were paid, tips were left. Time was wasted. Campbell had another cup of coffee. Was it worth trying to order decaff? Probably not, she imagined that the French scoffed at decaff.

She was both anchored and adrift. In the old world. An American in Paris. She should have a book with her. She should be reading James or Hemingway. Or maybe not.

It was nearly five o'clock by the time she meandered back to the hotel. Joel was lying on the bed watching an incomprehensible French quiz on TV. He glanced at her briefly and said, 'Why did you leave me in Les Invalides?' and she said, 'I didn't. You left me.'

'No, I didn't.'

They could have gone on for ever like that, Campbell supposed, batting right and wrong backwards and forwards, but she just didn't care enough to keep returning the argument. She went into the bathroom, stripped off and stepped into the shower.

He wasn't the heir, he was 'the spare'. That meant that if his brother Prince James ('Jamie') died, Alfie would be King. So only a teeny-tiny step away. Of course, the old King, their father ('Papa'), would have to die first. After Alfie it was some crazy cousin of their father's. ('The line of succession' it was called.) Jamie and Alfie weren't allowed to travel on the same plane because no one wanted the crazy cousin to inherit the throne if they went down together in flames. It was all written down in stone thousands of years ago. Skylar found it real interesting, being with Alfie was like being with living history. He was fun though, not like Jamie who was very solemn, like he already had that big, old, heavy crown weighing his head down. She didn't meet the King because he was off on tour somewhere but she did go to an official dinner where she was camouflaged (as Alfie put it) by the presence of lots of other celebrities. She was seated between the deputy prime minister and a man who made giant sculptures from trash. The flatware was gold.

Skylar had to be smuggled in and out of the palace. (The palace! It was awesome!) She hadn't told Mom yet because Alfie said it was very important that their love was kept a secret and if Mom knew about it she'd be on the cover of the *Enquirer* shooting her mouth off about 'Queen Skylar'.

They wrapped. Finally. And the rain stopped and Skylar had two whole weeks to herself. And, by chance Alfie had two whole weeks too. He was in the military. He'd just finished learning to be a soldier and now he was going to go on to learn to be a sailor. And after that, maybe a pilot. It was like they were expecting him to fight a war single-handed.

The English summer seemed to be a pretty busy time for people like Jamie and Alfie and their friends – a lot of boating and horse racing and garden parties which Skylar thought would be cool but Alfie said, 'God, I don't want to parade you round the season, I just want you to myself.' So they went and stayed in what he called a cottage but what Skylar would have called a mansion on 'the Sandringham estate' (it took her a while to work that one out).

Skylar didn't bother with make-up. She wore jeans or nothing. She didn't even need any pills, just a couple of Vicodin now and then. A woman (Sonia? Sylvia?) came every day in a big SUV and left meals for them in the kitchen. Someone came in and cleaned, but real quiet, so you wouldn't know they were there.

They had a lot of sex and when they were worn out with the sex they went into the woods and shot things. Skylar was a good shot, she'd been taught by a step-daddy called Hoyt, but she refused to kill anything as pretty as a deer so they just aimed at tin cans. 'You're good,' Alfie said. 'Between us we could take on the world.' Sometimes they took a picnic into the woods. Of course, they were never really alone, there were security guys everywhere, but Skylar was used to being watched by people.

She liked waking up every morning and seeing Alfie's cheerful face looking down at her. He woke up early, he said Eton had done that to him. Eton is a school. It was funny how when you got real fond of someone they started to look handsome. She began to imagine she could do this for ever. They'd get married and have little princes and princesses and Skylar would wear tweed and maybe even learn cross-stitch.

And then one morning Skylar, butt-naked, opened the door to Sonia/Silvia and, hey presto, the next morning, there was her photograph in one of the papers that a security guy showed them. 'Royal love nest,' it said. And a whole lot of other stuff as well, obviously.

There was a huge fuss, breach of royal security, Alfred could have been shot with a gun not a camera, etcetera, but a lot more column inches devoted to Skylar, of course. Alfie was real upset. 'They can't let me have anything,' he said. 'Even you.'

'Especially not me,' Skylar said.

Then it just went crazy, they were in every newspaper and celebrity magazine. Skylar thought she was famous before but this was awesome. She turned her cell off. Otherwise it just rang off the hook. Marty and Harry, Marshall, her Mom, hundreds of other people who all depended on Skylar. Their two weeks was up. She was supposed to be in LA, shooting had already started on her new movie. Alfie was supposed to be on a ship somewhere. Instead they were holed up on 'the Sandringham estate' like outlaws. 'We can't stay here for ever,' Skylar said to Alfie and he said, 'Why not?' and she felt real sad because she knew he really wanted to stay here for ever with her. And he knew he couldn't.

Then Skylar opened the door again. Fully clothed, she'd learnt her lesson, and who was standing there? Only the King with a capital 'K'.

'Can I come in?' he asked. As if he didn't own the place!

'Sure, your Royal Majesty,' Skylar said. (She'd been learning all the right things to say. Just in case.) 'Alfie's in the bathtub. Shall I get him?'

Turned out it was her he'd come to see. He wanted 'a word'. About how the monarchy was 'being brought into disrepute'. How things were pretty bad anyway for them (really?) without 'this kind of scandal'. He was nice, she liked him, she could tell he didn't want to upset her. He did though.

'Gee-whiz, Your Majesty,' Skylar said. 'We're just two young people who love each other, we shouldn't have to battle the whole world.' This was a line from a teen movie she'd done way back when, but she reckoned it was a pretty safe bet that the King hadn't seen it.

He had an attaché case with him and he fished inside it and came up with a DVD that looked blank and said, 'Do you know what I have here?'

'A blank DVD?'

'No, I'm afraid there is a film on it, Miss Schiller. Here

are some stills from it,' he said, digging into his case again. He handed over a folder of photographs to Skylar and said, 'Recognize them?'

It was just a movie. A lot of people got started that way. True, she was only fifteen and she'd lied about her age. It was just before the Dr Pepper commercial when she thought she was never going to break into the big time. And, OK, so the sex in the movie was real but it wasn't as if she'd never had sex before ('You may as well be paid for it,' Mom said) and it wasn't for distribution, just for some rich guy who wanted to star in his own porno show and was prepared to pay real big bucks for the privilege of doing it with Skylar in every room in his house. (It was a pretty big house.) Yeah, and so what if some of it wasn't very nice, life wasn't very nice, was it? And she'd managed to erase it from her head and now here was the King of England, no less, showing her a reminder of it.

It wasn't pretty. (Did he watch the whole thing? The scene in the bathroom?)

'I can have it held back,' he said. 'It's in all our interests. But only if you give him up. And believe me, Miss Schiller, I say that knowing how much pain it will cause the pair of you.'

'We have to sacrifice our love?' Skylar said, which was another line from the movie. The teen one, not the porno one.

By the time Alfie was out of the bathtub his 'Papa' had gone and Skylar was the one who had to tell him that she didn't love him anymore. And it was only when she said the words, and watched his face crumple like a kid's, that she realized that the words were a lie. Love pinched her heart. They said love hurt, and it turns out it did. Who knew?

*

A dead sky. Everything flat, like white paint. They endured a terrible afternoon at Versailles. Even getting inside was an endurance test in their ongoing stand-off with the French. 'Why can't they just have a sign that says *Entrée*?' Joel fumed. 'Everything's so perversely illogical with the French.' They didn't like Versailles, it was big and overblown, like every other European palace they'd ever been to. They'd done Europe one summer when they were students. They'd only had one day in Paris, that was one of the reasons they had come back here on honeymoon.

Campbell liked Le Petit Trianon, it was pretty and orderly and there was a cute donkey. She fed potato chips to the fish in the stream.

'How can you like it?' Joel said. 'It's artificial, a pretend place for a woman who was – rightly – doomed.' Yesterday they had argued about a friend who'd called their first child, a boy, 'Giuseppe'. They weren't Italian and Joel said the name was therefore 'stupid' and 'pretentious'. Campbell liked the name. She wondered what Joel would call a son if he had one. Not something Italian, apparently.

They were going to the Opera. The hotel concierge had got them expensive tickets to *La Traviata* and they got dressed up in their best clothes, which, being Americans, weren't much different from their ordinary clothes and had schlepped along the road to the Palais Garnier which Campbell thought was a gorgeous building and Joel, of course, thought was 'grotesquely overdone'. It turned out that it didn't matter what it was because it was the wrong building.

'Jesus Christ,' Joel said. 'Didn't you check?'

'Me?'

*

They managed to haul themselves into a cab and get to the Opera Bastille which Campbell thought was a soulless modern building and Joel thought was contemporary and sensible. They were cross and sweaty and only made it to their seats (right in the middle of a row, of course, and after many '*Excusez-moi*'s) with seconds to spare before curtain up.

'Which opera is *La Traviata*?' Campbell whispered as the overture struck up. She wasn't good with opera. Joel's parents had season tickets to the Met because that was the kind of people they were.

'Tragic inappropriate love, abandonment, death,' he whispered back.

'Yes, but *which* one?'

It was some kind of bank holiday in England and they were showing *101 Dalmatians* in the middle of the afternoon. Skylar and Marshall watched it on the hotel TV. He'd been a real friend. The security guys had driven her back to London yesterday and dropped her off at a hotel, 'very discreet, in Knightsbridge' one of them said to her. She wasn't sure who was picking up the check. She was flying out tomorrow. Both Marty and Harry said they were going to be at the airport to meet her and then she had to be straight on set next morning. They made it sound like she was going to be locked up and they were her jailers.

And so much for His Almighty Majesty being able to suppress anything because clips from *that* movie were all over the internet. Apparently it was called *The Baron* (Skylar didn't know it was called anything) and everyone was guessing who 'the Baron' was but Skylar remembered that was what he called his doohickey.

'You mean his dick?' Marshall said, lighting up a joint.

Skylar never did dope, she didn't believe in taking drugs.

'Can we not talk about it anymore? Please?' It was all shameful and horrible, worse than anything Lindsay or Britney, or even Paris, had ever done.

She took a couple of Xanax and then a couple more when they didn't kick in. They got through a lot of champagne before Cruella de Ville was vanquished. Marshall gave her some Oxycontin and then they got steak and fries on room service and more champagne, chased with a couple of Adderall. Then Marshall went to sleep at the end of Skylar's Emperor bed and she popped a couple of Ambien and phoned Mom but she wasn't in. Skylar was asleep before Mom got to the end of her answerphone message. She was real tired. Real, real tired.

'I hate modern interpretations,' Joel said in the interval. They stayed in their seats. Campbell would have liked a drink but not enough to get up and fight her way through to the bar. And Joel wasn't offering to go, which he would have done once.

'It's so self-referential,' he said. 'I mean why can't Violetta just be Violetta? Nineteenth-century courtesan, or whatever she was. Big dress, fans. Why does it have to be drugs and Hollywood and all that minimalism. The British royal family, for Christ's sake.'

'Why does it make you so mad?' Campbell said. 'It's just an opera.'

'Everything makes me mad.'

'Especially me?'

He made a funny little jerking motion with his head which could have been interpreted in a number of ways. And then the interval was over.

*

Skylar felt real comfortable. Like she had no worries and someone was taking care of her. Someone *was* taking care of her,
lots of someones. Nurses and doctors and she could tell they
all had her best interests at heart. A machine was keeping her
going. She could hear the tick and hiss of it. She loved that
machine. Her Mom was there. Harry and Marty were in and
out. Marshall had come with her in the ambulance but Marty
had kicked him out. Kirsty or whatever her name had been here
and Skylar remembered she hadn't given her the Birkin bag at
the end of the shoot. She felt real bad about that. She hoped it
wouldn't count against her.

She heard Phoebe Something-Or-Other's theatrical voice
saying, 'Poor lamb, I just brought her this,' and one of the
nurses said, 'It's lovely to meet you, Miss Hope-Walters, I'm
such a fan.'

He never came. Alfie. Skylar supposed he wasn't allowed. He
would have come if he could have done, she was sure. She loved
him. It was one true thought and it lived inside her and made
her shine with light.

Campbell didn't think the story had been cheapened. It moved
her in a way she simply hadn't expected. When it came to the
deathbed scene she couldn't hold back a noisy, hiccupy sob and
she saw Joel shrink away from her in embarrassment. Part of
her had been hoping the ending would change. It *was* tragic. It
felt more real than her own life. Perhaps that was the tragedy.

She was real, real sorry for the way things had turned out. If
she had her time over she would do things differently, but it
didn't really matter now. A life was what you made of it. And
Skylar had done her best. But gee-whiz, she sure would have

liked a bit more time. She hoped there was a heaven and that she'd done enough to get in. She hoped there would be dogs (no horses!) and she could eat all she wanted without getting any heavier.

And then he was there! She heard a nurse murmur, 'Your Royal Highness,' and then she felt him take her hand. He was crying and his hot, wet tears fell on her skin and burned right through to her bones and she felt the light inside her again.

It was funny but right at the end, after her lovely machine was switched off (by Mom) it was as if she was right there, awake and alive, and the last thing she saw was this cushion with a big pink rose cross-stitched on it. It was ugly. Real, real ugly. But as Mom would have said, 'It's the thought that counts.' And then that was it. The End.

The Growler
Julie Myerson

It was her nineteenth birthday and she was in Italy on her gap year, working as an au pair. She'd been in Florence almost six months - through an icy February and a long, chilly spring – and now it was June and she felt at home in this city, with its bright blue skies and dark frescoes and sudden virgin faces. She had freckles on her nose and shoulders and a pair of flat red espadrilles and, having arrived without a single word of the language, not even knowing the words for yes and no, she could now get by quite well. Instead of immediately guessing, 'You're English, aren't you?', people would frown and say, 'You're not from around here, are you?' She was incredibly proud of that difference.

She'd come in winter and now it was summer. Since late April the ancient, dusty bowl of the city had been heating up and now it was airless and tired. People walked slowly and stood around scowling in the shade, and those who could afford to were already getting out, heading for the mountains or the lakes or the sea. And their own bags were packed. They were leaving for Elba the next day, taking the ferry to Napoleon's island. The family she was working for had been going there since the early 50s when there were no hotels or houses, barely even a road. Just a rough dirt track, they told her proudly, a few peasants and a couple of hairy old mules.

She'd never spent a birthday away from home before. If she'd been at home, her family would have woken her with strong tea and presents in bed. Later, she might have met up with friends for a drink in town. Yates's, The Trip, The Bell. Andy, Sally, Caro, Mel. Names from another lifetime. The few letters she'd had from these people in the last months – hectic, biro paragraphs about parties and bars and who was going out with who – had made them seem less, rather than more, real.

Here in Florence, she knew some of the students from the language school – in theory many nationalities, but in fact mostly American or German. Sometimes they all went for a pizza together. She'd met an odd, mad English boy at the British Institute Library one afternoon and they'd had a surreal, whispered conversation and he'd written his phone number on the back of her Italian phrase book, but she hadn't felt any need to call it. And she'd been out for one, awkward, late-night ice cream with the waiter from the bar at the end of the street – wedged so tightly on the back of his Vespa that they couldn't talk to each other anyway. But that was all.

Actually, it was enough. She had the whole city to play in, a whole new self to invent, and anyway looking after a small child wasn't exactly peaceful and she'd begun to relish her time alone. She spent her afternoons off in Boboli Gardens, in the Uffizi, in the Bargello, in Santa Croce, in her head. Writing poetry, thinking, reading. On bad days she felt a little dizzy and dark, but on good days, her loneliness felt like a gift, a discovery.

*

This day, her nineteenth birthday, unrolled like any other. In the early morning, Niccolo, the three-year-old she looked after, presented her with wax-crayoned drawings of some long-tailed creatures he'd invented. Fat, toothy monsters, scribbled colour spilling furiously over their edges. Slowly, solemnly, snuggled against her in bed, he took her through the name for each separate beast, waiting for her to repeat it after him, before yelling his approval. Sometimes with Niccolo she had no idea whether the Italian she was learning was real or made up, useful new phrases, or a three-year-old's idiosyncratically deranged vocabulary. Maybe it didn't matter, since her principal companion was, in fact, a three-year-old Italian.

After the monsters, she put him on the toilet – he'd recently graduated from potty to toilet with the help of a plastic step – where he sat looking grave and careful while, still in her nightie, she made him breakfast. 'What are you making?' he called to her, leaning forward on the seat, his small elbows drooping over his knees. Every day the answer was the same: milky Earl Grey tea and melba toasts with black cherry jam piled on each one.

Things were going well with Niccolo. He was the first three-year-old she'd ever known apart from her sisters and she couldn't honestly say she really remembered them at that age. He'd come to live with his grandparents for a year while his mother sorted out her personal life in Bologna. 'Sorting out' was the grandparents' word for it. Basically, the man Niccolo's mother was trying to live with didn't want some little kid hanging around, and the mother was mad (or insecure) enough to want to give this living arrangement a go.

Life without her child. Life without this plump, dark-eyed baby who drew complicated monsters and wore a button-up sleep suit at night and woke you up by stroking your face in the morning. The girl couldn't ever in a million years imagine accepting such a thing. In fact she just knew she never would. She was conscious that her whole life stretched ahead of her, unpeeled, unchosen, unblemished by detail or desire. And she was determined that none of the choices she had yet to make would ever involve such compromise.

When Niccolo arrived in Florence he was a sullen, tired child, taking a lot of different medicines. He often wet the bed at night and screamed and cried if he didn't get his own way. He was terrified of water and wouldn't go near a bath, making do instead with brief flannel washes. There were loads of things he wouldn't eat, items of clothing he refused to wear, activities he wouldn't even try.

The girl had looked at him and remembered herself at the same age. The things that she had hated, the things that had frightened her: water, certainly, was one. And darkness. And clothes that fit too tightly and had to be pulled over her head. She looked at the child and she didn't really know what to do about him. She didn't speak his language in any useful way, so instead she pretended to fall down dead. He laughed. She pretended not to have noticed and did it again. He laughed louder. She walked away and he asked her where she was going. She didn't answer, so he followed her. She walked more quickly and he giggled and chased after her.

He chased her into the bathroom where she ran a bath but didn't ask him to get in it. Instead she played with the water, intent, absorbed, messy, ignoring him. Keeping his eyes on her, he played too. They both got wet. In the end he asked her if he could get in. She hesitated as if she was thinking about it, then shrugged and said, 'OK.' His grandmother came in and was astonished to find him allowing himself to be washed.

The girl did the same with food. She didn't force him to eat, but she ate enthusiastically in front of him. He gazed at her hungrily while, in her terrible Italian, she told him stories about bad cats and funny monsters and children who weren't at all afraid. She drew pictures of the pets she'd had back in England and told him what had happened to them. He especially liked the stories about the pets and their deaths. And as he listened to the stories, he picked up his fork without realizing and accidentally began to eat. The girl pretended not to notice. He finished his plate.

And the months had passed and now he was bright and happy and calm, sleeping through the night every night. He'd put on weight and got colour in his face and had stopped all the medicines – it was obvious there was nothing wrong with him. His grandparents observed the changes with delight and begged the girl to stay with them as long as possible. The situation was pretty much perfect, except that Niccolo sometimes called her 'Mamma' by mistake, which meant she had to be given the whole day off on the days his real mother visited.

She didn't know why she so enjoyed looking after this child, but she did. She was still only a teenager herself, and maybe she shouldn't have been feeling so maternal, but all the nights out in pubs with her friends, all the nightclubs and discos, all the fun she used to have shopping with her sisters, somehow none of these could compare to the satisfaction she felt when she tucked this small boy up in bed at night. Or folded his tiny pale blue and white striped vests. Or stirred fat musty yellow flowers into boiling water to make him camomile tea. Or polished his little brown button-up shoes. The grandmother was very particular that his shoes were kept polished.

The grandmother was a music teacher, a pianist and one-time

opera singer. She'd studied singing under someone the girl had had to pretend she'd heard of. The grandmother was so soaked in music that she just assumed everyone knew everything about it, and to say you never gave it much thought would be like saying you never got around to breathing air or eating food. The grandmother could be fierce. The child of a naval officer and a concert violinist, she'd told the girl she'd swum in the sea with sharks when she was a child, and the girl could believe it. She could just imagine those fine brown arms striking out through that dangerous water, circled by endless, ominous dark fins.

The grandmother had come to Florence and married the grandfather in 1949. He was fifteen or maybe twenty years older than her, a large but frail man with a lot of ailments, none of which stopped him chasing women. He flirted with the stout grey-haired cook who came in to make lunch. He flirted with the kind, blonde physiotherapist who came to do things to his damaged knees. And of course he flirted with her, his grandson's English teenage au pair. Every time he spoke a word of English to her – and he knew quite a lot of words – he seemed to think that gave him the right to touch some part of her body, an arm, a leg, her hair.

The girl didn't know whether the grandmother noticed all this flirting and touching. She and the grandfather had separate bedrooms and the grandmother took little notice of her husband, except to give him orders or pills or a piece of her mind. When she was around, he was docile, defeated. He seemed to give up and shut up. But when she was out, he acted naughty, like a big bad mouse creeping out to play.

At first the girl had thought him rather charming, a kind and harmless and quite fascinating old man. But one day he'd tried to kiss her on the sofa after lunch – on the lips, he'd actually taken her in his arms – and she'd pulled away in shocked horror. The smell of him. Hair oil and medicines and elderly skin. She wanted to be sick. And even though she knew it wasn't her fault, still she felt ashamed at having somehow attracted him.

After that, she couldn't look at him when he spoke to her. She told herself she wasn't frightened either of him or the grandmother, but it wasn't true. She was frightened of both of them in different ways. Of the grandmother's tight, compromised mouth and occasionally harsh manner. And her husband's sheep face – his helpless, shabby craving for physical contact.

The grandmother was old, in her fifties at least, but you could tell she had once been worth looking at. Her hair was silver, cropped defiantly close to her head as if she couldn't be bothered with something as trivial as a hair-style, and her skin was the kind that tans easily. She had a faint, dark moustache and her clothes were immaculate and sensible – tweed skirts and slacks and crisp linen shirts. Only her jewellery seemed gorgeously out of kilter: heavy amber necklaces, turquoise beads strung on silver, drop earrings made of jade and gold.

Her shoes were flat lace-ups or loafers, and she wore an ugly, sensible man's watch, but under her sensible skirts you could see she had nice legs. And she sometimes wore eye shadow, a sheen of olive-gold on her heavy lids. Or a faint trace of lipstick. And you'd catch her sitting alone at the kitchen table dreaming, no longer stern, her face unguarded and suddenly pretty. On the sideboard in the dining-room there was a black and white photo of a young, dark-haired woman, wearing an old-fashioned two-piece swimsuit, her head thrown back, laughing. She looked like a model or a movie star, the girl thought. So beautiful.

Because she taught music and singing at the *Conservatorio*, the grandmother was nearly always out. Lessons in the day, concerts and recitals in the evening. She'd leave in the early morning, tipping the dregs of her coffee into the sink, jewellery clinking, a shawl flung across her shoulders. And she'd arrive home late in the evening, long after husband and grandson were in bed, sometimes finding the girl still up, sitting alone reading or maybe mending Niccolo's clothes.

If the TV was on, she'd flick it off with a small shudder of impatience and, even if it was cold outside, she'd fling open the tall windows that looked onto the courtyard and put a record on the player and the girl would hear the click and wobble as the needle engaged, and she'd know then to hold her breath. Because at that moment, the moment when the needle pierced and probed the grooves, everything in the room would change – every atom of air, every ounce of colour, every tiny, sharp possibility. And though she tried to get herself ready, she was never really ready for it. How could she be when music burst like that into the room and the whole hidden world of her heart sprang to life?

Music burst in and she'd have to struggle to continue with whatever it was she'd been doing – pushing the needle in and out of the fabric, turning the cloth, making a strong seam along the denim rip in a pair of Niccolo's dungarees. In the end, though, the grandmother would demand that she put the work down, and she'd kick off her sensible shoes and pour them both a glass of wine and for a while she'd stop being a person to be afraid of and her whole face and self would change and she'd be the young woman in the black and white photograph – loose and beautiful and ready to be delighted.

The girl couldn't take her eyes off her.

Some of the music the girl thought she might have heard before, maybe at school or on TV. Other music threw her –

unnerved her, seemed to split her in two, making her feel as if one half of her was on one side of the room, the other half on the other. Spaces between one part of herself and another. What could she do? Huge, frightening spaces opening up inside her, spaces she had not even known were there. Spaces filled up with notes, with music, with sound. Sometimes she stole glances at the grandmother to see if what was happening to her, inside her, was obvious. She hoped it wasn't. If it was, the grandmother had either seen it all before, or else she let her off and made sure not to look too hard.

One time the grandmother put something on that was so achingly strange, a piece of music that seemed to conjure a vast, cool, spare landscape that so exactly mirrored her own state of longed-for loneliness, that the girl found tears standing in her eyes. It felt as if she'd been found out, recognized. She didn't know whether she liked the feeling or not.

'Mahler,' said the grandmother and her face was stern, 'You're telling me you've never heard Mahler's First Symphony? Eighteen years old! Whatever have they been doing with you all these years?'

Another time, another night, a hot early summer's night, the windows flung wide on the jasmine-scented courtyard below, something crept around the drawing room. Something? – an oboe? A flute? The girl didn't really know one instrument from another, though she'd never have dared tell the grandmother this. Whatever it was, it found its way in. A light, lean, shivery thing, alighting on pieces of furniture, winding its sly, melancholy way around pictures and under rugs, jumping and floating and leaping towards her. She almost recoiled. She wanted to pull back. Her stomach hurt. Her head felt peculiar. Terror and delight. Terrified and delighted at the same time.

'You like it?' the grandmother mouthed, and this time she was almost smiling, waiting for her to respond. The girl nodded. She couldn't speak and the grandmother seemed to understand that.

'*L'Aprés-midi d'un faune,*' said the grandmother and she closed her eyes as if that was all, no other words were necessary. Let's just give in to this monster, shall we? A thing on the prowl, on the loose. The terror and delight of submitting to music.

And now it was her birthday and the grandmother, swatting wasps as she sipped her breakfast tea at the window, said she had a surprise for her. She said they were going to lunch at the Country Club.

'The Country Club!' shouted Niccolo, pulling himself onto the girl's lap. There, she would play a round of golf and the grandfather could see his cronies and Niccolo and the girl could have lunch by the pool. 'At the snack bar!' yelled Niccolo, because the Country Club pool and its expensive, pink linen-tableclothed snack bar, where they served pizza and pannini and Coca Cola, were one and the same to him.

Then, continued the grandmother, that night she and the girl were going on a special trip, an evening out, just the two of them. 'Me too, me too!' yelled Niccolo. The grandmother smiled. No, Niccolo would be put to bed by his grandfather and—

'But you know I'll never manage that!' the grandfather began, indignant, reaching for his stick and pretending to shamble to his feet as if someone was asking him to do it right now this minute.

'Then we'll ask Delfina to come up and help you,' said the grandmother very firmly as if it was all sorted out and she wasn't really very interested in what happened after that. Delfina was the porter's wife, the fat, wide, black-haired lady who sat at the gate all day shelling peas. Delfina was strong. She could do anything, help with anything, carry anything. The grandfather always said it was because she was a peasant, and when he said it the girl could never tell whether the look on his face was one of loathing or of lust.

The girl was listening carefully to all these plans. Intently. It was her birthday. She was nineteen. Her mother was going to phone at midday. If she missed her at midday, she knew she would try again at six.

'Where are we going?' she said. 'Tonight, I mean.'

'Ah,' said the grandmother, and she smiled.

That evening they drove high up into the hills, high above Florence. They drove up past olive and cypress groves, past great black blotches of pine trees, up where the air started to feel fresh and cool and smell of resin and blue needles. Eventually, high up in front of them, gripping the hill as if it might slide down it at any moment, was a large, spread-out building with a turret on the top. More than a turret. It looked like a large building with a smaller one perched on top of it. 'There,' said the grandmother, indicating left and turning off the road onto a track that felt bumpy and kicked up dust. '*La Certosa*.'

The girl had never seen such a place. She thought it looked like something out of a fairy tale. She wouldn't have been surprised to see a ring of mist around it. 'We're going up there?'

'You bet,' said the grandmother, who sometimes talked like an American when she was away from the grandfather and feeling happy.

They got out of the car and walked up a steep chalky path strewn with poppies and wild orchids and floppy pink roses with huge yellow centres. Lizards skittered in and out of cracks in the walls. That morning, the grandmother had given her a birthday present of a white lace shawl, white with silvery stitching, and she drew it round her shoulders now and even the feel of the fabric made her feel like somebody else. Girl in a shawl.

The grandmother explained that *La Certosa* was a monastery but in the summer months they played music there. Opera, symphonies, anything and everything. And the girl asked – not out of politeness but out of sheer, honest, boiling curiosity – what were they going to hear? And the grandmother must have told her, but she's forgotten what it was now because all of this happened a long time ago, almost thirty years ago.

All the girl remembers is they heard some singing – maybe a recital, maybe something from an opera she had barely heard of – and that afterwards she and the grandmother went and had some dinner together. The dinner was in a rustic place with no windows – was it part of the monastery? – just gaps in the thick stone wall that opened out onto the darkening hills. And eventually, after the salad plates had been cleared and more wine had been poured, the grandmother somehow threw some different words in between the sentences she and the girl had been speaking, words that told her what she realized she had known all along: that she had a lover.

'A lover?' The girl frowned, trying to reassemble the words she'd just heard. She looked at the grandmother and saw that her eyes had changed.

'A colleague at the *Conservatorio*. A dear person. A person I've known my whole life.'

Her whole life. A whole other part of herself. The girl didn't know what to say.

'He plays piano,' said the grandmother as she laid her chin

in the soft brown cup of her hand and, for the first time ever, the girl noticed her clean oval fingernails. 'A marvellous pianist. I've been in love with him for twenty years. We are together as much as possible, whenever possible. Are you shocked?'

And the girl said no, she wasn't shocked, partly because she'd drunk wine and wasn't used to it, and partly because the music she'd just heard gave her the sense, as usual, that her life was just on the edge of something wonderful, just beginning, and that all risks of any kind were worthwhile and possible. Why did certain music – especially the piercing, under-the-skin kind of music the grandmother showed her – seem to do that to you?

She was thinking all of this as she drank her wine – nineteenth-birthday wine – and ate her chicken or her fish or whatever it was. She wondered if she was a little bit drunk as she didn't feel scared of the grandmother at all – just alert to her, pleased to be with her, interested to know about her life, her love.

She heard herself ask the grandmother why she hadn't married her lover.

'Ah well,' said the grandmother, and she told her that her lover was married, that his wife was very seriously ill, that she didn't know what she'd do if the wife died.

What she'd do? The girl shut her eyes and opened them again and looked at her and realized she really could ask anything she liked.

'You mean – you might leave – him?'

'Him' meant the grandfather. For the whole of the dinner, maybe, she realized, even for the whole of the time they'd known each other, neither of them had spoken his actual name.

The grandmother's mouth creased a little and the girl realized it had been ages since she'd noticed her faint dark moustache.

She tried to smile, then she stopped trying and she shrugged. 'Well, for goodness sake. No one knows how much life they have left,' she said, as if that was an answer.

The girl asked the grandmother if her daughter knew about all of this. The grandmother looked at her carefully. 'No one knows,' she said. 'You're the only person I've ever told.'

The girl felt she ought to be pleased about this, flattered anyway. So why did hearing it make tears come in her eyes?

'Something that I don't get about you,' the grandmother said after a moment or two. 'Something that's been bothering me a little bit.'

The girl looked at her and smiled, ready to answer anything, any question, ready to try and make sense of herself in the frankest possible way for this woman, in return for the confidences she'd bestowed.

The grandmother looked down at her plate, as though she was finding the words quite difficult to locate, to pull up. Her English was excellent, but all the same.

'You respond so deeply to music, to the music I've played you. But you seem to have no music in your life. I am sure you are very musical indeed. I can't for the life of me understand why you've never taken up an instrument, or learned to sing.'

The girl felt herself blush. 'Oh, I could never do that,' she said.

'What do you mean you could never?' the grandmother said.

Just as she was looking around for an answer, the girl realized it didn't have to be looked for. It settled easily in her head, in her mouth. 'Because I'm no good,' she said.

'No good?'

'I did a bit of piano, but I gave up. And I can't sing.'

The grandmother shook her head in the impatient way the

girl had come to know so well. 'How do you know you can't sing? Of course you can sing. Everybody can sing if they want to.'

'But I'm a growler,' said the girl, telling the truth as it came back to her, as it floated back up to her, then realizing what she'd just said. A growler? She hadn't even thought of that word in years.

'You're a what?' said the grandmother.

And there she was. There she is. Down in that dark old basement room with the bars on the windows, the room where they have assembly and gym and also music. Wednesday mornings. A dark morning. The headachy time before lunch. They're all singing and—

The teacher stops right there in the bright alert middle of a verse, hands lifted and held in the air like two frozen claws. She looks around her, eyes black and beady.

'Who's that growling?'

She feels her skin go hot to the roots of her hair. The backs of her knees. Her bladder. She can feel the wee waiting to come out, just at the edge. She won't wet herself.

The teacher scratches her head. Her dark green jumper is stained and her breath smells of smoke when she comes up close. She once said the word 'bloody' when she told someone off.

'I asked a question,' she says.

Slowly, because she has to, she puts up her hand. Blushing, her stomach falling away with fear. Everyone looks round. The teacher folds her arms. 'Is it you? Are you growling?'

She tries to nod.

'A simple yes or no will do.'

'Yes.'

And that's it, that's the end of her voice. So easy it's not even painful. After that moment, for days and days, for years and years, she makes no sound, she does not disturb the air with her singing. She moves through life – through childhood and on into the upper school, through a million assemblies and carol services – a deadly silent person, doing the actions, mouthing the words, her whole face moving but no sound coming out.

The grandmother was listening and she wasn't smiling. She pulled her cardigan around her shoulders and poured more wine into the girl's glass.

'How old were you when this happened?'

The girl thought about it. She felt the backs of her knees with her hands, held on to them to keep herself from feeling drunk. 'Six,' she said, 'Maybe six and a half.'

The grandmother's face was still. 'But your parents – they didn't complain?'

The girl thought about this. 'I don't think they ever knew,' she said, and she smiled because she didn't want the grandmother to feel too sorry for her. 'You're the only person I've ever told.'

The grandmother wasn't looking at her. She was looking out into the hot night. Orchards and olive groves. Far away, at some farm or in some village, woodsmoke curled and dogs were barking.

It was late when the grandmother and the girl made their way back down the hill to the car. The air was still hot, but thick and black with a peppering of stars above and the chirrup of crickets. The grandmother touched her arm.

'Hey, I wonder how he got on, putting the boy to bed,' she said with a little laugh. And the girl thought about the soft curve of Niccolo's almost asleep face. And then she thought of the grandfather making his slow way back down the long dark corridor with its rugs and paintings. And then her mind went to the pianist lover at the Conservatorio and the grandmother's heavy amber jewellery and the empty-yet-full look on her face sometimes when she came into the apartment, and the twenty years of being in love and no one and everyone knowing about it, and she laughed too.

'They'll be OK,' she said, and for once it felt as if she actually knew something.

They drove in silence for a little way. The night was black, not much moon. Once or twice the grandmother asked her what she was thinking and she didn't really know what to say until she remembered she could tell her the truth. 'Just about my life really,' she said. 'And the beautiful music tonight. I can't stop thinking about it all.'

'Nineteen,' sighed the grandmother. 'What an age. A lovely age. But the city's been so hot. So airless. You must be sick of it. Ah well, we'll get some good fresh breezes by the sea tomorrow.'

And the girl smiled because, what with her birthday and the music and the trip into the hills, she'd completely forgotten they were going to Elba. And the car window was open and she stretched her arm out into the night. Just at that moment, she needed to do it, she couldn't have told anyone why. Maybe she just wanted to see how it felt to touch darkness.

The Ghost
Toby Litt

Schleich, the German company that mostly manufacture plastic animals – horses, goats, pigs, ostriches – also make a tradition-ally recognizable ghost. It stands about three inches tall, is white-painted, besheeted, drags behind it a black-painted ball and chain. The two implied hands are raised to head level, and its mouth is open in the silent *whooo* of a wail.

My son, Jim, saw it in the local toyshop, wanted it and got it – I was, I'll admit, the parent who gave in.

A while had passed since his last gift, and as he and I were in there buying a pirate costume for my nephew, his cousin, it would've been mean to force him out empty-handed. Or so my argument went.

Jim held the ghost all the way home, with me pushing him in the McLaren buggy. We went through the park, Brockwell Park. That's in South London. It was autumn, and the trees had circular skirts of fallen leaves.

'Whooo!' Jim called, though I couldn't remember if I'd ever taught him that's what ghosts say.

He was two-and-a-half years old. 'What does a horse say?'

was a question he was quite used to being asked. And pig, and goat. Not so much ostrich.

To be honest, with Jim I had avoided the subjects of death, dying, the afterlife and the lack of an afterlife. My partner, Glenys, and I had had quite enough of all four.

The year before Jim was born, my father came to live – and die – with us. He had pancreatic cancer. We moved him in to my top-floor study, until he couldn't manage the stairs. Then we had him in the sitting room. (Ours is a standard Victorian terrace; the front parlour knocked through into the back.) After that, it was hospice, hospital, graveyard, goodbye.

All this time, we were trying to conceive. I wanted a grand-child to show him before he went – though his prognosis was only just longer than a full nine-month term. But the stress of nursing him, and the very fact he was in our house, made the thing impossible. I couldn't bring myself to penetrate Glenys directly above his head, even if he was so zonked on painkillers he'd never hear or, if he did hear, remember. Even after he had gone to the hospice, it was hard not to imagine him right beneath us, listening to the floorboard-creaks and bedsqueaks.

Jim, though, was born eight months after my father passed on – two weeks late. In the relief of my father being out of the sitting room, Glenys and I must have had sex – although, to be truthful, I can't remember it. We drank quite a lot, throughout that period.

We took the baby, only two months old, to the muddy grave-yard to show him to my father's headstone. My father's middle name was James.

Afterwards, we both wanted as little to do with the morbid as possible. Glenys had never liked horror films, though I'd been an addict since the onset of puberty. Together we now avoided documentaries, hospital dramas, in fact most dramas full stop.

Until Jim asked what death was, which he hadn't yet, we intended to allow him his blessèd ignorance.

Ignorance or innocence? I'd never really believed in the latter, but his gaiety seemed to be genuine – and to issue from some blank, blandly happy place. He uplifted us, and we were in need of uplift.

I once heard a story from a friend, Scott, also a father. He'd been a stand-up comedian, back when he had ambitions of fame rather than academe. But he was always funniest in private, coked up. Scott's wife was a good audience, complete with witty hecklers. When he got a position in an American university, they moved there and had a son, Josh. One Sunday afternoon, they went round to another couple's for tea. The man of the couple was in Scott's department; the woman stayed home to look after their strange daughter, Annalise. Even before Scott went to the house, he'd been warned that Annalise – in fact, that the whole family was strange. No one quite knew why. Only a year old, Annalise was in her high seat as the four adults talked. Josh was there too, with chocolate biscuits. In the course of conversation, Scott made a remark, his wife laughed loudly, and Annalise instantly became hysterical. Her mother removed her from the room, with apologies. Then the girl's father explained: 'I don't think she's ever heard anyone do that before.'

'What?' asked Scott.

'Laugh like that. We don't really laugh much. We don't really laugh at all.'

Glenys and I were agreed: for children, you had to make like you're happy. They might pick up on subtext but your job was to put the bunting out, always – that is, if you didn't want to be guilty of mental cruelty. So Jim brought us, and also enforced, joy.

I bought him the plastic ghost because he wanted it. If I had refused him, I would have had to deal with the issue of why. Easier far to give in, as he'd already trained me to do. There was no need to explain to him what a ghost was. He knew the word – for the moment, that would be enough.

Glenys was not happy, although she waited until Jim had fallen asleep before footnoting her disappointed frown – the one she'd given me on first seeing the small white figure in Jim's excited-sweaty fist.

'It's my *ghost*,' he'd said.

'Couldn't you have persuaded him to want something else?' Glenys asked, over dinner.

'No,' I said. 'He was determined.'

'I don't like it, that's all.'

This conversation was backwards to what you'd expect: I was the superstitious one. Out of the two of us, I was by far the most likely to believe in ghosts.

'He wanted it,' I said. 'I don't know why. Maybe because it's white.'

'But what's it going to do? He only ever plays with his animals and – I mean. Is there a ghost in the farmyard?'

'We'll see,' I said. 'Perhaps he'll lose interest, and we can just put it away somewhere.'

But, right from the next morning, it became clear that the ghost had entered into the universe of Jim's play. His most recent obsession had been the Three Billy Goats Gruff, and to begin with at least the ghost simply replaced the troll.

'Whooo-who's that trip-trappin' over *my* bridge?'

It was a defender of limits – a constantly defeated defender.

I looked after Jim on Tuesdays. Glenys did Mondays. For the rest of the working week, we had a nanny – though I was in the house most of the time, writing in my study. The weekends, we did together. And so I was able to follow the ghost's development quite closely.

He began by seeping out of the Billy Goat narrative and into others. Glenys' question was answered – there *was* a ghost in the farmyard, and in the jungle, and most particularly in the dolls' house.

This, Jim had never been all that interested in before. Not unless as an extra barn to house the chickens. It was of course made of plastic, bright yellow, and had come with tables, chairs, bedside tables, beds – plus a nuclear family. The manufacturer was Playmobil. Now the ghost began to play in the small, cramped rooms with patterned stickers for wallpaper. I noticed that the farmyard and jungle animals didn't join it. Jim seemed happy just moving it from floor to floor, saying *whooo*. When I came down from my study, walked in and asked him what the ghost was doing, he said, 'Hauntin'.' (Jim had a tendency to drop his final g's.)

I couldn't at all remember having told him this word. Perhaps the nanny, Eileen, had. But when I asked her if they'd ever talked about ghosts, she swore they hadn't – not before I bought him the figure. (This was later, when asking such questions became necessary.)

Jim went out to the park that afternoon, and I had a look through his picture books – trying to find a ghost that might have given him the idea of wanting one. Eventually, I discovered a single picture. It was in a book called *You Choose* – the idea of which was that, for each densely illustrated double-page spread, the child picked out whatever they liked most. There were likeable animals, foods, means of transport. And then there was a page of characters you might or might not choose to be friends with. They were shown as if in framed paintings hung upon a vast red wall. One of them was a ghost – a ghost a bit like a kiddy cartoon of the plastic ghost. But I couldn't remember, among all the other things, that Jim had ever chosen it. He tended to go for the the fireman or the cowboy or the farmer. As far as I was aware, though, this was the only ghost Jim had ever seen.

Later, they came back from the park and started playing in the playroom – the room where my father had lain on his pre-deathbed. Jim's *whooo*, rising up the stairs, left me in no doubt of what his game was.

'He really loves that ghost,' said Eileen to Glenys, debriefing at the end of the day. 'He makes it fly around all through the dolls' house.'

When she left, we went to join Jim in the playroom. The dolls' house was positioned on a clothes chest, in front of the French doors. That was where my father's head had been. He said he liked the cold air coming off the window pane.

'I don't want to be hot any more,' he said. He had always found hospitals intolerably stuffy.

Jim knew Daddy didn't have a daddy, but that wasn't anything special – Daddy didn't have a mummy, and Mummy didn't have a daddy or a mummy either. We had reached the end of our thirties before we started to want children; our parents, too, had started late. My mother, then Glenys' mother, then her father had all died in the five years before my father. So, the issue of grandparents never really arose for Jim. Until he went to school, and started comparing what he had with what other kids had, we would remain the absolute normality of his world. (And at least we *tried* to laugh.) We hadn't needed to explain that his grannies and grandpas were dead, they just *weren't*.

Jim was making the ghost bounce along the roof of the dolls' house.

'We saw my silver man,' he said. 'In the farmyard, where we went.'

I didn't like the sound of this.

'What man?' I asked.

'Silver man,' Jim said, not turning round.

'In the farmyard,' I repeated.

We had taken Jim to a city farm about a month before. I wondered if he meant that. But there had been no silver man.

'You mean where we had the pink ice cream?'

'No, the – this farmyard now.'

Jim turned around, the ghost in his left hand, and pointed to the farm buildings. They were on the carpet, beneath where my father's rotting abdomen had once been.

'A silver man?' Glenys asked.

'Long silver man,' Jim said.

'You mean Long John Silver,' Glenys said, expecting that Eileen had told him the story of *Treasure Island*.

'Long arms,' said Jim. 'Long head.'

This made him really laugh hard.

'Long head!' he said. 'Daddy's got a long head.'

He rushed towards me with the ghost out in front.

I was sitting cross-legged on the floor.

Jim hit me on the crown with the ghost.

'Jim, no,' Glenys said. 'Say sorry to Daddy.'

'Sorry, Daddy,' said Jim, immediately. He didn't want to waste playing-time on the Naughty Step. Then something changed and he said, 'It's a long head,' and hit me again with the ghost.

Glenys grabbed his hand and pulled him to the foot of the stairs.

'Two minutes,' she said. 'And no bedtime story if you don't start to be good.'

He was immediately reconciled to this, ready to sit it out. But then Glenys remembered our subsidiary rule: No toys on the Naughty Step.

She held out her hand. 'Please give it to me,' she said.

Jim shook his head.

'Give it to me, please.'

He shoved the ghost under his armpit.

Glenys reached in, and he bit her on the arm. He'd never bitten either of us before – or he had bitten Glenys, but only accidentally, on the nipple, whilst breastfeeding.

I went over and together we took the ghost away from him.

'And you're not having that back until tomorrow – if you're good.'

'Now say sorry to Mummy,' I said.

'No,' said Jim. 'Give me!'

'Say sorry.'

'I don't want *anything*!'

'Jim, please say sorry.'

'Nothing!'

That night he had no story, and no song either.

We talked it over. I thought the silver man might be my father. Once, when he was close to the end, I'd gone downstairs to make sure he was asleep. We used to check on dying-him just as, nine months later, we'd check on newborn-Jim. The curtains were open and a stripe of moonlight ran down the single sheet covering his body. He was so emaciated that there were deep dips between the bumps for chest, hips, knees and feet. At the time, and not just in the context of what Jim said, I thought of him as silvered. He looked like his own tomb – as if he were a knight.

'Don't be silly,' said Glenys. 'There's no way he could know that.'

'Of course not,' I said. 'Not really. But it felt as if he did, and that's what matters.'

'How you feel?' Glenys was about to become sarcastic. 'Yes, that's what everything comes back to, isn't it?' She was referring to my one affair, and my desire for time apart at various points in our relationship. In her staging of our lives, I had been cast as The Selfish Man.

'It's the only thing I have to go on,' I said. 'It felt…Well, I hate to annoy you by using the word, but it felt uncanny, *unheimlich*.'

'In what way exactly?'

'Him knowing something he couldn't have known.'

'You've already admitted he didn't know it.'

'Rationally, I believe that. But it's what I'd like to believe rather than what I really believe.'

'So now there's something you *really* believe, is there?' As well as The Selfish Man, I was also The Callow Relativist.

If I hadn't said uncanny, I would have said spooky – that might even have been more accurate. Because I'd started watching horror movies when hardly older than a child, I had never been all that scared by spooky children – or all that worried by nasty things happening to nice children. I rather liked it, in fact. Nice children were annoying, and nasty evil children were thrillingly powerful. But, over the years of rentals, I had been conditioned to beware of the tinkly music, to hear the playground chants as inevitably doom-laden. *Ring-a-ring*

*of roses. London Bridge is falling down. Incy wincy spider climb-
ing up the spout.* And since I'd become a father, I had suddenly
realized why these tricks are so effective. Parents are suckers
for them. You're programmed to react, and strongly. Children
are spooky – and the soundtrack to their early lives is all
music-box jingle, laughter, more laughter, and then scream-
scream-scream. Superadded to this is the terror they bring in:
a new death born into the world with each little one of them.
However, I didn't feel worried for Jim. Within the genre, he
was the spooky truth-telling child. And, as such, he couldn't
be harmed even by a whirlwind of spirits. The one in danger
was me.

I didn't sleep much.

Eileen was to be with Jim the next day. She had decided to
take him, and the clutched ghost, to the zoo in Battersea Park.
Before they went, I gave her some money and asked her to buy
Jim whatever animal he wanted from the gift shop. Perhaps a
sufficiently exciting lion or polar bear would oust the ghost;
new toys supplanted favourite toys all the time.

When they returned, around teatime, Jim's second fist was
clutching not an animal but a zookeeper.

'Let's have a look,' I said.

'He didn't want an animal,' Eileen said, getting in her rebut-
tal before my challenge.

Once Jim saw I didn't want to take away his ghost, he handed
over the small, dungaree-wearing figure. It was my father, in
miniature. Not as he had been when the cancer got going, but as
a man of around my age. I even had a photograph of him, interrupted whilst gardening, wearing a similar outfit and leaning on
a spade.

'Who is it?' I asked.

'Elephant man,' said Jim. And he was right, the spade was for shifting dung.

'Good boy,' I said.

He held his non-ghost hand out for the toy; I gave it back.

'Good boy,' I said again.

He went through into the playroom, and laid the man on his back in one of the downstairs rooms. The dolls' house had a very different layout to ours – it was double-fronted for a start – but he'd chosen the closest equivalent to the very place he was standing: my father's place.

'No, no,' he said. 'That's on the – there.'

He closed the front of the dolls' house and made the wailing ghost look in at the downstairs windows.

'He ate all his lunch,' said Eileen.

'Good boy,' I said, and realized I was doing one of the things I'd most hated my father doing, praising me as if I were a dog.

'I'll leave you to it, then,' I said, attempting a more man-to-man tone.

I didn't know exactly what *it* was, though.

Upstairs in my study, I found that I couldn't work. The thing I was writing was my ninth play, and it wasn't coming easily; I'd been commissioned, so had to stick close to what other people thought they wanted. With Jim wailing downstairs, I couldn't become sufficiently distracted. If my dead father really was speaking through him, then what did he want to say? The haunting – always assuming that's what it was – seemed different to classic possession, though. I had no sense of a message, more of a reenactment; as if my father, whilst living with us, had been visited by one of the ghosts already resident in the house – a Victorian ghost, perhaps. And, for whatever reason, he'd kept this terror to himself. He'd had enough of the more imminent terrors to concern him; pure agony for one. He often woke us with anguished cries – to the extent that we sometimes ignored the first or second occurrence; never more than that. They didn't always mean he was in pain, or even awake. He often dreamed of death (he told me this, latterly), and would scream from the deeps of nightmares in which he was fully interred.

I made a final attempt to pull myself back from these kind of thoughts. Jim *wasn't* possessed. I was projecting everything onto him, from a guilty, adult perspective. He had wanted a new toy, and I had distorted that into something far darker. Very often he said pertinent things without knowing it. But just as often, he spoke nonsense. Only the week before, a new catchphrase had entered family legend. Jim had walked into our bedroom, first thing, and sagely announced that 'Crocodiles eat broken toes, and smelly cheese.' What he was saying *now* issued from no different source to that statement of muddledness: Jim wasn't even old enough, according to Freud, to have developed a subconscious. It was more like the language itself babbling along, making combinations of words that might or might not go together. It was meaning testing meaning.

Just before six o'clock, I went down to the playroom to take over from Eileen. Glenys would be back in about half an hour. Jim had already been fed.

As I walked in, he was bouncing the ghost along the roof of the dolls' house, which was still closed – although I hoped he'd allowed the elephant-keeper out at some point in the previous two hours.

'Attic, attic, attic!' Jim was chanting, and then, 'Limp, limp, limp!' The ghost wobbled as it flew, although it didn't really have the feet for proper limping.

Eileen said goodbye to me and then to Jim. He blanked her.

'Say thank you for taking me to the zoo today,' I said.

'Thank you, attic,' said Jim. 'Thank you, limp.'

This was funny.

I gave Eileen a frowning smile. She knew the little bastard could be like this sometimes.

'See you tomorrow,' she said.

'Attic-limp,' said Jim. 'Attic-limp.'

But when I'd closed the door on Eileen, and gone back to Jim, this chant had achieved its true and significant form: 'Limp-attic, limp-attic.'

It was the spread from the pancreas to the lymphatic system which finally killed my father. And that had taken place right where Jim was standing.

'Stop it,' I said.

Jim kept going; the chant was his joy of the moment.

'Stop it, please.'

'He got limp-attic,' he said. 'He got limp-attic daddy. He got limp-attic mummy. He got limp-attic sister.'

I strode across, deliberated banging my heels onto the floorboards; I wanted Jim to know I was his father, was coming fast and that I was immensely angry.

I shook him, harder than I should have done – a lot harder. His head rocked on his shoulders, going in the opposite direction to the shakes.

'Shut up! Shut up!' I said. He couldn't speak – his throat was too distorted by the back-and-forth, but he could still cry; first with his eyes and then vocally; and he started to keen as soon as I let go and began to calm down. We were like the ends of a see-saw: he, rising to hysteria; me, sinking to catatonia.

'I'm sorry,' I said, and held him.

I couldn't allow myself to become a danger to him.

We watched television until Glenys returned, and as soon as he was asleep I confessed. He had been subdued all evening – not himself – had not done the usual bath-splashing or towel-swirling.

'Do you think you hurt him?'

'I don't know. It was so horrible. I don't think you could have chosen anything worse.'

Then I remembered one thing. Before he could properly speak, Jim had used to chant dad-dad-dad at me. And quite often it came out as dead-dead-dead. It had been just one of the many signs I'd had to dismiss as meaningless.

Glenys went and woke Jim.

'Does it hurt when you turn your head?' she asked, then tried to manipulate it. Jim was too bleary to understand. He didn't wince, though, or even resist.

Out on the landing, Glenys said, 'If you *ever* hurt him like that again, I will leave. I will take him and leave.'

'But I told you,' I said. 'I could have covered up and you'd never have known.'

'And that makes it better?'

She didn't speak to me again until we were in bed and the lights were out.

'I know you're still grieving for your father. I know it's difficult for you. But you must never take anything out on Jim. I would prefer it if he was alone in the house for ten minutes than that you stayed here as a threat to him.'

'I'm not a threat,' I said, but I knew that wasn't true; I had hurt him even if I hadn't injured him.

The simplest thing seemed to be – remove the cause of the trouble.

'Right,' I said, twisting out of bed. I went to the kitchen and fetched our torch from one of the drawers. Then I went into Jim's room and started to look for the ghost.

Glenys, worried, had come in after me.

I explained, in whispers.

'It was in his hand when he went to sleep,' Glenys said. And I found it still there. His grip was tight. I had to bend his fingers back a little to get it out. Glenys watched. The torchlight moved around on the walls and the shadows on Jim's face made him look skeletal.

'Right, mate,' I said, talking to the ghost, trying to make a joke of it. 'You're history.'

I carried it downstairs, out the front door and chucked it into one of the wheelie bins.

'He will miss it,' said Glenys. 'It'll be a big thing.'

'I'll buy him something else. Take him to the toyshop. Whatever he wants.'

Still, I didn't sleep. And Jim wailed for the ghost from the moment he woke up. The elephant-keeper was no consolation – and was ignored from now on. Jim seemed genuinely pained; Glenys made the connection to my roughness, and took him straight to casualty. I went, too. We left a note for Eileen, explaining we didn't know when we'd be back.

Jim hung on to Glenys and wouldn't come near me. I was terrified he'd tell one of the nurses what had happened, and end up getting himself taken into care.

We stayed an hour in the waiting room before he was seen. In the cramped blue cubicle, they asked for an explanation. I said he'd tripped over the stairgate and fallen downstairs. It had happened that morning, I said.

'Are you sure?' asked the nurse. 'These are bruises.'

I looked at Jim's shoulders. My thumbprints were there on either side of the double-swoosh of his collarbone, purple. I just prayed my fingers weren't there, four and four, on the back. The nurse turned him round. I realized I had to say something.

'That was different. He tried to run into the road. Yesterday. I pulled him back. I was a little rough, I admit.'

The nurse looked at me. 'Understandable,' she said. I was pretty sure she didn't believe a word. 'And you say he fell head first?'

'He was that way when we got there,' I said.

She looked to Glenys, who took a moment to nod.

'Well,' the nurse said, feeling Jim's neck once more. 'There's nothing broken I can find. We'll send him for an X-ray, though – just to be a hundred per cent sure. Alright?'

'Good boy,' I said, as we went back to A&E.

We waited another hour before they could do him. There was no fracture.

'Never again,' said Glenys, after strapping Jim in. We stood behind the car in the hospital carpark. I had parked in a space three along from the one I'd used when I came to collect Jim as a newborn. When visiting my father, I'd parked in just about every space there. 'You have no more chances,' said Glenys.

I insisted we stop at the toyshop on the way home. Jim went straight for the low shelf where the ghost had been before, but it seemed to have been the last of them. If one had remained, I suppose I might have bought it for him, and things would have turned out differently; perhaps better, perhaps worse. As it was, there was no replacement ghost. Jim, despite great persuasion, wouldn't accept anything else, in fact began to cry, and so we took him home.

'You can choose something next time,' said Glenys. She did

not, luckily, suggest they order a ghost in specially for us.

After scrambled eggs on toast in the kitchen, Glenys went off to work and I left Jim with Eileen. I put headphones on, so I wouldn't hear what he was doing. I think I already had a shivering suspicion what it would be.

At ten to six, I came downstairs to the sound of *whooo-whooo*. Jim was tiptoeing around with a drying-up cloth on his head, being a ghost.

'He's been like this all afternoon,' Eileen said. 'Running up and down. I can't find the little figure. Do you know where it is?'

The rubbish wouldn't be collected until Monday morning. I knew *exactly* where it was.

'No,' I said.

'Have a good weekend,' Eileen said, and picked her coat off the rack. Jim gave her a very affectionate goodbye, kissing her on the lips, then went back into character after she'd left.

Whooo was all he'd say. At least it wasn't *lymphatic system.*

He raced along the corridor between the kitchen and the playroom, the drying cloth over his eyes. He never bumped into the doors, as I expected him to. Eventually, I gave in and went upstairs to get one of the old sheets we'd used on his cot.

'Here you go,' I said. 'If you're going to be a ghost, you'd better look like one.'

I cut eyeholes and a mouthhole, drew round them with black felt-tip, then handed the costume over. Jim was surly, without gratitude. He put the sheet on, however, and immediately became a scarier ghost. His performance started to unnerve me; it was obsessive. I began to wonder whether us indulging this was completely psychologically healthy. Me shaking him had made things more intense, but the plastic figure was what

had begun the whole episode. I should have obeyed my super-
stitiousness and not bought it for him.

Whooo, he said, even when I turned the television on for his
favourite programme, *In the Night Garden…*

I sat down to watch, but a sheeted figure stood in front of
the screen, holding its arms out. The picture was completely
blocked by white cotton – all I could see were different colours
coming through.

'What do you want?' I asked. And as I spoke, I realized that I
was speaking not to Jim but to the ghost he had become. 'What
do you want me to do?'

'Play,' said the ghost-voice. This was an answer Jim might
give. 'Play, now.'

'Say "Play, Daddy, please,"' I said.

The ghost wavered about for a bit. Having got a word other
than *whooo*, I thought I'd lost Jim once more. But no—

'"Play, Daddy, please,"' he said. That, at least, was what I
heard at the time. Thinking back, the voice said it without the
implied comma and capital: 'Play daddy, please'.

'What do *you* want to play?'

'Play ghost.'

'What do I do?'

'You play.'

I grabbed the remote and turned the television off, then stood
up. The ghost, still quite substantial, pushed me through into
the playroom.

'Play here!'

'"Oh, no,"' I said, '"a ghost. I *am* scared. Oh, help, no!"'

'No,' said the voice, further from Jim's. 'Not *that*.'

'I don't know what you want me to do. What do you want me
to do?'

The ghost ran around me a couple of times, whoooing.

'Do you want me to lie down?' I asked.

'Lie down,' the ghost said, and it was as if I hadn't spoken at all, and the command was coming freshly from him.

I lay with my head towards the dolls' house and my feet towards the off-television – in the exact position my father had lain, when his bed and his death were there.

'Now what do you want?' I asked. 'You've got me here – what do you want?'

'Shhh,' the voice said.

He wafted past me several times. I tried to look up beneath the sheet – I wanted to see Jim's face; I wanted to make sure Jim's face was still there. His jeans and bare feet came out from the sheet's bottom edge, but the noises in the room seemed lower than anything Jim had made before.

I closed my eyes. This was usually an invitation for Jim to jump on me, then laugh.

He didn't.

I waited.

The ghost swished back and forth; I could no longer hear the slap of feet.

'I'm dying,' I said, with relief. 'I'm in the worst imaginable pain, and you can't do anything about it. It doesn't matter if you're my son or a ghost or what you are, because I'm the one that's about to die – and I'm scared. I'm scared. I didn't think I would be but I'm fucking terrified. I feel like I'm looking over the edge of a cliff into the dark only there isn't a cliff or an edge there's only dark. Someone's going to come up behind me and push me off, and that someone is Death with a capital D, and there's nothing I can do about it. I can't turn round and look at it, face him down. I've tried, all I see is more dark and more dark again. All around. Lots of people I know have died, and quite a few have died like this. Of cancer. I stayed away. I didn't like to visit and then have to remember them as skeletons rather than the living, friendly people they'd been before. And now I'm here and people are avoiding seeing me, and I can understand why. I look like shit – I look like something you wouldn't want anyone to see. I can't stop myself from smelling something fucking awful, too. I puke all over myself, when I'm not quick enough to make the bucket. And even when I do turn in time, I often miss. They have to clear up after me. My breath smells and I stink of old piss, too. Like some fucking wino. But I still get erections. Isn't that amazing? But I haven't got much longer. And it's not fair. I wasn't a heavy drinker. I never smoked. I shouldn't be dying like this. No one should die like this, but especially not me. This is a punishment for something I never did. It is. I'm in hell. Body and soul, in hell. And it hurts like nothing you've ever known. It's just terrible. And children are meant to make everything better. You're meant to make me feel like I've passed something on to the world. Made a positive contribution. But I hate you because you're so fucking healthy and young and I want your health and I want your life and all the years of fucking living you've got left. You little jammy fucking little bastard. You little cunting little fuck. You fucking little bastard cunt.'

Then it stopped, the language. I'd said it, and it had said me, and my father.

Just then, a key ground into the door and Glenys called *Hello* from the hall.

If I'd moved quickly, I could have stood up, or at least got into a crouch – that's what I think now. I could have *moved*. But I lay where I'd been, eyes still closed. I must have wanted her to see.

'What's this then?' Glenys asked, coming in.

There was a pause.

I didn't want to look, but I had to.

The ghost was still there. Glenys stood with her hand on its head. I could see Jim's big eyes through the eyeholes; I could see his open mouth, through the mouthhole.

'Cunt,' said the ghost.

Glenys did not laugh.

Nemo
Joanna Trollope

My mother thinks I have no ambition. She's always told me
so. In return, I think she doesn't know the difference between
ambition – which I think is aspiring to succeed – and bettering
yourself, which in her case means having a higher standard of
life than you were brought up to. That's what she likes about
my brother. She likes his BMW and cufflinks and poncy job in
the City moving money that doesn't exist round in circles. She
likes the swank of it all. I don't do swank.

What I do – no, what I *did* – was what I was good at. I was
a fitness instructor. Not the kind that arrives at five-million-
pound houses and puts bored spoiled women looking for
no-strings sex through their paces on their bedroom floors,
but the kind that helps fat unfit people escape from being fat
and unfit a while. I worked in the gym and the pool of a health
farm. Not a *spa*, you understand, not a sleek urban arrangement, all brushed steel and opaque glass, but an old-fashioned
kind of health farm, where the clients wouldn't be intimidated
by too much glamour and thinness. We didn't do wheat grass
and tonic vibration at Dulcie Farm, we did small portions and

water aerobics. And I ran the fitness side, with Judy, who was a swimmer, and Gianetta, who came from Turin, who taught yoga and Pilates.

My mother – something else to resent her for – christened me Nigel. I arrived at Dulcie Farm, newly qualified as an instructor after reading sports sciences at Loughborough University, as Nigel. But I arrived that day wearing a sports shirt I'd been given by my then girlfriend, a shirt hooped in black and orange, and at first glance, the manager of Dulcie Farm – more about her later – said I reminded her of nothing so much as a clownfish.

'I'll call you Nemo,' she said. She wasn't even looking at me, she was pinning something up on the board behind her desk. 'We'll all call you Nemo and then the clients can have a laugh, finding you. Can't they?'

I threw the shirt away, that same day. I got my team into navy blue with white trainers, but the name Nemo had stuck by then. Judy gave me a coffee mug with the clownfish Nemo on it and then the clients started. I had lockersful of Nemo junk, T-shirts and baseball caps and bath toys and even some nylon fur slippers with big plastic eyes stuck on. Gross, really. But if you work with the public, if you are paid to work with the public, you have to humour them. I humoured them all right. I humoured them because I'd chosen this job, and I was paid to do this job, and I humoured them because – well, because of *her.*

I didn't believe in love at first sight. I thought it was something girls fantasized about, like being carried off by a tall dark stranger on a white charger. But then it happened to me. She'd hardly looked at me, she'd hardly clocked me and then she stood up and turned to pin something on her office board and she said, 'I'll call you Nemo,' and I was a goner. I wanted to leap over that desk and flatten her against the wall and just *have* her, mind, body, spirit, the lot. It was all I could do to go on standing up straight. The room was spinning like a merry-go-round.

She was called Adele. She said her mother was French. She wasn't, really, even my type, she was too big, too blonde, too confident. She had the face of an angel and the bum of a balloon. I thought she was so gorgeous, my eyes crossed, just picturing her. She had little hands and little feet and when she let her brassy hair down, it fell almost to her waist. She pretended not to notice me, but I knew she had. I may not exactly have the face of George Clooney, but my physique's okay. I'm well set up. You have to be, if your mother's gone and called you Nigel.

The girls, Judy and Gianetta, could see how it was with me, almost at once. Women are like that: they never seem to miss an emotional second. Judy was sorry for me. Judy was okay, a nice girl, with a steady boyfriend. We bought lottery tickets together each week, and her dream, if she won, was to pay for a down payment on a house, and to buy an American fridge with an ice machine in the door. Gianetta was much trickier. Quite a looker, but temperamental. And jealous of everyone.

'What d'you want to fancy her for?' Gianetta said, 'She's fat and she's fake. She's like one of the clients. You got eyes in your head?'

I said, 'I think she's fantastic and she's my boss and she knows that.'

Gianetta was stripping off a T-shirt. She always did that in front of me, so that I could see how slim she was, how toned. She yanked the shirt over her head and then she said,

'Anyway, she's got a boyfriend.'

'Don't tell me.'

'Certainly, I tell you! What are friends for?'

I bent down to retie my trainer laces.

She said, 'It's Mr Belcourt.'

'Who?'

'You know,' Gianetta said. She was standing there, in her sports bra, and I could see how good-looking she was and feel completely unmoved by it. 'Mr Belcourt. He comes three times a year, and never gets any thinner. He comes to feel her up, in the consultation room. When his wife dies, he'll marry her. And *she*—' Gianetta began to pull on a singlet, very slowly – '*She*'ll marry his money and his car and his timeshare in Florida.'

It was my policy not to badmouth clients. If I caught Judy or Gianetta imitating or slagging off clients, I let them have it, in no uncertain terms. But I found myself saying, 'I'll kill him.'

'Cut him out, then,' Gianetta said. 'Cut him out. If that tub of lard is what you want.'

'She won't even look at me. To her, I'm just a penniless clownfish. I couldn't even – I wouldn't dare—' I stopped.

Gianetta picked up a towel and snapped it across my groin.

'All mouth,' she said, 'no trousers. See the English I learn?'

Mr Belcourt came to Dulcie Farm two months later. He had a new car – a Bentley, I ask you, what kind of a granddad car is that? – and new luggage and we were told to be particularly respectful to him as his long-ailing wife had finally released him and taken herself off to Paradise. I watched Adele like a hawk. She'd dressed herself in black, and veiled her amazing cleavage with a bit of black lace, and she knocked me out. I made a point of standing next to old Belcourt as often as I could, in front of her, so that she could compare and contrast, and it was during one of these triangular sessions that Dr Dulcie arrived.

Dr Dulcie started, and owned, Dulcie Farm. I suppose you'd describe him as a diet doctor – he certainly wasn't a qualified medical one – someone who had taken advantage of the dangers of early slimming pills, and worked out a regime of eating for people who love obeying priests and doctors and weird gurus. At Dulcie Farm, the clients were served Dr Dulcie's special muesli at breakfast, and had their portions weighed according to his proportional system. He had written several books – the first, *Diet with Dulcie*, had been a runaway bestseller – and been, in his day, something of a television star. I couldn't help thinking he wasn't a brilliant advert for his own advice. He was thin as a rail, I grant you, but his hair was dyed – badly dyed – and his face was so lined, it looked gnarled. But he had the confidence of the very devil. He'd walk into the treatment waiting area, where they all lay about like so many white towelling porpoises reading back numbers of lifestyle magazines, and it was like collective electric shock treatment. They seemed completely galvanized and when he bent over them, and took their hands, they looked like my mother looks when she plays her Tom Jones CD.

Dr Dulcie cornered me in the fitness area staff room. I was trying to tidy up a bit, picking up Snickers bar wrappers and takeaway cartons.

'You in trouble, young man?'

I straightened up. I looked at the junk food evidence in my hands.

'I'm afraid I can't stop them eating this stuff—'

Dr Dulcie glanced at the rubbish.

'I don't care what they eat. Put it down.'

I dumped the rubbish in the overflowing bin.

'You can eat what crap you like,' Dr Dulcie said. 'You can live like pigs. But I want my staff sexy. Sexy sells. And you aren't sexy if you ain't getting no sex.'

I looked at the floor.

'You're not getting any sex,' Dr Dulcie said. 'Are you?'

I felt the hot redness surging up my neck and swelling my ears.

'I've got ears,' Dr Dulcie said, 'I've got eyes. I know who you fancy. And I know you're scared.'

'I'm—'

'You're scared,' Dr Dulcie said. 'You're in such a state about her, you think you won't get it up or keep it up. Hold out your hand.'

I couldn't look at him. I held out my hand. It was shaking. I felt him put something light into my palm.

'Use them,' Dr Dulcie said. 'Use them and cheer up, for God's sake.'

I heard the staff-room door swing shut behind him. I looked in my hand. There was a bubble pack of four small pills. They were pale blue, and they were shaped like diamonds.

I never had such a night. It made me feel as I suppose marathon runners feel, that they've got to keep going because it's so fantastic when they stop and realize they've done it. I was amazed and utterly elated. I didn't know you could have that much sex and not have your eyes fall out. And Gianetta did it without any blue pills. Gianetta matched me, all night long, and in the morning she said, 'Not bad, big boy,' and I heard her singing Amy Winehouse in the shower.

I was grinning all day. I couldn't stop. I was on a complete high, and every so often I went to check on the three pills I still had left, and I bought Gianetta a red rose and she stuck it in a smoothie bottle in the staff-room sink and said she liked action better than attitude. That made me laugh. Everything made me laugh. I went up to a changing-room mirror, and breathed on it and wrote 'I am a sex god' in the mist, and that made me laugh too. I loved everybody and everything. I remember thinking that if this is being off my head, then I don't ever want to be back on it. I was just delirious.

Three days later, I was summoned to see Adele. She'd taken off the black dress, and she was in red, with sex-shop heels, and a diamond the size of a winegum on her finger. I didn't, at first, take in which finger.

She said, 'You know perfectly well, NIGEL [she emphasized the Nigel], that I can't have fraternizing among the staff.'

I gawped at her. What was she on about?

'Your free time is, of course, your free time. But you are to lay off members of staff. Do you hear me?'

'Yes,' I said. I wasn't entirely concentrating. I was looking, as usual, at her breasts and was suddenly a bit distracted, too, by the diamond.

'I know about you and Gianetta,' Adele said. 'I should think the whole *world* knows about you and Gianetta. What an exhibitionist and pathetic performance!'

I was about to say that it had hardly been pathetic and, as nobody had been watching, hardly exhibitionist either. But instead, I found myself staring at the diamond.

I said, 'What's that?'

'What's what?'

'That ring.'

'That,' she said, 'is my engagement ring.'

I suddenly felt sick. Sick and shaky. I tried to stand up, and I couldn't. I said, in a strangulated whisper, 'Engagement?'

She held out her hand, as if to admire it better.

'To Mr Belcourt.'

'Oh God,' I said, 'Please don't, please—'

She went on looking at her ring.

'Why should you care?' she said. 'What's it to you? All night shagging that little tramp from Turin, and you dare to question my engagement?'

I said weakly, 'It wasn't like that, it wasn't because I fancy her, I didn't mean to. It was the pills.'

She leaned forward and thrust the diamond at me.

'And this,' she said, 'you sad little jerk, was the *money*.'

'Ah,' Mr Belcourt said, 'it's my friend Nemo, isn't it?'

He laughed his loud and jolly laugh. His office was huge, with oil paintings and a desk the size of a ship. He patted his big belly.

'No good at the exercises,' he said, 'without you to bully me!'

'That's what I've come about, sir,' I said. It choked me to call him 'sir'. 'I've come to see if you can help me. Help me with – with my ambition, sir.'

I'll give him his due, he listened to me. I told him that I felt stuck at Dulcie Farm, that I knew I was good at what I did, that I wanted to work in a larger environment, and with people who lived in the real world rather than those in a health-farm cocoon. He leaned back in his chair and eyed me over his fat hands, held fingertip to fingertip. When I'd finished, he said, 'What did you have in mind?'

And I said, 'Working for a company like – like Belcourt Holdings, sir. I'm sure your staff would benefit from in-house fitness training.'

He eyed me.

'Is it the girls? Is it the money?'

I gave my pocket a brief pat. In it lay my bubble pack of pills. I put my chin up and looked him in the eye and said, quite loudly, quite seriously, 'Both, sir.'

He laughed. He threw back his head, and laughed and laughed. And then he brought his hands down flat on the desk, and leaned forward and said, 'You may well be on, my boy.'

'Thank you, sir.'

'Tell me – tell me why you came to me.'

I went on looking at him.

'Broken heart, sir.'

'My God,' he said. 'My God. We'll soon mend that.' He got up and moved towards the door. 'Come and walk with me through the offices. You never saw so many girls.'

I never had. Desks of them, floors of them, women turning to look at me like some teenage wet-dream fantasy. I walked through that building, with the magic still in my pocket, and I thought that maybe a new life would open up, could open up, and I'd be free of longing and longing for something I could never have because I was just Nemo, and a bit of a joke.

And then, when I got back to Dulcie Farm, Judy was there waiting for me. She was shaking with excitement. She put a piece of paper with numbers on it in my hand and she said, 'I stayed late to tell you – I haven't told anyone else. You've won! You've won!'

I stared at her. I stared and stared, as if I couldn't take it in.

She said, 'The lottery!' and I patted my pocket in a dazed kind of way and whispered, 'It's the pills...'

Nothing was real, after that. I was on a cloud: not a high, but more a dreamy, unreal place where everything seemed a bit distant. I had a million pounds. A million! I know a million isn't what it once was, but for a fitness instructor on twenty-five grand a year, it's a fortune beyond imagining. I also had Mr Belcourt's offer of a job and Gianetta's almost permanent offer of another kind. And the three pills. I looked at them often but I didn't touch them. The first one had proved so potent, potent way beyond just sex, that I felt respect bordering on fear for the remaining three. I also, despite all this wealth and promise and opportunity, felt a huge and overwhelming sadness. I had all this great stuff coming, all this stuff other people would give their eye teeth for, but it felt hollow, and pointless and empty, because the heart was missing, *my* heart wasn't in any of it. My heart was, miserably, painfully, where it had always been.

Probably, being a man, being a man in a muddle, it would all have just drifted on like that. I'd have left Dulcie Farm, gone to London and Belcourt Holdings, married someone called Amanda from accounts, been okay. But not wonderful. Wonderful is when you are living fully, when there's electricity in the air, when someone gets you to believe in yourself because they really believe in you. Wonderful is when the right person takes the right action.

She came to find me. I was cleaning up at the end of the day, picking up wet towels and scattered newspapers, and there she was, sitting on one of the loungers by the indoor pool, elbows on her knees, staring at the water. She was in her red dress and her hair was down her back, and the reflected light from the pool was speckling her face with sequins. My heart just turned over.

I dropped all the towels, and went over to stand next to her. She glanced up. Then she held her hand out.

'Look.'

'Look what?'

'No ring.'

I fell on my knees beside her and seized her hand.

'What happened?'

She turned to look at me.

'I can't marry him.'

'You can't—'

'I can't marry someone I don't love. I can't love him because I love someone else. You can't work for him because I can't lose you.'

My head was spinning. I said something incoherent, something joyful and incredulous, and then she seemed to waver a little and she put her arms out towards me and she said, 'Oh hold me, Nemo, hold me, I think I'm going to faint,' and she pitched forward, into my arms, just as I had dreamed and dreamed of her doing. And that, by a million miles, was the best fulfilled fantasy of them all.

We've been married a year. We manage Dulcie Farm together now, and Mr Belcourt – who came to the wedding and gave us our honeymoon in his Florida timeshare – is going to marry a widow he met on the next sunbed in the solarium. Judy left to have a baby and Gianetta went home to Turin. The million pounds is just waiting. It's in a high-interest account, and it's just waiting. It's waiting until we feel it has enough reality to do something with, until it can truly fulfil an ambition, something we both want, something that will mean aspiration as well as success. There's no hurry. These happy days – why hurry a single one of them?

As for the blue pills – I'm going to give them to Mr B for his honeymoon. Privately you know, just man to man. It's the least I can do for him.

The Pearl Fishers
Colm Tóibín

In the late 1980s Gráinne Roche and her husband Donnacha moved to Dublin, where Gráinne became a fierce believer in the truth. When she argued, in her weekly newspaper column or on the radio, about the state of the Church and the soul of the nation, her tone made some people dislike her intensely. Nonetheless, her country accent and her insistence that she and other like-minded lay people represented the true Catholic Church more than the bishops and priests gave her a role in most debates about the changing Ireland; she insisted always that she stood for some middle ground, dismissing the attitudes of the country's liberal smart class. The few times I saw her in the city I enjoyed reminding her that when I had known her in Wexford she was young and walked around the town in her school uniform chewing gum. But in general I kept away from her. I had long before lost interest in arguments about the changing Ireland. But that is not the only reason I kept away from her.

I live alone now and I work hard. And when I am not working I am away. I do not see anyone I have no desire to see. It is easy to screen calls and avoid answering e-mails, and then they peter out. I love a long day when the night promises nothing more than silence, solitude, music, lamplight, the time broken by maybe half an hour on Gaydar to see if there is anyone new, or even anyone familiar, in the city centre who might stop by for what they call sex with no strings attached.

Viewed in the morning, it often seems a perfect life; once darkness falls it is sometimes sad, but only mildly so. It is easy being middle-aged, needs and appetites reduced to a level where they can be satisfied without much effort or pain or hardship. I make enough money from the grim, almost plot-less thrillers with gay sub-plots I produce, which are popular in Germany and in Japan, and from overwrought and graphically violent screenplays, one of which paid for the top-floor apart-ment where I spend my days, to live as I please. I let no one irritate me unless I can expect in return some compensation such as sex or serious amusement, or unless there are old and intimate attachments involved.

Thus when Gráinne left a message on my answer machine one day when I was out, I did not reply. I had no idea why she might want to speak to me. I pressed 9, which meant her message would be preserved on the machine for a week and then would have to be erased. When the week was up I erased it without a thought. She called again, and said into the voice-mail that I was hard to get hold of. I might have smiled in satisfaction at the idea that this was as it should be, but I still did not reply.

Not long afterwards, however, I carelessly answered a call from someone with no caller ID and it was Gráinne. She had me now. She moaned at first about the number of calls she had had to make to find me.

'I have to see you,' she said eventually, 'and soon, and so does Donnacha. It is important.'

'Can you tell me what it is about?' I asked. 'Just a clue will help. Talk slowly. I am not as bright as you.'

'Don't start,' she said. 'I'll tell you when I see you. It might be best over dinner somewhere during the week. Somewhere quiet or where the tables are far apart.'

'Somewhere quiet,' I repeated. 'Will you be there?'

'Don't start. Do you hear me? Don't start. We both need to see you.'

I left silence and thought of saying that I was writing a book and was not seeing many people. I knew how pompous that would sound to her and almost relished the idea, but I also knew how ineffective it would be as a way of deterring her. The way she said 'We both need to see you' made me stop for a moment longer. She seemed to be suggesting that this was not about her and her work, the two subjects which interested Gráinne Roche more than anything else in the world, and it was not to be a social occasion either. It was about her and Donnacha, whom I had known better than I had ever known her.

There was a time, indeed, when I had loved him, but that was something which had not bothered me for years. I knew that he now worked in administration in one of the main Dublin hospitals. I had heard him once or twice on the radio sounding rational and competent and in full possession of a large set of complex facts. His voice, I remember noting, had not changed. Nor indeed had hers. She made me agree to see them in the Tea Rooms at eight o'clock the following Wednesday.

'Are you still in daily touch with the Virgin Mary?' I asked before we rang off.

'I am,' she said, 'and she is taking a very dim view of you.'

I laughed. She had a lovely way of making herself sound as though she meant everything she said. Even when she tried to be ironic or sarcastic or funny, she sounded earnest. I could imagine Donnacha liking that too, finding it even more amusing and refreshing than I did.

I almost looked forward to seeing them until the time came close. But as I walked slowly towards the Clarence Hotel I actually dreaded the prospect of meeting them and I wished I had not answered the phone to her that day. There was something dull about Gráinne and her urgent needs and her strong and half-baked opinions. And there was something about Donnacha which I had never been able to fathom, some deep laziness or contentment, an ease in the world, a way of letting nothing bother him too much, a way of never allowing anything happen to him that would require close analysis on his part. This beautiful nonchalance of his had made me want him at a certain time in my life more than I have ever wanted anyone, and it had made him tolerate me and enjoy things while they lasted until something more normal and easy to manage came his way.

Such as a woman who did all of the talking.

Most of us are gay or straight; Donnacha simply made no effort, he took whatever came his way. In the past I had found that exciting and satisfying, but I had not thought about him seriously for a long time. As I walked into the Tea Rooms, however, and saw that they were waiting for me, I was surprised that I still felt jealous. Of Donnacha's self-containment, of his way of making people want him, or trust him, or like him. And maybe jealous too of the idea that he and Gráinne had now been together for almost twenty-five years, that she had him all the time, every night. I hoped to get away from them as soon as I could.

'We thought you'd be late,' she said.

'Yes, I planned to be late, but it didn't work out.'

Donnacha was wearing a suit and a tie. I wondered if he had come straight from work. He stood up and shook my hand as though he did not know me well.

'You are still married to her?' I asked.

He smiled almost shyly and looked at Gráinne.

'What God hath put together,' she said.

'Well,' I said. 'I don't often meet a divinely inspired couple.'

I wondered if my question had been unfortunate, if they were in fact meeting to let me be the first to know that they were separating, but I did not think so.

Gráinne seemed to have arranged the table so that there were two places set opposite her, one for Donnacha and one for me. I had imagined that they would sit beside each other opposite me. She obviously wanted us both to look at her, or wanted to make sure that we were both listening to her when she spoke.

She handed me the wine list.

'We have ordered gin and tonics,' she said, 'but that might be too strong for you.'

'It's nice to see country people back in the Clarence,' I replied. 'I'm sure the band are delighted.'

'Bono was in the lobby when we came in,' Donnacha said.

'Give me Larry any day,' I replied.

'Order the wine,' Gráinne said.

Donnacha had not changed. His hair was grey now, but the grey did not make much difference. His face had thickened but not very much. His teeth were still perfect. He was as slim as ever. But none of his physical attributes added up to much – he was not beautiful, or physically striking – and it was something else which made me glad that I was not sitting opposite him and would not have to look at him all evening. His aura had not been affected by the years. He was lazily there, easy-going, comfortable, with a withheld feline sexuality of which he seemed utterly unaware as their drinks came and we ordered our food and our wine.

'I see you are still keeping the old-age pensioners on trolleys in the hospital corridors,' I said. 'They get their pillow stolen when they go to the jacks.'

He smiled almost impatiently and slowly began to explain how things in his hospital were improving, mentioning in pass-ing several meetings he had had with the Minister and what she had said, and one meeting with the Taoiseach. I had forgotten how much he loved an argument and how rational he was and unwilling to deal with insult and half-thought-out invective. Nonetheless, it was not hard to tell him that the problem began and ended with the doctors and their greed and their arrogance, and nothing would change until their salaries were halved and they had to clock in like everyone else.

'It is not as simple as that.'

I almost said that it was precisely as simple as that when my mother was dying in a public ward over long months in one of the Dublin hospitals, but I did not want to talk about anything personal. I knew that Donnacha's parents had died, as had Gráinne's mother. I had not gone to the funerals, nor had they come to my mother's.

I noticed that Gráinne, who was facing the main door into the restaurant, paid absolutely no attention to this discussion, instead looked around her like a bored child. She was behav-ing like herself, only more so. It comes with age, I thought. Donnacha was thus becoming all reason, all good sense. I was becoming all bored, or maybe all regret. I wished I could tell Donnacha that I had no interest in hospitals or health systems or Ministers or meetings with the Taoiseach, that I was interested in his face and his voice, in the darkness of his eyes, in the slowly growing smile as he made his argument.

In St Aidan's we had been distantly friendly for the first three years, although Donnacha was always in a different dormitory and was not interested in hurling, as I was then. Thus I never spoke to him much or grew close to him. He had friends from home and he spent time with them. I remember him as part of a group on semi-permanent watch for opportunities to cadge cigarettes, asking for a pull of yours, or a drag, or the butt. I remember that he could be trusted not to horse a cigarette if you gave him a drag, and, if he had borrowed a cigarette, he could be depended on to return it the next day.

In our fourth year we became friends because we both worked to get on the school debating team. Donnacha began as a useless speaker, but over time the logical, calm way he made points began to work, especially if he was part of a team with other boys who had greater skills at delivery and drama or humour. I could do dramatic openings and endings as long as I could keep my stammer under control. Sean Kelly could do imitations and make jokes and barbed comments about the opposition. We left Donnacha to do the quiet summing up. By the end of January we had won the internal competition in the school, and this meant we could now represent the school in debates all over the county, mainly against girls' schools. Sometimes we got the topic a week in advance and were allowed time together to prepare, but there were some debates in which the subject was not released until an hour or two before, and these were the hardest and the most exciting. This was how we met Gráinne Roche, who at sixteen was the most fiery debater in the county, with a skill at invective that thrilled the audience. Donnacha never rose to her bait. Nothing she said or did made the slightest different to his delivery, and he could take a sentence of hers, or a point she had made, and dissect it coldly to make her seem like a fool.

Later, everybody who took part in those debates must have read the evidence against Father Rossiter, the science teacher who organized them, and presumed that we, who travelled with him so many times, must have known about him or even suffered because of him. I suppose we knew that he took an interest in us which was more intense than normal, and that he was often very nosy. And of course he liked Donnacha and loved quizzing him about the smallest details of his life, almost blushing with pleasure the more diffident and remote Donnacha grew. I watched this and it meant that I knew about Father Rossiter. According to the evidence given, it was only after our time at St Aidan's that Father Rossiter brought boys to his room and fucked them. But maybe there was other evidence that would have implicated him much earlier, and maybe it all happened in front of our noses. The idea of a priest wanting to get naked with one of the boys at St Aidan's and stuff his penis up the boy's bottom was so unimaginable that it might have happened while I was in the next room and I might have mistaken the grunts and yelps they made for a sound coming from the television. Or I might have mistaken the silence they managed to maintain for real silence.

On a night driving back to the school from Bunclody, where Donnacha's incisive and quiet arguments had seemed oddly powerless and flat, Sean Kelly sat in the front passenger seat while Father Rossiter drove and Donnacha and I sat in the back. I don't remember how we began to move closer to each other than we needed to be. It might have been because one of us wanted to be heard and thus sat over towards the middle to be within easy earshot of Father Rossiter and Sean Kelly. We did nothing obvious. I would never have dared to reach down towards Donnacha's penis, for example. But we moved close to each other so that our legs were touching and maybe, in the heat of the car, we had our jackets off and our shoulders were touching too and our arms. I eased off, I remember, in case this was a mistake, but it soon became clear that Donnacha was deliberately moving towards me and that a few times, as though by accident, he touched my thigh with his hand. We continued talking as normal but by the time we arrived back to the school Donnacha and I were on fire. It was a question of what we could do now. It was late and all the dormitory lights were off. No one would miss us, as everyone knew that we were in Bunclody at the debate.

Donnacha and I were on fire, but as I was to learn, there was a great deal of difference between us. If I did not make a plan, or insist in some way, Donnacha's fire would happily go out. It would not cost him a thought to go to his bed on his own on a night like this. But if I said nothing, merely led him to a place that was easy and comfortable and not too risky, then he would follow, and in the dark especially and with no words being spoken or whispered between us he would be passionate in a way that I could never manage. It would be clear that he wanted this all along, planned it maybe, but always with the proviso that he could, if he was not led, walk away.

Years later, when we lay in beds together, I learned more about him. But here in the dark, in this old school, with many nooks and shadowy spaces and unused room, I learned first how slowly I would have to move, how, for example, he would not let me touch his penis or kiss him until he had abandoned all modesty. This would take time. At first he would touch the light stubble on my face, or the hair on my chest, or the beginning of my pubic hair. He would do this as though it was leading nowhere. I could touch his back and open his pants and pull him in against me, and slowly I could move my hands and touch his buttocks but only when I sensed from his breathing that he was ready for this.

That night we went silently to a place off the rehearsal room that was once used for storing musical instruments. It had two doors – one connecting it to the rehearsal room, the other leading to a dark corridor, both of which could be locked. There was no light inside. At first, as we stood facing each other, I moved too fast and Donnacha almost pushed me away. I thought then that he just wanted to play a bit before going to bed. I did not know that he was building up to something. Since he had not let me kiss him I thought he did not want to be kissed at all, only to learn that I had to wait and work him up until he was ready. I learned that I could run my hand around his crotch and each time let it linger more until I could put my hand inside his underpants. By the time he let me pull his underpants down and touch his penis he was ready for anything.

I wondered that night, as I sneaked across the school to my dormitory and then lay in bed, what Donnacha would do in the morning. I wondered if he would avoid me, if he would pretend that nothing had happened between us, that he had not, as he finally ejaculated, left marks on my back with his fingernails and made muffled sounds which went on and on as he came all over my chest and stomach, if he would try to make me forget to see him, he nodded and said that Mr Francis had mentioned me to him, and that he too was an admirer of Hopkins and Eliot. He suggested that I come back another time. I wanted

Midsummer Nights | 130

my cha...
done this before. We walked

It seems ludicrous now, and it is certainly embarrassing, but it was more or less at the time I began to have sex with Donnacha that I became deeply religious. I still believe that it had nothing to do with him. I believe that I became interested in religion because of a number of poems on the school course that I read and reread with considerable intensity. These were the sonnets of Hopkins and two poems by T. S. Eliot, 'A Song for Simeon' and 'The Love Song of J. Alfred Prufrock'. If I ever happen to read 'Prufrock' now, it is as a comic poem, but then, at the age of sixteen, I took seriously the idea of the 'over-whelming question' which Prufrock wished to ask. I believed there was such a question and it was up to us, students of the poem, to formulate it. I believed the question was existential, almost religious, and it concerned how we should live in the world, and how we should relate to God and to each other, and I grew so solemn and earnest on the subject that Mr Francis, the English teacher, suggested I go and see a priest who had come back from America and worked only with the seminarians. He was a theologian. His name was Patrick Moorehouse.

The first day I knocked on his door he was busy, but I was struck by how polite he was. When I told him why I had come went up to his room every evening after tea for some weeks but he was never there. One day I saw him on the corridor but he did not notice me.

And then one Sunday, when I had presumed that I was travelling to New Ross for a hurling match, I was told that I had been dropped from the subs bench and the bus would be full. I knew it was my own fault for not togging out on the appointed afternoons, for disappearing into the library when I should have been on the playing field, but I was not alone in believing that I had been singled out by not being allowed to travel on the bus as a supporter. Even Donnacha had managed to get on the bus and he had never held a hurley in his life. This meant that I had a whole afternoon empty, from one o'clock, when the bus left, to five, when those still in the school would be expected to turn up for Rosary.

When I went up to Father Moorehouse's room that afternoon I did so merely as a way of passing ten minutes; I did not expect him to be there. He opened the door brusquely. He seemed preoccupied, but once he remembered who I was and how long ago he had promised to see me he invited me into the room. I had been in other priests' quarters, but this one was different from the rest. The main room was smaller. It was full of books and papers and LPs piled on desks. I could see no television but there was a stereo record player and there were two flat speakers resting against the wall. Father Moorehouse had been working at a desk. He moved some books and pamphlets from the short sofa and made space for me to sit and then he began to talk. I had no idea what I had expected him to say, or why, in fact, I had been sent to see him, but I need not have worried. His voice was soft; he smiled when he stopped to think, looking for the right phrase, and a few times he would take a note of something he had said so that he would not forget it. I wish I had taken notes too, but I remember clearly some of the things he said that day because I wrote them down as soon as I left his presence. He said: 'We must turn our bewilderment in the world into a gift from God.' He said: 'We must merge the language of our prayer with the terms of our predicament.' He said: 'We must humbly understand that consciousness belongs to each of us alone, it is part of us as much as it is part of God.'

He asked me about prayer and when I said nothing interesting he found me books and warned that some of them were not Catholic books but they might help me understand Hopkins and Eliot. He asked me if I had read John Donne and I said that I had not. He told me I must and he quoted some lines. By the time I left his room, I had books by Lancelot Andrews, Jonathan Edwards, Simone Weil and Fulton Sheen. He suggested that I come back even before I had read these books because he would like to talk to me more about faith and about prayer. I thanked him and I left.

I suppose it must be said that my interest in Patrick Moorehouse's mind, my fascination at the points he made and the terms he used and the writers he quoted from, was entirely sexual. But maybe it should be said only once, and perhaps whispered or put into parenthesis, or consigned to the realm of the obvious. At that time, no one knew that a sixteen-year-old boy and a priest twice his age could or would have sex, and so it never awoke as a thought in my conscious mind at that time. Now, I have to say, even now, the idea of it – of Father Moorehouse naked, for example, or Father Moorehouse with an erection, or

Father Moorehouse's tongue – is exciting. I regret that I did not put more thought into it then.

Instead, I tried to read the books he gave me. They were difficult, and I was glad that he had given me permission to go back to his room before I had finished any of them. I had found some essays by Eliot in the library and a book about his religious belief and his poetry and thought that this might be an excuse to go to Father Moorehouse's room again, maybe with passages marked that had puzzled me, to see what he thought.

The next time I found him in his room I was surprised to see Gráinne Roche and a friend of hers. They were both sitting on the sofa. Father Moorehouse got a chair for me from what I supposed must be the bedroom. I knew Gráinne, of course, from the debates. Now Father Moorehouse informed me that she was asking the same questions as I was and he was glad both of us had met in his room to discuss matters of faith rather than in the false world of the debating chamber. Gráinne was very quiet and appeared almost embarrassed. Father Moorehouse completely ignored her friend, who seemed not to notice, or not to mind. When he stood up, he made it clear that he had to go. All three of us left before him, the girls to walk back downtown, me to return to the study hall.

For the rest of the term, then, and for some of the following year, I had permission maybe once a week or once a fortnight to take time from the study hall and go to Father Moorehouse's room. It was presumed, I suppose, that I was being groomed for the seminary, although Father Moorehouse never mentioned that possibility. Most times when we met by arrangement Gráinne was there too, often with a friend or two friends but sometimes alone. A few times another guy from my class, who later did spend time in the seminary, came. He was clever and asked interesting questions. Donnacha had no interest in poetry or theology. I must have talked to him about what I was reading but perhaps not much because I have no memory of us ever discussing what went on in Father Moorehouse's room.

It is hard not to squirm when I think of some of the things I said in that room. Father Moorehouse sometimes spoke about complex matters, about God's role in chance and choice, in accidents and in decisions made on the basis of free will, in faith and its paradoxes. He loved words like paradox and ambiguity, he loved speculating, finding phrases, and he often turned to poems or books to help him as he went along. At the end, and sometimes at the beginning, he asked us to pray out loud, to follow him in finding words to match our feelings. I have no memory of any of Gráinne's friends ever doing this, but she did it and so did I. Father Moorehouse disliked cosy platitudes, as he called them, and simple stories. He pushed us all the time towards working our doubts and fears into words and phrases, towards using only the most precise metaphors. Sometimes we would kneel, sometimes face each other directly. Only one of us would speak. Occasionally he would ask us to address God directly, sometimes as though God were in the room with us, other times as though he were far away, a distant presence with whom we needed to communicate urgently.

It was awful, some of it, like Teilhard de Chardin crossed with Donovan or bad Bob Dylan. I know that Gráinne must remember how involved I became in it, how profoundly I talked to God! One of my greatest worries when she came to Dublin was that I would meet her somewhere and she would remind me, or start telling others, all about it. Or even that she might remember stray phrases or moments. Instead, strangely, her silence on the subject made me wish to avoid her even more, and made me uneasy now as I sat opposite her in the Tea Rooms as the wine was poured and the starter served.

'We got one of your things out on DVD and watched it one night when the boys were out,' Gráinne said. She sounded for a second as though she and Donnacha were meeting me in order to discuss the screenplay.

'They go to dances,' Donnacha said and smiled. 'I have to wait around the corner in the car for them so as not to make a show of them.'

'I hope you found the movie true to life,' I said.

'We thought *The Silence of the Lambs* was bad. I mean it gave Donnacha nightmares. But yours was worse.'

'It didn't give me nightmares,' Donnacha said.

'It did. It gave you nightmares. You don't remember because you were fast asleep for them, but I do because I had to listen to you.'

Donnacha looked at me and smiled.

'I have never had a nightmare in my life. It would take more than a mere movie to give me a nightmare.'

'What was your film called?' Gráinne interrupted.

'*A Raw Deal*,' I said.

'It was raw all right. I mean – the dentist's chair! How did you think of it?'

'The director added it. I didn't think of it.'

'I thought you wrote it.'

'Originally, I had something much worse.'

'I don't want to hear,' she said.

'I hope you didn't let the boys see it.'

'God knows what they are looking at. Except in our house the computer is in the kitchen, so at least we know what they are looking at there.'

'Ruins all the fun,' I said. 'The smell of cooking is bad for a computer as well.'

She sipped her wine and ignored me and looked all around the restaurant. I wondered when she would get to the point. In her company there was never exactly silence, even when nothing was being said. The way her eyes took in the room made a sort of noise. I noticed a red patch, almost a rash, becoming more obvious on her neck. Suddenly she seemed nervous.

I had never worked out what to do if she asked me straight out if Donnacha and I had ever been together. One night – and it must have been the night I spent most time in their company since they came to Dublin – we were in a bar in Donnybrook and I was almost drunk and had probably made one joke too many at the expense of decency. I sobered up quickly however when, once Gráinne had gone to the bathroom, Donnacha turned and spoke to me with lines that sounded like something from a bad play.

'Gráinne doesn't know anything about us,' he said.

I shrugged.

'I'd like to keep it that way,' he said. He had been drinking as well and there was a hint of accusation.

'Well, you had best not tell her then,' I said. 'Wouldn't that be the best thing?'

'You know what I mean.'

'You mean – I shouldn't tell her?'

'I mean you should never say it to anyone. Anyone at all.'

'I never have.'

'I am glad to hear that.'

I remembered, during that scene, how soft and biddable alcohol used to make him when he discovered it first, when he was nineteen or twenty, how funny he could become, and how uninhibited, once the light was turned off in my flat in Harcourt Terrace. I remembered that nothing made him happier when he had had a few drinks than to have me lie on my back while he knelt with his ass in my face, his knees on either side of my torso. He would bend as I pushed my tongue hard up into his asshole while he sucked my cock and licked my balls.

What was strange about him even later, even when he would come to stay for a weekend, was that he remained part of the culture that produced him. In that culture no one ever appeared naked. In the school, there were doors with locks on each shower, and a hook to hang your clothes within each shower cubicle. Only one guy, who was from Dublin, would strip off after a game of hurling and then move bravely towards the shower. Everyone else, even on the dormitory, moved gingerly. And Donnacha, even when he was very drunk, wore his underpants to bed. A few times I enjoyed tossing his underpants across the room when he was not paying attention so that in the morning he would have no choice but to wander naked in search of them. I knew he was burning with embarrassment at the idea that I was lying in bed watching his thin back and his smooth soft buttocks as he made his way across the room.

Watching him now, I could sense that nothing had changed. He probably slept in pyjamas, sitting each night at the side of the bed and edging them on without standing up. He was someone who never saw any reason why he should change, who lived as he was meant to live, who could be trusted, who never in his life had wanted anything more than what he had.

When the main course was served and we had ordered a second bottle of wine, Gráinne began to speak.

'I don't know if you have been reading my pieces on the Hierarchy,' she said.

'I look at the pictures.'

'Seriously,' she said. 'I thought it was time. There has been a great change and I wanted to write about that.'

'You mean Mass is on Saturday night as well?'

'Stop making fun of me! I mean that there is a new humility among the Hierarchy. All of them know the Church has made mistakes.'

'You mean they have decided to stop fucking altar boys.'

'Hey, here now,' Donnacha said. 'You're in a posh hotel.'

'I mean,' Gráinne said, her face becoming redder, 'that they know they are servants of the people, and servants of the truth.'

'You sound like you are on *Saturday View*,' I said.

'I have seen the archbishop a number of times. I was involved in an advisory group to his predecessor.'

'For all the good that did,' I said.

'He did his best. No one anywhere else did any better. But what I am saying is there has been a change, a real change.'

'Lovely,' I said.

'But it was something the archbishop said which stopped me in my tracks,' Gráinne said. She had put her knife and fork down and I thought I saw tears in her eyes. This, I said to myself, is unbearable.

'He said that it was important not only for the Church now that the truth be known, but it was something that the Church of the future would demand from us. The Church of the future would, he said, stand for truth.'

'I see.'

'I came home and I spoke to Donnacha, and then with his support I spoke to the boys and then all four of us knelt down and prayed and we asked our Saviour to guide us, and then we decided that the truth should be known. And I want nothing to do with tribunals of inquiry and I want no compensation but I can no longer hide the truth.'

'What is the truth?' I asked.

'And I need you to know before I speak out,' she said. 'The priest in question is no longer in the Church and there have already been other allegations against him.'

'Which priest?'

'You know which one,' she said.

'I don't.'

'Which one do you think?' Donnacha asked.

'You tell me.'

'Patrick Moorehouse.'

'Are you saying you had sex with Patrick Moorehouse?' I asked. I quickly wiped the beginning of a smile from my face.

'Keep your voice down for God's sake,' she said.

'Hold on. Did you?'

'I have told you I did.'

'Sex? Actual sex?'

'Is that not what I said?'

'When?'

'Sometimes before those little prayer meetings we had, and sometimes after.'

'You were often there with one of your friends.'

'On those days I doubled back and went to his room later.'

'And on the other days?'

'I arrived early.'

I tried to think back, to remember evenings when I had arrived from the study hall to find Gráinne and Father Moorehouse alone in that room. I realized that there was nothing, not a single detail, not a blush, for example, on either of their faces, not a thing unusually out of place, that I had noticed or could now recall.

'What has this got to do with me?'

'I need a witness.'

'To what?

'That we were in that room, that we knew him, and we were vulnerable.'

'Speak for yourself.'

'I was vulnerable. That is me speaking for myself. And you were vulnerable too, just in case you don't remember.'

'You were vulnerable enough to arrive early and double back?'

'He had us in his thrall.'

'Speak for yourself.'

'I repeat – he had us in his thrall. Are you denying that?'

'I didn't have sex with him.'

'That is hardly the point.'

'What is the point?'

'Keep your voice down. The point is that I was taken full advantage of, aged sixteen.'

'And you want to talk to Joe Duffy on his radio show about it? Is that right?'

'I have written a book.'

'And you want my imprimatur and the archbishop's nihil obstat?'

'She already has the archbishop's nihil obstat,' Donnacha said drily.

'Is it a long book?' I asked.

'It is as long as it needs to be.'

I realized that I wanted to ask her how much about me was in the book, how much about that room where we said prayers, and then it struck me that I did not care what she put in her book.

'I am going to tell the story of my life,' she said. 'And it is going to be the truth.'

'I thought you said you had already written it.'

'I have.'

'When does it start?'

'It opens on the night I met Donnacha.'

'When was that?'

'You were there too. Do you remember that awful opera they let us go to in Wexford one year? I checked back the year and then we both remembered. It was called *The Pearl Fishers*. My book starts that night.'

She smiled at Donnacha. I put my knife and fork down and poured another glass of wine for each of us.

'I vaguely remember it,' I said.

'That was the first night for us,' she said. 'I mean the first time I knew I fancied him. And vice versa.'

As she went on I pretended for some time more that I barely remembered the night, and then I excused myself to go to the bathroom. I hoped that neither of them had noticed that I had been telling lies and trying to change the subject. I hoped that I could soon get away from the high drama of Gráinne's life, which was now on display for me and Donnacha as a sort of preparatory gesture to the world, a piece of recitative for a great diva who would go on to sing many great arias. This supper was merely a way of warming up her voice, letting her know how wonderful she herself sounded, especially in the upper register.

In those first months when Donnacha and I began to have sex whenever we could in the school, it was announced that any pupil in the senior years could attend a dress rehearsal of *The Pearl Fishers*, which was running as part of the Opera Festival, as long as he came to the music room every afternoon and listened to the opera on record and attended a lecture on its form and its meaning from one of the priests who was also a music teacher. Since I was still sulking about being turfed off the bus to the hurling match and refusing even to tog out between class and Rosary in the afternoon, this seemed an opportunity for revenge on the hurling coach and the captain of our team. I could tell them that I was busy in the music room listening to an opera. I convinced Donnacha to come too. We were informed on the first day that anyone who missed one of the five sessions could not attend the dress rehearsal. By the last day, because the music and the explanation of the plot and the motifs in the opera had bored the majority so badly, there were only seven or eight of us left.

I stayed because the music took me over, especially one of the duets by Zurga, the baritone, and Nadir, the tenor. I was also interested in the idea of a motif, a set of notes which played, say, on a harp could remind you of the same set of notes as sung by the soprano, or by the baritone and the tenor in the duet. Zurga and Nadir's duet was about eternal friendship sworn between two men who were in love with the same woman, Leila. By the end of the opera that same melody would be sung as a duet by Nadir and Leila, who had found love, thus leaving Zurga alone and miserable. I found this beautiful and compelling. Donnacha liked it too, or maybe he just tolerated it; he was never very enthusiastic about anything much. He came along perhaps because I did. It mattered to us both maybe that the room, where the music teacher's personal stereo had been specially set up for us, was just beside the smaller room where we had gone that first night. I never for a second thought anything as banal as that I was the tenor or the baritone and Donnacha was the other singer in the duet. But the music lifted me, and the aria they sang haunted me. It made me feel happy that I was close to Donnacha while I listened to it, and afterwards back in the study hall I composed some poems in response to it, and, I am almost ashamed to say, some prayers which I later showed to Father Moorehouse.

Students from St Aidan's and from the convent in the town filled two rows of seats at the dress rehearsal. Because there were only eight of us, we had been allowed to walk down to the opera house without supervision but with instructions to come straight back to the school once the opera was over. Walking to the opera house that evening was like being free. I had never been to an opera before; I think I may have heard a live orchestra once or twice, but only a chamber orchestra. I was surprised by the lighting and the costumes and the set, how yellow and stylized everything was, and how rich the sound coming from the orchestra and the chorus. But I was overwhelmed when the two men began to sing. When we were told about the difference between a baritone and a tenor I had understood it but it had not meant much to me. Now the tenor's voice seemed strangely vulnerable and plaintive, and the other voice masculine and rich and strong. I was surprised at the real difference between the voices, much greater here than on the recording. You could hear each voice clearly when it came to the duet and when the voices finally merged in harmony I was almost in tears. I could not take my eyes off the two men. What they had done together in that aria was the beginning of a new life for me, not only because I would follow music and singing from then on, but because it had given me a glittering hint of something beyond the life I knew or had been told about. That made all the difference to me, and

I presumed that it had made a difference to those around me as well who applauded warmly when the aria was over.

I was surprised, then, when the interval came and we got outside, to find Gráinne Roche in high good humour, laughing and gathering her friends around, delighted that she would not be going back in to the second half. Instead, she was going to lead a posse, she said, down to Cafola's for a hamburger and chips. No one would notice our departure, she said, and we would even be able to smoke there in freedom. I stood apart and remained silent. I watched other people standing outside who seemed, like me, to have loved the first half. I waited for Donnacha to come over and join me, but he was busy talking to Gráinne and her friends so I left him there.

It was a strange feeling, looking up at the tall buildings in the narrow street, and at the night sky, knowing that backstage here the singers were in dressing-rooms preparing for the second half. And that over the next two or three weeks people would come from all over the world to see *The Pearl Fishers*, people who lived their lives in a way which seemed to me that night glamorous and exotic. People rich enough or free enough to travel a distance to be beguiled by music. I wondered what it would be like to be among such people.

Donnacha walked over to me looking happy.

'Are you coming?' he asked.

'Where?'

'To Cafola's. We're all going.'

'Are you going to miss the second half?'

'I am starving.'

He seemed utterly impervious to how I felt, and that came as a shock. I thought he surely must have realized from my response to the music as I sat beside him that the idea of going to Cafola's to eat chips and hamburgers instead of going back into the opera would be pure dull madness. I saw that that did not occur to him. I saw that the music had meant nothing to him. I saw that he did not notice how much it had meant to me.

'No, I'm going back in.'

By that time Gráinne was standing beside us. She had a packet of cigarettes in her hand. She was chewing gum.

'Listen to goody-two-shoes,' she said.

'We won't get caught,' Donnacha said.

'I'm going back in,' I repeated.

When his eyes caught mine I knew that he sensed there was something wrong.

'I'll be waiting outside when it's over,' he said.

'Let us know if there is any more screeching,' Gráinne added. 'God that woman did more screeching! My nerves are in bits from her.'

'Do you mean the soprano?' I asked.

Gráinne did a loud, jarring imitation of a soprano hitting a high note until a few people turned around to glare at her.

'We're off,' she said. 'See you.'

'I'll be waiting outside when it's over,' Donnacha said again. I did not reply but turned and walked back into the opera house.

Afterwards he was lurking in the shadows and slowly we walked back to the school together.

'How was the second half?' he asked.

'It was great. How were the chips?'

'They were great.'

I enjoyed the idea of us walking together through the empty streets of the town. Neither of us spoke much; we had different things to think about. Donnacha could not have known or even suspected that ten years ahead, when he was working as an accountant in one of the midland towns, Gráinne Roche would be the star journalist on one of the local papers, covering sport and local court cases, and they would meet again and within a year they would marry. I could not have suspected that the music which had lifted me out of myself that night, which had seemed like a great new beginning, would within a decade seem sweet and silly to me, not Germanic or hard enough. The future is a foreign country; they do things differently there.

Once we got in the back gate to the school that night and were in the dark we held hands as we walked across the playing fields. It was cold. We made our way silently to the room behind the music room. As always, it took time to get Donnacha going. I was always the same on these occasions, excited from the minute we started, ready for anything, holding myself back. He changed every second. I could tell by his breathing and where he let me put my hands.

It was only when he began to ejaculate that I noticed the line of light under the door and knew that if there was anyone in the next room they would hear him now. His orgasm took time, the slow moan he made grew louder and, while he did everything to control it, it often was accompanied by a set of gasps which he tried to muffle but not always successfully. As I felt his hot jets of sperm hitting the skin of my belly I heard footsteps and then a voice in the rehearsal room, something like 'What the hell?' In that second Donnacha, who had not finished coming, unlocked the door leading to the dark corridor and ran out. I moved quickly to the door between our room and the music room and put my foot against it, preventing whomever was there from entering. It became a small battle between the force of the foot and my shoulder and someone trying to open the door. I knew I had one quick second before whoever it was began to push harder to get across the small room and out the same door through which Donnacha had departed. The voice I heard as I ran was the voice of the music teacher. He did not see me and I ran down the dark corridor and then along another, illuminated corridor, and then through the narrow doorway which led to the dormitory. I knew that the music teacher could have seen me from behind as I made my way along the second corridor if he was following closely enough, and the trick now was to take my shoes off and get straight into bed, cover myself with blankets and pretend to be asleep. It was not long before I heard footsteps in the dormitory. All he had to do was use his sense of smell and he would smell semen or stand silently watching me until I turned to check that he was gone. I was careful to lie still, to do a perfect imitation of someone sleeping for at least half an hour, before quietly undressing, tasting what sperm was still caked on my skin and then getting into my pyjamas and going to sleep.

In the morning I felt drained and guilty – the sounds Donnacha made would have been unmistakable – but I knew there was nothing the music teacher could do. After breakfast when I looked over I saw that Donnacha must have slipped quietly out of the refectory. It was a few days before he began to speak to me again, and when he did he was guarded and I knew he did not want to talk about how close we had come to being discovered.

I took my time drying my hands in the toilets of the Clarence before returning to the table. When I got there I found that Seamus Fox was sitting in my chair having an animated discussion with Gráinne Roche. I knew Seamus because we had served together a number of years earlier on a jury at a film festival in Galway. I found him friendly and funny, which was surprising since the columns he wrote were notable for their sourness and a level of support for rural and traditional values which at times made Gráinne Roche seem radical and cosmopolitan. I tapped him on the shoulder.

'Get up,' I said.

He turned and grinned.

'I now declare the meeting of the Catholic cranks of Ireland suspended,' I said. 'Go back to your own table.'

'What are you doing together?' he asked. 'How do you know each other?'

'We are the only two people who have read your book "Reading the Bible with Bono", and we often meet to discuss it,' I replied.

'Okay,' he said. 'Wexford. I get it. The Wexford mafia.'

'Our aim,' Donnacha said, 'is to rule all Ireland.'

'Wash your hair,' I said to Seamus Fox. 'It's too long and too greasy.'

'Fuck off.'

'Here now,' Donnacha interrupted.

'If the bishops heard that,' I said.

'You can take them out of Wexford,' he said, 'but you can't take Wexford out of them.'

'Tell me something,' I asked.

'What is it now?'

'Is the Church still against fornication? Or has that gone the way of Limbo and the Easter dues?'

'Fuck off.'

Seamus Fox stood up and grinned and then turned and walked back to his table.

'How to make friends and influence people,' Donnacha said.

'Hey, it worked,' I said. 'He's gone.'

'You are worse than ever,' Gráinne said. She then caught the eye of one of the waiters and did mock handwriting in the air as a way of calling for the bill.

'Are you paying?' I asked.

'Yes, I'm paying,' she replied.

'Are you going to send me the book?'

'When it's published.'

'What do you want me to do with it?'

'Read it.'

'Is that all?'

'There are things about you in the book. I used your name. I thought it was polite to tell you.'

'What about me?'

'About the prayer meetings we had.'

'I don't remember much about them,' I said. 'And I don't care much about them either.'

'What do you care about?'

'Don't try that stuff on me. Save your sincerity for Seamus over there. He needs it more than I do.'

'I just want you to say something that is true, that's all.'

'Do you? Do you really?'

'Yes, I do.'

The bill came and she paid by credit card.

'It was nice to meet the two of you,' I said, pushing my chair back and standing up.

'Do you remember the poem you wrote,' Gráinne asked, 'called "There's Blood Flowing out from the Rose-Bowl"? I still have the copy you gave me in your handwriting. I have quoted from it in the book. The publishers will be writing to you asking for permission.'

'Blood flowing out from what?' I said.

'A rose-bowl,' Donnacha said. 'I thought it was a bit strange myself.' He laughed.

'Tell the publishers no,' I said.

'I told them you'd be fine with it, that you are actually a big softie,' Gráinne said. 'So when they write to you, just reply that there is no problem. There's no reason to be ashamed.'

'No reason to be what?'

'Ashamed. It's a good poem for a sixteen-year-old.'

I sighed and stood up. The three of us walked out of the restaurant together. As we passed Seamus Fox's table, Gráinne and Donnacha waved goodbye to him. I ignored him.

'Can we give you a lift? We are parked over on Lord Edward Street.'

'No. I'll walk.'

We stood and looked at each other. Donnacha grinned.

'Good to see you anyway. Thanks for the dinner,' I said.

'You're a nice guy,' Gráinne replied.

'I wouldn't bet on that,' Donnacha said and grinned more. I looked at him for a second but he did not give me even the slightest hint of recognition. They turned and walked towards Parliament Street as I walked towards Temple Bar.

When I came to Dublin first you could walk home alone on nights like this alert mainly to the dampness and the shabby poverty of the city. You would pass lone drinkers who had been ejected from public houses at closing time. There would be almost no traffic. It was too sad to be dangerous; no one had the energy to commit crimes. The route I took now varied only slightly from the old route. Meeting House Square and the Curved Street were new, but the streets which led to Dame Street had always been there. Further up it was a new city once more with gay men in two or threes or hungry ones alone coming out of the George on their way to the Front Lounge or Gubu or some new joint that I have yet to hear about. If I know them, we nod or smile.

I have always liked corners and side streets and thus I made my way quickly across Dame Street and left at the sign saying 'Why Go Bald' and by the side of the Stag's Head and then into Andrew Street and Wicklow Street, hitting Grafton Street at McDonald's. I love these turnings, and now, in these years of change and prosperity, I love the untidy crowds in the streets, the sense of a night not finished, the Garda car edging its way along the pedestrianized street with young Gardai looking out at us suspiciously as though they were thinking of having furtive sex with us. I love seeing half-drunk people on their way elsewhere.

It is the last stretch I cannot bear, when I come to the top of Kildare Street and have no choice but to walk in a straight line along Merrion Row and Baggot Street towards Pembroke Road. This is the grim city with a few damp bars and creepy nightclubs and places to buy chips and hamburgers and kebabs. The street lights are dim and there is a sense in behind the façades of houses, of murderous old spaces with half-rotting floorboards, with crumbling brick and rattling windows and creaking stairways and alarm systems in urgent need of repair. Front rooms tarted up or shiny signs outside for solicitors and auctioneers and public relations firms make me shiver even more as I pass them on my way to my nest of attic rooms, my wireless broadband, my stack of CDs, my new printer, the closets half full of clothes that soon won't fit me, the wall of books, the lamps that all turn on from a single switch. Each time I take this route I marvel at my foolishness for not finding another way home.

Across the city I imagined Gráinne and Donnacha driving to their home in Terenure; I imagined her going over the evening, indignant about some of the things said, satisfied at others. And Donnacha in the driver's seat nodding mildly, making the odd amused remark, or turning serious when a matter of fact was in dispute. I imagined the drive of their house where the car could be parked, the single tree, the flower beds, the mowed lawn, the PVC French windows leading from the dining room to the long back garden. Their sons up watching television. I imagined her in the kitchen, where they kept the computer, making tea and Donnacha sitting with the boys not saying much. I thought of the two of them going up to bed, wishing the boys good night, a biography of someone or other on the table at Donnacha's side of the bed, some new books about Ireland and its ways on the table on the other side where Gráinne slept. I imagined lamplight, shadows, soft voices, clothes put away, the low sound of late news on the radio. And I thought as I crossed the bridge at Baggot Street to face the last stretch of my own journey home that no matter what I had done, I had not done that. No matter how grim the city I walked through was, how cavernous my attic rooms, how long and solitary the night to come, I would not exchange any of it for the easy rituals of mutuality and closeness which Donnacha and Gráinne were performing now. I checked my pocket to make sure I had my keys with me and almost smiled to myself in satisfaction at the bare thought that I had not forgotten them.

Key Note, or, *Che Gelida Marina*
Anne Enright

At about five o'clock, on an afternoon in October, Ollie noticed the folded piece of paper that had been slipped under his office door. It was a fresh white sheet of A4, temptingly aslant and held aloft by a thousand fine hairs on the carpet of grey cord. He could see, as he bent to pick it up, that the message inside was brief and recently scrawled. He could feel the letters under his fingertips as he opened the sheet wide.

Inside, he read the words, 'Nice work, professor'. Ollie paused for a moment, noting the disturbances in the text; the lower-case p, the comma but no full stop. The writing seemed familiar – there was, at least, a familiar madness about it. 'Nice work.' He could not imagine what the writer might mean. He had done nothing 'note worthy' in the last few weeks – Ollie gave himself a small smile, as he folded the page along its own crease, then folded it once again and let it fall into the bin.

He kept the next one, the one that arrived in November. He slipped it in under the sheaf of unanswered correspondence that was dying slowly in a heap on his desk. Ollie wasn't exactly threatened by the note, but you couldn't say that it made him laugh, either. It said, 'The professor Takes a Shit.' Again, the arbitrary capitalization; again, the words were written so vigorously, the shape of them came through the reverse, making you worry that paper might be able to feel.

In December – was it on the same day of the month as the others? – the note said, 'mary Christmas'. The writer was getting cutesy, Ollie thought, as he put it with the others – cutesy and less interesting. Though the fact that his wife was called Mary brought the whole business a little too close to home.

When he took in the assessment essays at the end of term, Ollie found himself looking, not at the points the students were making, but at whatever handwritten scraps might accompany them. 'I'm sorry about the footnotes, I couldn't get them to sit at the bottom of the page.' 'I know this essay is very short but my father had a stroke. Apparently, I have to speak to my tutor about this.'

After the break, he came back to the calm of his office and sat there, and waited for the next one to arrive. He had a sense that, whatever way this business was going, it might contain a revelation. Unlike the rest of his life. For a while, he played with the theory that he was writing the notes himself – he tried to make a poem out of it, but the thing he dashed off was too tricksy and premature. Ollie hadn't written a good poem in a while, but he thought – he was certain of it – that he would write a good one when he knew more about the notes and what they had to tell him. Ollie was fifty-five. His schedule was light. On the first Wednesday of term, he looked around his one difficult lecture; 150 first years chewing through Browning, and declaimed:

'That's the wise thrush; he sings each song twice over,

Lest you should think he never could recapture
The first fine careless rapture!'

But there was no answering unease in the hall – at least none that could be detected. What was he supposed to do, look each of them in the eye?

Actually, he knew what he was supposed to do – he was supposed to inform the Dean. The note maker was clearly a female student, and she was probably distressed. But Ollie did not want to tell the Dean, he did not want to go up the corridor to the faculty office and ask who had passed that way recently. He did not know why. Some of the girls were hopelessly beautiful, but that was not the point (he had been there and done that – some years ago now – he had already crashed that particular car). No, he thought the girl was probably plain. Or let's not call it plain; 'Unprepossessing'; the way clever girls can't do the signals; get their lipstick wrong and are humiliated, all the way up to their backsides, by their own high heels.

Plain or pretty, Ollie would keep his distance from this girl. He did not want an entanglement; he did not even want sex. He wanted a poem – was that too much to ask?

Over the next few weeks, he took out his work folder; an ordinary file in ointment pink, the cardboard made fuzzy by long use. Maybe he should get a new folder, maybe that would help. He had been working for some years on a sequence entitled 'The Lives of the Saints'. This was a collection (he hoped), which started with the classical saints – Lucy, who plucked out her too-beautiful eyes, Cecilia who heard celestial music on her wedding day – and then moved on to more modern variants: the first man ever to be cured of rabies, who spent much of his life tending to the grave of Louis Pasteur; the astronauts who spent so long in the Space Station that they couldn't walk when they finally came to ground. There was also an imaginary secretary, who spent her lunch-hour Googling phrases like 'I died and no one noticed' – for which only four results would be found.

It was proper work, he thought, even though it was not working properly for him. The ideas belonged, in some way he couldn't name, back in the 1980s. Ollie looked through his scraps; his photographs and notes: 'Real People: 1) Sal Orifice, hairdresser to Elvis 2) Donald Turnipseed, took the fatal right turn into James Dean's car.' Such flotsam. All this was young man's work. He should write something about the person he had become, about the coherency of his life now. And he should write about the notes.

The next one, which arrived on the 21st January – he checked the date before he picked it up – was horrible and banal. It said, 'The professor does His Job.'

There it was: the capital 'H', the divine pronoun. The professor does the work of God, she was saying. Or perhaps the professor thinks that he is God. The poet-professor suffers, like Job in the Old Testament; leprous, railing against a God who will do anything except fail to exist. This was the God of Ollie's own work; this bastard absence. He was the void out of which Ollie's poetry sprang. How did she know all this, the bitch?

'The professor does His Job.'

Ollie felt the flatness in the phrase. This woman was not so much overwrought, as psychotic. She might even be a male.

He crumpled the note in his hands, remembering, as he did so, that 'job' was the word his mad Irish mother used for shit or turd; for the action of shitting or the result. As in, 'Have you done a job yet, Ollie?'

He fired the paper into the bin.

He really must tell the Dean.

He must tell the Dean about this girl who understood his work better than anyone, and yet was laughing at him. This girl who knew what he, Ollie, should be writing next and yet would not say.

It was weeks before Ollie picked up the folder again. He sifted through his various fragments to find a photograph he loved, clipped from a catering magazine. It was of a girl at a butcher's counter and she looked as though this was exactly what she wanted – a picture of herself smiling, with her hands pressing down in a confident, springloaded arch. It was so perfect. She looked as though she had imagined this picture: that the camera should be looking up at her, and she should be smiling. Behind her, on a steel rail, there would be cream and red meat, each piece on a separate hook. The walls behind the meat would be white, her coat would be white and spotless, the plastic mesh trilby hat on her head would be at its proper tilt. And, lo! this was just the photograph she got. The only flaw was the colour of her hands, which were red to the wrist, either from the cold, or from the dried blood that is so engrained, and hard to wash away.

Ollie wanted to write about this butcher girl; her smiling face, her way with cleaver and blade, but the poem had already died on him, several times. He went back to an earlier draft to see was there anything fresh there; an impulse he had missed and could take again, and there it was: the name of a road in Harold's Cross, and contained in that, like a secret, a girl he once knew, who had such cold hands.

Miriam. His first…what do you call that? Do you lose your virginity that way, or just a tiny bit of it? There was no technical term for it, anyhow, and no romantic one either. She was his first touch, his first 'real' girlfriend.

Did he love her?

Well.

He certainly loved her parents. They were what was called, in the Dublin of 1969, 'bohemians' – meaning they played the piano, and kept drink in the house. It was his first year out of school and Ollie still thought he would go into his uncle's business, but there they were, Hazel and Henry Mooney, splendid on poetry and whiskey, with paintings on the walls, and not enough money between them for two pork chops. And there also, behind the drinks tray, was their daughter, Miriam. An excruciation.

It was not that she was stupid – far from it. No, the thing that mortified him about Miriam was that she was so plain. It wasn't just a question of grooming, or smiling, or making the effort – though she did not, in fact, make the effort – it was the conviction she brought to the whole business of being ugly. And it had nothing to do with the shape of her mouth or her eyes – if you examined her sitting still and unaware, she was quite fine. It was just, perhaps, that her father, Henry Mooney, had never once noticed his daughter except to sneer, and a lifetime of this had broken her looks for good. By the time Ollie arrived, there was no curing it; this duck and flinch from a male gaze, this covert aggression. Despite which, he walked out with her once – it seemed inevitable. Indeed he nearly kissed her. It had been her father's idea, of course. Good old Henry Mooney pushing them out into the cold evening with a snigger.

It was the winter of 1969. Ollie had already secretly decided that he would abandon commerce and write poetry, and he was in love with his new future as he was with the Mooneys, who had opened his eyes to it. And he did his best by their daughter, Miriam, who was so plain. He offered his arm, and looked at the night sky, and slowed his pace to hers; two strides for every three she took, in silence beside him. He thought that this was all they would do, he thought they might just *commune*, but as soon as they were out of sight of the house, she started to speak. Ollie had never heard her say more than two sentences – now there was a flood of words, all of them sour and some of them amazing and true. He took her frozen little hand and was suddenly in love with her; this ugly scrap, this woman he could hardly even look at, head on. They were strolling along the canal by now, and when they stopped to embrace he couldn't kiss her. Even with his eyes closed. It was like holding a pain in his arms. Her intelligence – those eyes – her intelligence was so raw, it was a thing of blades and lacerations, and her hands were still freezing as they pulled his shirt up and grazed his belly and tugged at his waistband.

Ollie looked at the photograph of the butcher girl again. There she was, still cheerful. Her stupid white mesh trilby was still jaunty, and her hands were still mottled with old blood.

Those hands. The thing the girl did to him was not like anything he had ever imagined – and Ollie had imagined plenty, by the age of nineteen. Her hands were so cold, and they were real. Too real, when it came down to it. He let her do what she wanted, and he did not kiss her, and then he walked away.

He couldn't write a peom about that. How awful. How finally untrue of his life.

Even now, Ollie did not feel like a professor of poetry, he just felt like himself; a pleasant enough man in his early fifties, who had done no more than anyone else to hurt people, who had blundered around a bit, that was all.

Christ, where was she now?

He Googled 'Miriam Mooney' and found nothing. Which is

to say he found several women of that name: a manicurist, a woman who did fundraising for the Special Olympics, the third partner in a legal firm. Any of them might have been her – or none of them, more like.

But Ollie started to write for them all, remembering how he had loved her – to his own great embarrassment – remembering, too, how he refused her kiss and suffered the reality of her cold hands.

He had never written a real word in his life. He knew that now. He had never written a single poem that was real. This was the first one: this was where he would begin.

Another note slid under the door.

First Snow
Andrew O'Hagan

At closing time in the summer months, the light would fall through the ceiling windows of the library to reveal the dust that had settled on the cabinets. It was the kind of light with a golden tone and a scent of cinders. Hazel's eyes would go to the clock, scanning its face for evidence of something new before she capped her pen and dreamed of the magic that must exist in the workings of clocks. As she put the computer to sleep and placed her pens in the pot, Hazel often thought of her father's fish stew or of men she had known who were too stupid to contemplate. There was a bottle of scent at the back of her drawer and she took a few dabs of it before fetching her bag and coat. Recognition is a sort of bliss and you can't argue with Essence of Limes to see you on your way.

Hazel liked watching box sets of American television shows and she knew her way around a bottle of Pinot Grigio. She was fastidious, in keeping with library custom, yet she often smirked at the image of the person she was supposed to be: she wore cardigans, but only cashmere ones in pretty colours, and she hadn't kept her hair in a bun since Intermediate ballet class. She remembered the whiskery old ballet teacher, Mrs Ferguson, who smelled thrillingly of sweat and perfume, resin and cigarettes. 'Hazel Campbell,' Mrs Ferguson had said, 'you will never get off the ground unless you change your attitude. One must aim to be light, my dear. Light!'

'How come?' asked Hazel at the time. 'I don't have any interest in being a princess or a fairy. Why would anybody want to be that?'

'This is classical ballet, dear,' said Mrs Ferguson. 'Don't get me started. I know you are perfectly content to be a galumphing girl all your life, but at the heart of our calling is a traditional respect for celestial beings.'

'It's idiotic,' Hazel said. (She had never wanted to go to ballet in the first place.) 'And what kind of art form is it, anyhow, that always depends on making women look like they're about to break?'

'I don't think you're suited to us, dear. I really don't think you want to be elegant.'

That was the beginning of Hazel as her own person. She established her character along such lines, and she stuck to it, only now and then feeling confined by the requirements of loyalty to her own views. In recent years, Hazel Campbell had come to read all the books about women doing it for themselves, about men coming from Mars and women coming from Venus, about chicken soup for the soul and Does My Bum Look Big in This, but none of it really added to her basic principle and her first commandment, that she had a natural talent for laughing at romance. People liked to ask her about books and she knew plenty. 'That one's a crackpot from the minute she appears,' she said of Emma Bovary. 'But at least the novel knows it. I could tell you the barcodes on the books that drive women mad and I'd avoid them all if I were you.'

Then she began seeing this man. She was sure he only came into the library during that last hour of the day when the place was quiet. She'd just look up from whatever she was doing and he would often be there, smiling at her. He was spick and span – the hero, she reckoned, of meticulous ablutions, walks in the park – and he arrived through the doors like someone accustomed to being watched by people less confident than himself. With his ironed jerkin, his grey hair parted and combed and his teeth manifestly clean, the man immediately appeared to Hazel like someone who might be naturally gifted in answering to other people's helplessness, whilst knowing, all the while, rather attractively, that helplessness is native to everyone. His response to problems was in his very bearing: his confident, firm jaw, his tanned, coping brow, his patience. When she got to know him better, she saw he had what the beneficiaries of helplessness always have, be they parents, teachers, nurses, or God: they have a perfectly reasonable but not always obvious streak of violence. Yet these thoughts may simply have been typical of Hazel. She never saw any violence from the man she got to know. The man was simply charming and blameless in his brushed shoes. He just walked through the stacks like a fresh-air ghost – lifting a volume, casting a look – and Hazel found it enhancing to see such a person taking an interest.

Hazel was good at pretending not to see people: it was a skill she had mastered over the years. Fluff on her skirt, a pencil suddenly needing to be sharpened, a rubber band on the floor; she could always find something urgent to conceal her attention, but over time she wanted the man to register her own small satisfaction in the fact that he wasn't just anybody. She had one of those smiles that served itself up quite reluctantly to men, not so much a smile anyhow as a compressed and muscled grin, which her mother used to say flattered neither her looks nor her intelligence. To hell with all that: she wasn't in the business of making eyes at men, and anyway she knew the visitor understood well enough that she was not unreceptive to his presence. The thing that mattered most to Hazel was the man's obvious willingness to think, and so she began to enjoy speaking with him in the library. She spoke to him until she had established the terms and the scope of his arrogance, which she always sought to do with men, and this in turn led to jokes and lots of cheek from Hazel. Sarcasm had always been her preferred currency with half-decent men, and she imagined that might suit his view of himself, too.

He didn't have membership of the library but she saw that he liked the reference section and hated Self Help. Early on, he gave the impression of being someone whose sophisticated taste in literature wouldn't be satisfied by your average branch library, and after his conversations with Hazel became regular she found that he was bringing in books that interested him and leaving the books on her desk to look at. It may be that his growing affection regressed him over time, so that he became almost childish in his keenness to impress the librarian, yet he found his way into her head nonetheless. His special interests were American and Russian literature and he was able to say clever things off the cuff about literary life in New York in the years of the Cold War. It took time for her to see his comments as expressing not just cleverness but something of his own values. 'Did you know,' he said one afternoon when he caught up with her in among the Westerns, 'that Mr Nabokov always arrived to deliver his lectures at Cornell in the company of his wife?'

'Quite weird,' said Hazel.

'Many people thought so,' he said. 'She carried his books. He called her "my assistant".'

'How vomit-making,' said Hazel almost involuntarily, yet aware in that very same instant how she didn't want to sound like a hater of men. Her friend appeared to push his glasses up his nose and she noticed his lips looked very soft.

'I don't know,' he said, quickly awakening to sides of Hazel he agreed with himself to ignore, 'I don't know if marrying a writing genius counts as fulfilling one's literary ambitions, but Vera had no shortage of ambition. She married him in 1925 and that appears to have been enough for her. Is that wrong?'

'Not wrong,' Hazel said. 'Just depressing.'

'I don't know,' he said again. 'Everybody has his reasons to be cheerful. It is said Mr Nabokov couldn't fold an umbrella without the help of his loving wife.'

Hazel was slightly excited by the fact that she'd heard him say 'his reasons' – to her it showed he wasn't as clever as he thought. But overall she decided the man wasn't aggressive and she liked the way he managed his uncertainties, kind of grandly. 'Anyway,' he said, standing with his back to the window and a fake fern, 'I'm more interested in what happens when two people don't get on. I'm talking about that other relationship I mentioned to you before, not Mr Nabokov and Vera – but Nabokov and Edmund Wilson. There was a lot of mutual respect there. Next minute, they're arguing about Pushkin and the friendship is under pressure. In this world, you've got to pay attention when people don't get along.'

'Why?' Hazel asked, lifting a group of Larry McMurtrys from a trolley and then feeling a vague, small, distant panic on realizing she was about to file them in the wrong place. 'I'm not clear about any of this. Wilson writes a review saying Nabokov doesn't understand Russian.'

'That he gets *Eugene Onegin* all wrong.'

'So what?' Hazel said. 'People get things wrong all the time. I'm sure even you get things wrong, Mr Wonderful. Wilson was admired for saying what he thought and saying it very elegantly – admired by Nabokov for just that. Except when he says very elegantly that his friend's translation sucks, then suddenly he's out of touch with reality and an absolute non-friend.'

'Nicely put.'

'Bog off.'

'Nicely put.'

'Are you playing with me?' Hazel tried to put a little scold into her smile. She decided to shelve some of her worries about how she might seem. 'Look, Mr Wonderful. You know what it is? Male vanity.'

'Ahhhh.'

'Never mind "ahhhh". I know there's nothing new in your wonderful universe, but I'm afraid you just can't see male vanity, just like you can't ever see yourself asleep.'

'It seems to me you have a bit of a talent for seeing.'

'Never mind that,' she said to herself. 'I'm making a point about male vanity. Men can admit it, they can describe it, they can show all the signs of not liking it very much, but you can't see it – not if you're a man. The whole world is run by male vanity so maybe it's not such a party as you think when great men fall out. It's just more of the same old same old.'

'The librarian speaks!'

'Bog off.'

'Garbo laughs!'

'Time to go home now. We're trying to close up.'

'But we're only getting to the interesting bit,' he said. 'The bit where we fall out and I get to find you even more interesting.'

'Vain pig,' she whispered.

'*Eugene Onegin*'s first words,' he said. 'The French master's motto: "*Full of vanity*".'

'God, you like the sound of your own voice.'

'We were talking about the exchange between these two great men of letters. Now. My argument is serious: two people who wanted to get to know each other could do worse...they could do worse, you know, than looking at the moment when these two clever men stopped speaking. That's a black hole right there. The letters stopped. But, I'm telling you, if you traced the letters back into the heart of the friendship you could probably trace the birth of the disjuncture.'

'You should get out more,' Hazel said. She lost sight of him for a second and shivered to see herself alone, before she heard him on the other side of the stack.

'Mrs Overdue. Mrs Overdue. There are ways to get to know the world, if you wish to.' He was only playing but she found him creepy when he wasn't being serious.

'Some of us have work to do,' she said, lifting a crumpled Coke can from one of the book bins and making to go. As sometimes happened, she suddenly felt uncomfortable to be having the conversation.

'I always say, getting to know yourself is the only work that's really worth doing. Getting to know yourself and getting to know the people you care about. Now there's a job of work.'

'Vain pig,' she whispered again.

He was in the library the next day and she noticed again how nicely ironed were his shirts. She imagined he worked in a lawyers' office, but they never spoke of that. More interesting was this quite likeable obsession of his with the evolution of dislike. Hazel tried to imagine that it didn't emerge from anything small. The fact was there had never been anyone like him in the library, nor had any man, anywhere, for that matter, any man with so many potentially disagreeable assumptions, impressed her as having such a gift for taking an expansive interest in life. And he always seemed so unbelievably solid. He was an oddity, for sure, and Hazel was often surprised by his lack of crudity. Not all men were crude, but most of them were, and after a while she imagined this one might present a positive danger to her calmness.

He must have left the photocopy on her desk. It was of a letter sent by Nabokov to Wilson, a late letter, and the man was saying it showed the ruins of the literary pair's friendship. Wilson had sent it to his old friend at the Montreux-Palace Hotel. It was dated 8 March 1971: 'Dear Volodya: I am now getting together a volume of my Russian articles. I am correcting my errors in Russian in my piece on Nabokov-Pushkin; but citing a few more of your ineptitudes...' The man had copied another letter. It was one sent to Wilson by Nabokov six days earlier. 'Dear Bunny,' it said, 'A few days ago I had the occasion to reread the whole batch of our correspondence. It was such a pleasure to feel again the warmth of your many kindnesses, the various thrills of our friendship, that constant excitement of art and intellectual discovery.' Hazel looked down at it under the library's yellow strip lights. 'Please believe,' she read, 'that I have long ceased to bear you a grudge for your incomprehensible incomprehension of Pushkin and Nabokov's *Onegin*. Yours, Vladimir Nabokov.'

'It doesn't sound very convincing,' said Hazel.

'Exactly,' said the man. 'The disagreement was bubbling

away for years before. I could show you how it started in the very days when they were bonding.'

'Why do you care?' asked Hazel.

'Oh, don't ask,' he said. 'One thing follows another, that's all. I'm interested in cause and effect. One doesn't want to take everything for granted. It's a new hobby of mine. I've been reading these guys for years and I think I've found something that nobody else notices.'

'Eureka!'

'Hold on,' he said. 'Mr Wilson resented Vera at some level. He hated too much Vera-ism.'

'Here we go,' said Hazel, pushing the papers to the back of her desk. 'Time for the woman to get it in the neck.'

'No,' he said. 'But one thing follows another. Mr Wilson's wives were, shall we say, less given to ventriloquism. I deduce that Wilson saw Vera as his friend's typist, agent, muse, translator, editor, aide-de-camp, and his little dislike started there, years before they got to *Onegin*.'

'You deduce that, do you?' Hazel said.

One of the assistant librarians looked up from her terminal and Hazel saw her speaking.

'Nothing,' Hazel replied. 'I was just thinking.'

Hazel was having dinner a week later at a restaurant in Prestwick. 'Real feminism failed,' her friend Anya said in the middle of a Chardonnay rush. 'I'm sorry to say it, but lipstick won and that's that.' Hazel said she still felt like a woman in full command of her choices. She wasn't a firebrand, Hazel, not at all, but her hackles could rise when the male world advanced, which it did every other minute in her experience. She had been President of the Labour Club at university, back in the days of anti-Apartheid and the miners' strike, when girls like Hazel were socialists and feminists with a full-time hatred for Mrs Thatcher. Like everybody else in the Labour Club, Hazel had come down from the holy mountain and joined the carnival of everyday compromises, and so had Anya, who was once the pints-drinking editor of the students' newspaper, *The Sandinista*.

Over the wine glasses and the shared pudding, Anya spoke like she was declaring something big. 'It's not as if I've changed that much, Hazel. I don't think I have, not inside. But now that I'm actually in the situation, you know, I don't want Tommy hanging out the washing. Know what I mean? I don't want him taking the children to school or baking bread. I'm not inter-ested in him doing the bloody hoovering. I know we all said we wanted that stuff, right, but see when I go to the nursery to collect Ruby, it makes me feel there's something I own. And you know what? We shouted for years about men being more like us, or us being more like men, but the truth is...the truth is we don't want that even for a second. And the reason...' She took a gulp of wine. 'The reason is that no woman with any actual experience cares about equality as much as she cares about being happy and being loved. We didn't fight all those years to snuff out romance.'

'That's nonsense, Anya.'

Hazel really hated what her friend had said. She hated 'actual experience' and she hated 'equality', but more than anything in her old friend's speech she hated the breezy needi-ness of 'romance'.

'I'm happy you're happy, Anya, but what you said is total rubbish. I don't see why we should be expected to give a woman a round of applause every time she transforms herself into her mother.'

'That's not fair.'

'I'm sorry.'

'It's not fair. And it's something a man would say. I think you've started to think like a man.'

'Oh, get a grip, Anya.'

'I don't want any prizes, Hazel. I'm simply telling you that not one of the people down at the nursery school collecting their kids is a man. And do you know why that is? It's because the women fundamentally don't want their men doing it. They choose to do it themselves or get their child-minders to do it. They don't want their men taking it away from them.'

'Men are too lazy...'

'Aye, they're lazy shites. But that's no' why there are no men down at the surgery when the babies are getting their jabs. The room is absolutely choked with women and that's because women want to be there. They don't want to be manning the barricades, Hazel; they want to be making their lives nicer and choosing dresses from the Boden catalogue. And they want their men working. They want a man who is admired for the things he can do and the woman he was clever enough to choose and the children they made, all right? She wants someone who can take over the wheel when she's driving on a frightening road and she wants a man who can unfurl a hose and put the water into the paddling pool in the summer. I've seen it a million times. Every woman we know wants to be looked after. More than that, they want to be seen to be looked after. I mean, seen by other women. That's the truth. Feminism is a joke, Hazel, because the people it is meant to benefit don't want it and have never really wanted it, except when we were too young to know how easy it was to have views.'

'That's just *you* you're talking about,' said Hazel.

'I don't think so.'

'You should broaden your circle of women.'

'I don't think so, Hazel.'

After a while they got back to laughing. Into their second mint tea, Hazel felt more relaxed about things, deciding she might want to make a concession. 'There is one big mystery,' she said. 'And that's why feminism didn't, you know, make me more sympathetic to my mother.'

Driving away from Prestwick, Hazel knew she had been suckered by Anya's declaration of satisfaction. People who are happy sometimes seem so terrified of losing what they've got and Hazel was looking out for that. Driving home she was partly ashamed to think of how keen she had been to see some sadness in Anya's clear green eyes. Anya had been right in some of the things she had said, but where did Hazel's certainty come from, the certainty that Anya didn't really like women, that her old friend was on the run from reality? As she drove the car and disappeared into a tunnel of privacy, Hazel began to wonder if there hadn't always been a basic dislike in her relationship with Anya. Maybe it was there in the beginning, on those demonstrations at university, when they were all so radical and so certain of male failures, the whole thing now come to fruition twenty years later with Anya's story of the hardworking Tommy and the brave little Ruby and the caravan they were thinking of buying on the pretty side of Loch Lomond.

One Friday afternoon, Hazel could have sworn the man in the library put his hand over hers as she mended the spine of a book. She withdrew her hand quite silently and looked at his face, his neat ears: he wanted to rip up his life for her, she could tell that much was true. Hazel might not have known how bluntly she avoided her own feelings. She merely looked past him towards the bright glass of a window and saw a tree moving in the breeze outside, then she closed her eyes and opened her mind, asking him a question about Lionel Trilling and his true feelings about Diana and the moral life. The man didn't answer and she knew he wouldn't.

Driving to her flat that same evening, Hazel looked from the bypass and saw how the Isle of Arran was about to be obscured in grey mists. She had some American books piled on the passenger seat, the words Harper & Row catching her eye, 'Wilson' and 'Vladimir' and, right at the bottom, *Eugene Onegin*. From the driving seat, she could still make out the shape of the sleeping warrior formed by the peaks along the ridge of Arran. The sleeping warrior: she smiled to see the shape of him, the bumps on the horizon a distilled, lilac vision of male grace, the warrior at rest after his noble efforts. Sometimes in the night, Hazel would drive over to the harbour at Troon, down to the place where the men from the boats would stand in the dark in yellow oilskins, smoking and talking of the things they endured. And looking now at Arran she saw the throat, the chest, and the knees of the sleeping man; perhaps she simply envied him his permanence. Her father used to sing folk songs that had always seemed to connect the enchantment of the island to the reality of their speeding car, and she missed him, the way he was able to love her very plainly and the way he once strived to gather all the beauty and strangeness of life to her loving attention, the rock formations, the poems, the different species of fish, all the better to draw her intelligence into company with greater things and show her how to be happy. She looked again at the shape of the silent man on the horizon. He never raised his voice or got involved in other people's busy dislikes and his favourite novel was *Pale Fire*.

Hazel pushed a CD into the car stereo and heard the same old pleasant whirring. You couldn't always be sure the stuff from the music section of the library was good, half the CDs were covered in scratches, but soon the car became a vibrating cell of woodwind and trumpet. Hazel pressed the arrow for fast forward without taking her eyes of the road. She wanted to hear enveloping strings and the beginning of the women's voices, the girl and her nurse singing so perfectly and yearning for life in the Russian language, something that Hazel couldn't speak herself but whose meaning she followed to the letter.

'Tatyana, *c'est moi*,' said Hazel to the dashboard. 'Eugene, *c'est moi*.'

She caught sight of herself in the rear-view mirror. Why was the composer's marriage so short? she wondered. The recording hissed as the car passed Hazel's old school near Irvine; it was always there at the edge of her consciousness, a sting of memory as she passed the hockey fields and the dining hall. At that moment Hazel felt one of those lurches in spirits before another thought took over and she held fast to the steering wheel, thinking about Tchaikovsky leaving his wife and fleeing to St Petersburg after a terrible eight weeks. She remembered the man at the library sitting on a small blue chair in the children's reading area the week before, the sight of his shoelaces tied in a bow so charming to her, and how he spoke with obvious pleasure about the bad character of Mary McCarthy and Hazel looked at him and ruminated, without saying a word, on the advantages of knowing that his contentment would never be able to make her angry. Of course she knew there was no future with him, and so there would be no need to punish him for finding life so pleasing and for being happy, which is what she felt her mother had specialized in doing to her father. As the car sped on and a flake or two of snow hit the windscreen, Hazel realized she might soon be ready to visit his grave.

Hazel had learned by magic how to live alone and how to find the joke in standard miseries. That's why men liked her. She coped slightly too well by herself and her imagination made her peaceable more than it led her astray, which is not something she could say about all the people in her life. Nevertheless, Hazel was the sort of woman whom elderly women couldn't understand being without a husband and children. 'What a waste,' they would say, as if her powerful self-sufficiency could only serve to underscore her failure. 'That girl could have had the pick of the men if she wanted to.' Hazel was good with the local wisdom and didn't mind being one of its victims: the older women had survived more entanglements with male vanity and boorish intolerance than Hazel could ever have faced, and it made her want to be nice to them even as they marked her down as a woman of misfortune.

The music was very sweet on the car stereo. Maybe it was the sound of the music, or something inside the music or inside her head as she passed over Ayrshire, but Hazel, at the last minute, suddenly pressed down the indicator and took the exit into Kilmarnock to have her hair done. Driving past nature, past hedges and farms and unburst gorse, Hazel decided she had become a substantial person, the sort who could achieve a good, clear, moral feeling in the afternoon as she drove the roads. The sun was going down over the Loudon hills and she realized as she drove, pouring herself into the orange distance, that there was something distinctive about herself, something articulate with the past and perhaps even free, or nearly free, of other voices. She felt herself very much in the world just then, with the snow falling over the fields. For a second she pictured Tatyana, wild as a forest deer, high on the fancies of Richardson and Rousseau, hungry for life's particulars. Hazel asked herself a pair of questions that seemed to blend with the passing trees and disappear into the car stereo and the opera. The questions were quick and personal. 'Is romance Tatyana's only food? And is hunger an anti-depressant?'

She had slowed down, turned the music off, and could hear her tyres licking the mud. She was scanning the fields on the passenger's side when she saw a gate: I want to climb over and run and keep running, she said, to feel the first snow on my face. In less than a minute the cold top bar of the gate was in her hand and she was pulling herself over without a coat, her body freezing but her mind excited by the look of the field and the smell of manure. She thought she had seen life at the edge of the field and she was right: three rabbits of varying sizes were mysteriously alert by a rusted bath, the sleet blowing across them. Hazel was sure the rabbits stood still for a second to check if she was as real as they were. She could feel the cold muck breaking under her heels, and seeing the rabbits move she suddenly thought she would run after them, just keep running over the field and not stop until she could be among them. She saw the rabbits leap through some wire and Hazel laughed as she chased them, but they turned into a gully and vanished.

The salon had the buzz of a nightclub, chatter, laughter, the drum and bass of female secrets. The staff seemed impossibly skinny and fashionable, roaming over the floor with their large belts and flip-flops and striped hair, living in perpetual syncopation with the shop's music, rolling their eyes over the interminable complications of weekends, a time that seemed equally alive in staff memory and staff anticipation. Hazel felt the weight of herself in the chair, she felt her age, but not without pleasure and a sense of arrival, because the coming and going of youthful certainty among the chrome, the fairy lights, the acrid chemical weather of the salon, only made Hazel feel glad to have sunk into a region of personal doubts. The youngsters had a strong sense of community, which was temporary, but they couldn't be expected to know that as they wielded the scissors and tapped the straightening irons for heat. They gossiped like there was no tomorrow, but there was only tomorrow, a place where business beyond their present cares and conversation, beyond their belief, was waiting very patiently to show them things they never suspected. How nice it was to be absent.

'If he doesnay text me back before my break, he's chucked,' said the girl behind Hazel. The girl was very tanned and she wore glitter on her cheeks, as well as a very tight T-shirt with the words 'You Wish' printed across her chest. 'A waste a space and I'm no' kidding you,' she said. 'Guys like that. I mean, guys like that. They come up tae you and ask for your number and everything. Then you don't hear from them again. What's that all about? He can sling his hook, well. Is that no' right, Michelle?'

The girl further along was attaching a diffuser to the nose of a hair-drier and was already agreeing. 'Waste of space,' she said. 'You're too good for him, Mary. I told you that.'

'He can beat it.'

'Totally.'

'Like, who is he anyhow?'

'Right. Who is he?'

'Some guy frae Troon.'

'Some guy.'

'Exactly!'

'Some guy frae Troon who wants to talk about football and his mother still irons his shirts.'

'Ewwwwww.'

'Exactly.'

'Mammy still irons his shirts.'

'Totally.'

'And everything.'

'I know.'

'He should text you, but. You don't just take somebody's number then give it "see ya", sure you don't.'

'I think he will,' said Mary. 'Text me. He was quite drunk but I think he will. Nice eyes as well.'

'Totally.'

'Really nice eyes.'

'That's right.'

Hazel often felt the juniors looked on her as a kind of warning. They admired her things – her wraparound dress, a bangle, an appliquéd handbag – as if her individual choices showed bravery in the face of terrible odds. 'That's so nice, intit?' they said. 'That's totally gorgeous.' But they felt without saying anything that their bookish client, who always gave good tips and never spoke intimately, was somehow guilty of major crimes against dependence, and even as the stylists' scissors did their chatty semaphore about her head, you could see in the mirror's traffic of eyes something amounting to pity. But Hazel was experienced in getting along with herself: she knew that other people's sense of your failure can sometimes be quite galvanizing, and as the hairspray wreathed about her face like the mist over Arran, she looked ahead and smiled at that, too.

Only when she was paying the girl at the desk did she look down and see the dried mud that was caked to her shoes.

Hazel was on the phone later that night. She was eating a rice cracker and speaking to her sister Carla in Inverness. 'Never mind,' said Carla. 'I'm talking about any supermarket. I'm trying to think ahead all the time, thinking: "What are the things none of them are going to remember to do?" Like with this holiday to Greece. Bernie and the kids are only interested in whether there's an Internet connection at the hotel. Meanwhile, I'm buying tennis rackets and spending half the day on the phone to these idiots from Europcar, trying to make sure when we get there the car's going to be automatic.'

'You love it,' Hazel said down the line.

'I don't know about that,' said Carla.

'Of course you do.'

'Well, I'll tell you something for nothing. I'm going to sit down in Mykonos and read a magazine. Five magazines! Drink a bottle of wine and read a magazine, that'll be me. Bernie's got to take them jet-skiing. They'll probably freeze to death: it's eleven degrees out there.'

'That's not bad.'

'Aye. I suppose that's not bad. Anyway, it's Bernie's job. If he wants winter holidays then he has to take his chances on the jet-skiing, right?'

'That's right,' said Hazel. 'And you can sit in a taverna and enjoy yourself.'

Carla took a second.

'I'll be happy just to sit back and think about their costumes,' she said. 'That'll be the next thing. Soon as we get back, it's costumes for the school play.'

'Carla,' said Hazel. 'Fuck the costumes. Just go and find a

nice pool somewhere and swim. Just by yourself. Swim and eat what you like and walk on the beach if it's not too blowy.'

'It doesn't get blowy in Greece,' Carla said. 'That's one of the nicest things. The sky's blue in January.'

Carla was always ready to accept her sister's advice as saying more about Hazel than it did about her. But she was glad of it all the same, feeling it brought them closer. Hazel was the one that went to university and Carla tried to respect that, but secretly – or quite obviously, to Hazel – she felt that her sister didn't really understand the fundamentals of everyday life. Hazel cared about things that didn't really matter. She made things up and her head was in the clouds. She created unhappiness for herself and was far too serious about men and everything. Hazel could really get under your skin sometimes. 'Just be sure and make some time for yourself, Carla,' said Hazel.

Carla took another second. She waited and then said what she wanted to say. She knew it would upset her evening if she rang off knowing she'd failed to put Hazel right. 'You know, Hazel,' she said, 'I'm looking forward to Greece with Bernie and the boys. It's something I've been looking forward to.'

'I know that, Carla.'

'Well, that *is* time for myself. It is *all* time for myself as well as time for them. It's not separate.'

There was a noise in the background of the kids bumping past and shouting. Hazel could hear Carla telling one of them to get his skateboard out of the hall. When she resumed talking to her sister, there was no panic in her voice. Carla felt she had given a firm account of herself in the conversation and she didn't always feel that way after talking to Hazel. 'Well, mind and send me a postcard,' Hazel said. 'It sounds lovely.' Carla wondered if she hadn't said too much to her sister. She watched the boys out on the grass and suddenly imagined she'd been cruel.

'You know, Hazel,' she said. 'I just wouldn't know how to cope on my own.'

'Well, don't worry. There's no need.'

'You were always good at that. You're a leader, Hazel. That's what I always say to people. And it's true.'

'True nothing. All's I did was fail to marry any of those fucking idiots my mother liked. Away and feed your weans, Carla, before they cause a riot.'

'But I'm glad Daddy left you the car,' said Carla. 'I know how happy he would have been to see you driving around in it. That was Daddy and you, wasn't it? Long drives and long books. That was you two, happy as Larry. You know it's a year this week?'

Hazel went quiet. She didn't want her sister's life, she didn't envy Carla her choices, but she might have said yes to having a little more of her simplicity. 'Have you phoned Mum?' Hazel said eventually.

'This morning,' Carla said. 'She was moaning about not hearing from you.'

'Nothing new there,' Hazel said. 'Listen, I had better let you go. Enjoy your holiday. Sunny or not.'

'Love you,' said Carla.

'Hate you,' said Hazel.

'You're as daft as a brush, Hazel! You make me laugh, so you do. But I wouldn't have it any other way. That's the truth from yer wee sister, right?'

'Whatever.'

'Whatever nothing. It's your sister talking.'

'Go and feed your weans.'

'Love you.'

*

Tchaikovsky's opera played in the room. It seeped through the polished floorboards and travelled like a penetrating dampness over the roses on the wallpaper. Hazel seemed to rise with the music and find herself imbued with borrowed drama, as if her freedom, her feminine brilliance, lay in a talent for totally inhabiting herself, which in her case was the same talent as that exhibited by the great impersonators. Outside now there was proper snow and the cold light poured past the curtains onto her bed, seeming an incursion, an interesting dispute, bringing the plain spirit of Russian winters over the coloured weave of her bedding. Hazel at last accepted the season was over. For months she had thought of him with naked feeling. She had lately begun to wonder what he was doing when he wasn't with her. At night, she imagined him walking a dog or taking off his shirt, conceding a point to a man in a pub or accepting the admonishments of some terrible wife. By and by, Hazel had come to wonder whether she had the power to imagine things without finally conceding to them.

She turned up the heating for cosiness and stayed all day in her nightdress. Her books of Nabokov and Wilson were stacked on the kitchen table. For the hell of it, Hazel began writing a love letter of the most scenic profusion: she touched on rivers and moons and hosts of natural ornaments that disappeared quite breathlessly towards a distant horizon. In her mind, as she wrote, she saw Russian peasants gathering golden wheat; she saw Highland warriors smitten with adoration for rose-cheeked maidens in the hidden parts of the glen. She went in and out of the letter all day and then began more pages after dark. As the night wore on, her pen tripped believingly from sentence to sentence, and she grew excited at the slow and precise orchestration of her farewell to the man. Perhaps she was thinking of Tess Durbeyfield as she noted how flushed she felt the second time he appeared at the library carrying a bag of strawberries. Maybe it was Molly Bloom in her own nightdress, lying in bed but thinking of himself and the way he kissed her that first time they were roiling in the grass on the headland at Howth. Hazel felt able to play many parts and to disgust herself in the process.

Around three in the morning she stopped writing – she ended with something about Yeats and Maud Gonne, the white swans at Coole, the rose upon the rood of time, and Maud's great majesty in the face of Willie's unrepentant desire – and put down the pen as if she found it wanting. She put her letter in a folder beside some photocopied documents, letters that bore the names and addresses of Bunny and Volodya in Wellfleet and New York. Indeed, the season was over. She brushed her hair at the dressing table and drifted to the window. Looking at the citrine shout of the streetlights she imagined she was ready for the outside world, the world of people in search of one another, the snow, the dark, the reality of life outside the brain. It suddenly felt good to know you could keep your own hours.

Hazel felt safer in the car than anywhere. Before she turned on the engine she laid the folder down on the passenger seat and placed her own letter on top, then she drove towards the coast, taking her time on the freezing roads, but unzipping the trees and the lovely dark as she passed the familiar shops and houses, stopping at last before the harbour lights. She parked up beside the boats and turned off the windscreen wipers so that the snow could build up and close her in. She turned up the opera, hearing Tatyana's voice climb the scale and back again, wanting Onegin, yes, but making the Onegin it was possible to want. In the months after the end of his sad marriage, Tchaikovsky is said to have wandered each night in the snow of St Petersburg, finding streets in the old city that ended in flights of steps going down to the Neva. Hazel could see the composer looking behind himself to see the many footprints that led to the water's edge. He saw Pushkin's, Onegin's, and those of his short-lived wife, Antonina. Which were Tatyana's? Which were Lensky's and which of them belonged to kinsmen and strangers, ghosts and fictions? She imagined the composer looking into the snow and feeling the frost he would feel at the ends of his toes, Tchaikovsky asking in complete silence, asking with nobody watching, with the opera composing itself in the recesses of his mind, if any of the footprints belonged to him. And then the snow would come, covering all things, covering the world, as if the world was new.

Hazel loved the harbour at night. You could buy fish straight off the boats and in winter, as now, the men would gather round a brazier to smoke their cigarettes and to talk about the size and the quality of the catch. She turned on the wipers again and saw the flames licking out of the metal drum, and as the music calmed and the strings reduced, Hazel tucked her hair behind her ears and lifted the papers off the seat. 'Oho, the talent's arrived,' said one of the fishermen as she approached.

'Easy boys,' she said. 'Cold night.' As she paused for a second and felt the heat it passed through her mind that any of these boys could be the boy from Troon who failed to text back her hairdresser. She clutched the papers to her chest.

'Aye,' said the youngest one. 'A lassie like you should be tucked up nice and warm, eh?'

Hazel laughed without effort and dropped the letter and other papers into the fire. 'Don't tell me that's oor homework yer burning, Miss,' said one of the fishermen, whilst all the others stood around and grinned. 'Don't tell me yer away and burning oor jotters? We did oor best.' Hazel Campbell just smiled at the men and walked back to her car at the top of the harbour. It is nice to feel warm in your coat, she said to herself, gripping the keys in her pocket as snow fell into the sea.

Goldrush Girl
Jeanette Winterson

When you meet someone for the first time, you forget it fast, or you remember it forever.

We went to lunch.

It was an expensive restaurant with small tables angled to give the illusion of space. At small tables shamming space it is necessary to judge distances carefully – between wine glass and plate, food and fork, especially when you do not know your host/your guest, and especially when you have ordered food, not out of politeness, but because you are hungry.

I felt that the distance between us was immense and tiny. We didn't know each other, and your life was quite separate to mine. We were polite, formal, we had our feet tucked back under our own chairs, and we made sure that each of us had enough room.

But seeing the way you cut into your sausages, I understood that you were someone who got hungry too.

We talked – what did we talk about? I forget. Whatever we said was lost under the pressure of everything not said. You cannot say to someone you have just met *I want to kiss you.* Sometimes it is as simple as that.

Not for long. But sometimes.

I wanted to kiss you in the way that I want to eat cherries from the greengrocer's stall. I don't want them in plastic boxes half dead from cold, I want them warm, slightly sweating, stalky, random. I want to eat them while I walk round finger-and-thumbing the limes and throwing handfuls of rocket into brown paper bags. I want the smell, the taste, the surprise, the disagreeable stone.

I smiled at you. I remember that, and that you blushed.

We drank pink wine; I remember that.

If I am going to tell the truth I can say that I was looking for a way out. I was married, I was elsewhere, I was solid, I was stable, I was waiting the way people wait for spring. There was nothing I could do about the winter but I was waiting for the sun.

So when I met you, and I felt what I had not felt in such a long time – simple desire – I did not want to let it go. We walked for a long time after lunch because we did not want to let go.

Sometimes life is simple and sad. There was a sadness even already because nothing in this life holds – the only chance is to move with the moment, to move with the flow of life, but that is hard. Already I was wondering what would happen, what would happen to us, and the mind moves ahead of the flow of life, and the heart hangs back, afraid, and the rhythm is wrong, and all you can trust is your body. And you do.

The golden of your skin was unexpected. I thought you would be pale like me and instead I looked like a white cat lying in a pool of sun. The spread of you, like sun on the steps, the climbing of you, step by step. The warmth of skin and the colour of skin and the most known thing in the world – a body, becoming like a pan of gold that has lain all this time on the riverbed, and now it's in my fingers.

My own body was like a mine where the sun didn't reach. A dark place, dug but not lit. Sun on me now, and the shine of it, and the colour of it, and the gold of it, and these riches.

Goldrush girl.

Minnie runs a bar high up in the Sierra Nevada. Her customers are rough miners trying to make a fortune. They are all in love with her, and each believes he is the favourite. But Minnie doesn't have a favourite; she loves all and none. When the snow is too deep to go out she teaches the men to read and write.

There's a bandit called Ramerrez – big price on his head, WANTED posters everywhere. Minnie keeps the gold hidden in a barrel of water. He'll never find it.

One night a stranger shows up at the bar – Johnson from Sacramento. He says to Minnie, *Do you remember me?* And she answers, *If you remember me…*

I decided to take you to the opera and Puccini seemed like a good choice, because he is shamelessly romantic, and because – and this is strange – Puccini is where opera usually begins for beginners, but less said is that after a long long journey round Mozart and Strauss and Handel and Britten and even Wagner, back you come to Puccini. But not *Tosca*, or *Turandot*, or *Madam Butterfly*, no, where you come back to is *Fanciulla del West*.

I am speaking personally, but how else is there to speak?

*

You knew a lot about opera. It was tricky going to the opera with you. Later, much later, when we were at the end, I took you to *Tristan and Isolde*. I cried all the way through. You said that you didn't like the set.

But this is the beginning, not the end, and there is a rush of gold to my head.

In spring, in the Sierra Nevada, the blue violets push through the snow. I was sitting next to you at the opera, feeling the blue violets pushing through me, and the force of new life, and the colour of new life, and remembering that in spring the sun warms the ground, yes it does, but as soon as that happens the ground warms itself too, by the energy of growth, the movement of roots and shoots.

I realized that the sun of you had warmed me to growing temperature again, and although I was still covered in snow, there were blue violets.

In the dark I held your hand.

Johnson takes Minnie's hand. She asks him to come to supper in her cabin in the mountains. She's excited. She gets out her Monterrey shoes and shawl and dresses up. The fire is bright. She checks her hair. The door opens and in he comes – wild, handsome, shy, the stranger who travels by the sun.

Do you remember me? Yes, if you remember me...
They want to talk to each other. I remember that. Memory is dialogue. When we talk the brain is prompted towards connection. I am a solitary person and I need connection. I have it with plants and animals, and all invisible things, but with

people it is harder for me. I am not stand-offish, or too shy, it's just that I don't like superficialities. I can't do small-talk. I would rather not talk at all.

You and I talked best when we had made love. Then both of us could talk. In fact, at other times, you were rarely there for me to talk to, and I was lonely. In my marriage I could talk but I didn't want to. With you, I wanted to talk, but you wouldn't let me. When you left me, you stopped talking to me altogether. You never returned my calls, or my calls for help. It was a shock, but in a way, it was only more of the same. Silence and separation.

In fact, you were always in love with someone else, but that was never going to work in the way that you had hoped. But your deepest self was not with me. You loved me, and sometimes you longed for me, but your deepest self was elsewhere.

Minnie knows that; it's why she can't marry rich Jack Rance or romantic Sonora. Her deepest self stayed with the stranger who rode out of Sacramento. She made a life. He made a life, but because of each other, they couldn't make a life with anyone else.

In the cabin it starts to snow, and Minnie gets her bedding out and says that she will sleep by the fire and Johnson can sleep in her bed. She doesn't want him to leave. She doesn't want him to stop talking. He wants to make love to her but her gold is her own, and he can't take it by force.

The men are all out searching for the bandit Ramerrez... when...

When the door bursts open and Johnson has only just time to hide, and there's Jack Rance telling Minnie that her precious Mr Johnson is Ramerrez himself, and the trail ends at her cabin...

*

The stranger is never what he seems. Never what we imagine he'll be.

I wasn't what you thought I'd be, though I was the miracle you needed. You weren't what I hoped for, though you were as glorious as May time, and as rich and full.

The stranger is always a trickster.

Walk home with me, the music in our heads. Sleep with me, the music in our bodies. In the night give me courage for the day. In my dreams, sneak out of your body and come into my head. Stand there. Call out. Find me.

In the night the softness and the darkness are reassuring. I feel safe. I feel happy. I needed this whatever the cost, whatever the price of gold I have to pay it. Sometimes life is so close to running dry that any price is worth paying for thawed rain, for the sun on the water, for the river that runs, for the clear, cool moisture that was locked in the earth and nothing grew.

The buried treasure is really there, but buried.

I didn't think it would cost so much to find. It costs everything.

Minnie is so angry. Ramerrez the bandit came to steal the gold. Johnson the runaway lover came to steal her heart. But Minnie doesn't want to be stolen from; she wants to give. It is hers to give, not his to steal.

Ramerrez runs out of the cabin, guilty, confused. Minnie slams the door against his back then she hears a shot. He falls back inside, bleeding, wounded, and she hides him in the loft.

Sheriff Rance is at the door now, and in spite of Minnie's dissembling, Ramerrez is bleeding, and his blood is dripping slowly from the loft. The blood falls on Rance. He knows what

Minnie is up to now. Now there is another price to pay; she has to stake her own life for Ramerrez. She and Rance play poker for him. If she loses, Rance gets her for good.

She cheats. She wins.

But nothing of any value is ever won that way. At best there is a reprieve, and then the true price has to be paid.

But that's how we end it, at the curtain of Act Two. Minnie has won her man at cards.

You and I went out for an interval drink. I was so nervous I ate crisps. I was nervous because I knew the stakes were high, but I didn't understand what I was playing for – not really – or how much it was going to cost.

I had the feeling of something important and simple, blindingly obvious, like a kiss or a wanting to kiss. My heart was beating too fast. I was gambling the lot. I was going to lose my house, my marriage, and I wouldn't be winning you, because you were not to be won. It was myself I had to win. That is very hard, and there are no cards to hide in your skirt. You play you win, you play you lose, you play.

How long have we got? you said. Not meaning the interval.

Will you stay with me? I said. Not meaning the night.

The rhythms are wrong – the mind runs ahead towards the inevitable end. The heart holds back out of fear. Only the body, only the body, only the body stays true. Poor body, faithful body, that so often must do the work of both head and heart, like an animal made to carry much more than it should.

Act Three. The snow is deep. The gibbet is ready. The miners have caught Ramerrez and he isn't Minnie's anymore. *Hang him quick before she comes.*

He's brave. It's cold. He thinks about love, and how for one brief lit-up moment he found it, true gold, unstealable, gift only. She loved him. She risked her life for him. He slipped out one night, his wound half-healed, to save her, to let her start again. He misjudged it because he's a long-haul bandit who can calculate a raid, but he's only just a lover, and so he can't measure a gift. He doesn't know that the gift is so big that there is no measurement.

You take it or leave it. Love is not barter. Love is not theft. Love is not cards, though it is a gamble. Love is a gift. Take it...

Minnie woke up, alone at dawn, once more betrayed, one more betraying man, but love is real and not so easily cheated. This is not a game at all.

As they push him up the frozen gibbet, his hands tied, the men hear her voice off-stage, and there she is, running through the snow, through the past, through the impossibility of love to make love happen. She's standing there, in his head, and in his body and in the world as it is, and as she claims him, she says, *This man is mine.*

Up on the gibbet, standing beside him, she asks the men one by one to forgive – and to each man she tells a story – a story of the night she sat up with him when he was sick, a story of how she taught him to write, a story of a letter, a story of a window iced with snow, and a fire she made on her knees, a story of love, because this is a love story...

Is it?

My goldrush girl, we rescued each other with a pot of gold of the rainbow kind, and the lit-up days were real. But you had a person and I had a past and we got trapped somewhere and I was wounded.

I guess I could not judge the distances right; we both got too close, and yet stayed too far away. I guess you could not accept the gift. Love is such a difficult gift to accept.

Minnie has to leave everything, right there and then; her bar, her home, all the life she had made. And Ramerrez the bandit, she tells the men, died that night in her cabin. It's true, he did, but not by a bullet. Love's renewal never happens without a death of some kind.

She takes his hand and their tracks disappear in the snow.

After you left me it felt for a long time as if the world had darkened. I slowed, I was cold, I was underground again. But anyone who strikes gold can keep it. And the sun-gold that warms the ground is faithful and fiery. Whatever is found well is found forever.

I didn't want you to go because in spite of everything that was wrong, you felt right to me. I have been in mourning, and mourning is dark and shrouded. But the dark and shrouded place that is mourning is not the same as the dead place where there is no life.

I don't know if I will see you again. And if I do what we were will be long gone, the tracks in the snow disappeared.

But the sun will come again.

And there are blue violets.

The Martyr
Ruth Rendell

'I can't tell you how pleased I am,' said Eudoxia. 'It was making things rather awkward for Alexander and me. What arrangements have you made?'

'Arrangements?'

'I mean, is it to be Venus or Flora? And are you going to have some kind of ceremony? If it's to be Flora I know one of the priestesses. She dines here. I'm sure she could fix it up.'

'I thought,' Theodora said, 'that I could just buy some incense and go along to the temple and – well, do it.'

'Just as you like,' her sister said rather coldly, 'but do remember not to go out unaccompanied. At least take a slave with you. It was different when you were one of those Christians. Everyone expects them to behave like hippies.'

So Theodora asked Berenice to go with her. 'Asked', not 'commanded', because until the night before she had considered slaves to be her equals. Berenice was a Circassian and as well-born as she, a princess like her until her father had been killed, her city sacked and she carried off into slavery. They went first to the market where Theodora made her essential purchase and then to the temple of Flora, a circular building with white columns and suitably floral friezes. The few priestesses who happened to be about stood around, watching with interest, while Theodora scattered incense on the altar. She thought the haughty-looking one was probably Eudoxia's friend.

'I'm sure you're doing the right thing, madam,' Berenice said afterwards. 'They've been saying in Antioch that neither Venus nor Flora delight in the woe which disfigures their fairest resemblance below. That means you, of course.'

Septimius had already told her this. She wondered what he would say now. What would Didymus? In an extravagant moment he had said he intended either to live with this princess or die with this Christian, meaning her in both instances. She did not want to think about Didymus just now.

'I have some calls to make, Berenice,' she said. 'First I must go to the Grove.'

'Where the Christians are, madam?'

'I wish you'd call me Theodora.'

Shocked, Berenice said, 'That wouldn't be proper.'

'No, I suppose not. I hate propriety and all that. You can't imagine how free I was when I was a Christian. It was lovely. I could go where I liked and be friends with anyone I wanted and I could go out alone – oh, I don't mean to hurt your feelings but it is so nice to be free. I never will be again.'

Theodora heard the singing from a long way off. Members of the choir – and that was all of them – were expressing their devotion in one of their favourite hymns, 'Lord to Thee, each night and day, strong in hope, we sing and pray.' It reminded her so powerfully of those happy days before the soldiers came for her that she was afraid she might begin to cry. The sound swelled in a crescendo and then died away on its final sweet notes. She saw them standing in a circle under the trees. The Grove, as they called it, was a wood on the far bank of the Orontes river, a cool shady place in a hot climate.

Now she had arrived, Theodora hardly knew what to do. Two nights ago she had believed she would never see this place or any of them again. The kind of disgrace the Romans had planned for her, a degradation which men justly called a fate worse than death, would have been followed by death itself. Heaven afterwards and a martyr's crown. But heaven and glory look different when death stands before you as a reality. She lifted her head and saw that one of the women on the other side of the river had recognized her. Once Irene would have waved. She would have smiled. Not now. Her whole demeanour, her body language as Eudoxia would have called it, indicated something near despair. But aware perhaps of Theodora's unwillingness to cross the river, she picked up the long skirts of her robe and began to cross the bridge. Theodora waited.

In all the time they had known each other they had never met without exchanging a kiss and an embrace. Not any longer. But Theodora could tell Irene was not angry. She was only sad.

'I understand,' she said. 'It was too much to ask of you. You are so young, Theodora. Have you sacrificed yet?'

Theodora nodded.

'And have you somewhere to stay?'

'I'm with my sister and my brother-in-law.'

'Didymus came to tell us how he managed to get you out of prison. He doesn't yet know what the consequences to himself will be. I fear – I'm sorry to say this to you – but I fear he will be disappointed in you. Who is that young woman?'

Berenice was standing meekly a little distance away, her head bowed and her hands folded.

'A slave from Circassia.'

'Would she not join us? So many of us are former slaves.'

'She's not mine, she belongs to my sister. Goodbye, Irene.'

Theodora walked away and waited for Berenice to join her.

'I have another call to make,' she said.

The projected visit demanded a steep climb up the mountain-side. Like all the best soothsayers, Sybil lived in a cave or, rather, conducted her business from a cave. Her home was a house in the same street as Eudoxia and Alexander's. And like all soothsayers worth their salt, she dressed in grey robes and wore her hair in dreadlocks. Theodora gave her name to the acolyte who sat at a table at the entrance and made her way into the dim interior where the soothsayer stood, staring into a shallow bowl of water. When she saw Theodora she beckoned to her and Theodora also looked into the bowl but she could see nothing, only the clear water and greenish sides of the bowl which seemed to be made of some glittering crystalline substance.

The soothsayer said, 'Yes?'

'I want to know what will become of me.'

'Nothing new in that,' said the soothsayer. 'That's what they all want. You've given up your faith?'

Knowing that was not much to be proud of, Theodora thought. The whole of Antioch must know by now. She looked about her. The walls of the cave were covered in curtains of thin fabric like cobwebs which hung limp and still. It had a strange and not very pleasant smell of dead things, half-masked by a perfume which might have been civet. It was said that the soothsayer consulted entrails for some of her divinations and that would account for the decayed meat smell. As for the civet, she had seen the cave-cat strolling about when she approached the entrance.

'I want to know what will become of me,' she said again. 'Tell me my fortune.'

The soothsayer's eyes were as clear and pale green as the water in the bowl. She stared downwards, then lifted her eyes. 'I see nothing now but hundreds of years ahead I see people listening to an opera about you – or it may be an oratorio.'

'What's the difference?'

'I don't know,' said the soothsayer irritably. 'It's not my field. Please don't interrupt. An opera or an oratorio by a man called George Frideric. George like your saint and Frideric – well, it's a Barbarian name. I can hear the music and some of the words if I listen carefully.' She bent over and lowered her right ear to the water. '"Angels ever bright and fair, take, oh take me, to your care..."'

'What did you mean when you said "nothing now"?'

'Well, nothing is what you've chosen, my dear, apart from what there always is for a woman and a princess, marriage, babies, that sort of thing. It was your choice.'

'Oh, if I on wings could fly.'

'Easier said than done,' said the soothsayer. 'That will be two pieces of silver. You can pay my girl on your way out.'

In the heat of the day the atrium in her sister's house was a cool place. A slave created a breeze by the rhythmic waving of a large feather fan. Several women, enslaved and free, were stitching a tapestry. It was to be a picture of Apollo pursuing Daphne and caught at the point where the young girl is metamorphosed into a tree to escape the god. Eudoxia's friend Helena was at the loom, hung with pearls as usual, her fingers stiff with diamonds, while Eudoxia herself sat at the spinning wheel, distaff in hand. She got up when she saw Theodora and came over to greet her at the doorway.

'Some very good news, my dear. I can't wait to tell you. Didymus is here and – what do you think? – he has asked Alexander for your hand.'

Theodora looked at the busy women, then back at her sister. 'He wants to *marry* me?'

'Yes, of course. That's what I said.'

'He loves me still? After everything?'

'I don't know about love,' said Eudoxia. 'He's a soldier and an honourable man doing the honourable thing. After all, you spent a night alone with him in the prison, singing songs and exchanging clothes.'

Together they went into the house. Alexander and Didymus were in the library where a slave was filling two cups from a flask of wine on the table in front of them.

'Here she is, my boy,' said Alexander. 'Better drink up.'

Didymus drank up. He smiled at Theodora. In spite of what Irene had said, he did not look disappointed and Theodora reflected on the size of her dowry. When Alexander and Eudoxia had discreetly retired, he took both her hands.

'Well, here we are, my sweet rose and lily, and isn't this the best outcome? Between you and me, I never quite believed all that stuff about martyrs defying the sword and enjoying the encircling flame.'

'Are you going to stay in the army?'

'Happily, yes. The centurion's been very generous. He's agreed to overlook my springing you out of jail. But I'm going to be transferred to Laodicea and that may be the best thing. No one knows you there, you see.'

'They blow neither hot nor cold in Laodicea. Like you and me. Because they blow neither hot nor cold the Lord spews them out of his mouth.'

'Is that right?' Didymus looked a little uneasy but he spoke heartily. 'We have to put all that Christian stuff behind us. Give me a kiss, my girl.'

After he had gone Theodora sat with the women, re-learning the skills she had almost forgotten in the Christian years. When she pricked her finger for the third time, Eudoxia took pity on her and the two sisters went down to the perfume shop, accompanied by Berenice and a male slave. Though it was very hot, Eudoxia wore a long silk veil wound round her head and gave one to Theodora.

'In your peculiar position,' she said, 'you can't be too careful.'

When they came home again they took childless Helena with them to the children's quarters where Eudoxia's three girls and two boys were with their nurses. 'These are my jewels,' she said with a glance at Helena's pearls and to her sister, an arm round each of the two littlest, 'I don't think you've seen Hebe and Philemon before, have you?'

Theodora agreed that she had not. She had been a Christian when they were born, working for the kingdom of heaven, singing hymns, spreading the good news, bringing converts to the fold. In her own room she took off the veil, folded it carefully and put it in a drawer. There had been no slaves to do these things for her among the Christians and old habits die hard. She stood at the window, watching the western sky, feathered with red and gold, darken as the sun sank. In the atrium below the women were putting away their work and slaves were bringing lamps. When the sky was the green of a peacock's tail she wrapped a robe round her shoulders, for in that climate the nights are as cold as the days are hot.

Alexander and Eudoxia were dressing for dinner. Servants

were busy everywhere, preparing specialities. Didymus was invited and had been given a pass by the centurion until midnight. Theodora had misgivings about Didymus, small qualms which bothered her – but it could not be for long, could it? Nothing now could be for long.

She had walked no more than a hundred yards when she became aware that someone was following her. She stopped, looked back and saw it was Berenice.

'The mistress will have me flogged if I let you go alone, madam. I could carry your bag.'

'I have no bag, Berenice,' said Theodora. 'See? I have nothing but what I stand up in. I shall need nothing where I'm going.'

It was growing dark. The stars were coming out, radiant stars, especially Venus herself who shed light almost as bright as the moon. Venus lit their way and this amused Theodora, considering where they were going and what she was to do. The Orontes river gleamed like a silver belt, the bridge a dark buckle spanning its course. On the far bank none of the Christians could be seen but Theodora who knew their habits could just make out shapes moving among the trees and then the glimmer of a fire.

'I must leave you here,' she said to the slave and, in words she had thought she would never use again, 'The living God be with you.'

She began to walk across the bridge. Perhaps those goddesses still had hopes of her, for Venus shone more brightly as she came to the other side, showing her to Irene and her friend to her as Irene came out from under the trees.

'You've come back to us, Theodora.' Irene held out her arms.

'I have come home,' said Theodora, 'for a little while.'

On the Antioch side Berenice watched and waited until the

two women disappeared into the wood where the fire was. She
thought for a moment of that other fire which awaited Theodora
and then she turned and walked back to the city.

String and Air
Lynne Truss

Flippancy at short notice was always Caroline's speciality, of course. Yet I think she surprised even herself by the swiftness and certainty with which she christened those rescue cats of hers, and set in train the events I will recount. 'Rescue cats, Adrian?' Peter had said to me, with an eyebrow raised, when I told him what Caroline was planning. 'Trained in life-saving, are they? What a novel idea. Cats and deeds of altruism are so rarely mentioned in the same breath.'

As usual, I ignored the jibe. It's a well-established fact that Peter does not approve of cats. I tell him it's because their self-ishness outweighs even his own, to which he replies (usually) that people in glass houses would be well advised not to practise for any Olympic-standard discus-throwing events, at which point we leave it amicably and move on to other topics.

The point is that Caroline was going to choose her cats care-fully, taking her time, and not rushing into any decisions. One Wednesday morning – it must have been June two years ago, because I remember that my *Agrippina* costumes meeting was to take place in the afternoon – I went with her to the shelter in Paddington. 'Just to look, Adrian,' she said. 'Keep reminding me. I'm only here to look.' And that's what we did. To be frank, I thought it was quite noble of me to accompany her to this dank and cheerless place. But we did look at any number of pathetic specimens behind glass, some of them mewing piteously, and then we went away. So imagine my surprise when, on the following Sunday, Peter and I arrived at the Gaskell Square house for lunch, and the first thing we saw was a pair of handsome black cats with huge green eyes sitting at the top of the stairs, watching in eerie silence as we shook the rain off our jackets to hang them beside the front door. (I may have mentioned it was June.)

'Caroline?' I said. 'But on Wednesday, I thought you'd decided—'

'I went back on Thursday,' she said. 'I'm sure the reason we didn't notice these two properly the first time was that a) they didn't miaow, and b) they were called Doozles and Blackie.' Casting my mind back, I couldn't remember Doozles and Blackie, but I let it pass.

'You'll love what I've called them, Adrian.' Barely able to contain her excitement, she gestured up the stairs and indicated the larger, left-hand cat.

'That's Miles,' she said. And then she indicated the tiny right-hand cat: 'And that's Flora.'

'What?' I said.

She laughed. Peter saw my dismayed face and laughed too.

'Oh don't look like that, Adrian,' she said. 'They're brother and sister, you see. He's about three years old, probably. And she's about one. And they're incredibly spooky, that's the point. I mean, look at them. The way they just stare at things that aren't there; it's hilarious! I gave Flora a little dolly to play with this afternoon—'

'Oh, please, don't!' I said.

'But you'll be relieved to hear that she didn't sing anything creepy to it. In fact, she kicked it to bits.'

I didn't know what to say. I was truly shocked. Caroline surely knew how much *The Turn of the Screw* meant to me. I sang Miles on umpteen occasions in my youth. I've directed it twice. Caroline was a dear friend of twenty-five years' standing (we'd met at the Guildhall, when she was training to act), but her devotion to glibness would ultimately undo her; I had always said that.

'Oh come on, Adrian, don't be such an old stiff about it,' Peter said. 'I think the names are entirely appropriate for cats. It's very clever. Cats inhabit a parallel reality. They are patently able to see things we can't see. They are never grateful for love; in fact, they bite any hand that succours them; and perhaps I go too far, but there is quite strong historical support for the cat as the willing little helper of Satan. I think probably *all* cats should be called Miles or Flora. It's the only thing that makes sense.'

Caroline looked at me. 'I thought you'd think it was funny, Adrian,' she said.

I looked up at the cats again. Those solemn faces. Those pointed ears. That graceful posture. They were both focusing their silent attention on something unseen, something between our heads and the ceiling in the hall.

Peter shivered, and that was an end to the introductions. The cats were evidently not coming down to be sociable. Caroline led the way to the kitchen. I felt guilty. Obviously, she'd been expecting me to tell her how clever she was, and I had missed my cue. I tried to make amends.

'I suppose I just think you'll never surpass Furry Lise,' I said. 'That was the best cat name ever.'

Peter stopped in his tracks. He'd forgotten. 'Oh, Furry Lise was a very funny name, Caroline,' he pronounced.

Caroline stopped and turned, and put her hand on my arm. 'Oh, Furry Lise,' she said, her eyes welling with tears. 'I miss her so much, Adrian. My lovely, lovely Furry Lise.'

I have to admit that I took more of an interest in those cats because of the names Caroline had given them. Had she called them, well, Itchy and Scratchy, I would probably have forgotten about them altogether. And I appreciated that, in a way, her naming of the cats had been in reference to her friendship with me. We had always argued about Britten, and especially *The Turn of the Screw*. It wasn't the music she objected to so much; it was the libretto. Being a wordsmith by trade, she said the banality of some of Myfanwy Piper's lines simply tortured her ears. She would parody Piper's humdrum recitative at the drop of a hat – even when I strenuously begged her not to.

'How was your JOUR-NEY?' she would sing.

'Caroline, please stop it,' I'd say. But she wanted to finish, and she did.

'Well, would you BELIEVE IT, Mrs Grose? There was no TROL-LEY...on the train.'

'NO!'

'YES! It was SHOCK-ING! I was hoping for PRINGLES, or at least a frothy COFF-ee!'

'That's enough, please. I do get the point,' I'd say. But she could keep it up for hours.

'They shouldn't get AWAY WITH IT, dearie. You should write to SOMEONE. I can't believe there were no PRINGLES for you ...on the train!'

And of course I would explain – again – that the everyday language gave all the more power to the supernatural theme. And I also made the point once or twice that *The Turn of the Screw* was actually a very suitable opera for Caroline to identify with. You've got an irresponsible and vulnerable imagination, just as that poor governess has, I said. And, like her, you have a great protective love to bestow, but unfortunately no children of your own to bestow it on, so it's terribly thwarted and frustrated and comes out in forced, contorted, perverse and unnatural ways.

'Thanks for pointing that out,' she said. 'Only a dear friend would sugar the pill so perfectly.'

'Have they miaowed yet?' I asked on the phone, a couple of weeks after their arrival.

'Have *who* miaowed yet?' she said, pointedly.

'Oh you know: Miles,' I said, as casually as I could. I still hated to say the names. 'Miles; and, what's-her-name, Tiddles.'

'Not a peep, Adrian,' she said. 'I look at them all the time and think, who are you and where on earth do you come from? I try to stroke them and they back off and run away. They're really conforming to type. I've started singing *Lavender's blue, diddle, diddle* all the time, to make them feel at home.'

I suppressed a harrumph.

'Peter thought a rescue cat might be one who performs daring rescues,' I said, hoping to change the subject.

'Well, he'll say anything for effect. He didn't really think that.' This was a noticeable thing about Caroline, by the by: how other people's flights of fancy never amused her as much as her own. 'Oh, but I did find out a couple of things about them, by the way. About the cats.'

'What? When?'

'Well, the man from the shelter came to check I was looking after them properly, and he said that, between him and me,

Miles had been so unpopular with the volunteers, they'd been relieved to see him go!'

'What?' I said.

'It's true. They said he had a bad effect on the other cats; that the other cats were actually scared of him. Isn't that amazing? Just like in *Turn of the Screw*, when Miles gets expelled. I *knew* I'd been inspired when I chose those names.'

I spent much of the following six months abroad, during which I heard little about Caroline or her Jamesian household. Perhaps I vaguely hoped that the joke had quickly worn thin, and she'd renamed the cats something sensible like Nero and Poppaea. However, nothing could have prepared me in any case for the change I saw in her when we next met. It was in Marylebone High Street, outside that old BBC annexe building, in the week before Christmas. I'd just given an interview about my *Fledermaus* and had come outside, and was about to cross the road to that splendid bookshop with all the travel books when I spotted Caroline standing on the kerb at the other side, looking straight at me but apparently so deep in thought that she couldn't see me. I waved. She frowned. She was evidently talking to herself. I waved again, to no effect. Her hair was long and wild. And her eyes – well, I was just glad Peter wasn't there, because she looked frankly insane and *had just bought some fish for her cats from the most expensive fishmonger in London*. That's the sort of thing that Peter makes quite a lot out of, given the opportunity.

Of course, once she saw me, she was transformed. In fact it was extremely gratifying to have such an effect on someone's mood just by grasping them firmly by the shoulders and saying, 'Hello, Caroline, it's me.' And it started out quite pleasantly. I bought her a coffee and a cake at that old Viennese place, and told her about my bat opera, my plans for 2012, and the new flat in Milan; in her turn, she said that the cats hadn't really settled down.

Obviously, I had hoped the subject wouldn't turn to the cats quite so quickly, but it seemed there was nothing for it.

'Do they miaow now?' I asked, meaning only to show a friendly interest. Sometimes, I admit, I'm quite pleased with myself for remembering the details of my humbler friends' lives. It's an empathetic gift that many politicians I'm sure would trade a limb for.

'No, Adrian,' she said, and she gave a rather tragic little laugh. 'No, they don't miaow.'

She poked at the remains of a millefeuille with her pastry fork. I smiled at her.

'Car-o-line?' I sing-songed, encouraging her to smile back. But she didn't. In fact, she looked down, bit her lip, frowned, and then wiped away a rolling tear. Under the cuff of her coat, I caught a glimpse of her forearm, etched with slashes.

Now, I should explain that I'd known Caroline a very long time, and when I told her she had a vulnerable imagination, I knew whereof I spoke. In her work, which involved coming up with far-fetched comedy plots for an animation company, this imagination of hers had served her very well. She was a genius of the extended 'What if?' and she had made a very decent living from it. The only trouble was that, quite often, her robust brain could construct a funny idea that her frail little psyche couldn't cope with afterwards. And this sometimes caused her best friends to worry seriously about her sanity.

For example, we were once together in a ship's chandlers in South Devon, choosing lightweight waterproof jackets, when the rather haughty assistant took us both by surprise by snatching the jacket I was holding ('May I demonstrate something, sir?') and with a few alarmingly quick motions, opening the pocket, shoving the whole garment inside, and zipping it shut. I looked at Caroline in astonishment, and she looked at me. Her face simply shone with delight. 'Well, Adrian,' she said, straight-faced, 'I hope it doesn't do that when you're wearing it!' Of course, we laughed so hysterically we were obliged to leave the shop. A day or so later, however, when I said it might be safe now to go back now and buy one, she pulled a face and asked me not to.

'Why?' I said, puzzled.

And she explained that, although it sounded daft, she would always be a bit worried now, you see, that it would actually happen: that we'd be standing on a cliff top together, watching the sunset, and then there'd be a sinister synthetic zippy-uppy noise and she'd look round – and there would just be this over-stuffed plastic pocket writhing about on the ground, with me inside it, suffocating, screaming, punching to get out.

'Oh come on, Caroline,' I had said. 'It was a joke. A good joke, and quite a vivid joke. But still just a joke.'

'I know,' she had laughed. Was she serious? Was she semi-serious, or maybe serious in inverted commas? Either way, her lip had wobbled, and she'd shot me a pleading-for-understanding look; a look I've always remembered, of someone fully aware of the utter silliness of the situation, but still helpless. Helpless to dismiss this preposterous fear she'd created, herself, out of nothing.

I recognized the same look now, in the Viennese coffee shop.

'Caroline, calling those cats Miles and Flora was your own idea.'

'I know. But they really won't let me love them, Adrian.'

'You gave the impression you could handle it.'

'They shun my affection; they fight me.'

'Oh, Caroline. They're *cats*.'

'They live in a separate reality, staring at the hall as if there's something there.'

'As I said, for heaven's sake, they're *cats*. And they grew up somewhere else, with someone else, so it will take time for them to relax and bond with you, that's all. Think about it, please. Be reasonable. If they'd come from a lovely happy home like yours, they'd still be in it, wouldn't they?'

She just looked at me, then looked down again. I knew what she was thinking.

'They are not possessed, Caroline!'

It was time to lay this card firmly on the table.

'How do you know that?' she said.

'Look.' I was quite impatient now. 'They don't sing *Tom, Tom, the piper's son* in a spooky way. You are not a governess in a crinoline. I'm sure Miles-the-cat never tore up a letter you wrote to your employer, in order to protect a malevolent red-headed ghost. And just in case you are beginning to think so, Britten did not base the story of *The Turn of the Screw* on one overly suggestible woman's relationship with some unresponsive big-eyed cats she took into her home without sufficient research.'

I wondered if I should mention the old waterproof jacket incident by way of illustrating how overly suggestible Caroline could be. I decided it might make things worse.

'What happened to your arm?'

She pulled up her sleeve and looked at the wounds. She shrugged.

'I watch them all the time, Adrian.'

'Well, don't. That one's easily solved. Just don't. Go out. Watch *University Challenge*. Shut the door. Wear blinkers.'

'Something evil is in the house.'

'Oh, that's nonsense.'

She bit her lip and sniffed.

'I've seen it,' she said, quietly.

I actually thumped the table when she said that. The woman at the next table dropped her cream bun.

'What?' I demanded. 'What have you seen? Of course you haven't seen anything. What do you mean, "I've seen it"? What have you seen?'

She gave a little cough. And then she pushed back her chair, stood up, and *sang*. I'm not joking. In that rather staid and quiet patisserie in Marylebone High Street, she suddenly did her old Myfanwy Piper recitative thing, with full projection.

'I've SEEN IT, Adrian!'

'Caroline!' I pleaded, as people looked round. I grabbed her hand, but she pulled it away.

'I've SEEN...what the cats see! It has a POWER over them. But you don't BE-LIEVE ME! What ever shall I DO?'

Having apologized publicly to the other customers, I paid the bill quickly and accompanied Caroline back to her house. On the way, I telephoned Peter and asked him to meet us there. I think I did ask myself briefly whether Caroline would have done the same for me if the positions had been reversed – but then I couldn't imagine I would ever have talked myself into such a preposterous state of mind in the first place, so it didn't seem worth pursuing the question.

'Did you ever try just giving them a lot of cat treats shaped like little fishies?' I said, as lightly as I could, as we crossed

Baker Street going west. 'Or waving a toy on a piece of elastic? Many a cat's heart has been won with less.'

These suggestions were evidently not worthy of reply.

'You won't be able to see it, Adrian,' she said, as she put her key in the door. 'But that doesn't make me mad.'

And then, as the door opened, her manner changed completely. She put on a false smile, and called out to the cats in a tone of desperate, wheedling ingratiation. It was the creepiest – and possibly the most degrading – performance I've ever been made to witness.

'Darlings!' she called. The cats were at the top of the stairs again. They did not respond to the call. The big green eyes were wide and round.

'Hello, Mi-iles,' she said, very emphatically, and smiling. 'Hello, Flor-a!' She used that tone we use for ga-ga old people, or people in a coma. It has the sub-text, 'We're pretending everything is absolutely normal here, and that this conversation really has two sides!' Then, in a low voice she said to me, 'Say hello to Miles and Flora, Adrian.'

'Oh, all right. Hello, you cats,' I said. 'Who's up for some Friskies?'

But I did not manage to leaven the tone.

Caroline, having removed her coat, climbed the stairs towards them on hands and knees, I suppose because it would be less startling to the cats. She seemed to have forgotten all about me, the minute she saw them.

'What a lovely cat you are, Miles.'

He looked down at her, and then away again.

'What a beautiful, beautiful, clever, lovely cat.' Having arrived at a point of eye-level, she put out a hand to stroke the back of his head, and he ducked away.

'Please, Miles,' she said. 'Please. I love you.'

It was quite embarrassing to hear this, it goes without saying.

'Please, Miles. I wouldn't harm you. You're my darling boy. Please.'

And then, to my alarm, she burst into tears and came back down, sobbing.

As I comforted her in the kitchen, I did feel a smidgeon of impatience. I mean, no one likes to watch a friend suffer a mental breakdown at any time, but I felt that a) Caroline was having her particular mental breakdown on an extremely flimsy pretext, and b) there was some vital element missing from the picture. It took me a while to work out what it was. Here was Caroline, sobbing, losing her mind, on the very precipice of unreason. Here was I, her old friend, being noble and staunch, holding her hand. We formed a pleasing tableau. Yet something...? And then it came to me. Music! That's what was missing! A scene like this just won't come alive without the music.

Luckily, Peter arrived quite quickly, because I'd formed a plan.

'I'll be back by six,' I said; and, pausing only to call goodbye to the cats (hoping this would please Caroline), I left the house and caught a cab. Looking back, I often wonder whether this was indeed the best plan of action in the circumstances. Removing Caroline to San Francisco until her head got better would have been a much better solution, but unfortunately it didn't occur to me until a couple of weeks later. So, while Peter kept my mad friend company, I took the taxi to the Paddington shelter, to ask about the origins of Doozles and Blackie. In particular, of course, I wanted to know whether, as kittens, they had been horribly maltreated, causing some feline version of post-traumatic stress disorder. But if they hadn't been maltreated, my next question (based on nothing more than a hunch) was whether they therefore might have been exposed – likewise as impressionable kittens – to improbable quantities of *grand guignol,* on screen, stage or radio.

'You're in luck,' sighed the woman at the desk, having checked laboriously through some old ledgers. She coughed and sniffed, and manoeuvred a cough lozenge with her tongue. From the wafting aroma, it was eucalyptus.

'Doozles. Blackie.' She ran a finger across the page. 'June, June, June.' She sighed again, causing another gale of menthol. 'Brought in in March. Oh yeah. That was Officer Ron. I thought so.'

She picked up a battered walkie-talkie, but luckily the requisite Officer Ron appeared in the doorway at that moment, and the woman explained my inquiry to him. He was a tall man with a comb-over, big glasses and a kindly expression. I expected him to have no recollection of two very ordinary black cats, with unmemorable names, released a full six months before, but he evidently did. In fact, I noticed that, at the name Doozles, his face drained of colour, which wasn't exactly encouraging.

'Can we use the office, Mo?' he said. And then he got a big white handkerchief out of his pocket, and – I was quite worried now – he actually wiped his brow.

Half an hour later, I was back in the street, and I was running, running back to Caroline's house as fast as I could, and I emphatically did not require a 13-piece orchestra to make it more dramatic. Maltreated? *Grand guignol*? Post-traumatic stress disorder? Well, I'd certainly been on the right track. Ron had come close to weeping as he described the scene in that terrible house in Wembley. People had reported this evil old woman several times, apparently; even though Ron had tried to get entry on two separate occasions before he finally broke in, he still blamed himself for leaving it so long. He found the woman swinging lifeless, of course. She'd been dead for at least two days – and she had chosen hanging, Ron had deduced, because it was the only way of guaranteeing the starving cats couldn't get at her to eat her corpse. Around the house, which stank so badly that he and his fellow officers could hardly breathe, were eventually found, both living and dead, sixty-one cats. Doozles and Blackie were the names Ron had given Caroline's pair himself – at the end of a very long day. But he remembered them especially because, unlike the others, they didn't try to hide. Flea-bitten and thin, their green eyes huge in their heads, they sat together at the top of the stairs, seemingly transfixed by the body of that evil old woman hanging; hanging in the hallway below.

I was too late, of course. By the time I arrived, the ambulance had gone, and Peter was alone in the house with little Flora, who was miaowing loudly, ceaselessly, and following him around. I felt sorry for her. For six months, Caroline had begged her to make a noise, any noise. Now that she'd started to pipe up in earnest, these two distraught strangers kept telling her, please, please, please, for pity's sake, shut up.

'It all happened so quickly,' Peter kept saying. I had never seen him discomposed before. He was always so – well, the opposite, composed. 'Why weren't you here?' he said to me, as he cupped the generous glass of brandy I'd poured for him. 'Why weren't you here?'

Evidently, Caroline had crawled back up the stairs after I'd left, and Peter had heard her pleading with Miles in that ghastly cloying humiliating manner I'd witnessed earlier, and then – well, then she had called out the words he didn't understand.

'There she is!' she called. 'Peter, she's here!'

What did she mean? Who was 'she'?

He went into the hall and looked up to where Caroline and the cats were all staring back down.

'Look, Caroline—' he began.

And that's when he felt it: the electrical jolt of sheer, bottom-less dread. In that hallway, a sense of evil seemed to congeal around him. He froze. Silence buzzed in his ears. His body shrank inside his clothes and the rings dropped from his fingers. He confessed he actually shook with fear.

They were all looking down – but not straight at him: at something above his head. He had no idea what they thought they could see. Was it real? Had they summoned it up between them? Suddenly he felt angry; he felt deeply, madly angry. And what made him utterly furious was that, at a time like this, Caroline was mewing words of comfort, words of reassurance, not to him, but to a cat. To a resistant and uncomprehending bloody-minded *cat*.

'Oh, Miles, Miles, don't be afraid,' she was saying. 'My darling, I'm here to protect you. Don't be afraid.'

Poor Peter broke. He couldn't stand it. He grabbed his coat and opened the front door. He remembers the gust of cold air and the look on Caroline's face.

'Shut the door!' she yelled. But it was too late. She grabbed Miles as he jumped, but he tore his way out of her arms, shot down the stairs and ran outside, straight into the road, with Caroline following, screaming; screaming after him to come back.

*

Flora lives with us now. I thought adopting her was the least we could do – and Peter feels it's good for his soul that she miaows non-stop and never lets him forget the fatally irresponsible part he played in the dramatic last moments of her brother and adoptive parent. She lets us pet her, and she seems to be positively enchanted by games involving toys on lengths of string. Released from the psychodrama that propelled Miles and Caroline under the wheels of that Ocado van, she seems to have no imagination whatever – which is normal for cats, I dare say, but a welcome surprise in the circumstances. I quite worship Flora. I feed and protect her and she repays me by clawing the furniture. Isn't that exactly how things ought to be?

La Scala has asked me to direct *Turn of the Screw* again, but I have to say, there's not a chance I can go back to it now. The piece is completely ruined, as far as I'm concerned, unless the world is ready for the somewhat bathetic cat version in which the heroine – instead of heartbreakingly realizing Miles is dead in her arms – gets run over by a vehicle doing home deliveries for Waitrose. Once you get an idea in your head, you see – well, I don't need to spell that one out. I could never direct even the first scene again now; not now that I think my eager Victorian governess is actually desperate for a tube of Pringles on the train.

I miss Caroline very much. They said in the obituaries that her imaginative skill was to make 'something out of nothing'. Well, she certainly did that. And she paid the price, alas. Sometimes, to torture myself with Caroline's memory, I sing to Flora from Act Two of the opera, the lines about the cat's cradle.

Cradles for cats / Are string and air.
If you let go / There's nothing there.
But if we are neat, / And nimble and clever
Pussy-cat's cradle / Will go on for ever.

'String and air,' I say to her, lightly tickling her ear. 'String and air. If you let go, there's nothing there.' And Flora rolls over on her back in the sun and looks at me through narrowed green eyes as if to say, 'You're mad.'

The Empty Seat
Paul Bailey

Although my beloved Uncle Rudolf died thirty-two years ago,
he is still a constant presence in my life. For a few minutes each
day, I listen to one of the tracks on the Golden Age compact disc
of the recordings he made in Vienna in the mid-1920s with the
soprano Hilde Bernhard. As Rudi Petrescu, he had studied singing under the strict but affectionate tutelage of Jean de Reszke,
considered by many to be the finest lyric tenor of the nineteenth
century. It was de Reszke's wish that his exceptional pupil would
claim his own glorious repertoire – Florestan, Don Ottavio,
Tristan, Ferrando, Don José. Yet when Rudi became Rudolf, and
Petrescu Peterson, the roles that he was offered were of a kind
that his master and mentor regarded as 'froth'. Alfred in *Die
Fledermaus*, Barinkay in *The Gypsy Baron* and Count Danilo in
The Merry Widow brought him international fame and made
him very rich and lastingly discontented.

Alfred and Danilo are parts that continue to be coveted, but
who would dream of resuscitating Zoltan Kassák, the brigand
with noble blood in his veins in *Magyar Maytime*, or Igor, the
unknowing heir to the Boldonian throne in *The Gypsy Prince*,

or the dare-devilish Shahah, the pirate who is crowned King of Balkania in the closing tableau of *The Balkan Buccaneer*? Zoltan, Igor and Shahah were created especially for my handsome uncle, who deployed his formidable skills as both actor and singer the better to render them credible. It is true to say that this preposterous trio dashed every remaining hope he possessed of being a respected – as distinct from a popular – musician. Froth destroyed his talent, as Jean de Reszke and the composer Georges Enesco had predicted it might in letters I found among his papers in the weeks following his death. De Reszke wrote to him in 1924, urging him to 'number Messieurs Verdi, Bizet, Mozart and Wagner among your musical acquaintances' and not confine himself to operetta. Enesco's letter, dated May 30, 1929, was harsher and sadder, admonishing his fellow Romanian for his frivolousness and pleading with him to 'put music before such transient matters as fame'. Enesco had heard him sing *Dalla sua pace* from *Don Giovanni* at the Bucharest Conservatoire in 1919 and had recommended the promising young tenor to his friend Jean de Reszke, then living in retirement and teaching in a grand villa in Nice. How often, I wonder, did Rudolf Peterson reread those two heartfelt messages when it was no longer possible to heed them? He could have torn them up or burnt them, but chose instead to preserve them carefully. It pleases me to think that he penned equally sincere replies, assuring his heroes that he would consign Johann Strauss and Franz Lehar to his past. Perhaps, like the youthful Augustine of Hippo in more elevated circumstances, he was contemplating his future operatic chastity. He could see it on the near horizon. He was on his way to it, but not quite yet.

I came to England in February 1937 for what my father convinced me would be a short holiday. I was Andrei Petrescu on arrival at Victoria Station, and Andrew Peterson thereafter. It was my uncle's mission to comfort me and protect me from the terrors afflicting our family in Romania, the details of which he revealed to me when I was eighteen. Those details sound the stuff of crude melodrama when set down baldly, but they are real even so. My mother was seized by a group of men who dragged her into a forest, raped her, slit her throat and left her for dead, for the sole reason that certain people in the small town where I was born remembered that her father had been a debt collector, and the debt collectors in Eastern Europe were invariably Jewish. She was bearing a second child – a brother or sister for the little boy she already cherished. My father announced one evening that I had been invited by my famous uncle to spend some time with him in the city of Big Ben and Westminster Abbey and that we must leave home very early in the morning. Roman Petrescu accompanied his son to Bucharest, where they boarded a second train that took them across the Hungarian plains in darkness, through Austria and Switzerland, until they reached the centre of Paris three days later. At the Gare du Nord, my father entrusted me to the care of a French guard, and kissed and hugged me to him as he told me the biggest of all big lies – we would be together again, the three of us, as soon as my holiday was over. My holiday never ended, and my despairing Tată hadn't the strength or will to make the return journey. He gave himself to the Seine instead.

The melancholy Rudolf Peterson, the star of *Magyar Maytime*, which was playing to full houses throughout 1937, was determined to create a bright new life for his orphaned nephew. During the Christmas season of that memorable year, Santa Claus brought Andrew wonderful presents when he emerged from a chimney in his uncle's Elizabethan manor house in Sussex. Yet the most enduring present was neither tangible nor destruct-ible. After dinner on Christmas evening the guests assembled in the music room, holding their glasses of port or brandy, ready to be entertained. My uncle requested everyone present to forget Danilo and the Gypsy Baron and the Vagabond King, and that bloody idiot Zoltan, and all the other halfwits he had imperson-ated, and listen to something different. His friend Ivan Morris, who was known as Ivan the Terrible if he played off-key, seated himself at the Bechstein piano and accompanied my uncle as he sang the aria from Handel's *Jephtha*, in which the anguished father offers up his child for sacrifice:

> Waft her, angels, through the skies,
> Far above yon azure plain;
> Glorious there, like you, to rise,
> There, like you, for ever reign.

I was seven, soon to be eight, and I was moved to my first happy tears. I knew nothing of Jephtha's plight, and I was unaware who Handel was, but I understood that I had just heard something – 'something different' – that was radiantly beautiful.

My uncle abandoned his career in 1945, after a charity perfor-mance in aid of the survivors of the Nazi camps. He gave his adoring public what they wanted – Johann Strauss and Lehar, and several lesser composers – and for the last of many encores he sang 'Dalla sua pace' in memory of Jean de Reszke. From then on, he devoted himself to my wellbeing. He took me to Besançon in France for what transpired to be Dinu Lipatti's final recital. Uncle Rudolf held Lipatti's dedicated musicianship in the high-est esteem. His self-effacement at the keyboard was rare in the autumn of 1950, as it is rare today. On the way back to London, my uncle said he would make sure that my finely tuned ears would stay unsullied by operetta, which he now hated with an intensity that verged on the manic. It was the music of prewar Vienna, that city of cream cakes and incipient Nazism.

I received a superlative education, mastering my adoptive language with diligent patience. I married, fathered a son, and was quickly deserted by my English wife, who had fallen in love with a much older American. Billy, who calls me Andrew, occasionally visits me from the States, and I have no doubt that he is my own child since we could be mistaken for brothers. Once Mary and I were divorced, I went to live with my uncle, working as his secretary and amanuensis. It was joyous employment for me, despite his frequent complaint that I was wasting precious years looking after a singer who was deservedly forgotten. I endured these bouts of self-pity, reminding him that his postbag was in a very healthy state for someone who was a relic from a bygone age.

Uncle Rudolf died of a hasty cancer with my mother's maiden name on his lips. I knew that he had loved Irina Aderca and had proposed to her, but she had chosen the plain-looking, shy Roman Petrescu for her husband. Uncle Rudolf's love for me was deepened and enriched by his abiding adoration of the woman who had brought Andrei into the world in that blessed time before madness descended on the town outside Botoşani. His care for me was the gift he offered to her, as I once heard him whisper as he prayed in front of an icon of St Nicholas.

He was in his sixties, I recall, when he reached the considered decision that the music that most consoled him, that exercised and renewed his spirit, was 'melodiously dissonant'. Bartók comforted him, and so did Alban Berg, and so – miraculously

– did Janáček, whose characters (in *Jenufå* and *Katya Kabanova*) he found recognizably human and believable. He was an early admirer of Ligeti's playful seriousness, or was it – he asked me, with comic pedantry – his serious playfulness? Rudolf Peterson and his doting nephew were a familiar sight, or fixture, in the capital's recital rooms, concert halls and opera houses. The ageing survivor of operetta listened with a rapt attentiveness that beatified his features to sounds that often reminded him of his pogrom-ridden homeland.

One evening in 1985, on the tenth anniversary of my uncle's death, I had the misfortune to be seated next to a fidgety woman with a passion for sweets that needed unwrapping, during a glowing interpretation of Berg's Violin Concerto. I fled from the hall the moment it ended, and walked by the Thames to ease my mind and calm my nerves. I was determined that no fidgety woman or abstracted man would ever spoil my pleasure again. I saw my uncle's beatific expression and decided on the instant that I would always have an empty seat beside me whenever I listened to music in a public place. This has been my practice for two decades now: I reserve two seats well in advance of the event, one of which is on the aisle and thus ensuring that no stranger can distract or irritate me. Uncle Rudolf is the occupant of that empty seat, his ears as finely tuned as mine to Beethoven's last quartets, or *The Art of Fugue*, or *Wozzeck* and *Lulu*, or *Bluebeard's Castle*, or the limitlessly inventive songs of Schubert.

His soul was with me as I watched, and listened to, the unparalleled Anja Silja in *The Makropulos Affair* at the opera house in Sussex that isn't far from the Elizabethan mansion he bought with the money the likes of Alfred, Danilo, Barinkay, Zoltan, Igor and Shahah had secured for him. I sent their insubstantial shadows scampering off as Emilia Marty achieved her ambition to be embraced by death. At the bar, afterwards, with the melodious dissonance still in my head, I saw the great singer approaching and summoned up the courage to thank her for the profound happiness she had afforded an elderly, but ardent, fan. She accepted my awkward compliments with smiling grace, but I couldn't say that the compliments were Rudolf Peterson's too. Of course I couldn't. That would have been the act of a madman.

When the train drew into Victoria at midnight, I stopped and remembered the far-off day in February 1937 when my impossibly handsome, famous uncle lifted me up and held me in his arms and kissed me on both cheeks and called me Andrew Peterson, the new name that would rid me of my demons and make an English gentleman of me. And standing there, I shed tears of the happy variety for his melancholy thoughtfulness. I had tickets to reserve the following day for the two of us. There was a concert devoted entirely to the music of Georges Enesco coming up in September and that was something different to look forward to.

My Lovely Countess
Antonia Fraser

'*Dove sono...*' questioned the dulcet, plangent voice of Emily Nissaki during the third act of *The Marriage of Figaro*. And 'Where indeed are they, those previous happy moments?' silently echoed Leila Hopper from the third row of the stalls.

'*Dove andaro i giuramenti...*' sang the handsome black-haired American soprano, in the role she was rapidly making her own. And: 'Too right, where have they gone, those vows of a deceived tongue?' recited Leila bitterly to herself. She felt at that moment that she had all too much in common with the Countess Almaviva since both of them faced a predicament caused, essentially, by an unfaithful man.

'Oh heavens! To what humiliation am I reduced by a cruel husband!': those words also found a tragic echo in Leila Hopper's heart. Except that Leila intended to deal with her own off-stage predicament rather differently. No masquerade for her, no changing clothes with her maid – what maid? Leila didn't have a maid – and above all no sweet reconciliation at the end of the day.

'*Più docile io sono...*' Yes, the forgiving Countess on stage was going to be good deal kinder to her husband than Leila was going to be to Charlie Hopper. For what Leila had in mind was murder.

Not the murder of Charlie himself however: reared on the fine old traditions of operatic vengeance, Leila planned something subtler, crueller and finally, she hoped, more devastating. For Leila intended that at the post-opera party in the theatre bar – a party for the theatre's patrons – Charlie should personally administer poison to his mistress. Not for nothing had Leila thrilled to the macabre and tragic plight of Rigoletto, convinced the wayward Duke was inside the sack which actually contained the body of his daughter. And then there were the twists of the plot of *Tosca* by which the singer finally delivered her own lover's death warrant. Charlie Hopper should hand the poisoned chalice – actually the free glass of wine for the patrons – to Magdalen Belport. Thus he would always know that he personally had brought about her agonizing death.

What about Leila's own position in all this? Did she really expect to elude discovery for very long? It was true that she had persuaded Charlie in one of his good-husbandly moments to purchase the poison in question on her behalf. (A peculiarly nasty garden potion destined to reduce errant lawns to scorched earth, it was accompanied by a list of warnings which had caused Charlie to observe mildly, 'What price the ecology these days, darling?' But when Leila had retorted, 'If you weren't away so much and helped me in the garden...' Charlie had dumped the poison and hastily changed the subject.) Since Charlie had indubitably purchased the poison, it would be Charlie's word against hers when it came to the question of who had actually administered it.

At the same time, more grandly, Leila did not expect and did not want to avoid discovery for very long for the crime of passion she was about to commit. After all, what did life hold for her, now that she had lost Charlie?

'*J'ai perdu mon Eurydice...*' – Leila adored Gluck – even if she was an unlikely Orpheus and Charlie, handsome broad-shouldered Charlie, an even more improbable Eurydice.

But Magdalen Belport, of all women in the world! It was not that Magdalen Belport lacked beauty. The late Earl of Belport had died childless some years ago leaving Magdalen, his fourth, much younger wife, a large fortune and the right to queen it at Belport Castle for her lifetime. Whatever his faults, he had known how to pick a woman who would in a sense grace the role of Countess. Previous countesses had been renowned for their looks in periods which stretched back into the Thirties. Magdalen, a former model (as the newspapers never failed to point out), had the long legs, the narrow hips and neatly catlike features of her original profession. With her elegant, unchanging leanness – she had to be well over forty – and an endless fund of money at her disposal, Magdalen Belport could cut more dash at a patrons' function in a white silk trouser suit than all the other women in more conventional evening dress. Leila knew. She had seen her do it...

No, the fearful cruelty of Charlie's behaviour lay in the relative positions of Leila Hopper and Magdalen Belport within the Festival organization. And who knew the facts of this better than Charlie himself? As Countess of Belport, by far the most glamorous local figure, Magdalen acted as titular Chairman of the Festival committee. This meant that she attended at least one committee meeting, and bought a great many tickets (some of which she always gave away, whether she attended the performance or not, since Magdalen's friends were not exactly passionate lovers of the opera). If Magdalen did attend the pretty red-and-gilt theatre in the Regency Gothic castle, she could be guaranteed to behave with the utmost benevolence (if her spiky-heeled Manolo Blahniks did ruin the lawn, it was after all her lawn), and make remarks which were on the whole gracefully innocuous – Magdalen liked to please. Then she always went on to accept all the credit for the work of the Festival. That was the work which had actually been carried out, dutifully, devotedly, day in, day out, or so it often seemed, by Leila Hopper.

Leila's love of opera might be verging on the obsessional – she knew in her heart of hearts that it was – but then so, she had always thought, was Charlie's own passion for the subject. And yet he had not appreciated the sheer disloyalty of an affair with Magdalen Belport. It was as though to denigrate all their shared feelings for the Festival, the pooled task of finding singers, arranging programmes, in all of which Charlie had so often said, 'You *are* the Belport Castle Festival. Don't worry about the public thank you. Magdalen Countess of B. is just our essential figurehead, a publicity-mad mermaid on the prow of our ship. A woman who actually thinks the late Pavarotti was a bass' – Leila had laughed at the time, much reassured by Charlie's words – 'just because he had that wonderful deep barrel-chest. No, she actually said that to me. You'd think even Magdalen noticed that wasn't exactly a bass singing *Nessun dorma*.' And surely Charlie had laughed too.

Given Charlie's essentially lighthearted temperament, the wayward nature which Leila both loved and deplored, she had often thought that a passion for opera was the deepest, most stable thing in her husband's life. Had it not drawn them together in the first place – that magic evening at Glyndebourne listening to *Eugene Onegin*? Yes, opera was Charlie's greatest passion – until his passion for Magdalen Belport, that is.

'My lovely Countess': Leila would always remember how she found out: those words spoken by Charlie into his mobile when he had imagined she was working late in her tiny Festival office. They followed immediately on the highly disquieting incident of the trip to Venice. Charlie Hopper had always travelled a great deal, mainly to America, since his work as a corporate financier demanded it, and Leila, since she had no choice, accepted the fact. Charlie did after all in consequence get to hear of rising young stars in the States who might be prepared to visit Belport Castle: that was part of the way in which the Festival work had drawn travelling Charlie and homebound Leila together. (Emily Nissaki, whom Charlie had heard sing Micaela in *Carmen* while in Chicago, was an example of that kind of happy serendipity between husband and wife.)

What she did not accept, could never accept, and was now going to take violent action to end, was Charlie's new passion for Magdalen, which meant that since that Venetian trip – as it turned out to be – he had hardly seemed to cast an affectionate glance in Leila's direction, let alone a caress. No Micaela bewailing her lost happiness with Don José had ever felt more piercing sorrow than Leila recalling how long it was since Charlie last made love to her.

'Charlie Hopper! Last seen in Harry's Bar in Venice!' Odd that those seemingly innocent words of international travelling snobbery could have destroyed Leila's peace of mind for ever. It was some party at Belport Castle in aid – as usual – of fund-raising for the Festival. Leila did not know the man concerned, a big man with receding brown curly hair and a well-cut suit which probably concealed rather too many years of good living. At Harry's Bar, Venice and elsewhere.

Now Charlie had never, so far as Leila knew, been to Venice; the reason she thought she knew this was that La Fenice was one of those opera houses, described but never visited, which they had both yearned to see for themselves. The person who had been to Venice, many times, no doubt, but certainly very recently, was Magdalen Belport. In her generous way she had even brought Leila a present back – some elegant gold and glass beads. The necklace was intended, Magdalen said, as a thank you to Leila for all the hard work she had done in the run-up to the present Ballet Festival.

At the word 'Ballet' Leila had felt a moment's genuine bewilderment. Surely even Magdalen...

But Magdalen had quickly corrected herself. 'Whoops, sweetie, opera. Trills not spills. It's just that I'm on so many committees. You know the feeling.'

Leila, who was on only one committee herself, smiled forgivingly and allowed Magdalen to fasten the beads around her neck. (What treachery! Leila had later smashed them to pieces.)

'Harry's Bar?' questioned Charlie; he was using his lying voice; Leila who loved him could tell immediately. 'I don't get it.'

But Magdalen interrupted him. Unlike Charlie, she spoke rather too fast, as if concerned to override whatever Charlie might be going to say.

'Venice!' she exclaimed. 'Don't you remember? We bumped into each other. There was that vast mass of people, all making a terrible noise, a lot of Italians, well, I suppose that was hardly surprising. You were alone. I was with a large party.'

'Oh Venice,' said Charlie after a pause as though he had somehow thought the conversation to be about quite another place, New York, Boston, Chicago (to name three cities he had recently visited). He gazed steadily at Magdalen, which meant of course that he avoided looking at Leila. 'Harry's Bar in *Venice*,' he repeated, still staring at Magdalen with that yearning intensity.

Later that night, Leila was first of all informed by Charlie that he had only briefly visited Venice from Munich (where he also sometimes went on business en route back from the United States) and had hardly thought it worth mentioning to Leila. Then he changed his story. The truth was, he finally blurted out, after some hours of talk in which the subject never quite went away, that Magdalen Belport had asked him to escort her to an opera gala at Le Fenice. She had been let down, she needed an escort – 'You know what she's like' – Charlie had been in Munich, they had been in touch over some matter to do with the Festival, he had flown down. There was nothing else to it. Absolutely nothing. And now would Leila stop all this and leave him in peace?

Charlie Hopper closed the conversation at this point by going out of the room abruptly and slamming the door. But Leila watched him slip his mobile into his pocket. She knew he was going to make a call. And when Charlie did come to bed, once again he turned away from his wife.

The next morning all he said was, 'I thought you might be jealous. Missing out on La Fenice. You can ask Magdalen if you like. Nothing else to it.'

Jealous! It hardly seemed an adequate description of her bewildered feelings. Nor did she intend to raise the subject with Magdalen Belport. It was Magdalen who raised it with her, the next morning paying one of her rare visits to the Festival office. She used exactly the same phrase as Charlie had, Leila noticed.

'An escort, darling. Nothing else to it.'

'What was it?' asked Leila suddenly and, for her, very

sharply, so that Magdalen opened her slanting cat's eyes in astonishment.

'The opera!' Leila almost shouted. 'What opera did you go to?'

But at this Magdalen merely smiled in her most feline lazy way. 'Oh, darling, you don't expect me to remember that. That's your department. But I do know what I wore: grey satin blazer from St Laurent, very pretty with paler grey crêpe trousers. My new Christian Louboutins with the red soles. Everyone admired them.'

It was quite possible, thought Leila rather wearily, that Magdalen was actually speaking the truth.

Then: 'My lovely Countess.' It was those words, overheard twelve hours later, which finally convinced Leila that the unbelievable had to be believable: her adored Charlie had transferred all the passions of his nature to Magdalen Belport. And after that, of course, in a terrible brutal way, everything began to fit in. Charlie's increasingly obvious desire to please Magdalen, for example, notably during the meetings of the Festival committee. His flattery of her taste, even her taste in opera and possible singers for the Festival…now that was really going too far. 'My lovely Countess', perhaps, but knowledgeable about opera, never!

There was one peculiarly humiliating incident which actually took place in the committee. Leila was as a matter of fact used to smoothing over Magdalen's not infrequent cultural gaffes. She had brought it to a fine art – or so she thought. A quick change of subject, and a quick correction of the minutes afterwards, seemed to result in satisfaction all round.

But now Magdalen insisted that *La Bohème* was the story of a fun-loving courtesan called Violetta; one who went on a glorious spree to the country with her lover, and then came back, only to die of TB in his arms. And Charlie agreed with her! Leila could hardly believe her ears. For the first time she actually contradicted Magdalen, instead of merely altering the record.

Maybe Leila's voice did rise as she began: 'You are thinking of *La Traviata*, for heaven's sake. Isn't she, Charlie! In *La Bohème* there are those students—'

But that was no excuse for Magdalen to lean back delicately in the face of Leila's passion, and confide to Charlie, 'I've always identified myself with Violetta. That's why *La Bohème* is absolutely my favourite *numero uno* opera.' And still Charlie, Charlie of all people, did nothing.

On stage the opera was almost over and the Count, a short fat man with none of Charlie's handsome looks, was asking his wife to forgive him. '*Contessa, perdono!*'

'I am kinder: I will say yes,' his wife responded in the rather better-looking incarnation of Emily Nissaki. It had always been one of the moving moments in all Leila's canon of opera. No longer. For Charlie Hopper (and Magdalen Belport) there was to be no forgiveness. Doomed people: yes, indeed. In a very short time the post-opera party would begin in the theatre bar. And a very short time after that Magdalen, Countess of Belport, would be dead.

How convenient that Leila, as secretary of the committee, generally looked after the doling out of the patrons' free drink! It was with special care that Leila handed the fatal glass to Charlie in order that he might – equally fatally – pass it on.

'I've got something special for her. She really wants champagne, of course. But this is at least better than the usual plonk. Take it to her.'

Then Leila could not resist adding – what madness overtook her when she had held her tongue for so long? – 'Go on. What are you waiting for? Take it to your lovely Countess.'

For a moment Charlie, now holding the glass, stood staring at Leila. His expression was one of total amazement, followed almost immediately by guilt.

'She knows.' That was what his expression said to her, as clear as words. 'She's known all the time.'

Leila's own expression, which had been momentarily triumphant, changed to blandness.

'Darling, just give it to her.' It was her usual polite, affectionate tone, the tone of an organizer who needs to make everyone happy. '*Figaro* is not exactly short. She must need it.'

'She must indeed,' replied Charlie levelly, the amazement and the guilt by now well concealed. He turned away. Leila followed the direction of his tall, black-dinner-jacketed figure, that formal guise which set off his fair English good looks to perfection. She watched Charlie edging his way through the crowd, polite, skilful, not spilling a drop. There he went, remorselessly towards the corner where Magdalen Belport, svelte as ever in one of her elegant jackets which surely came direct from Chanel, held court. Despite the crowd which surrounded her, Magdalen Belport looked up to give Charlie a special intimate smile. Leila watched Charlie, holding her breath. Now, now, let him hold out the glass, let him perhaps kiss her on the cheek – for the last time – but let him at least hold out the glass, let his be the hand, let her drink from it—

But wait – No, for God's sake—

'No!' screamed Leila involuntarily. She stopped. 'No, Charlie, no,' she wanted to cry. 'Not her...'

It was too late. Already the wine was coursing down the

throat of Emily Nissaki, that pampered throat soon to be closed and silent for ever in death, as she flung back her handsome head with its abundant coils of dark hair, the relic of her Greek ancestry, smiling her thanks with her bold black sloe eyes fixed on Charlie Hopper who had handed her the drink.

Beside her, Magdalen, Countess of Belport, wondered when Charlie Hopper, or at least that hard-working opera-mad wife of his, would bother to bring her a drink. After all she was Chairman of the Festival. Hadn't there been something about a special glass of wine? Yet Leila had been behaving so curiously lately, sulking really, she who had always been so grateful for everything. Could she possibly have found out about Charlie... Magdalen hoped to God she wasn't planning to leave the Festival office or anything drastic like that. Leila was so clever, so inventive...

So when was that special glass of wine coming? The plonk in the theatre bar was famously disgusting, poisonous one might almost say, even if that face the lead singer was now pulling was surely slightly over the top even for a dramatic soprano.

The death of Emily Nissaki, described by the tabloids as being on stage – the theatre bar was surely near enough to count as that – created a predictable sensation. There were those, it is true, who suggested that her macabre ending cast a false retrospective glamour on her actual talent. But then none of those critics had probably heard her sing in person: those few records so far released did not quite do her justice. These same critics had not, for example, as Charlie Hopper had done, ecstatically followed Emily Nissaki round American opera houses – and to Venice – throughout her brief career; following that first *coup de foudre* meeting with her in Chicago.

Finally Charlie had secured, with some quiet manipulation,

that 'my lovely Countess' as he was wont to call her – a reference to that glorious night together following her performance in *Figaro* at La Fenice – should come to the Belport Castle Festival. (Even if it had involved flattery beyond the call of duty to Magdalen Belport: luckily still a remarkable-looking woman.)

To the rest of the spectators, the way in which Leila Hopper, shortly before confessing her crime, cried out, 'The wrong Countess!' made no sense. She then quoted the general exclamation at the end of *Figaro* of 'Heavens! What do I see?' 'The wrong Countess!': what could that mean? She had known, surely she had known – of Charlie's affair with Emily Nissaki – otherwise why poison her? She must have known. It was Magdalen Belport for example who reported seeing Emily Nissaki and Charlie Hopper together in Venice.

'Not that I told Leila,' Magdalen added quickly. 'In fact after Geoffrey's gaffe I tried like mad to cover up for Charlie by pretending he was alone; whereas of course he was hanging round the neck of that wretched singer, Emily Whatnot. And then I backed him up with Leila to the hilt. Some cock and bull story about going to the opera. As if one didn't have better things to do in Venice! Absolutely to the hilt.'

It was only Charlie himself, broken not only by the death of Emily but also by the part he had unwittingly played in it, who knew exactly what his wife had meant by her frantic cry of 'The wrong Countess!' And her use of those words from *Figaro* confirmed it to him. 'Heavens! What do I see?' exclaimed all those on stage when the 'right' Countess finally stepped out of the alcove to reveal herself. (Not that he could ever tell Magdalen Belport, unaware both of Leila's suspicions and of the peril which had threatened her.)

'Take it to your lovely Countess': how could Charlie have

looked in any other direction than towards Emily Nissaki?

Yet in the end popular sympathy swung surprisingly in the direction of Charlie Hopper in a way which would have infuriated his late wife Leila, had she lived. This swing was something to do with the blatant manner of Leila's own self-sought death. An obsession for opera was all very well, and even a *crime passionnel* committed against her husband's mistress could be understood (if not condoned). But for Leila Hopper, a mere administrator after all, to run to the top of the battlements of Belmont Castle and throw herself off, crying something like, 'The soldiers will never get me' – that was surely carrying things too far.

'Poor Leila, I'm afraid she was no Tosca.' purred Magdalen Belport. She did her purring in the ear of Charlie Hopper himself, having for once taken the precaution to check that she had the right character in the right opera. In the unavoidable absence of Leila, she had consulted a huge opera dictionary usefully adorning the Festival office. She looked forward to doing it again. That was the measure of her newly-awakened interest in Charlie Hopper, who, with the loss of his wife and mistress all at once, had definitely got some gaps in his life.

Indeed, the way things were going between Magdalen and Charlie, it might not be very long before the fortunate fellow was murmuring those thrilling words yet again – but this time in a more appropriate ear: 'My lovely Countess'.

La Fille de Mélisande
Kate Mosse

White is the colour of remembrance. The hoar frost on the blades of grass that cling to the castle walls, the hollow between the ribs and the heart. A shroud, a winding sheet, a ghost. Absence.

The trees are silhouettes, mute sentinels, slipping from green to grey to black in the twilight. The forest holds its secrets.

Mélisande's daughter, Miette, presses herself deeper into the green shadows of the forest. She can see glimpses of La Fontaine des Aveugles through the twisted undergrowth and juniper bushes. It is late in the day and already the light has fled the sombre alleyways of the park, from the gloomy tracks that cross the woods like veins on an old man's hands.

White is the colour of grief.

This is the anniversary of her mother's death when, according to the mythology of the land, the paths between one world and the next are said to be open. It is not a night to be abroad. It is also Miette's birthday, although this has passed without celebration or comment these past eighteen years. The date has never been marked by feasts or fanfares or ribbons.

The story of Mélisande, forbidden love, tragic beauty, a

heroine dead before her time – this is the architecture of legend, of fairytale, of poetry and ballad. How could the prosaic existence of an unwanted, resilient daughter possibly compare? A watchful daughter biding her time.

Miette presses her small hand against the velvet of her robe, feeling the reassuring shift of the paper in her pocket. It is her testament, her confession. She knows her father has murdered once, twice, if not three times and yet kept his liberty, but this is not how it will be for her. She needs to explain, to make herself understood. In this, as in so many other ways, she is not her mother's daughter. Everything about Mélisande's life – her delicate heart, her fragile history – remained as indistinct as a reflection moving upon the surface of the water. Where had she come from before Golaud found her and brought her to Allemonde? What early grief had cracked her spirit? What were her thoughts as her wedding ring fell, twisting, down into the well? How shifted her heart when she looked at Pelléas and saw her love reflected in his eyes? Did she know, even then, that her story would escape a happy ending? Did she catch her breath? Did he?

Miette grew up in the shadow of these stories, now cracked and battered around the edges. Of her father, Golaud, and his jealousy. Of her mother, Mélisande, and her gentleness. How her long hair tumbled down from the window like a skein of silk. Of her uncle, Pelléas, and his folly. Of the others who stood by and did nothing.

Green is the colour of history. Not the white and black of words on a page or notes on a stave. Not the frozen grey of tombstones and chapels. It is green that is the colour of time passing. Olive moss, sable in places, covering the crow's feet cracks in the wall. Emerald weeds that spring up a path long unused. The lichen covering, year by timeless year, the inscription on the headstone, the letters, the remembered name.

At her nurse's knee, Miette learned the history of Pelléas and Mélisande. It is the mythology of Allemonde, a tale perfect in its construction – *un amour défendu*, a sword raised in anger. Always the balance of the light with the dark, the ocean with the confines of the forest, the castle and the tower. The colours, the truth of the story, Miette pieced together from what was left unsaid between her half-brother, Yniold, and her father. The truth, she learned from her grandmother, Geneviève.

The truth is always shabby. Always mundane when set next to the stuff of legend.

Miette sighs, caught between boredom and terror.

Il est presque l'heure.

Her father's customs are well known. From the white-haired beggars at the gate to the servants that process the sombre corridors of the castle, all of Allemonde knows how Golaud, the widower, the murderer of wives, makes annual his pilgrimage to La Fontaine des Aveugles on the anniversary of Mélisande's death. To mourn, to pray, to weep, to pick over the bones of his life. No one knows if it is remorse or relief that guides his steps. He has never shared that chapter of his story and Miette never asked for fear it would strip her purpose from her.

In the distance, the chiming of the bell. The sheep in the fields begin their twilight lament, the mournful bleating, grieving for the passing of the day. Out at sea, the sun is slipping slowly down beyond the horizon, as every day for centuries. And in the palace, the slow and steady business of lighting the candles will now begin. The dancing yellow flames skipping up along the stone walls and grey corridors.

The legend of Mélisande holds that she dreaded the dusk.

They say that Mélisande feared the night. The ringing of the Angelus bell, the closing of the gates in a rattle of wood and metal and chain – all this made her think of the grave where the worms and spiders dwelt. Mélisande looked always, or so Miette's nurse told her, to the west, to the setting sun and the shore, as if looking for that first ship, long departed, which had brought her as a child-bride to Allemonde. As if hearing, still, the cries of the sailors and the rote and the gulls.

Miette glances down and sees the tips of her satin slippers are stained with the first touches of the evening dew brushing the grass. She shivers and pulls her cloak tight around her with slim, strong arms. Deep in the folds of cloth, she presses the tip of the knife against her thumb, softly at first, then harder until her skin is pierced. She draws her hand free. A single, red pearl of blood hangs suspended, a jewel in the twilight.

There are beads of perspiration at the nape of her neck now beneath the canopy of her hair, worn long in remembrance of her mother. The mother who never held her. The braids are a symbol of the connection between them, although an inconvenience. Brushed, plaited, smoothed, demanding. Miette is more her father's daughter than her mother's. Quick to temper, easily frustrated, vengeful.

Beneath the trees, Miette shifts slightly from foot to foot, feeling the cold seeping up from the earth, the roots, into her young bones. She does not know how long she has been waiting, entombed in the green embrace of the wood. Long enough for dusk to fall, it seems both an eternity and a moment. She feels panic rising in her throat, nausea, sour and bitter, and wills herself not to lose her nerve.

Pas maintenant.

Red is the colour of dying. What else?

The violent rays of the setting sun through glass, flooding the chamber crimson. The petals pulled from a rose, strewn on the cobbled stones of a garden no longer tended. The colour of the damaged beating heart. Blood dripping through the fingers.

It is not the first time Miette has come to this place. To test herself. To attempt the business of breaking the cycle. To act so that the story can begin again. She shivers in the damp air. Her body vibrates with possibility, an open string on a violin.

To steady her nerves, Miette sends her thoughts flying back to the castle. She remembers herself at seven or eight years old, carried on Yniold's shoulders. Laughing, sometimes. Content, sometimes. But, quickly, the darker memories come. Her past opens out in her mind like the decaying folds of a paper fan. Older, eleven or twelve, tiptoeing alone down dusty corridors. Or, later still, hidden beneath the covers in her cold chamber, hands over her ears, trying not to hear her father shouting or Yniold weeping.

A bird flies up out of the trees, the abrupt beating of its wings upon the air mirroring the rhythms of her own resolute heart. Miette narrows her eyes, sharpens her ears. In the distance, now, she can hear something. The subtle snap of twigs on the path, the scurrying of rabbits seeking cover in the undergrowth, the shifting of the atmosphere. Someone is coming. Her father?

Miette stiffens. She has imagined this scene so many times. The single strike of the blade. How Golaud, wounded, will reach out his hands as once Mélisande had reached for the baby daughter she was never to know. He will ask her forgiveness. She could give it.

'Je te pardonne. Je te pardonne tout.'

Miette waits, holding her breath, wishing the deed could be over. Or not need to be done at all.

The light from a lantern, jagged and uneven, is getting closer. Miette can distinguish the sound of breathing above the twilight sighings and whisperings and chitterings of the forest. The rattle of an old man's chest.

Golaud walks out of the darkness, out of the cover of the trees and into the glade, following the well-worn path to La Fontaine des Aveugles. To the place where Pelléas fell.

He moves slowly, pain in every step. Miette watches and feels nothing. His body is failing him. He is old. His wounds sing loud in the damp evening air. The scars, beneath the velvet of his robes, remind of hunting accidents and the memory of metal and spear. The crumbling of sinew and bone, eating him away from the inside out, grief or regret or anger, all or none of these.

But she does not pity him. She thinks only that he must be called to account. In Yniold's absence it falls to her. A daughter to avenge a mother, a less familiar story.

It is dark now. Golaud places the lantern uncertainly on the edge of the well. Miette waits. It is not yet her turn to step upon the stage. Her father is muttering, talking, but so softly that she cannot distinguish one word from the next. She moves a little closer, picks out the words.

'La vérité. La vérité.'

Over and over, like a chorus refrain, the syllables bleeding one into the other and back again. The words he said to Mélisande as she lay dying.

Tell me the truth.

Golaud leans forward, two twisted hands in the yellow halo of light on the grey stone of the well. Miette steps forward, in silence and without drama. For if she is to rewrite this story, it cannot be in noise and emotion, but rather enacted with cold purpose. It is a practical ending, not a theatrical one.

One step forward, then two. *Un, deux, trois loup.* A game of grandmother's footsteps played by two lonely children, she and Yniold, in a desolate palace so long ago. With a third silent step, she is on him.

As her father stoops forward to gaze into the blind eye of the water, Miette has the sudden advantage of height. Thinking of Mélisande, perhaps of Yniold's mother too, Miette lifts the knife. She has heard it said that the soul takes flight alone and in silence.

With the strength of both hands, and the weight of her body, she brings the blade down between her father's shoulders.

He cries out, once, like an animal caught fast in the metal jaws of a trap, then silence. Miette relinquishes her hold on the hilt and steps back, half stumbling on the hem of her cloak beneath her heel, sodden now with dew.

She, too, is silent. She wills him to turn, wishing her act of revenge to be understood. At the same time, she does not want to see the life leaving him or her own image reflected in his dying eyes.

Golaud falls forward, as once Pelléas had fallen. His hands slip from the wall, empty fingers scratching down the stone surface of the well, down to the ground. No crash of cymbals, no crescendo to mark the moment.

Miette remains motionless, unwilling to disturb. A nightjar calls, a spur to action. Taking the letter from her pocket, she places it upon her father's body. The testimony of Mélisande's daughter, eighteen years in the telling.

'*La vérité,*' she whispers. This is the truth of it. That stories can be rewritten. Acts of love and death.

Miette stretches to take the lantern from the rim of the well, taking care not to touch, then turns to walk back through the forest. How easy, it seems, to kill a man. So easy to separate the spirit from the skin and bone?

In the distance, the bell strikes another hour. It marks the end of one history and the beginning of another.

Gold is the colour of loyalty. Of a duty fulfilled.

Now the Great Bear...
Andrew Motion

1

My friend Michael had tickets for the opera; would I go with him? It was in London and we could stay at his sister's flat. Why me, I wondered. I knew nothing about opera – my family were country people who did country things. Sure, now I was sixteen I'd started to veer off a bit – reading poems, going to the Tate sometimes, but music was... Well, if music wasn't rock 'n' roll it just wasn't. Don't worry, Michael said. You'll like it. It's set in your part of the world. He meant East Anglia and he was right – that was our place. For the last hundred years, Dad's family had lived in Stisted, midway between Halstead and Braintree. We were in the old rectory now, and his parents were up the road. Grandpa in Nedging, where he had a pig farm, and his ex-wife Betty in Westleton on the coast. The coast! Michael said. She practically *is* Peter Grimes, then! Crimes? I said. Grrrrimes, Michael growled, then went on more quietly. Well, no, not Grimes perhaps. Ellen. This time I said nothing. Granny was a sore point.

2

Dad never talked much about anything that mattered, and because his parents mattered a lot, he said almost nothing about them. My brother Kit and I pieced together his childhood from pictures in the album and things Mum said. We had to be careful, though, because Mum liked stories, which meant she exaggerated. Had Granny really been a nymphomaniac? Probably not. But she'd definitely run off from Grandpa, which was unusual in those days, the 1930s, and Dad still hated thinking about it. Back then, he'd felt angry and ashamed, and everything peaceful in him had started to get complicated. Even though he went on living with Granny during school holidays, and in the gap between school and joining the army, he stopped liking her.

That's what Mum thought, and Kit and I could see why: we called her Granny Sunbeam but that was only because of the car she drove; really she wasn't sunny at all. Her house in Westleton was a pink cottage on the village green which looked pretty from the outside but turned out to be made of dark corners. It smelled of soot and rosemary. And so far as we could tell, all Granny ever did was sit around drinking gin with her hair pulled back so it looked like a helmet, laughing at us when we bumped our heads on the ceiling. Don't worry, Dad whispered, but his mouth was pursed up like a little boy's. He didn't enjoying our visits any more than we did. Never mind, though; we only came once a year, and we'd be home soon. It was what Mum called a penance.

3

Michael and I dumped our overnight bags with his sister then set off for the West End. I didn't know my way round London yet but I loved it – like being an ant crawling through long grass. At home in the village everyone always knew what I was doing. Here I could be anyone I wanted – a completely different me. In fact I'd already started being a new me while I was mugging up the opera. It just wasn't the kind of thing anyone had done at home before. Going in to Hannay's in Braintree and buying a book of poems by Crabbe – that was a revolution. So was reading it in the sitting-room with everyone watching. It was a cruel story I thought, but interesting all right, even though it had a weird flat feel, like sitting in a car with hard wheels and no suspension.

Michael had already said the story happened in Aldeburgh, which helped because I knew the coast round there. We'd explored it after one of our visits to Granny – it was a way to let off steam. Dunwich first, where we'd climbed the muddy cliff and Mum explained there used to be a village, but it had fallen into the sea and if we listened carefully we'd hear the church bells ringing underwater. I closed my eyes and saw mackerel whizzing through the windows of the tower, flicking the bell with their silver tails. Then Minsmere because Dad wanted to see the arctic plovers, which had just arrived from their feeding grounds in the north. Then Aldeburgh, with its wonky shacks, and its giant-toy-lifeboat, and its shelf of flints running down to the sea. None of us could walk across them without looking drunk, or as though we were fainting, so we hammed it up and staggered around like halfwits. All we meant was: thank God, we've escaped Granny with her metal laugh. Then we sat down in a row with our arms round our knees and stared at the water. Big brown waves falling like horses' manes, but gouging up handfuls of stone every time and flinging them about, even though it was a calm evening. There was no ssssh, ssssh like at Bideford where we went in the summer. Here everything was crash, crash. It was exhausting to listen.

4

Feeling different had a lot to do with thinking about death. Mum said it was morbid, which was a word I liked, but I could tell she thought it made me grown-up too, and that was what I wanted. Being a teenager didn't suit me; I needed to cut short this part of life and move on to the next, where I could decide for myself how I wanted to live. The trouble was, I didn't know much about dying. There'd been Great-granny Jessie – but she was ninety-four so of course she wasn't going to last much longer. Brookes and Mr Catchpole at school were more the kind of thing I meant – Brookes who was funny and popular, and kept a radio hidden in a book with a cut-out middle, but still got leukaemia and died; Mr Catchpole who walked as though he was being attacked by wasps; he'd told a boy he loved him, then killed himself when the boy turned him down. These deaths weren't natural like Jessie, they were terrible. Tragedies. All the same, part of me accepted them because they showed my instincts were right. If things could go wrong in life, they would. Unhappiness was stronger than happiness. Whenever people were having a good time, and laughing, and thinking they'd got away with something, misery was waiting to punish them for being stupid. That's what Brookes and Mr Catchpole proved. And now Granny Sunbeam proved it too, though in a different way.

5

On one of my trips to the Tate I'd seen a picture by Walter Sickert. It was long and thin, not the usual square shape, so looking at it gave me vertigo, as if I was falling off a cliff in a dream. That was all right. Vertigo was the subject, sort-of. Sickert had set up his easel in a huge old London theatre, a music hall probably, and painted the audience watching the stage. Amazing. He must have painted in the dark. There were shadows like curtains tumbling from top to bottom, and all around them, in between them, breaking them apart and joining them together again, he'd put splashes and dashes and splotches of gold light to pick up the faces and fancy hats, the furs and watch-chains, the warm skin. Not to mention the plaster everywhere – the smart boxes and tighter seats rising almost vertical into the ceiling, as if the whole place were really some kind of parliament, or the senate in Ancient Greece, or a meeting of fallen angels in Hell, deciding how they'd get back to Heaven.

That's what I was thinking when I sat down beside Michael waiting for the lights to fade. We were almost under the roof ourselves, and even though the cherubs on the ceiling looked clumsy in close-up, it didn't matter. Being here was what mattered. I was a step nearer my new life. I turned to face Michael, wanting to thank him, but he looked at me with a long face, his mouth hanging open a little. I could see his dead tooth, the grey one in the middle, and it made me realize how much I liked him. He wasn't my best friend exactly, but near enough; we were hitching to Greece together next summer. He was going to look after the money because he was sensible – but he was fun, too, and came smoking with me in Bagley Wood most afternoons at school, even though he was a prefect. What is it? he said. Nothing, I told him. Pleased we're here, that's all. He nodded, and as if it was a signal the lights went down. Good, he whispered. Just didn't want you to be worrying about your granny or anything.

6

The waves at Aldeburgh must be gentle sometimes, not always throwing stones around, because now the music had started it was like quiet water. Sunlit and glittery, more cobwebs than water, but steely too, unbreakable. Nothing can stop water, the notes were saying, it goes and comes back, goes and comes back, and when it's like this, peaceful, count your blessings because soon it'll change its mind and want to smash the world to pieces. In fact it would start doing that any minute, judging by the way darker waves were creeping under the bright ones; there would be a storm for sure, and that was because of what Peter was going to do to his boy, beating him and maybe worse; there would be a storm and the village would turn against Peter, which was understandable too, but cruel at the same time, all that gossiping and poisoning like in the village at home; more than cruel in fact, murderous, because in the end the sea which had been Peter's life was going to be his death. He was going to sail towards the horizon and drown.

7

That's what Michael had meant about Granny, of course. He didn't have to explain. I didn't have to say anything either – I'd already told him at school, which was where I'd first heard. I'd been lying in the bath after games – one of those revolting baths, where the water was like gravy speckled with grass-bits, because nobody could be bothered to change it, including me – and Bidwell had come in to say there was a telegram waiting for me on the noticeboard. My heart missed a few beats then calmed down: it couldn't be anything too bad because otherwise Mr Way would have asked me into his study and made me sit down then told me. So the telegram didn't mean my parents had been killed in a car accident. In fact I might even have won something. The Premium Bonds, for instance – I had a few of them, according to Dad. I hauled myself out of the water and picked the grass-bits off my skin before drying myself.

The telegram was from Mum; she wanted me to ring her at home. No clues, and no 'It's not serious, don't worry'. What did that mean? Dad? Not as bad as that. Maybe one of the dogs. I looked at my watch. There was half an hour before chapel, which meant I had time to ring now, immediately, in the cupboard by the dining hall, which was the only place we were allowed to make calls. Usually there was a queue, which I hated because people could hear what you were saying, and if they thought you were going on too long they rapped on the door with their money. Today I was in luck. Just some stig I didn't recognize, who hung up and scarpered when he saw me glaring through the glass.

Mum sounded out of breath. While she nipped through the usual How-are-you's and I-miss-you's, I thought it must be because she'd run indoors from the garden when she heard the telephone. But it wasn't that. She was nervous. I told myself not to worry. Of course she was nervous; she'd sent me a telegram hadn't she; she had something bad to say and didn't know how to start. 'What's the matter, Mum?' I asked in my grown-up voice, so she'd know I wasn't hurrying, just trying to be helpful. 'What's happened?'

It was about Granny Sunbeam, that was the first surprise – normally we didn't think about her much, except when we had to make one of our visits. Mum said Granny Sunbeam was dead, and she wanted me to know about it now, so I'd understand why Dad might sound upset when I next talked to him. Of course, I thought. He's bound to be upset. Granny Sunbeam was his mother, even if he didn't like her much. No, especially upset, Mum said, because this is what happened. Last Friday evening, during that bad weather, Granny drove from the cottage in Westleton to Dunwich, and parked in the carpark by the cliffs. I remembered the cliffs, didn't I, and the shed where we bought the ice creams? Yes, I said, and saw the silver mackerel again, gleaming through the windows of the church underwater. Well, Mum went on. After that nobody's quite sure what happened, but it looks as though Granny decided to go for a walk on the cliffs. I interrupted: in the dark, you mean, even though it was raining? That's the thing, Mum said, it's all very peculiar. It was raining, and the middle of the night, and probably Granny was a bit drunk. Anyway, she fell in the sea. That's how she died.

There was a pause, and the line bounced between us, as if crows were tightrope-walking somewhere between my ear and Essex. You mean she threw herself in the sea. There was another pause. That's another thing, said Mum, using a voice which wasn't quite her own, but more like someone my own age. It looks like that, but they've checked the cottage and there was no note. So the answer is: we don't know. The police are saying it was an accident, because otherwise things get complicated – something to do with her life insurance. If you ask me, she did chuck herself in. She was very unhappy, Granny, you could see that couldn't you? Always very unhappy. Poor her, though. And poor Dad.

Yes, I said slowly; poor Dad, but Mum didn't answer immediately. I thought of her standing by her desk in the sitting-room, with green light falling through the French window, and the dogs curled on the central heating vent, so the hot air blew straight onto their stomachs. It made me homesick, which I hadn't been for years. I'd been wrong about death making me grown-up. Death was frightening, that was all. Frightening and everywhere, even when I couldn't see it.

Are you there? Mum said suddenly. Yes I'm here, I said. Then, Hang on a minute. I opened the door of the phone-cupboard and found the stig I thought I'd scared off, leaning against the wall. He'd obviously been crying – his eyes were red, and there were orange smears on his cheeks. Was he homesick too, or had something worse happened? Maybe he was finding out about death as well. I smiled at him and mouthed I won't be long, and shut the door again. Mum? I said. I've got to go now, but I'll ring you later and we can finish then, OK? Are you all right darling, she said, dropping back into her normal voice, I haven't upset you have I? No, I said. It's just that I've got to go, that's all. I'll call before bed. Then I hung up and held the door open for the stig, closing it quietly behind him so he could see I was sorry.

8

What did people think about when they were listening to music? That had always bothered me. With rock 'n' roll it was easy – dancing was the main thing. But with opera? All that sitting still, not moving – wouldn't it be excruciating?

As things turned out, it was easy. Now the action had started, and the villagers were surging in and out of the pub in their long black coats and dresses, my brain had decided it knew exactly what to do. It was as though I'd been waiting to hear these sounds all my life, and already understood them. When the tarty nieces were tarty I laughed. When Bulstrode ordered people about I thought of Mr Saunders the church warden at home. When Ellen tried to help Peter it reminded me of Ruby, who'd been Mum's nurse when she was a girl. And when the hubbub suddenly died down, and Peter sang his lines about the Great Bear and the Pleiades, the whole universe ground to a halt on its axis, and the star-map of the heavens stretched clear and brilliant to infinity, drawing me into it like mist off the sea. It was the most beautiful sound I'd ever heard, and when I landed back in myself again, I realized my face was wet. I was crying! In an opera! I looked sideways at Michael, sliding my eyes into the corner of their sockets so I didn't have to move my head. He hadn't noticed, so that was OK. Was he crying too? No, but his mouth had dropped open, and the glow from the stage made his teeth look evenly white; I couldn't see the dead one.

I fixed my eyes back on the stage again, and waited for the tears to stop. They did, but the feeling that made them didn't. I'd been caught in a current that was going to carry me for miles, and only let go when it was good and ready. It was a kind of floating, like being asleep, but I was completely awake at the same time. Awake and crammed with thoughts – not like whether that note was a minim or a crotchet, or whether those were violins or cellos. Thoughts that were feelings. Elongated achy feelings when the music was pulled tight. Big clumsy feelings of sadness when Peter blundered from bad to worse. He was trapped in himself – the music was telling me that, with its overlapping circles. It didn't matter how beautiful it sounded, because beauty didn't help. Everything Peter had ever done, all his hopes and chances and accidents and unkindness – they were being gathered together into a gigantic wave that was about to thunder down and obliterate him. There was no escape. The only question was: could he go under still feeling he had some goodness left?

9

I rang Mum later that same evening, after prep, when most boys had gone to their dormitories and the corridor outside the phone-cupboard didn't have a queue, just supper-smells and dead echoes. She said Dad was home now, watching telly in the sitting-room, so she couldn't be long. That was all right, I told her, there probably wasn't much more to say; I just wanted her to know I was sorry I'd had to rush off earlier – it wasn't because I was upset. It seemed easier that way, not speaking to Dad directly, and I expected Mum to say Yes, of course, and leave it at that. But she said Poor Dad again, in the same voice she'd used earlier – dramatic. I know, I began, but she cut me off. They didn't find Granny's body for nearly a week. They knew she was missing, but they didn't know where. Eventually the sea spewed her up, miles down the coast. And you know what the sea does to people when they've been in it for a while, don't you? Mum paused, not long enough for me to say anything, then hurried on. It takes all their clothes off and blows them up like balloons. That's what made it especially tough for Dad. He had to go and identify the body. It was in Ipswich, in a morgue by the ring road. Can you imagine? It wasn't a real question, or not one Mum wanted me to answer, so I kept quiet, staring at the wall of the phone room. Someone had scratched a swastika in the black paint by the A button. Dad would hate that, I thought. He'd fought the war, and watched his friends being killed, then sent me to a school where someone thought a swastika was OK. Don't tell him you told me about the morgue, I said eventually, and Mum promised she wouldn't. After we'd said goodnight and hung up, I realized I hadn't asked about the funeral. That must have happened already, but they'd obviously decided I was too young.

10

It was nearly finished now, and I knew what was going to happen. But the strange thing was, I wasn't a hundred per cent sure. Why was that? Because I felt sorry for Peter, and didn't want him to die, and thought maybe the director felt sorry for him too and would change the ending. But of course that wasn't going to happen. We'd all seen Peter walloping the boy, and heard the boy scream when he fell through the wall of the hut on the cliff, onto the stones below. That meant there would have to be punishment. Even so, Peter was like the monster in *Frankenstein*, which I'd read last term: his badness wasn't all his own fault. If the villagers knew that they were keeping quiet about it – all except Ellen. They were just standing and watching, while he sailed his boat towards the horizon. Standing, and watching, and swaying as their voices sank and the music took over.

I closed my eyes and let it carry me. I saw the boat scrape down the flint shelf at Aldeburgh, swing round as the wind filled its sail, then straighten into the brightness with Peter standing in the stern to untangle the anchor. In a minute, when he was far enough out to sea, he was going to smash a hole in the hull and the boat would sink. He was almost ready now, turning to look at the shore for the last time. There was the line of brown shingle with a lavender haze behind it, and there was the cliff at Dunwich. I closed my eyes tighter and the weather changed, the sky darkened, and Granny Sunbeam swerved through the rain into the carpark by the fishing hut, then scrambled up the cliff wearing her shiny black fisherman's coat. Mum had said there was no note, but there didn't have to be. Everything was written down in her head. Her marriage. Her running away. Her children. My father's anger. Our shadowy visits. She wasn't a monster, and no one had died. But there was too much unhappiness. I watched her step towards the edge of the cliff and lean into the wind. She was waiting for the silence to break, and the drowned church bells to reach her through the water. Nothing. She put her hands to both ears, the rain running down her fingers and into her sleeves. Nothing again, not even the waves. Then applause.

Forget My Fate
Marina Warner

I

Someone was standing in the middle of the road when Barbara
May left her house to walk in the opposite direction towards
the corner shop, but her steps were drawn to the knot of tension
tightening in the street and the mounting noise of the stalled
traffic. Then she saw that the commotion was caused by Lello,
Lello Sanvitale, her neighbour, and a kind of friend from the
school where he used to teach music and where she was still
teaching classics. He was airily tickling one driver with an
index finger to brighten his rhythm, then patting another to
slow her to an andante. Barbara began waving to him from
the pavement, trying to bring him over out of the mêlée, but
he was alight with excitement as he turned this way and that,
now sweeping his arm over the traffic on the downhill run, now
chivvying the other stream that was grinding up the incline.

That stretch of the rise to Highgate is a bad boy's dare to
cross, a death sentence for the elderly: a bus route and a thor-
oughfare for heavy freight, with residents' cars parked on both
sides, and she saw that Lello Sanvitale was beginning to lurch

and twist as drivers started to hoot at him, leaning out of their windows and shouting. He paid no attention to them or to Barbara's beckonings. Flecks of sweat and spittle flew around him; his gestures were choppy and loose, windmilling with clownish heaviness. But he plunged on, his eyes half-closed, his sparse hair, a tangerine glow, awry.

At first, Barbara laughed. The drivers could have responded with a foot on the accelerator, wipers sawing, tootles and blasts, dips and swells of their radios as if playing a piece by Steve Reich. But she began to realize that the trouble which had begun to show at school towards the end of Lello's time there, the garbled words, erratic timekeeping and sudden blanks, now had him in its grip, and the mood in the road was turning ugly.

She was staff at a former Direct Grant school that had become an Independent, but Lello was supply; he'd come in now and then to give music lessons – piano, chiefly, but he'd also stand in as choirmaster and conductor. He didn't have papers or formal qualifications; all had been lost, he said, in the many upheavals in his life. So the school never gave him a secure position.

When the cars eventually halted long enough for Barbara to make her way to him and fetch him to the safety of the pavement, he didn't know who she was. He was stained, and she smelled the staleness off him; he'd painted his eyebrows in crookedly. His shirt stuck to his chest in dark patches; the tangerine showed white at the roots against his hennaed, flaking scalp. Lello, the immaculately manicured musician with his signet ring of carnelian engraved with his name in Arabic script and his brushed careful suits made by a tailor in Cairo – his name was inked on the inside of the breast pocket he had once turned out for Barbara to read – was dandified in an old-fashioned way. Everyone took him for gay, and she knew he would be ashamed if he knew the state he was in.

She coaxed him back to the house where he occupied the top flat, which, he always sighed, was sad for his cat, sitting in the upstairs window gazing at birds in flight in the trees. In earlier days the two of them had often talked together there after school, once they'd discovered in the staffroom one day that they were such close neighbours. Both her children were grown and Desmond her husband didn't miss her, unless she was very late. So she'd dawdle behind with Lello, drinking Turkish coffee like toffee in thimbles while he played her old LPs until she began to think crackle was part of the music, enhancing flaws in a master's ceramics, and she learned how he'd grown up among the long-rooted Italian–Jewish community in Egypt that his parents joined when they emigrated with his sister and himself, then a tiny baby, from Ancona in 1935 to avoid the Fascists.

'They could sense it coming,' he said. 'Like dogs howling long before the earthquake gives its first rumble.' And he jerked his head back and howled, but in a throaty hiss; then brought his face close to hers and grimaced. That was when Barbara first glimpsed the disorder that was already breaking up his mind.

The family settled among other Italians in Cleopatra, a suburb of Alexandria. 'But it wasn't anything like the name suggests – it was a poor suburb. It was a "sink estate".' Lello laughed. 'The women left to become nannies for the families of the rich in Cairo. Nannies, and sometimes, Pappa's...well, you know what – his *trick*.' Lello's English was pretty fluent, but he picked up the odd incongruous word or turn of phrase from his pupils.

Lello looked Italian and moved his body like an Italian, as if his feet and hands were small and light, though in fact he had pianist's hands with strongly developed muscular pads to the thumb and on the palm. He'd first come to London in the wake of Suez. 'Foreigners' businesses were gradually closed down, one by one, and my father had a small draper's shop nearer the centre of Alexandria – but all assets were being frozen, property seized, no matter how small. We weren't posh – no way. But it made no difference.'

The evening Barbara found him conducting the traffic, she left him at the door. She couldn't face the state she suspected prevailed in his flat, if it were only half as frowsy as he was. She made some excuse about not going in. He turned his face to hers, full square, and she quailed from the blind milkiness in his blue eyes threaded with red. But then something clicked and came into shape behind them and he mouthed her name, 'Barbara, Barbara May,' slowly, and then added, 'teaches the girls and boys about Dido and Aeneas...' His look fell slowly to her lips, and he sung almost soundlessly a thin line of a melody she did not know.

Barbara shivered; it reminded her of the time she'd met a parrot, and the bird's black tongue played between the two hooked nebs of its beak and pecked at her coquettishly.

Her hand flew to her own mouth to cover it, and she turned and almost broke into a run.

When Lello alluded to a wife in the past and mentioned children, Barbara assumed they were all long behind him, part of a world of custom and opinion when protestations of heterosexuality were necessary to survival. But after he died, a note arrived from someone who identified herself without further explanation as his daughter. Written on a scrap of paper, the note said simply, 'Dear Barbara, Your name is on a list my father left among his effects on his desk. He specifically wanted you to have the enclosed.

'Enjoy!'

The envelope had arrived by hand. There was no return address. She must have been clearing his flat. Had she rung the doorbell? Barbara wouldn't know, and anyhow, she'd probably been at school.

Inside, there was a plain brown folder with a single phrase pencilled on the cover, almost like a doodle, 'Elissa–Cairo, 1950'.

Holding the folder in her hands, she had a flash: she'd been talking to Lello, grizzling in the staff room about teaching Virgil to sixteen-year-olds, when Lello said, 'Try playing them *Dido and Aeneas*, the last lament, with the great, incomparable Flagstad – Kirsten Flagstad. Surely then, Barbara, even the hardest of hard nuts will begin to...' his hand passed over his heart, 'to feel. To feel something happening inside. They act tough, but they're not that tough.'

'You don't know the half of it.'

When Barbara first taught Virgil, the class used to snigger and even blush at the cataract of Dido's passion and then her fury. Now the intensity of her love made them snort. They laughed in disbelief that she felt she had to kill herself. Brutally, they wanted her to turn on her lover, kill him instead.

'When she sings, "Remember me, but ah! forget my fate," Dido is right, you know,' Lello went on.

'Yes! She doesn't want anyone to suffer afterwards on her account. She's thinking of us.'

'No, no,' cried Lello, and when he became excited his Italian tones came back more pronouncedly. 'We must forget all that. None of that happened like that – it's all Virgil's invention.'

Barbara was discomfited; he was showing how much he

knew, and about her subject. Stiffly, she interrupted him: 'Dido says that because she's ashamed. She's disgraced in the eyes of society and of her world. She isn't really married at all. It's an old story – she's been tricked like a silly goose of a girl. That's what she wants us to forget.'

'But nothing in it is true. Not a word of it. Roman slanders. Official lies. Politics. Piety...'

'Stories and poems don't have to be true!' Barbara was now sure of her ground. 'In fact, they'd be very dull if they followed history – so, good for Virgil, if he did make up such a terrific, tragic love affair!'

'"I think you'll recognize this,"' Lello replied. 'That's what the storyteller must always say to the listener to capture his atten- tion. Or, "Do you recognise this?" Virgil brings off this great stroke of recognition because his Dido suffers what everyone longs to suffer, extreme passion. It's an ideal state, to love more than one's loved in return. Ah! to be *sedotta e abbandonata*...of course it is.' He laughed, quietly, and went on, 'But you can push a story in other directions – ones that are less frenzied. Not quite so familiar from the epics and the tragedies. Ordinary moments of love and satisfaction and happiness. The big epic poets don't bother with those. They like Dido dead or dying. Widow Dido. Dead as a Dodo Dido.

'Her real name, as you know, was Elissa.'

Lello's notion that Virgil's tragedy was somehow clichéd made Barbara very cross.

'Virgil loves her being crazy, unleashed, and bent on destruc- tion,' Lello was going on, 'destructive of herself and others – don't you think? He loves making us watch her throw herself into the flames.'

'That's unfair! We're on her side,' Barbara protested. 'The

poem is with her in her passion against Aeneas' duty. Virgil makes her magnificent, powerful, and tragic. And when we glimpse her later, in Hades, that's one of the most haunting moments in all of literature, surely? Virgil doesn't admire Aeneas for abandoning her the way he does. He can't help making us feel a kind of... contempt for his hero, that perfect specimen of the repressed English public schoolboy, compelled by duty, out of touch with his feelings.'

'Virgil had Egypt in mind,' Lello had also said in the course of that conversation, making a sour face as he tasted the cafeteria coffee they were having together in the lunch break at school. 'Dido is an Oriental queen, and you know Oriental queens are bad news.'

Before the close of that conversation, Barbara had wanted to get away, but Lello laid his hand on hers. 'One day,' he said, 'we'll talk about Elissa, the true Dido, before Virgil got to her.'

She didn't pull her hand away, though she was uneasily aware of its pressure.

Even so, in spite of her irritation, Barbara tried out Lello's idea in her class: she turned on the overhead projector, and an image of Elizabeth Taylor floated on the screen, her eyebrows in arcs like swallows' wings, her eyes like birds with eyeliner tails; she was wearing the cobra diadem.

'Virgil is writing for his Emperor,' she began. 'For Augustus, the very same Augustus who, when he was younger, defeated Cleopatra, Queen of Egypt, Cleopatra who was having a scandalous love affair with Mark Antony, the great hero of Republican Rome – you know the story.' Most of the classicists were doing English Literature too, and she could count on some of them knowing Shakespeare's play.

'And what happened? Mark Antony made a fatal move at the Battle of Actium. He turned back his ships to follow the Queen – to follow Cleopatra – because he saw her apparently quitting the scene. And all for love!'

More images materialized of Egypt: triremes and lighthouses, tasselled flails and amuletic sceptres, triple-tiered mitres on high-shaven foreheads, lapis lazuli talismans and opulent cosmetics, obelisks, ibis, pyramids, dhows. Barbara projected this pageant of Oriental sexiness and allure, and the class began to look; some of them began commenting, in an undertone. She caught the name of Amy Winehouse whispered, and a reference to extravagant eyeliner.

'Virgil was writing for—' she continued, 'no, he was *sucking up* to that very same Augustus Caesar who had defeated Antony and Cleopatra. Before Mark Antony got to Egypt, Julius Caesar, who was Augustus' adoptive father, was also seduced by Cleopatra – turned into another plaything. But he managed to get away. *He* didn't idle and kiss his kingdom away with an African Queen.

'You can see why Oriental female rulers were a danger in the minds of Romans. Cleopatra was a dangerous woman – *the* femme fatale of history. Virgil was modelling his dangerous woman on her – and saving his hero from her clutches.

'Look through Dido and what do you see? Cleopatra.'

Barbara thought of Cleopatra killing herself, of the asp and its poison. Of Cleopatra, fierce and proud, who won't live on in shame – she would never have allowed herself to be captured and paraded as her sister had been in Julius Caesar's triumph. Cleopatra's erotic energy beat under the surface of Dido, rich, hospitable, decadent, pleasure-loving, and smitten.

'In Dido's case, Virgil shows another queen from the African shore killing herself. Dido's mad passion's made her forget her promises and her dignity. It corrupted her, and she feels utterly degraded. Of course it's the fault of the gods and goddesses, especially of Venus and Juno. But that doesn't mitigate the shame.'

She was trying to make her class imagine a time when a love affair would lose you the respect of your whole world.

Lello had said, 'There's another story, you know.'

So at work Lello Sanvitale had been someone she considered an ally, fussy and a bit of a know-all, but a 'good citizen' as the phrase went, who'd take on any task he could manage – and show grace in doing so. At rehearsals of the school orchestra, Lello would treat the tone-deaf player on the triangle with as much courtesy as the first violins.

There were some letters in the folder, still in their envelopes lined with blue tissue paper and addressed in a hesitant hand with curly capitals and lots of loops, the script of someone who does not write very much. The stamps were Egyptian. She held the bundle close to her nose, expecting the perfume of an expensive milieu, jasmine and Turkish cigarettes, but London damp from Lello's cupboard had overlaid them with a mushroomy bloom. Underneath it were some sheets of a text, a carbon copy of something composed on an old typewriter, and several closely written pages of a score.

The first letter was signed in clear letters Banou Zafarin; it was dated 25 March 1949, and was written in French: Barbara could grasp that she was inviting Lello to meet her the following day to discuss the musical idea he had submitted to His Majesty for consideration. She gathered that King Farouk was going to turn thirty the following year, and Lello was offering to compose something to celebrate the birthday. His correspondent was polite but eager; she talked of her two daughters, Lello's pupils in piano and musical harmony; of her husband who had been very musical, with a wide repertory, and how she herself loved to play, but wasn't gifted like *feu* M. Zafarin. Her husband's brother was now her guardian and the responsible man in the life of her girls, and he was in a position of some influence at court – hence the indirect approach Lello was attempting.

Mme Zafarin referred rather often to this second M. Zafarin, Abdel, her *beau-frère*; it was clear that he did not share the qualities of her own beloved husband, the first M. Zafarin, whom she had so sadly lost the year before to a congestion of the lungs.

Nostalgia for the days when *Aida* was created for the opening of the Suez Canal seeped from the letters Mme Zafarin was writing to Lello; she hankered after the splendour of Mohammed Ali's festivities, when the Khedivial Opera House greeted the *haut ton* who flowed to Cairo as his guests, no expenses spared. No matter that Verdi lagged behind with the commission and failed to complete the score for the night, or that the costumes and sets didn't arrive in time – a tradition had been established in Egypt. Italian opera, Italian lavishness of spectacle and passion.

In her tentative hand, Mme Banou Zafarin informed the *cher maître*, Lello, that his idea had been received with interest at the Palace and the *beau-frère* would be soon raising it with the splendid young King.

The messages Mme Zafarin sent Lello were formal and reticent on the face of it. Each of them began, without variation, '*Cher maître*' and never progressed to Lello or even M. Sanvitale; but the phrase began to acquire a skittish, ironic tone, as if it were becoming a pet name between them. For beneath the courtly phrasing and necessary decorum, Barbara could sense excitement growing: the rhythm of their sending (the first twelve letters arriving in as many days) conveyed how Banou Zafarin was glimpsing the chance of something igniting. Her writing became more rapid and fluid as her hopes mounted that something – that Lello's plan would lift the stultifying round of her existence beyond ladies' lunches and wealthy widows' charity dos.

Barbara had agreed with Lello that they would have another Dido–Cleopatra conversation, another time. But that time never came. Rumours about his forgetfulness grew, his air of worn-out cosmopolitanism became a reproach, as if he were posted at the school gates, begging. There were stains on his forlorn tie. An inspector recommended restructuring, and Lello's arrangement, such as it was, wasn't renewed.

'Dido,' Lello had said to Barbara. 'Dead Dido. Widow Dido... her real name, you know, was Elissa.'

II

Elissa, ou Le Triomphe d'Afrique
Epopée Lyrique en Six Tableaux
Dramatis Personae

Elissa, reine de Tyre...................................*Mlle. Amina Zafarin (soprano)*
Sichée, son mari, grand prêtre du temple d'Hercule...à suivre (mezzo-soprano)
Pygmalion, son frère.................*Mlle Zubayda Zafarin (mezzo-soprano)*
Iarbes, roi de Mauritanie, prétendant d'Elissa........................*(la même)*
Anna, la soeur d'Elissa.....................................*à suivre (soprano)*
Assassins, Tyriens; Mauritaniens; Carthaginiens; vierges et nymphes;
courtisans et suivantes etc. etc...............*Ensemble des choeurs des*
écoles du Caire et d'Alexandrie

So: no Aeneas, and a *school* production, with the principal roles given to two girls, surely the daughters of Lello's correspondent.

A synopsis followed, two closely typewritten pages on sheeny, ancient onionskin.

> *1ér tableau: Sichée abattu au temple – Intérieur d'un vaste*
> *temple en rond* – interior of a vast, round temple – play of
> reflections on the walls and ceiling reveals the invisible presence
> of the sea beyond – it is midsummer and moonrise – murmuring
> under the palm trees – we are in the temple of Hercules in Tyre
> – Sichaeus presiding at solemn sacrifices – Enter Elissa –
> her sister Anna with her—

A trio was to follow, in which Elissa, her husband, and Anna exchange pledges of their love of one another, of their country and its gods, and evoke the Phoenicians' prowess. This was the first melody in the piano score, Barbara realized, a melancholy sweet tune in D minor.

But the idyllic harmony in Tyre was soon to be devastated:

> – two assassins enter silent and hooded, fall upon Sichaeus
> with poniards drawn, and kill him on the steps of the altar
> (key change from D minor to F sharp major). As invisibly and
> as furtively as they appeared, they steal away – great and
> terrible sorrow of the women – and lamentation from the chorus
> – ('*Sombre destin*', tutti, C minor)

Interleaved, Barbara found a note:

> 'The story so far: in Tyre – principal city of the ocean-going
> Phoenicians – one of the richest kingdoms (gold, skills, maps)

– home of the alphabet – the king is dying – Elissa his heir – her brother Pygmalion enraged – passing on power in the female line is barbaric (aria, mezzo – your younger daughter Madame has a deeper timbre than her sister) – declares it a custom no longer to be followed...

'Dido of poetry = Elissa in history – Elissa NOT one who gives up in despair – Elissa a strategist – founder of a nation – a North African nation – like Ulysses also condemned to wander she is *polymetis* – Elissa of the many devices – a survivor – *bref*, a new woman (tall – graceful – intelligent).'

2ème tableau: Le trésor des Phéniciens – Elissa knows it was her brother who ordered her husband's murder – but dissimulates to protect herself and her allies – grief now moves her to abdicate (aria: *'Le goût amer des cendres...'*) – she has offered up all her treasure to the gods to obtain knowledge of his assassins' identity – again she is deceiving him – she quits the stage – Pygmalion savours his triumph (aria F major: *'Le soleil de ma gloire se lève...'*) – meanwhile Elissa in secret prepares her escape – smuggles out her wealth – loads ships in the harbour –

3ème tableau: The Departure for the West: Anna and a group of followers board the ships at night – Elissa will found a new empire to the west – in Africa – a grand chorus of hope – (*tutti fffff: 'Afrique, Afrique! Je rêve de vos douceurs, du vent qui balance les palmiers, du soleil qui caresse vos côtes...'*)

The passage was marked in the margin: *'C'est très bien! J'aime beaucoup!'*

4ème tableau: La plage à Cythère – the island of Aphrodite – young
women, handmaidens in the temple of the Goddess, come down
to the beach to greet the Tyrian fleet – baskets of fruit and ewers
of spring water to rinse their salt-caked limbs – to soothe the
sting of sun and wind – hibiscus and jasmine – they are singing a
sweet traditional ballad, a simple tune, ballad-like (NO vibrato)
– Elissa sees the gay company milling on the beach – resting
in the shade – she knows that her new city will need children
– she invites all the young priestesses of the Goddess to come
to Africa—

General rejoicing – a full chorus of sailors, courtiers, islanders,
etc. joins the female voices to consecrate their venture to the
goddess of marriage...

At this point, when the Queen cheerfully takes on board all
the sailors' sweethearts to populate Carthage, Mme Zafarin's
occasional marginal comments took a different turn:

– *Mais, non non, Monsieur, quand-même, vous rigolez!* She proposed instead that the young girls should be played as peris
and nymphs. 'This would be much more appropriate for *des
jeunes filles bien élevées,* and besides the costumes will be much
more attractive.'

5ème tableau: The foundation of Carthage – they reach
Carthage – Iarbas meets them at the head of massed troops of
Mauritanians – a gorgeous sight (your daughter will be splendid
and amuse herself greatly in the role) – Elissa asks for land for
her city – the extent covered by an ox hide – merriment among
the Mauritanians – Iarbas grants it willingly – the famous
episode – the Queen takes the sharpest of blades and pares the
edge of the leather so finely that working continuously round

and round the hide she achieves a string – and pegs out a plot with a sea shore and a harbour – this will be the emplacement of Carthage – centre of the new empire that will defy Rome – that will stand up to the west.

The chieftain marvels – her skill, her cunning, her authority – he falls in love.

Finale (6ème tableau): Elissa has refused Iarbas – she promises to marry but only when she has finished mourning Sychaeus – this time might never come – Iarbas grows fretful, complains.

Duet: Elissa protesting, Iarbas wooing (*'O doux souvenir du temps passé des noces...'*)

– But Elissa is herself tricked when her people remind her that she has asked them all to promise they will do anything for the new city that is necessary to its flourishing.

'Marry,' they beseech her. 'Marry Iarbas.' She is cornered – she laughs.

Wedding March (*allegro vivace*): Triumph of Elissa in Africa.

III

This Dido Lello Sanvitale had invented – this triumphant Delilah, Judith, Armida, Amazon, and Wonder Woman all rolled into one – made Barbara May smile as she stood in her kitchen with the folder open on the table.

To her husband she explained, when he came in that evening, that unaccountably she, who couldn't play the piano or sing a note, had been left a score of an unperformed opera by a colleague who had died that year. She added that he was 'That Egyptian – with the carroty dyed hair—'

Desmond looked vague, but when Barbara frowned, said, 'Ah,

yes, indeed I do. Left you something, did he? How very nice.'

'Can't think why,' said Barbara, fighting impatience.

Lello's bare-faced flattery of the Fuad dynasty was pretty sickening, she thought, but even so, had there ever been a smidgeon of a chance that Lello could have written the opera he was outlining? Or that the work could have been produced at all, let alone in a girls' school in Egypt during the last gasp of the reign of King Farouk?

– 'Cher monsieur,' wrote Mme Zafarin, 'Je vous remercie de votre partition qui vient d'arriver, et ce matin de bonne heure j'ai commencé à jouer... La musique est bien jolie mais...' She needed a fellow player, she wrote, as Lello had composed the piano medley for four hands and so far, even under his tuition, her daughters were not quite able to play his work.

Barbara looked again at the score – and there it was, another pair of hands was involved – the piano piece was a duet, with Lello the teacher taking the harder part, the student at his side on his right the less demanding.

She thought back to the times Lello had invited her in, charmed her at his table with his records, his conversation, his wine, his coffee. Had she missed something?

But then she paused – she was a woman who did not like to imagine things.

'The idea of taking a picnic in the desert during the interval before the last act begins is very tempting,' wrote Mme Zafarin. 'We should see whether His Royal Highness' birthday coincides with the full moon. However I do not think, Monsieur, that you should place so much emphasis on what you term "the glorious history of feminine influence and female power in this north-ern part of Africa". After all, we shall be celebrating the King's birthday, not his sisters'!'

Then Barbara found another letter, the last in the series.

'*Cher maitre, Je regrette...*' Banou Zafarin was leaving Cairo for the summer to spend it at her house in the country – far from the whirl of the city where her *beau-frère* was however detained on palace business. It was too hot to stay in town, she said. She included a vague invitation. 'If you yourself happen to be in Alexandria this summer, you will be able to find me with the children on the beach at Sidi Basr 2', and she gave an address.

'PS I am having our piano brought from Cairo so that my girls will be able to keep up their practice.'

Did Mme Zafarin mean something particular when she wrote that it was beginning to get too hot in town? Did Lello find a way of joining her for the summer in Alexandria? Of continuing the piano lessons? It seemed that that was where their contact on the page came to a close. And when something else began?

Madame Zafarin was testing the ground very cautiously in her letters as Lello coaxed a melody from the exchanges she allowed him, and together perhaps they managed to compose music that was different from the piece in the folder he had left Barbara – or at least, she thought, as she felt the sharp prick of opportunities missed, that was what he had wanted her to see.

IV

When Barbara and Lello had talked, either in the common room at the school or in his flat after teaching, she'd always felt the need to get away from him: work, home, her own routine, friends and family called to her in a kind of *obbligato* pulsing away under whatever tune Lello was playing. She realized that even though she liked being with him, he'd never really counted for much in her life – or, rather, she had never noticed that he did count. His attention flattered her and did not reach her at any depths at all. Which is why she could leave him at the door after she found him in the street that last time she saw him.

Then she began to remember more things about him, how he liked to say, 'Think of the world, think of your world, like a band. Everyone in the band is different. Every one has a different voice. But together you can express something effectively. You can charm us – as well as yourselves, hold us captive to what you are playing. Make that moment mean something that is not like the rest of life, that is not dull.'

She began to see something in herself that was uncomfortable in a different way from her moments of uneasy contact with him when he was alive. Lello had presented her with a design that didn't possess familiar features; the plot he was living in wasn't one she recognized. He had said to her, '"You might recognize this,"' and she'd failed to do so. She had taken him for one thing; or rather, she'd mistaken him. And so she was now beginning to feel the pang of unattained intimacies. It would all be so much easier, thought Barbara May, if you could direct your own life's affections the way you can make up a story and move the characters in it, change their ways of behaving and modify their feelings, stretching them according to your highest ideals of what you might be capable of feeling yourself. But something inside you stays fixed and stubborn, and unlike a story, won't let itself be prodded and shaped. But then not all stories are supple. Perhaps Dido's usual story, Virgil's great tragic queen, is recognizably close to everyone's experience: as Lello remarked, it's the fate of us all to love more than we are loved in return. Recognizing a particular story does add to its pleasure: it's safe too, it's home. Funny that tragic self-killing should be such a place of satisfaction, of comfort.

Maybe there is an alternative story – one that isn't so compelling, she thought, but one that fits closely if not obviously to another kind of experience, a little more commonplace, with a happy ending. That story also invites us to enter: 'I think you'll recognize this.'

V

Hesitantly, Barbara showed the score of the duet to the school Music Director; when he tried it out on the piano (she had to nudge him), he was intrigued – much to his surprise. He began mentioning it to friends. One of these, a trombonist who lived with someone involved with arts funding, showed it in turn to the director of the Kempley Music Festival. The programme he was planning for the summer included a strand, 'Cross-currents: East Meets West', and it was to feature other works by composers from countries along the shores of the Mediterranean, Arab, Israeli, et al., including some of the earliest electronic music written by a compatriot of Lello's, Halim El-Dabh (who had won first prize in the Piano competition at the Cairo Opera House in 1942 and had known Lello then). So the director copied the score to the celebrated P. sisters, the star performers of the 2008 season, and Yvette and Tanya P. were captivated: besides, they had Algerian roots, for one set of grandparents were born in Oran. The *Suite Levantine* was full of poignancy and sweetness, of life and laughter, of fun and mischief, they said; it was flirtatious; it had some of Busoni's architecture and melancholy, of Poulenc's ironic wit and Satie's playful spirit. But it also had its own chromatic harmonies and its own pulse, in which they could detect something definitely non-European.

'*Six Chansons d'Egypte, or Suite Levantine*' by Lello Sanvitale received its première at the Kempley Music Festival on June 25 2008. Barbara May was invited to contribute a note to the Festival programme. She found it difficult, and struck out one line after another. When the deadline arrived, she sent what still seemed to her awkward, vapid clichés. But she couldn't find another way.

'Lello Sanvitale was an unforgettable character,' she began, 'with what used to be known as a mysterious past, some of which infuses the musical compositions which he was too modest to talk about and bring to our attention when he was alive. The *Six Chansons* were first discovered among his papers after his death, half a century since they were first written but as fresh as if conceived yesterday.' She went on to give some background for the story of Elissa, 'the other Dido', and the opera that never was.

The Albanians
Alexander McCall Smith

'It's one of the silliest of Mozart's operas,' said Mark. 'In fact, it's *the* silliest, without a shadow of doubt.'

His friend, Hugh, fiddled with a rubber band that he had twisted about his fingers. '*Così fan tutte?*' he said. 'Actually, I must admit I love it. We saw it at Glyndebourne, you know. One of those wonderful evenings when you might die and go to heaven and find that heaven is just like the place you've left. No difference. A seamless transition.'

'I've always had a bit of trouble with heaven,' said Mark. 'The same trouble that I have with hell, now that I come to think of it.' He glanced at the twanging rubber band. 'The music is fine in *Così*, but the story...well, it's absurd, isn't it? Two lovers testing the constancy of their girlfriends – fiancées really – all to satisfy a bet with a cynic. And dressing up as Serbians, of all things, to test them.'

'No. Albanians. They dress up as Albanians.'

'Albanians, then. Ridiculous. Do you think for a moment that any woman would be fooled for a moment if her boyfriend dressed up as an Albanian? Do you imagine that it would work?'

They were both silent for a moment. He had intended the question to be rhetorical; but it was more than that.

'Actually...' Hugh began.

Mark would have none of it. 'No, it wouldn't. It just wouldn't work.'

'You don't think so?'

'No.'

Hugh looked out of the window at the Edinburgh landscape. The city sloped away from them to the north, and beyond that the hills of Fife were shrouded now with veils of rain. He had called in to see his friend on the way to the wine bar where he was due to meet his girlfriend, Rose. Rose lived in Glasgow and came to Edinburgh for weekends. She was friendly, as it happened, with Lottie, who was Mark's girlfriend of several years' standing. Everybody thought that Mark and Lottie were ideally suited and would marry in due course. They also thought that about Hugh and Rose, but perhaps not as strongly as they thought it about Mark and Lottie. Rose, they felt, would be more difficult to tie down. Hugh certainly thought that. Rose, he had once confided to Mark, has certain, unspecified *commitment issues.*

'I'm not absolutely sure about her,' he had said. 'She blows hot and cold. Most of the time I feel quite secure with her, but then on other occasions, I feel that she wouldn't find it hard to leave me.'

Mark looked thoughtful. 'If somebody better-looking came along?'

Hugh frowned. 'Do you think I'm not good-looking enough for her?'

Mark laughed, but it was a nervous laugh. 'No, there's nothing wrong with you. You're...you're fine. It's just that I thought that maybe *you* thought that. I don't know of course.'

What he could not say, of course, was that he thought that Rose was exactly the sort of girl who would be swayed by something as superficial as good looks. And poor Hugh; he had many merits, but he was hardly glamorous. Solid, yes; reliable, exceptionally so; but not the sort of man one could describe as glamorous.

'Well, you may be right,' said Hugh. 'I don't really know. But there's no way of telling, is there?'

But now, in the middle of this conversation about *Così fan tutte*, it occurred to him that perhaps there was a way of finding out – a way which would enable one to test both fidelity and the operatic proposition that a lover could never be fooled if one were to disguise oneself as an Albanian, or anybody else for that matter.

'I've had an idea,' he said to Mark. 'Isn't it Geoffrey's thirtieth birthday party coming up? And I seem to remember your saying something about organizing his party for him. Is that still on?'

Mark nodded. 'That's the general idea. I haven't done anything to arrange it yet, but I'll get round to it. It's still six weeks away.'

'Make it a fancy dress party,' said Hugh quickly.

'Aren't we a bit old for that?'

'For fancy dress? Certainly not. It's very fashionable. Look at the glossy mags. They're full of fancy dress parties. Extravagant occasions.'

Mark stared at his friend. Was he really imagining that they would mount some sort of Mozartian love test?

'I'm serious,' said Hugh. 'I've been unsettled for a long time. I've suppressed my doubts, I've told myself that I'm imagining things, that it's all down to groundless insecurity on my part. But I do feel insecure. I do doubt her. I'm sorry, but I can't help it.'

Mark was gentle. 'All right, I understand what you feel. Rose is a very attractive woman. She could easily get a man who was more...' He stopped himself. He had been about to say that Rose could easily find a more attractive, more desirable man that Hugh, but that would not have been tactful. So he tailed off, leaving his comment unfinished, and thereby lending to it a far greater potency than it would otherwise have had.

The argument so far: Two young men, Mark and Hugh, are in love with two young women. Mark is in love with Lottie, while Hugh is in love with Rose, whom he suspects to be fickle. He has no evidence of this, however, and when Mark mentions the unlikely plot of a Mozart opera, he decides to dress up as an Albanian in order to test Rose's constancy.

'An Albanian?' said the woman in the fancy dress agency. 'Are you sure that's what you want? We've got pirates and sea captains and...well just about everything, but Albanians, I'm not so sure...' She paused. 'What do Albanians actually wear?'

Hugh smiled. 'Well, I use it just as an illustration, really. I don't really require anything specific. It's just that in Mozart's Così fan tutte two men dress up as Albanians in order to deceive...' He trailed off. The young woman behind the counter was staring at him intently. There were some people, Hugh reminded himself, who did not think allusively. Young men in computer shops fell into that category generally, but there were others.

'What I need,' he said, 'is something that will really disguise me. Something with a beard, for instance. And a wig, perhaps.' He thought for a moment. If Rose's head was to be turned, then he *would need to have something dashing. He looked about him in desperation. This encounter was becoming embarrassing.*

'Here's something,' said the woman, reaching for a box behind her. 'It just came in. You see these green trousers here and this shirt. And we've got plenty of beards and wigs. No problem there.'

'Wonderful,' said Hugh quickly. 'Actually, that's an Albanian costume, as it happens. I'm pretty sure of it.'

With the box tucked under his arm, he went out into the street. The shop was on the High Street, and as he walked back up towards the Bridges a man in an elegantly tailored dark suit walked down towards the Parliament in the other direction. Behind him a teenager dressed entirely in black, his face studded with piercings, his hair slicked down over his forehead, his thin legs encased in the most clinging of trousers, provided the sharpest of contrasts. We all dress up, thought Hugh, all the time; we profess our social and aesthetic allegiances in the simple act of donning clothes. Yet clothing can be misleading. The man dressed in the business suit, the badge of rectitude, may be the purveyor of a lie; the boy in black with the piercings, wants only to belong, to be seen to be strong, but may be lonely and unsure of himself, as only adolescents can be.

All of us, thought Hugh, are alone and frightened.

Act Two: The two young women, Fiordiligi and Dorabella, bid farewell to their lovers, Ferrando and Guglielmo, whose regiment must leave for war. They are wished well on their journey in the moving trio *Soave sia il vento* – may the wind that carries you on your voyage be a gentle one. Despina, their maid, claims that old lovers are readily forgotten once new ones are to hand.

'I'm sorry about this,' said Hugh. 'I was looking forward to Geoff's party. I really was.'

'Well, I think it's really inconsiderate of them,' said Rose. 'Why can't this wait until Monday? Or until tomorrow? They can't expect you to work Saturday night and all of Sunday.'

'They can,' said Hugh. 'And they do. We see the client on Monday. There's a meeting with counsel and we simply have to have everything ready. It's a really complex case. You should see the papers.' He made a gesture; a mound of papers, feet high.

Mark, who was also a lawyer, nodded in sympathy; he knew how it was. Turning to Rose, he said, 'Sometimes these things crop up, you know. I was in a case once where we had twenty-four hours to get ready. That's all. I worked for eighteen hours non-stop and had six hours to go back to the flat and get some sleep before we were in court.'

Lottie had been quiet until now, but now she made an observation. 'It's brutal,' she said. 'People shouldn't have to live like that. That's not what life should be about.'

'Everybody has to work,' said Hugh. He looked at his watch. 'Anyway, you three should get along to Geoff's place. Everybody else will be getting to the office.'

Lottie rose to her feet and reached for the bag containing her outfit. She was going as Marie-Antoinette. 'I hope that things go well,' she said. 'Poor Hugh!'

'Yes,' said Rose, also rising to her feet. 'My poor, overworked darling!'

Mark looked at Hugh, and smiled. 'I hope you get a good wind behind you,' he said to his friend. 'Soave sia il vento.'

Rose turned her head sharply. 'What was that?' she asked. 'What did you say?'

But Mark did not answer her question, as the taxi had arrived, and could be heard outside, its diesel engine noisy and insistent in the way of hard-working diesel engines.

*

Act Three: At the party, the young lovers mingle in the crowd of friends, all disguised in fancy dress. There are Venetian masks; there are comic policemen; there are burglars in the striped jerseys of their calling. A short time after the arrival of Mark, Lottie and Rose, a bearded Albanian slips in and joins the party, on the opposite side of the room. There is much jollity, and presents are heaped upon the host.

It was obvious to Hugh that Geoffrey did not recognize him when he opened the door to him.

'It's me,' he said, pulling the beard down across his chin. 'See?'

Geoffrey laughed. 'I wouldn't have known that,' he said. 'What are you meant to be?'

'An Albanian,' said Hugh.

The noise from the music further inside the flat was loud, and Geoffrey misheard.

'An albino?' he said.

'An Albanian,' *Hugh repeated, enunciating the word carefully.*

Geoffrey looked him up and down. 'Is that how they dress? Albanians?'

Hugh shrugged. 'I've never been there. But it's not important.' *He leaned over towards his host and whispered to him.* 'The important thing is this: don't let on to Rose that I'm here. I want to surprise her.' *He pointed to his beard.*

Geoffrey smiled. 'All right. That's what fancy dress parties are meant to be like. Full of surprises.' *He paused, and looked down at the drink in his hand.* 'Thirty,' *he said disconsolately.* 'Thirty.'

Hugh put a hand on his shoulder. 'Cheer up. Next time it'll be forty. Think of that. Forty.'

'I hardly remember being twenty,' *said Geoffrey.* 'I mean, it was *hardly any time ago. And it's gone – a whole decade has gone. Just like that. Pow!'*

'But it gets better,' said Hugh. 'At least I think it does. Life becomes more interesting.'

Geoffrey was not convinced. 'Maybe.' He took a sip of his drink. 'You know something about getting older? You know what? You become invisible to people who are younger than you. Have you noticed that? You gradually fade away, as if your light is getting dimmer and they can't see you. You're just not there. You no longer count as far as they're concerned.'

Hugh thought about this. Invisibility. Being there but not being there. That resonated with his current position, he thought. He was here but not here. He was there but Rose thought he was not. And did that mean that she would behave any differently? That he would find out, and he saw her now, across on the other side of the room, talking to a man wearing the outfit of a naval captain. Mark and Lottie were nowhere to be seen. He looked at Rose. She was dressed in the outfit of a Flamenco dancer, and was smiling. He saw her reach out and touch the naval captain on the arm, laying her hand there on his forearm, and leaving it for a moment before she withdrew it again. Her expression was one of rapt attention, and the captain smiled back at her. He leaned forward and whispered something to her. She laughed and turned her head away. He could not see her face now.

He moved through the crowd. People glanced at him – people whom he knew – and then looked away. None of them recognized him.

'A bearded man,' said one woman as he made his way past her. 'Very mysterious! Is it itchy under there?'

He did not stop to talk, but continued until he was stand-ing directly behind Rose. The captain, who was facing him across her shoulder, looked up from their conversation. He did not seem pleased to be interrupted, as an expression of slight irritation crossed his face. This confirmed what Hugh felt: this man was flirting with Rose. And then the ancillary, awful thought came to him: she must be encouraging her suitor.

Rose turned round. At first her eyes fell upon the outfit itself – on the baggy green trousers and the rough shirt of Balkan hodden. Then her gaze moved upwards and fixed itself upon the beard.

Hugh cleared his throat. He had decided that he would disguise his voice by talking in a lower register; a natural tenor, he would become a basso profondo.

'Hugh!'

She half turned to the captain. 'Excuse me,' she said. Reaching forward, she took Hugh's arm and led him away into a corner. With her other hand, she touched the beard.

'My darling,' she said. 'My lovely, hirsute darling! How did you get away?'

He hesitated. 'I...I just didn't go. I decided that I had to have a life of my own and I didn't go.' He laughed, nervously, unsure as to whether he sounded convincing. 'Stupid case! Plenty of time for that next week.'

'You brave, sensible darling,' Rose said. 'Smelly old office!' She looked at him appreciatively. 'And you're such a handsome, convincing Albanian! You really are. All these boring old pirates and captains and so on. And you're such an interesting Albanian. So different.'

He stared at her. 'How did you know I was an Albanian?'

She smiled, and gently pulled the beard away from his face, 'I just knew,' she said. 'Women understand these things.'

She took his hand. 'You know something,' she began. 'I was standing there talking to that other man and all the time I was thinking of *you. I had to make a real effort to follow what he was saying because I was thinking so much about you.' She paused. 'I always think about you. All the time.'*

'Do you?'

'Oh yes. All the time.'

He felt the pressure of her hand in his. He loved her. He knew that, just as she knew he was dressed as an Albanian.

'You know,' he said, 'I can't speak a single word of Albanian. Not one.'

She laughed. 'But there are occasions when Albanian will simply not do. When it has to be Italian.'

'And this is one of them?'

'Yes,' she said. 'Soave sia il vento/Tranquilla sia l'onda/Ed ogni elemento/Benigno risponda/Ai nostri desir.'

He lowered his gaze. He was ashamed of himself, that he had doubted her. And she had not been angered by this doubt, but had forgiven him, as women will forgive men who do all sorts of things because they are just weak, insecure creatures – as I am, he thought.

'I've been so silly,' he said.

'Operas are like that,' she replied.

Notes on the Operas
Peggy Reynolds

Jackie Kay, 'The First Lady of Song'
Leos Janacek (1854–1928), *The Makropulos Affair*

Opera in three acts premiered in 1926, set in the 1920s in Prague with a libretto by the composer based on Karel Capek's play. Emilia Marty (soprano) is an opera singer with a glamorous career and a strange interest in the long-running inheritance court case of Gregor *v.* Prus. As long ago as 1827 Baron Prus had died apparently intestate and his estate was to go to a cousin, but a new claimant appeared who declared he was the Baron's illegitimate son. Emilia tells the lawyer now dealing with the case where to find papers that will solve it. In fact, Emilia is also after a paper that contains the secret of the elixir of life. Backstage at the opera house Emilia wins admiration from all, including the present Baron Jaroslav Prus (baritone) and his son Janek (tenor). But she herself is strangely cold and world-weary.

An old man appears – Count Hauk-Sendorf (tenor) – who is drawn to her because she resembles his long-ago mistress Eugenia Montez. He realizes, with amazement, that she is the same woman. Emilia spends the night with the Baron and in the morning comes the news that Janek has committed suicide because of her rejection. Prus gives her the paper she had requested, but everyone's suspicions are aroused. At length Emilia explains. She is Elina Makropulos and she was born in 1549. Her father discovered the secret of the elixir of life and she drank it. Every few years she has changed her identity, always retaining the initials E.M. Now, after three hundred years, she longs for death. The recipe for the elixir is thrown on the fire. As she ages before their eyes Emilia sings herself to death.

Ali Smith, 'Fidelio and Bess'
Ludwig van Beethoven (1770–1827), *Fidelio*

Opera in two acts after a drama by Nicolas Bouilly premiered in Vienna (in three acts) in 1805. The 1806 revision was in two acts, and in 1814 there were further revisions to text and music. There are also four versions of the overture. Set in a fortress near Seville in the eighteenth century, the opera opens with Marzelline (soprano), daughter of the jailor Rocco (bass), who is being wooed by Jaquino (tenor) but who is in love with Rocco's assistant, Fidelio (soprano). Pizarro (baritone), the governor of the prison, arrives and orders Rocco to kill the prisoner who has been incarcerated in the most secret part of the dungeon for many years. This is none other than Florestan (tenor), a nobleman and husband of Leonore, who has disguised herself as Fidelio. Rocco refuses. Pizarro resolves to do the deed himself.

At the end of Act I, at Fidelio's request, the prisoners are briefly permitted into the air of the courtyard in honour of the King's birthday. Fidelio seeks Florestan among them but he is not there. Rocco summons Fidelio to help him dig a grave, but as they enter the dungeon Fidelio recognizes her husband.

When Pizarro arrives to kill Florestan, Fidelio/Leonore stands between them and declares herself. A trumpet sounds as Jaquino enters to announce the arrival of the Minister (bass). Pizarro's moment is gone. Florestan is freed.

George Gershwin (1898–1937), *Porgy and Bess*

Opera in three acts with text by DuBose Heyward and Ira Gershwin, first performed in Boston in 1935 and set in Charleston, South Carolina, in the 'recent past'. The scene opens as Clara (soprano) nurses her baby to the famous 'Summertime'. When Porgy (bass-baritone) appears, getting about in his little goat-cart, the assembled inhabitants of the tenement of Catfish Row tease him about the foolishness of his romantic aspirations given his handicap. Porgy is sweet on Bess (soprano), the mistress of Crown (baritone), a well-built stevedore. In a row over a crap game Crown kills Robbins (tenor) and Bess urges him to flee. Sportin' Life (tenor), a dope pedlar, offers to take Bess to New York but she refuses and begs for shelter in Catfish Row. Only Porgy will help her and together they visit Serena (soprano), Robbins' widow. The detectives arrest old Peter (tenor) as a 'material witness'. Together Porgy and Bess lead the spirituals in lament.

In Act II Sportin' Life is still pursuing Bess, but she and Porgy express their love for each other in 'Bess, you is my woman now'. As everyone goes on a picnic to Kittiwah Island Crown reappears and Bess stays with him. After two days she returns to Porgy, ill and incoherent, but says again that she wants to stay with him. Crown orders her to come with him when Clara rushes in saying that her husband Jake (baritone) is lost at sea. Crown leaves to help her seek him, but when he returns again for Bess, Porgy kills him. Porgy is taken to identify the body, but refuses to look at Crown – now acknowledged as Robbins' murderer – and is jailed for contempt of court. Sportin' Life seduces the distraught Bess with his 'happy dust' and she leaves with him. When Porgy returns after a week and finds Bess gone, he sets off for New York in his goat-cart – 'Oh, Lord, I'm on my way' – determined to find her and bring her home.

Sebastian Barry, 'Freedom'
Victor Herbert (1859–1924), *Natoma*

One of the earliest 'American' operas, to a libretto by Joseph D. Redding, first performed at Philadelphia and the Metropolitan Opera in New York in 1911, *Natoma* is set on the island of Santa Cruz off Southern California in 1820 and features Spanish and 'native Indian' themes in the music. The Scottish-American soprano Mary Garden sang the title role, with the Irish tenor John McCormack as Paul.

Natoma (soprano) is an Indian girl serving as a maid to Barbara, who is now returning to her home. Among the group awaiting her is Alvarado (tenor), a suitor favoured by her father Don Francisco (bass). Also present is Paul Merrill (tenor) of the United States Navy. Natoma is in love with Paul and happily praises her mistress to him until she realizes the effect of her words.

Paul and Barbara are immediately attracted to one another. Seeing this, Alvarado plots with Castro (baritone), a half-breed, to abduct Barbara, but Natoma overhears their plans. At a fair in the public square of the old town of Santa Barbara, Castro distracts everyone's attention by challenging all comers to a knife dance. Natoma throws her knife into the ring, and just as Alvarado is about to seize Barbara, Natoma stabs him. As the townsfolk rush to take her, Natoma seeks refuge in the local church. Admonished by the priest, Natoma finally gives up hopes of earthly happiness and says farewell to her mistress as she joins the sisterhood.

Kate Atkinson, 'To Die For'
Giuseppe Verdi (1813–1901), *La Traviata*

Based on the popular play by Alexandre Dumas *La Dame aux Camélias*, itself based on Dumas' affair with the courtesan Marie Duplessis, Verdi's *La Traviata* has a text by Francesco Maria Piave and was first performed in Venice in 1853. Set in Paris in 1850, the story begins at the house of Violetta (soprano), where she is giving a party to celebrate her recovery from a severe illness. She is introduced to Alfredo (tenor), who has admired her from a distance. Alfredo overcomes her scruples, and Violetta leaves her patron Baron Douphol (baritone) to live in the country with Alfredo. Here she is visited by Alfredo's father Giorgio Germont (baritone), who persuades her to leave her lover for the sake of his family. Though broken-hearted, Violetta writes that she has returned to the Baron. Alfredo turns up at a grand party given by her friend Flora (mezzo-soprano) and throws all his winnings from the gaming table at Violetta and challenges the Baron to a duel.

In the final scene Violetta is dying, but Germont has written that he will bring Alfredo back from exile to her. When they arrive, it is clearly too late, but Violetta rises up and in her final moments cries that she feels well and leaps into the air, only to fall dead in Alfredo's arms.

Julie Myerson, 'The Growler'
Richard Strauss (1864–1949), *Ariadne auf Naxos*

The original was a one-act opera to a text by Hugo von Hofmannsthal first performed in 1912. The revision, dating from 1916, consists of a prologue and one act and that is the version generally performed today. The prologue opens on the house of the richest man in Vienna. He has commissioned a serious opera on the theme of Ariadne abandoned on Naxos from a young composer (soprano, in a cross-dressing role). As the curtain rises we see the beautiful and sophisticated Prima Donna (soprano) – who will sing Ariadne – and the Tenor (tenor) – who will sing Bacchus – preparing for the performance later in the day. The rich man's Major Domo (speaking role) appears to announce that the opera will be followed by a Harlequinade performed by Zerbinetta (soprano), Harlequin (baritone), Scaramuccio (tenor), Truffaldino (bass) and Brighella (tenor). Moments later, he returns to say that the rich man has decided that there is no time for each piece to be performed consecutively – both tragedy and comedy must be played simultaneously. Which is what happens in the second half. Ariadne bewails her lot in dramatic terms. The comedians attempt to cheer her along. In an extended aria, *Grossmachtige Princessen*, Zerbinetta advises Ariadne on life and love, and encourages her to take her pleasure where she can. In the climactic scene of the opera, a godly Bacchus arrives to take the transported Ariadne in his arms. Zerbinetta comments that she knew this would happen. In the most imaginative productions, the young composer is also present, witnessing the truth of life that art can teach us – that comedy and tragedy, happiness and pain, often do go hand in hand.

Toby Litt, 'The Ghost'
Wolfgang Amadeus Mozart (1756–1791), *Don Giovanni*

An opera in two acts with text by Lorenzo da Ponte, first performed in Prague in 1787, *Don Giovanni* is a powerful meditation on sex, death, betrayal, responsibility and liberty. It begins with a rape as Don Giovanni (baritone) waits with his servant Leporello (bass) for an opportunity to insinuate himself into the bedroom of Donna Anna (soprano). When the girl cries for help her father, the Commendatore (bass), comes to her assistance but is promptly slain by the licentious hero. Don Ottavio (tenor), Anna's betrothed, attempts to comfort her. Leporello and the Don meet a woman who turns out to be Donna Elvira (soprano), whom Giovanni had abandoned in Burgos. Elvira, Ottavio and Anna track Giovanni to his country estate. Here Giovanni is thwarted in his seduction of a peasant girl, Zerlina (soprano), by the three nobles and by Masetto (baritone), Zerlina's fiancé.

As the Don pursues yet another seduction, he and Leporello take refuge from an angry crowd in a graveyard by the tomb of the Commendatore. Giovanni commands Leporello to invite the statue to dinner. Much to the servant's horror, the statue accepts. In the last scene Elvira tries to warn Giovanni of his impending doom. The statue appears at Giovanni's table and invites the Don in return. The Don takes his freezing hand and is dragged down to hell. The remaining characters are left to contemplate his end.

Joanna Trollope, 'Nemo'
Gaetano Donizetti (1797–1848), *L'Elisir d'Amore*

This comic opera in two acts set in a small Italian village, with a libretto by Felice Romani, was premiered at Milan in 1832. Nemorino (tenor) is a young peasant in love with Adina (soprano), who owns a wealthy farm. When a detachment of soldiers arrives, Adina seems to be interested in their sergeant Belcore (baritone) and Nemorino confides in a travelling quack doctor, Dulcamara (bass), wondering if he can supply him with Isolde's elixir of love. When Nemorino gets drunk on the fake elixir and flirts with Giannetta (soprano) Adina is piqued and agrees to marry Belcore.

Desperate to buy another dose of the magic potion, Nemorino enlists in Belcore's regiment for the sake of the twenty *scudi* incentive. Nemorino realizes that Adina does love him, in the opera's most famous aria *Una furtiva lagrima*, and Adina buys him out of the army. Belcore accepts that he has lost Adina, and when the news comes that Nemorino's uncle has died, leaving him a rich man, Dulcamara sells his remaining stock of elixir, which promises not only love but money too.

Colm Tóibín, 'The Pearl Fishers'
Georges Bizet (1838–1875), *Les Pêcheurs de Perles*

Premiered in 1863 at the Théâtre-Lyrique in Paris with a text by Michel Carré and Eugène Cormon, *Les Pêcheurs de Perles* was first performed at Covent Garden in 1887 under the title *Leïla*. The opera opens as a group of fishermen meet to declare Zurga (baritone) their chief. Nadir (tenor) returns from a long absence and sings the so-called 'friendship' duet *Au fond du temple saint* with Zurga as they recall their old rivalry over Leïla (soprano), a priestess of Brahma. Nourabad (bass), the High Priest of Brahma, arrives with a veiled priestess who will pray for the success of the fleet. But Nadir recognizes Leïla and when the two acknowledge their love they are condemned to death by fire – she for breaking her vows, he for betraying the fishermen's trust. Zurga, realizing that Leïla once saved his life, arranges their escape and the opera ends with Leïla and Nadir singing *Au fond du temple saint* as they reach safety.

Wexford Festival Opera specializes in works that are rarely performed, but in recent years *The Pearl Fishers* has been included in the repertoire of many major houses.

Anne Enright, 'Key Note, or, *Che Gelida Manina*' Giacomo Puccini (1858–1924), *La Bohème*

Based on the novel *Scènes de la Vie de Bohème* by Henri Murger, to a book by Giuseppe Giacosa and Luigi Illica, an opera in four acts first performed in Turin in 1896. Rodolfo (tenor), a poet, and his friend Marcello (baritone), an artist, live in a poverty-stricken garret with Colline (bass), a philosopher, and Schaunard (baritone), a musician. They cannot afford to pay the rent, but when Schaunard arrives with some unexpected money they decide to go out on the town. Rodolfo stays behind to finish a newspaper article, but is interrupted by a timid knock. Mimi (soprano), a young seamstress, has come to ask for a light for her candle. Rodolfo explains that he is a poet. In lyrical terms, Mimi tells him of her quiet life. Then she loses her key, Rodolfo blows the candle out again and seizes her cold hand in the moonlight – *Che gelida manina se lasci riscaldar*. As they are quickly drawn together, Mimi joins Rodolfo and he introduces her to his friends at the Café Momus by saying 'I am a poet, and she is poetry'.

The idyll is soon over. Mimi is seriously ill with consumption and Rodolfo, alternately jealous and despairing of her life, cannot cope. They agree to stay together until the spring. In the final Act, Musetta (soprano), Marcello's estranged girlfriend, arrives with Mimi, who is dying. The four leave Rodolfo and Mimi alone together as they relive their first meeting. When

Musetta returns with a luxurious muff Mimi's hands are warm at last and she falls asleep. Rodolfo is hopeful, but Musetta sees that she has died and the opera ends as Rodolfo calls her name, 'Mimi, Mimi'.

Andrew O'Hagan, 'First Snow'
Pyotr Ilyich Tchaikovsky (1840–1893), *Eugene Onegin*

Based on the poem by Alexander Pushkin with a text by the composer and K. S. Shilovsky. Madame Larina (mezzo-soprano) and the old nurse Filipievna (mezzo-soprano) make jam as they listen to the singing of Madame Larina's daughters Olga (contralto) and Tatyana (soprano). Olga's fiancé Lensky (tenor) introduces his friend Onegin (baritone). Tatyana, reserved, romantic, and a great reader, is immediately impressed. In the famous 'letter scene' she writes to him, but next morning Onegin rejects her with cold condescension. At Tatyana's birthday party a bored Onegin flirts thoughtlessly with Olga. Lensky challenges him to a duel and is killed.

In the final scenes of the opera Onegin returns from long years abroad to find Tatyana married to the elderly Prince Gremin (bass), who truly loves her. Onegin is overwhelmed by passion as he sees Tatyana's sophistication and poise and he writes to her. Tatyana admits that she still loves him, but refuses to leave her husband and commands Onegin to leave her for ever.

Jeanette Winterson, 'Goldrush Girl'
Giacomo Puccini (1858–1924), *La Fanciulla del West*

Opera in three acts based on a play by the American writer David Belasco (who also wrote the play that Puccini turned into *Madame Butterfly*) which Puccini first saw in 1907. The premiere was at the Metropolitan Opera in 1910.

The story is set in a mining camp in California during the gold rush of 1849-50. The curtain opens on the bar of the Polka Inn, which is owned and run by Minnie (soprano). We do not meet her at first, but see the boys returning from their day's work in the mines. They set up a gambling game, but when one of their number enters singing a melancholy song longing for home, one of the hard men breaks down. Also present is Jack Rance, the Sheriff (baritone). Nick the bartender (tenor) has persuaded Rance that Minnie might be interested in him and Rance is keen. He picks a quarrel with Sonora, another of Minnie's admirers, then, Minnie herself enters – to much adulation from the boys – and attempts her reading-cum-bible study class. Ashby (bass), agent of the Wells Fargo Transport Co, explains that he is on the trail of a noted Mexican bandit named Ramerrez who he believes is in the vicinity. A stranger appears, asking for whisky and water. He asks Minnie if she remembers him. She does. He is Dick Johnson (tenor) from Sacramento. They recall their first meeting when they picked blackberries together. One of Ramerrez's men is captured. Minnie is left to guard the gold. Dick Johnson tells her she has 'the face of an angel'.

Act II opens at Minnie's cabin. Johnson enters and they admit their love for each other. Minnie makes up a bed for him, but then Rance and Nick come to tell her that Johnson is none other than Ramerrez. They leave. Minnie calls 'Johnson' to account and throws him out into the snow. Sounds echo outside, then comes a violent knocking. Minnie opens to Johnson, who has severe gunshot wounds. She takes him in, just as the posse is approaching. Minnie hides the unconscious Johnson but Rance spies blood. Minnie and Rance play cards for the bandit. As she sees that she is about to lose, Minnie slips the winning ace into her stocking. The curtain closes on Minnie's hysterical laughter.

When the men recapture Johnson they plan to lynch him. In *Ch'ella mi creda* Johnson begs them to let her imagine that he has escaped. Minnie appears and persuades the men to give him up to her. They leave California for ever.

Ruth Rendell, 'The Martyr'
George Frideric Handel (1685–1759), *Theodora*

Strictly speaking, not an opera but an oratorio in three acts, set to an English libretto by Thomas Morell and premiered in March 1750. *Theodora* was staged as an opera in the Glyndebourne Festival of 1996 in an acclaimed production by Peter Sellars, with Dawn Upshaw in the title role and the late Lorraine Hunt Lieberson as Irene.

In Roman-occupied Antioch in the 4th century AD, the governor Valens (bass) decrees, on pain of death, that all citizens must sacrifice to the goddesses Flora and Venus in honour of the Emperor Diocletian's birthday. Didymus (alto), a Roman officer, requests exemption for those whose consciences will not permit them to worship these gods, but it is denied and his friend Septimius (tenor) is given the task of carrying out the decree. Theodora (soprano) and her friend Irene (mezzo-soprano) are converted Christians. When Theodora refuses to comply, she is condemned to work in a brothel and threatened with rape. Didymus persuades Septimius to allow him to see her in prison and he coaxes Theodora to escape by changing places with him. The Christian community celebrates Theodora's safe return, but Didymus is condemned to death. Theodora gives herself up and each of the two lovers begs to die to save the other. Septimius wants to be lenient, but Valens is adamant and both are executed.

Lynne Truss, 'String and Air'
Benjamin Britten (1913–1976), *The Turn of the Screw*

This opera in prologue and two acts, based on the novella (1898) of the same name by Henry James, was premiered by the English Opera Group at the Venice Festival in 1954. At Venice, the part of Miles was sung by the young David Hemmings, who as an adult was to go on to star in Antonioni's *Blow-Up* (1966) and Tony Richardson's *The Charge of the Light Brigade* (1968).

In both the short novel and the opera, the theme of thwarted or misplaced desire is key, whether – in the case of the James – the love of the overall narrator Douglas for the Governess, or that of the Governess for her reclusive employer, or – as in the opera – the illicit relation between Miles and the 'ghost' of Quint. In the novella we can never be quite sure whether or not the ghosts are real or only a figment of the Governess' imagination. In the opera they are real, in so far as they are cast parts who sing and influence the action. Myfanwy Piper's understated and spare libretto with its incorporation of many children's nursery rhymes (appropriately scored by Britten) is generally reckoned to be a masterpiece.

'It is a curious story. I have it written in faded ink,' sings the Prologue (tenor) as he sets out the facts of the Governess' acceptance of a post offered by the guardian of two children inhabiting a lonely country house that will put her in sole charge of them both. Act I portrays the Governess' (soprano) journey to Bly, and her meeting with the housekeeper Mrs Grose (soprano) and the two children Miles (treble) and Flora (soprano). Then the Governess discovers that Miles has been expelled from school on the grounds that he constitutes 'an injury to his friends'. The Governess sees a man on the tower of the house. Mrs Grose identifies the vision as Quint (tenor), a former manservant, who we then see manipulating Miles in a haunting Latin rhyme which plays on meaning: 'Malo, malo, malo/ I would rather be/ Malo, malo/ In an apple tree...than a naughty boy...' Flora is similarly shadowed by Miss Jessel (soprano), who was once a governess in the house and is now – like Quint – dead.

In Act II Quint and Miss Jessel egg each other on in 'the ceremony of innocence is drowned'. The Governess challenges the shade of Miss Jessel when she finds her sitting at her desk and resolves – despite orders – to write to the children's guardian. Miles, persuaded by Quint, steals the letter. After a traumatic episode by the lake with Miss Jessel, Mrs Grose takes Flora away. The Governess is left alone with Miles and attempts to extract a confession or admission of evil from him while Quint tussles for the child. In the climactic final moments of the opera the Governess clutches Miles to her and then, realizing that he is dead, repeats the 'Malo, malo' theme.

Paul Bailey, 'The Empty Seat'
Leos Janacek (1854–1928), *The Makropulos Affair*
(see under Jackie Kay)

Johann Strauss II (1825–1899), *Die Fledermaus*

Operetta in three acts premiered in Vienna in 1874. In the house of Gabriel von Eisenstein (tenor) his wife Rosalinde (soprano) is hoping to meet her lover, the singer Alfred (tenor), while her husband is away for a few days fulfilling a prison sentence for some trivial offence. Meanwhile Rosalinde's maid Adele (soprano) is hoping to escape to a party at the theatre with her sister and has pleaded having to look after an ailing aunt. Dr Falke (baritone) appears. He is the 'bat' or 'fledermaus' of the title, having once, after a fancy dress party, been left drunkenly asleep by von Eisenstein. He is still bent upon revenge for the indignity of having had to make his way home in broad daylight in his bat costume. Falke persuades von Eisenstein to lie to his wife and have one last night of freedom at the theatre before surrendering to the authorities in the morning. Eisenstein agrees, and leaves in full evening dress. Alfred settles down to enjoy a tête-a-tête with Rosalinde when the police appear to arrest the man having dinner with her – her husband, of course! Act II takes place at Prince Orlofsky's (mezzo-soprano) party backstage at the theatre. Adele is there in one of her mistress' dresses. Eisenstein is there, and Rosalinde is there disguised as a Hungarian Countess. In this seductive role she 'proves' herself to be truly Hungarian as she sings a rich Czardas, 'the music of my native country shall speak for me', and she persuades Eisenstein to give her his precious watch. In the last act all misunderstandings are resolved and the cast sing an anthem to the restorative power of Champagne.

Johann Strauss II (1825–1899), *Der Zigeunerbaron*

Operetta in three acts first performed in Vienna in 1885. 'The Gypsy Baron' is Sandor Barinkay (tenor), the son of a Hungarian landowner who has fallen on hard times. When Barinkay returns from exile the gypsy woman Czipra tells his fortune and declares that he will marry a faithful wife who will bring him a lost treasure. Though he should be marrying Arsena, the daughter of the miserly farmer Zsupan, Barinkay is attracted to Czipra's daughter Saffi and declares that he will marry her, much to delight of the gypsies. Saffi dreams of the whereabouts of a treasure trove and, when investigated, the hoard is indeed there. Czipra reveals that Saffi is not her own daughter, but the child of a Turkish pasha and a true princess. Barinkay enlists and departs in despair as he cannot, as a commoner, marry anyone of noble blood. In the last act, which takes place in Vienna, all is resolved as Barinkay is ennobled after success in battle and so can claim his bride and her treasure. *Die Fledermaus* is regularly performed in serious opera houses, *The Merry Widow* (1905) by Franz Lehar (1870–1948) is performed very occasionally, while *The Gypsy Baron* is rarely performed in full but its many sparkling waltzes and polkas are popular concert offerings.

Antonia Fraser, 'My Lovely Countess'
Wolfgang Amadeus Mozart (1756–1791), *Le Nozze di Figaro*

Four-act *opera buffa*, text by Lorenzo da Ponte, from a comedy by Pierre Beaumarchais, first performed at the Burgtheater Vienna in 1786. As the curtain rises Figaro (baritone) is measuring up a room and planning where to put the marital bed after the celebrations of his imminent marriage to Susanna (soprano). He favours this room on account of its proximity to his master Count Almaviva's (baritone), and to that of the Countess (soprano), Susanna's mistress, but Susanna points out that for *her* being close to the Count's room is not necessarily a good thing. Figaro's next problem is the duenna Marcellina (soprano) who, with the help of Dr Bartolo (bass), plans to make Figaro marry her because he has defaulted on a debt. Cherubino (soprano) appears hoping that he will be reinstated as the Countess' page, but Figaro urges him to accept his fate and commit to the military.

The Countess herself appears in Act II with *Porgi amor* and we realize how she regrets the loss of her husband's love. In Act III she follows this up with another aria of loss and longing in *Dove sono*. Cherubino comes to plead with her and Susanna, but when the Count is announced Cherubino jumps out the window and Susanna locks herself in the Countess' dressing room. Convinced that he has discovered his wife's lover, the Count breaks down the door to find – Susanna.

In an effort to bring the Count back to his wife, Susanna and she swap clothes and Susanna agrees to meet the Count in the garden. Of course, the person he actually meets is his own wife - who has to suffer the pain of hearing her husband woo her while believing that she is someone else. In a scene of unparalleled musical beauty and philosophical tenderness the Countess forgives all when the Count's planned infidelity is revealed. He and she are (apparently) reunited, Figaro and Susanna are reconciled, and Marcellina and Dr Bartolo are discovered to be none other than Figaro's own parents.

Kate Mosse, '*La Fille de Mélisande*'
Claude Debussy (1862–1918), *Pelléas et Mélisande*

Based on Maurice Maeterlinck's symbolist play of the same name, it was premiered at the Opéra-Comique in Paris in 1902. Debussy's opera is true to the dreamlike quality of the original story, and offers no explanations or resolutions. Golaud (baritone) finds Mélisande in a wood by a stream. He writes to his mother Geneviève (alto) and his blind father Arkel, King of Allemonde (bass), that he has married Mélisande but still knows nothing about her. Mélisande and Pelléas (tenor), Golaud's brother, are drawn to each other. Mélisande loses Golaud's ring in the fountain in the park. At the same moment, Golaud is wounded in the hunt. Mélisande leans down to Pelléas from her tower, showering him with her long hair.

Golaud warns Pelléas to keep away from his wife. He makes

his small son Yniold (soprano) spy on his uncle and his step-mother. Mélisande arranges to meet Pelléas by the fountain. Golaud surprises them and kills Pelléas. Mélisande flees back to the castle. Mélisande lies desperately ill while Golaud alternately begs her forgiveness and demands the truth. Arkel brings her the girl child she has borne. Mélisande dies.

Andrew Motion, 'Now the Great Bear...'
Benjamin Britten (1913–1976), *Peter Grimes*

This opera in three acts with Prologue and Epilogue is adapted from a long poem by George Crabbe (1754–1832) called 'The Borough' and is set on the East Anglian coast in the early nineteenth century. In the Prologue the residents of the village attend an inquest into the recent death of the boy apprentice to the fisherman Peter Grimes (tenor). The verdict is 'accidental circumstances' but feeling runs high. Peter's only friend is the widowed schoolmistress Ellen Orford (soprano). In Act I a new apprentice for Grimes is found as Ellen promises to help look after him, but as a great storm blows up at sea, Grimes stays out and his isolation from the community is clear. When he does return to the Boar Inn Peter takes no notice of the company but contemplates the strangeness of human life and the power of the natural world as he sings about the stars and the sea in *Now the Great Bear and the Pleiades*.

On a calm Sunday morning Ellen notices that the boy's jacket is torn and that he has a bruise on his neck. While she tries to coax Peter into gentler ways, the people mutter against him. The Rector and various others set out for Peter's hut, but the boy is lost, fallen down the cliff to his death. Peter sets sail and holes his boat at sea.

Marina Warner, 'Forget My Fate'
Henry Purcell (1659–1695), *Dido and Aeneas*

This opera in three acts with a libretto by Nahum Tate was first performed at Josias Priest's boarding school for girls in Chelsea in 1689. It comes from the story of Dido found in Book IV of *The Aeneid*, an epic by the Roman poet Virgil written in the 1st century BC.

Aeneas is a Trojan who survives the slaughter at the end of the Trojan war. It is his destiny eventually to settle in Italy and found the city of Rome. During the course of his travels he lands at Carthage on the coast of Africa. The first scene of the opera discovers Dido (or Elissa, soprano), the Queen of Carthage, with her lady Belinda (soprano), who correctly surmises that the cause of the Queen's melancholy is their 'Trojan guest'. Belinda assures the Queen that Aeneas (tenor) is also in love with her. But in a cave by the shore a Sorceress (mezzo-soprano) plots to destroy the Queen and all Carthage. While Aeneas is out hunting with Dido, Mercury appears to him to issue Jove's command – he must leave Carthage and continue on to Italy. In truth, this vision is a spirit sent by the Sorceress, but Aeneas obeys and prepares to set sail. When he sees the Queen's distress, he relents, but the Queen proudly dismisses the man who could even consider leaving her. After his departure the Queen succumbs to death: 'When I am laid, am laid in earth, may my wrongs create no trouble in thy breast. Remember me, remember me, but, ah! forget my fate.'

Alexander McCall Smith, 'The Albanians'
Wolfgang Amadeus Mozart (1756–1791), *Così fan tutte*

To a text by Lorenzo da Ponte, first performed in 1790 and sub-titled 'The School for Lovers', the thin plot of *Così* yields some of Mozart's most sublime music. Don Alfonso (baritone) argues with two younger friends, Ferrando (tenor) and Guglielmo (bass), about the fidelity of women. Each declares his belief in his fiancée, Dorabella (soprano) and Fiordiligi (soprano) respectively, and finally they agree to put the women to the test. They pretend to leave Naples and then, aided by the girls' maid Despina (soprano), have themselves reintroduced to the women as two Albanians. Each man woos the other's betrothed and – eventually – each succeeds.

Just as the two marriages are to be solemnized (with Despina acting the part of the notary), Ferrando and Guglielmo return and all is resolved. Or maybe not – because directors' interpretations sometimes have the lovers end up the 'wrong' way round, disillusioned by the whole experience, or – as in this story – indicate that the women knew the score all along. *Soave sia il vento* from Act I is a trio for Alfonso, Fiordiligi and Dorabella as the young men depart across the sea. It is the single most chosen piece of music on BBC Radio 4's *Desert Island Discs*.

About Glyndebourne

The internationally renowned Glyndebourne Festival was founded in 1934 by John Christie and his wife, Audrey Mildmay; their grandson Gus is now executive chairman. The Festival repertoire includes operas from the baroque to the contemporary, including seven of Glyndebourne's own commissions and thirteen British premieres. The opera house itself was rebuilt in 1994 and now seats 1,200. Glyndebourne on Tour was founded in 1968 taking productions to a wider audience and offering increased performance opportunities to young singers. Additionally, Glyndebourne's education department has an enormous commitment to new opera and community projects; it currently hosts over 230 different activities each year.

With 124 opera performances annually reaching over 140,000 people, Glyndebourne's continued employment of inspirational directors and performers, and the ongoing drive to commission new work, now goes hand in hand with digital innovations to reach new audiences.

Glyndebourne would like to extend its sincere thanks to Jeanette Winterson and all the authors who have contributed to this

and is very grateful for the innovative
they have supported Glyndebourne's 75th
y.

Notes on the Contributors

Jeanette Winterson is the author of over twenty books for adults and children, including *Oranges Are Not The Only Fruit* and *Why Be Happy When You Can Be Normal?* She adapted her novel *The Powerbook* for the National Theatre in London and the Theatre de Chaillot in Paris. Her books have been published all over the world and she has won numerous awards, as well as being appointed OBE. She lives in London and the Cotswolds.

Jackie Kay was born in Edinburgh. She is the third modern Makar, the Scottish poet laureate. A poet, novelist and writer of short stories, she has won prizes for her books which include *Trumpet*, *Why Don't You Stop Talking* and her memoir *Red Dust*. She is Professor of Creative Writing at Newcastle University.

Ali Smith was born in Inverness and lives in Cambridge. She is a prize-winning author of five short story collections and nine novels, including *How to Be Both* and her latest, *Spring*.

Sebastian Barry has written several plays, including *Our Lady of Sligo*, and seven novels, including the Costa Book of the Year 2016, *Days Without End*. He lives in Wicklow, Ireland.

Kate Atkinson won the Whitbread Book of the Year for her first novel, *Behind the Scenes at the Museum*, and has been an international bestselling author ever since. Her four novels featuring former detective Jackson Brodie became the BBC television series Case Histories. She has won the Costa Novel Award twice for her novels *Life after Life* and *A God in Ruins*. She lives in Edinburgh.

Julie Myerson is the author of ten novels, including the best-selling *Something Might Happen* and three works of non-fiction, including *Home: The Story of Everyone Who Ever Lived in Our House*, which was dramatized on BBC Radio 4, and *The Lost Child*. She lives in London and Sussex.

Toby Litt is a *Granta* Best of Young British Novelist and a short story writer. His most recent book is *Wrestliana*.

Joanna Trollope has written eighteen highly acclaimed contemporary novels. *Other People's Children* was adapted into a major BBC drama serial. Under the name of Caroline Harvey, she writes romantic historical novels and has also written a non-fiction book, *Britannia's Daughters*. She was appointed OBE in 1996 and lives in the Cotswolds.

Colm Tóibín is the prize-winning author of several books of short stories, non-fiction and novels, including *Brooklyn*, *The Testament of Mary* and *Nora Webster*. His work has been translated into more than thirty languages. He lives in Dublin.

Anne Enright lives and works in County Wicklow, not many miles from where she was born. She is the author of several novels, including *The Gathering* and *The Green Road,* as well as short story collections and essays.

Andrew O'Hagan is a *Granta* Best of Young British Novelist and an award-winning author of several novels, including *The Illuminations*, and non-fiction, including *The Missing*. He lives in London.

Ruth Rendell is the author of twenty-four detective stories featuring Chief Inspector Wexford and many other novels and short story collections. She also wrote fourteen novels under the pseudonym Barbara Vine. She became a Fellow of the Royal Society of Literature and held the CBE. She died in 2015, aged eighty-five.

Lynne Truss is so well known for her bestselling book on punctuation *Eats, Shoots & Leaves*, that people are often surprised she has other interests. In fact, she has written several novels and many radio dramas and comedies; as well as an account of her years as a sports writer. In case anyone is wondering, she shares no traits with the heroine of 'String and Air' other than a small problem with the recitative in the works of Benjamin Britten. She lives in London and Sussex.

Paul Bailey has written eighteen books, including the Somerset Maugham Award-winning *At the Jerusalem* and a biography of Quentin Crisp, as well as plays for radio and television.

Antonia Fraser has written many internationally bestselling historical non-fiction books, including *Mary Queen of Scots*, as well as several novels and memoirs. She holds the CBE and has been awarded prizes for her books, including the Historical Writers' Association Norton Medlicott Medal and the CWA Gold Dagger. She lives in London.

Kate Mosse wrote the multimillion number-one international bestselling historical novels *Labyrinth* and *Sepulchre* as well as several other novels and plays. She is the Honorary Director and Co-Founder of the Women's Prize for Fiction and was appointed OBE. She lives in Sussex and Carcassonne, southwest France.

Andrew Motion was Poet Laureate from 1999-2009. As well as publishing many award-winning poetry collections, novels, biographies and works of criticism, he founded the online Poetry Archive and now teaches creative writing at John Hopkins in Baltimore.

Marina Warner has published several novels, collections of short stories and essays and studies of myths and fairy tales, including *From the Beast to the Blonde*. She is Professor of English and Creative Writing at Birkbeck University, President of the Royal Society of Literature, and lives in London.

Alexander McCall Smith is the author of over seventy novels for adults and children, including the prize-winning No. 1 Ladies' Detective Agency series, which have been translated into more than forty languages. He lives in Edinburgh. Both he and his wife are members of an amateur orchestra, The Really Terrible Orchestra, in which he plays the contra-bassoon.

Margaret Reynolds is Professor of English at Queen Mary, University of London. Her books include *The Sappho History* and (with Angela Leighton) *Victorian Women Poets*.